JOURDYN KELLY

Copyright © 2017 by Jourdyn Kelly

Published by Jourdyn Kelly

All Rights Reserved.

No part of this book may be used or reproduced, scanned, or distribu.   ·· rinted
or electronic form without permission. Please do not participate in or enc.
of copyrighted materials in violation of the author's rights. Purchase only auth.
editions.

ISBN Number - 978-0-9982725-2-8

This is a work of fiction. Names, characters, places, and incidents either are the
product of the author's imagination or are used fictitiously, and any resemblance to
actual persons, living or dead, businesses, companies, events, or locales is entirely
coincidental.

Cover Art by: Jourdyn Kelly

Interior Design by: Drue Hoffman, Buoni Amici Press

food and teasing each other mercilessly. Speaking of, she turned her attention to her frustrated daughter.

"What's the problem?" she asked innocently. "I was just beginning." *A story I should never have agreed to tell.*

"That is *not* how you start a story!" Jessie huffed.

"I'll have you know that it is a perfectly acceptable way to start a story! Some of the greats have used that line!" Ellie gave her daughter an exaggerated insulted look, causing Blaise and Piper to laugh even harder.

"Stop! You're going to make me pee!" The *greatly* pregnant Blaise rubbed her protruding belly lovingly.

"It's only *acceptable*," Jessie began. She tossed a *look* at Blaise that only teenagers can pull off, then focused on her smirking mother again, "when there are a campfire and s'mores involved!"

"S'mores?" Blaise sat up quickly — well, as quickly as an eight-month pregnant woman could. "Do you have s'mores?"

"Fantastic. Now, look what you've done. You woke up the Beast," Ellie laughed teasingly.

Blaise sent her a mocking glare, "scratching" her nose with her middle finger.

"Blaise?" Jessie called out sweetly. "You do realize that I'm almost seventeen, right? That gesture is *not* lost on me."

"Geez, she really *is* your daughter!" Blaise chuckled as two pairs of hazel eyes rolled at her. She looked at her own daughter, who shook her head in amusement and winked.

"Yes. Yes, she is." Ellie pulled her long, honey-colored hair back into a sloppy ponytail that made her look younger than her thirty-two years. It was more often than not that she was mistaken for Jessie's older sister instead of her mother.

Of course, being the mother of an "almost seventeen" year old meant a roller coaster of emotions and many surprises. Not the least being her willingness to tell her *daughter* about her "first time". Shit, she couldn't even blame alcohol since she wasn't drinking in solidarity with Blaise.

When Jessie had asked Ellie about *that* night, Ellie thought that maybe she should have told her about everything when they had

Chapter One

"It was a dark and stormy night . . ."

"Mom!"

Ellie Montgomery somehow managed to keep a straight face. Not an easy task when her daughter, Jessie, stretched the word out into several syllables. Obviously, the others in the room had less control than Ellie as snickers filled the room.

It was girls' night, and Ellie happily found herself surrounded by her favorite people. When Jessie, Blaise, and Blaise's daughter Piper – a surprising new addition to the group – were with her, Ellie was largely content with life. *Who needs anything more?* She glanced at Blaise, who was lounging on the sofa. Was it seriously just a few months ago when everything had changed?

Ellie knew that Blaise's life had been content, as well. Then she met her now husband Greyson Steele. Little did either of them know how that meeting would change everything. Hell, if Ellie hadn't been there, she would have thought it was a plot for some Hollywood movie. Instead, her best friend of fourteen years was the star of her own drama. Kidnappings, murders, secrets, all the elements were there. Ellie was just glad that the outcome was a successful conclusion and they could all be here together, eating junk

Other books by Jourdyn Kelly

Eve Sumptor Novels:

Something About Eve

Flawed Perfection

The Destined Series:

Destined to Kill

Destined to Love

Destined to Meet

LA Lovers Books:

Coming Home

Fifty Shades of Pink

"the talk". She knew she should have done it sooner than now and when they were alone. But, alas, here they were.

Having had Jessie when she was sixteen, Ellie certainly couldn't fault her daughter for having questions. And she wasn't naïve to think Jessie hadn't been in a situation where peer pressure had gotten to her. Her only solace at this point was Jessie swore she was still a virgin.

"I don't have everything to make s'mores, believe it or not." Yes, Ellie was aware she was avoiding the subject. Permanently if she could help it. *Maybe Jessie will wait until she's in her thirties to have sex. Ha! And, maybe I'll have sex in my thirties.* "But, I have cake and pie. I'm sure we can find something to satisfy Blaise's monster." She made a move to get up but was stopped by Jessie's hand on her arm.

"Mom, you agreed." That fact in itself was surprising to Jessie. If there was one thing Jessie's mother had always been reluctant to talk about, it was sex. Jessie had always chalked it up to the normal uneasiness a parent feels talking to their kid about this stuff. But even when the subject came up – no matter how innocent – during girls' night, Ellie shied away from it.

"I know. It's just . . ." Ellie sighed, glancing at the only other adult in the room. Blaise shrugged slightly. Even though she had a daughter the same age as Jessie, they had only just found each other. She had about as much experience at this as Ellie did. "Sweetie, nothing good came out of that night, except you." Ellie immediately dropped her head into her hands. *Damn it. I did* not *mean to reveal that.* When she looked up, three pairs of wide eyes stared at her.

"You got pregnant your *first* time?" Piper asked shyly. The poor girl was still getting used to her new life. She had grown up in New Zealand with people who had raised her to believe her mother had died. Only a few months had passed since she found out Blaise was very much alive, and Piper's life turned upside down. Or perhaps it turned out to be exactly how it should have been, finding her place within her new family. Ellie certainly couldn't blame the young girl for being bashful. The fact that Jessie and Piper became fast friends had helped considerably.

"Yep." Ellie took a deep breath. "It really *can* happen."

"So, my father was your first?" Jessie was shocked, and a little upset. Her mom never shied away from telling Jessie about her father when asked, but she *never* mentioned this. "Why didn't you ever tell me that?"

"I — I didn't think it mattered. Jessie, sweetie, I wasn't trying to hide anything from you." Ellie faltered. What no one needs to know is *why* she slept with Jessie's father that night. "The outcome is still the same."

"I knew I was a mistake, but . . ."

"You are *not* a mistake," Ellie replied vehemently. She took Jessie's hand and held it to her heart. "What I did that night was a mistake. *You* are a miracle." *Especially considering it took longer to get our clothes off than the actual act*, she thought miserably.

Blaise cleared her throat. "Okay, someone said something about sweets and did not bring me any. It is not nice to tease a pregnant woman!"

Ellie gave her best friend a grateful smile. "Calm down, kiwi. Do you want chocolate cake or banana cream pie?"

"What? No red velvet?" Blaise asked incredulously. She smacked her forehead with the back of her hand in a "woe is me" gesture, letting out a dramatic sigh. "What kind of best friend are you?"

Ellie raised an elegant eyebrow and snuck a peek at her daughter. At least she seemed to be distracted by the drama queen that is Blaise Knight. *Small miracles.*

"The kind that keeps making red velvet, and letting you take the *whole* thing every time you come over." Ellie crossed her arms and waited for a response.

"Oh. Right. You know what? Chocolate sounds good."

Jessie and Piper laughed at their mothers' antics. They both wondered if — and hoped — they would be as close when they were old(er).

"Wait!" Blaise stopped Ellie once again. "Banana cream sounds good, too."

Ellie put her hands on her hips. "Which one do you want, heiress? Please, I'm here to serve you."

"Banana cream," Blaise answered confidently. "No. chocolate

cake." She rubbed her belly as though the baby inside would give her words of wisdom. Or at least the answer to this undoubtedly hard question.

"Girls, do you know what you want?" Ellie asked, secretly entertained by Blaise's shenanigans.

"Chocolate cake!" they answered in unison and then giggled hysterically.

"See how easy that was, Blaise?"

"*See how easy that was, Blaise?*" Blaise muttered mockingly. "*You* try being pregnant!"

"Been there, done that. Got the daughter to prove it," Ellie retorted playfully. "Now get your butt up and help me."

"Aww, come on! I'm as big as a house! People are supposed to be waiting on me," Blaise pouted to an unrelenting Ellie. "All right, all right. Girls, help me up." Blaise raised her arms and wiggled her fingers with feigned impatience.

The two teenagers dutifully helped Blaise up as Ellie looked on with amusement. If she thought Blaise was in any real discomfort, she would never have asked — or demanded, whatever — help. The fact was, it was disgusting how great the woman looked being only weeks away from giving birth. It almost pissed Ellie off. She couldn't remember ever having this 'glow'. *Different circumstances, Ellie.*

"You okay?" Blaise asked quietly as she joined Ellie in the kitchen. Ellie's apartment boasted a large, open concept, and the two women were able to have a semi-private conversation.

"Mmhmm. Are you?" Ellie nodded towards the big belly Blaise was absently massaging.

"Hmm? Yes, of course. This isn't my first rodeo, you know."

"No, but you're older now. Can't be any easier." Ellie grinned at Blaise's indignant look.

"You're avoiding what you *clearly* know I got my pregnant ass up for." Blaise tapped her neatly manicured fingernails on Ellie's granite countertop. Something she knew annoyed the hell out of Ellie. "Why haven't you told me about Jessie's father? How did I not know he was your first?"

And only, Ellie added silently. "You know I don't like talking about it, Blaise." *It* meaning sex in general. She knew it sometimes bothered Blaise not having a "normal" best friend that talks about this stuff all the time. Hell, Ellie sometimes wished she could *be* normal. She shook off those feelings and brought out both desserts.

"This is about more than just sex, Ellie." Blaise leaned as far over the counter as her belly allowed. "Did something happen? Did he . . . Ellie, did he hurt you?"

"No!" Ellie glanced over at the girls who were too busy taking selfies and laughing to worry about her little outburst. "No," she repeated quieter. "He was . . . I am the one who initiated it. He was just as nervous as I was."

Blaise eyed Ellie as though she were trying to discern if she was telling the truth. Finally, she nodded. "Does she ask about him?"

"Not as often as you do," Ellie remarked snidely, immediately regretting her attitude. "Sorry. Not my favorite subject. To answer your question, I think Jessie doesn't want to care about someone who never wanted her. She's asked about him once or twice. And, as much as I've wanted to shield her from that kind of hurt, I couldn't lie to her about his willingness — or lack thereof — to be her father. He was young, and just wasn't ready for the responsibility." *Among other things.*

Blaise snorted. "*You* were young, too. You didn't shy away from the responsibility."

"No, that's true." Ellie divvied the treats up like a pro and transferred them to beautiful dessert plates as she spoke. "It was offered, of course. But I couldn't bear the thought of having an abortion." Tears gathered in Ellie's eyes as she gazed adoringly at her daughter. Right at that moment, Jessie looked up from her phone and smiled brightly at her mom. *I'd do anything to keep her love and trust. Anything.*

"Hey." Blaise placed her hand over Ellie's. "Where did you go?"

Ellie gave Blaise a bittersweet smile but avoided the question. "I know why Jessie is interested in my story. She's feeling the pressure."

"Pressure? What kind?" It finally dawned on Blaise what exactly Ellie was talking about, and she gasped. "But, she doesn't even have a boyfriend!" Terrified eyes moved to the teens. Blaise was definitely not ready for Piper to have these feelings. "Oh God! Do you think Piper? . . . ." She couldn't even bring herself to finish the question.

Ellie patted Blaise's trembling hand. "Ask her. I know that you two are just getting to know each other, but you're her mom." Ellie tried not feeling the hypocrisy of the statement. "Besides, if *I* must have this conversation with Jessie, it's only fair that you should go through it, too."

"I hate you," Blaise mumbled.

"You love me," Ellie answered in a singsong voice as she pushed two plates towards Blaise, and took the other two herself. It was most certainly time to get off this topic and get this night back on track. No way did Ellie want to keep fielding questions about her non-existent love life. Facials were obviously in order.

"JESUS, I AM exhausted!" Dr. Hunter Vale practically threw herself into the booth, barely resisting propping her feet up. *At least it's clean*, she thought, giving the place a tired glance over. Oh, how she longed to lay her head down, and sleep for at least three days. *Work be damned!* She glared at her wide awake, smiling friend. "Why did you bring me here? And if you're *this* awake after a shift like that, you clearly need more work."

Maureen "Mo" Vanelli knew better than to tease her friend when she was in a pissy mood. And Hunter was definitely in a mood. It had been a hard night at the hospital for the doc, which was the exact reason Mo brought the tall, brooding woman here. She knew if she had let Hunter go home, she would have ended up going over every fine detail of the night wondering what she could have done differently. Better to have her worrying about what kind of pie to get than something she can't change. And from what she's heard about the sweets at this place, Hunter would be distracted in no time.

"I need food. You need food. We're getting food," Mo answered in her usual no-nonsense way. She sensed Hunter's impending snarl and cut her off before she could even curl her lip. "Stop. You did what you had to do. You know it, and eventually, *she* will know it. Let it go."

"Easy for you to say," Hunter mumbled grudgingly. She *did* know it, but that didn't make the decision any easier. Nor did the fact that her patient was upset. She looked over at the stout woman with short, dirty blonde hair. It amazed her sometimes that they were still friends after all these years. They couldn't have been more different.

Though Mo was nowhere near overweight, she had muscles on top of muscles that gave her short stature a husky look. Hunter, on the other hand, had a trim, athletic body. At the ripe old age of forty-one, Hunter had to work a little harder to keep her almost six-foot frame in shape. But the effort paid off when heads turned her direction wherever she went.

"Yeah, it is easy for me," Mo said, cutting into Hunter's musings. She smiled at the young waitress that seemed to materialize out of thin air with menus.

"What can I get ya to drink?" the young woman asked, a slight twang in her voice.

Probably a wannabe actress, Hunter thought, blue eyes lifting to make eye contact. She couldn't help but smile slightly at the exuberant girl. *Oh, to be young and full of energy again.* "Coffee, black. Biggest cup you have."

"Um, we only have one size cup," the young waitress apologized, obviously taking the request seriously.

Hunter chuckled. "That's okay. Just keep it coming."

"You got it! And, for you?" she asked as she turned towards Mo.

"Coffee sounds good. Lots of cream for me," Mo said with a saucy wink.

"Jesus, Mo! You're married!" Hunter hissed as soon as the oblivious waitress was out of earshot. She shook her head at her oldest friend's antics. Having years of knowledge of this kind of behavior didn't make it any easier to tolerate.

The two women had grown up together, braving high school in Ontario (California, not Canada), before Hunter left for higher education at Harvard Medical school. Mo opted to stay local, studying nursing at UCLA. Ending up at the same hospital years later was a happy coincidence. Even so, sometimes Mo's juvenile outlook on life could be a little too much for Hunter.

"Not dead," Mo muttered defensively.

"That could certainly change once I tell Patty you've been flirting with some young thing!" Hunter felt no guilt whatsoever about threatening to tattle on her best friend. Not even when Mo's eyes widened in fear.

"I was not flirting!" Mo argued quickly. "I just asked for coffee creamer! Please don't tell Patty I was flirting. I'm begging you, Hunter! The woman will kill me for sure!"

Hunter chuckled wickedly. "Just one more thing to hold over your head. You know, it's getting to the point where you owe me so many favors you should just become my personal slave."

"Didn't know you were into me like that," Mo shot back smugly.

"Not like that, you perv." Hunter picked up her menu, effectively blocking out her blockhead of a friend. This was their routine. Insult, threaten, laugh, repeat. It may be a strange relationship that not many would understand, but it worked for them. Mostly. That's all that mattered.

"What are you getting?" Mo asked. She hoped that if she changed the subject, Hunter would forget about snitching on her. "I hear the pies are "to die for". Patty and her girls swear by them."

Hunter peered over the menu, narrowing her eyes at her friend. "Why am I just hearing about this now?" Hunter was known for her sweet tooth. A self-proclaimed 'dessert connoisseur'.

"Uh, because you've been *busy*."

Mo's annoyance was not lost on Hunter. "I have not. At least not for a while," she said softly. "I told you, I'm done with that shit."

"Yeah, until . . ."

"Until nothing," Hunter interrupted firmly. "I'm done. Believe me, I've been disgusted enough with myself. I don't need any help in that department. Okay?" She waited for Mo's sheepish nod. "I just want to find . . ."

"Here ya go!" Their peppy waitress – too peppy for this early in the morning – set the coffees down on the table, along with an overflowing bowl of creamer. "Did you decide on something to eat?" she asked and took out her pad, pen poised to write.

"Yeah," Mo began at Hunter's go ahead. "I'll have one of those deluxe breakfasts, a big glass of chocolate milk, and, um, a slice of that lemon meringue pie." She caught Hunter's wide eyes. "What? I haven't eaten since dinner!"

"Dinner was less than four hours ago," Hunter reminded her with a shake of her head. "I'll just have a slice of apple pie, and a glass of milk for now, please."

"You got it. Would you like the pie now, or when I bring out the rest of the food?"

"Together is fine," Hunter answered, and glanced at the girl's nametag. "Thank you, Charity."

The girl smiled and trotted off. *Either she's too damned perky, or I'm too damned grumpy. Or both*, Hunter thought with a hidden grin.

"Now who's flirting? Think she's?"

Hunter held up her hand. "Absolutely not! Don't even go there. That kid is *way* too young for me."

"Bah! If she's eighteen, she's legal." Mo was too busy stirring in her fifth shot of creamer to notice her friend's irritation.

"Sometimes I wonder how we're still friends."

"Hey!" Clearly hurt by the statement, Mo glowered. "I stood by you for all these years while you did whatever the hell it was you were doing. I didn't judge you. That was uncalled for."

"You're right. I'm sorry," Hunter apologized sincerely. "Still, no one under thirty-five." She was firm on that.

"Oh, come on! At least make it twenty-five." Hunter shook her head. "Okay, thirty. Give yourself a little wiggle room." Mo wiggled her eyebrows to emphasize her point.

Hunter laughed. What else could she do? Mo was a nut, and that wasn't about to change. It had surprised the hell out of her when Mo settled down and got married. But if Mo could find a woman to tame her, it gave Hunter hope. "Fine. *If* it's a mature thirty, I'll consider it."

They fell into a companionable silence after their food arrived, deciding to enjoy their food without their usual banter. Mo dug into her breakfast with gusto, while Hunter tried to savor every delectable bite of her apple pie.

"This is the best damn pie I've ever tasted," Hunter exclaimed with enthusiasm. Another bite, another unbidden moan of satisfaction. She winced as she glanced up, surprised that Mo wasn't making lewd comments about Hunter's obvious enjoyment. *She must really be enjoying that food.*

"Tole you," Mo mumbled with a mouthful of eggs, bacon, hash browns, and whatever else she could stuff in there.

"I can't believe you kept this from me. Mmm, guess whose birthday is coming up. She would *love* this!" Hunter took another bite. "Do you think they sell whole pies?" She wished now that she had kept the menu. If the apple pie was this good, she could just imagine what the others were like.

"Don' know," Mo muttered around another forkful.

"Don't talk with your mouth full." Hunter glanced around. She smiled when she found their waitress, who quickly made her way to their table at Hunter's signal.

"Need a coffee refill?"

Hunter frowned. The pie was so good she had completely forgotten about her coffee. Or the nectar of the Gods as she preferred to call it. Weird. She actually found something good enough to make her forget about caffeine.

"Um, yeah. Maybe a new cup? This one is cold." She handed the girl her cup. "Also, do you sell whole pies?"

"Oh, uh, I'm not sure. Sorry, I just started working here like a couple days ago. Hang on, let me get Miss Ellie for you." She scurried away before Hunter could say anything else.

"See?" Hunter threw a crumb at Mo who looked up with a scowl. "I could never date someone who says 'like' in the middle of a sentence."

That brought a snort from her friend. "Well, maybe you can ask 'Miss Ellie' out. I'm sure she's older than thirty-five."

"Ha, ha. Miss Ellie," Hunter repeated with a smile. "I bet she's some white-haired, little old lady who's been making pies for fifty years."

Mo's eyes rounded comically when she saw the woman coming towards them. "Uh, maybe not."

"Huh?"

Ellie gave Mo a smile. "Can I help," she met Hunter's startled eyes, "you?"

Chapter Two

"Uh." *Hell, yes, you can help me. In so many ways.* "Um." The beautiful woman's hazel . . . mostly green . . . eyes were hypnotizing, and they held Hunter's blue eyes hostage. Apparently, Hunter's brain was being held hostage as well since she had completely forgotten how to form a complete, intelligent sentence. A sharp pain on her shin shocked her brainwaves into working again. "Pie!" *Shit. Apparently, it didn't help that much.*

Ellie's eyebrows rose as she glanced down at the plate in front of the gorgeous woman. *No, Ellie!* Nothing but crumbs remained.

"Was there something wrong with your pie?" she asked pleasantly, ignoring the little flutter she felt in her stomach.

"Huh?"

Mo couldn't take it anymore. In all the years she'd known Hunter, she'd never seen her confident . . . almost arrogant . . . friend this tongue-tied before. "You'll have to forgive my friend here. She had a rough night. Hunter? You had a question for the nice lady?" Mo prompted. Hunter was doing a good enough job at embarrassing herself. No need to help her out there.

Hunter tore her stare away from the golden-haired beauty and glared at Mo. Her so-called best friend could do more to help her out here. "Yes, um, do you?" *Goddamn it! What the hell is wrong with me? Work, brain!* She made a circling gesture with her hands and tried to ignore Mo's sniggering. "Do you sell these pies in more pieces?" *Oh, God, kill me now. Please. Just open the floor, and let me disappear.*

Ellie's jaw worked double time trying to keep her smile from turning into a laugh at the flustered woman. *Hunter,* she thought. *Interesting name. Interesting woman. Stop it!* This was *not* something Ellie needed. "You're asking me if we sell whole pies?"

"Yes!" Hunter had to laugh at herself. Otherwise, she would start to cry. "Sorry, yes. Do you sell whole pies?" she asked again with some semblance of normalcy.

"Yes, we do."

The woman's smile brightened, blinding Hunter with perfect, white teeth. *Dear God, she's beautiful.*

"What kind would you like?"

"Oh, um." Hunter shook herself mentally. *Focus, dummy. She's going to think you're some kind of weirdo.* She glanced at Mo. "What kind do you think she would like?"

Mo tapped her chin in thought. "What kinds do you have?" she asked finally.

Ellie stubbornly tamped down the surge of disappointment that coursed through her. *Don't.* "One moment, let me go get you a menu." Ellie hurried away, irritated with herself for feeling jealous.

Mo watched her walk away, then turned her attention to Hunter. "What the hell is wrong with you? I've never seen you like this. It's like you've never seen a beautiful woman before."

"I've never seen her," Hunter answered simply. She somehow resisted turning to look for the woman occupying her mind.

ELLIE PUSHED HER way through the door connecting to the

kitchen. She leaned on a counter as her legs threatened to give out. "*No. No, no, no, no, no.*"

"Ellie?"

Ellie took a deep, cleansing breath before she raised her head, a smile plastered on her face for the diner's day manager, Rosa. The older woman was the only one Ellie trusted to open the diner in her absence. It helped that Rosa was almost as good at baking as Ellie is. *Almost.*

"Yes?"

"*Esta bien?*"

"*Si*, Rosa. Just came in to grab a menu." She picked up and waved a paper to-go menu that she could have easily gotten from the front counter. Either Rosa took the answer at face value, or she was respectful enough to not pry any further. Whatever the case, Ellie was grateful.

You're going to go back out there, and everything will be normal. You're going to see that you feel nothing for the goofy, stunning woman. You weren't affected at all by those sapphire blue eyes or the long, dark hair that looked as though it was made of silk. Stop! You can't.

You promised, another voice sounded, though not as strong. She knew exactly where that voice came from, and as much as she wanted to, she couldn't ignore it. Ellie sighed, and told herself to remain calm, cool, and collected.

"COME ON. YEAH, she's pretty, in that non-assuming way. And, her eyes are amazing. Okay, she's really hot . . ."

"It's more than that, now shut up before she comes back and hears you," Hunter whispered harshly.

"I can see if she's coming, Hunter. Calm down. Think she's family?" Mo chugged down the rest of her chocolate milk and peered over the rim to gauge her friend's reaction.

"I don't know." *God, I hope so. It would really suck to feel this way about someone that's off limits.*

"Well, here she comes. Maybe we can find out. Try to be cool. You know, act like you have the ego of a surgeon."

Hunter flipped Mo off quickly, then smiled as the beauty from whom she assumed was Miss Ellie filled her vision again. Before Hunter could react, Mo plucked the menu out of Ellie's hands. *I hate her*, she thought grumpily. That "hate" became a healthy dose of jealousy when the woman bent close to Mo to go over the menu with her.

As the two of them went over the types of pie, Hunter made herself feel better by letting her eyes roam over the woman. Definitely not a white-haired, little old lady. Dressed simply in a white, V-neck t-shirt that boasted the Ellie's Diner logo, and faded jeans that fit just right, Hunter had never seen anyone sexier. Ever. The morning light that flowed in through the windows caught the highlights in the woman's honey golden mane, giving her an almost ethereal glow. The thought almost had Hunter chuckling out loud. She had never been one for romance or poetry. But one look at this lovely, green-eyed, woman and all Hunter wanted to do was shower her with flowers and promises.

"Hunter?"

Mo's elevated voice brought Hunter out of the romance book in her head. *Silly. She's probably not even . . .*

"Hunter?" Mo called again, exasperated at her friend's continued weird behavior. "Did you hear all of that? You have a lot to choose from."

Chagrined, Hunter realized she didn't hear a word that was just said. "Um, what would you recommend?" Hunter asked as she tried to hide the fact she wasn't paying attention. At least not to anything having to do with pies.

"Well, is this for a special occasion?" Ellie asked nonchalantly. *Whatever the answer, it doesn't matter.* She would keep telling herself that as many times as she had to in order to believe it.

"My mom's birthday is coming up," Hunter answered,

exceedingly happy that she could respond like an educated human. "She, um, loves all kinds of sweets, and envies anyone who can bake. She's a great cook, but when it comes to baking, it's just terrible."

"I'm sure she's not that bad," Ellie responded politely. Her damned heart betrayed her with its little happy dance at finding out the pie was for Hunter's mother.

"Oh, yeah she is!" Mo snorted and echoed Hunter's first assessment.

Hunter laughed, and Ellie felt that laugh deep down. *Shit*. It was a rich sound, full of memories from what Ellie hoped was a happy childhood.

"No joke. Mo," Hunter gestured to her friend, "and I used to take her cookies and play street hockey with them!"

Ellie joined in their laughter, and only faltered slightly when she saw Hunter watching her with interest. *No!*

"Well, we could do a sampler for her," Ellie suggested.

"Sampler?" Hunter could – and would – sit here in this booth all day long if she could just watch Ellie. She no longer cared about sleep. It's amazing how wide awake you can become when your heart has received what feels like an electric current. *Geez, Hunter, calm your tits. She's given no indication that she's interested.*

"Mmhmm. Eight slices of any pie of your choice," Ellie explained. "You can mix and match whatever flavors you want."

"Is that an everyday deal? I'm going up to see my parents this weekend," Hunter explained when Ellie gave her a questioning look. "I thought maybe I'd get it fresh by coming back here right before I drive up there." *And every day in between if I can.*

"It's every day," Ellie smiled. She tried not to think about how happy she was about the possibility of seeing Hunter again. "However, the types of pies can change depending on my mood."

"*You* bake these?" Hunter asked with interest. Ellie nodded. "So, you really *are* Miss Ellie?" *Oh, man. Mom would love you.*

"Just Ellie," Ellie laughed softly. "Miss Ellie makes me sound like a 'white-haired, little old lady who's been baking pies for more than fifty years'."

17

"Oh God!" Hunter sank down in the booth and covered her face with both hands. *Seriously, kill me now. I'm begging anyone who's listening to put me out of my misery.*

Ellie felt a little bad for teasing the brunette, but the attractive blush that crept up that long, exquisite neck made it all worth it. *Ellie, stop. Don't wish for something you* know *you can't have.* She ignored the other voice that said she could.

Mo tried to hide her laughter behind a cough. "You're really deflating Hunter's God-like ego." If Hunter wasn't going to help herself out, Mo would have to do it. "After last night, that's probably not so hard to do." Oh, yeah. Hunter is going to kick her ass for sure.

"You mentioned a rough night," Ellie remembered. "Work or play?" she asked Hunter. *Please don't be a heavy partier.*

Hunter didn't know what stunned her the most. Mo saying what she said, or Ellie giving Hunter her full attention. *Don't blow this!*

"Work," she said quietly. "I don't have time to play." *I hope you're not a party girl.*

"Yeah, she gave up her right to having fun when she became a surgeon," Mo threw in and sat back. She got the conversation started, now all Hunter had to do was keep it going.

"A surgeon?" Ellie raised an eyebrow, intrigued even more. "What is your specialty?"

"Trauma," Hunter answered shyly. She didn't understand why she was acting this way. If it had been anyone else, there would be no hesitation, no worry if it would be impressive enough.

"Trauma," Ellie repeated. "That must be . . ."

Hunter silently sighed. *Here it comes. All anyone thinks about is how exciting it must be to be a trauma surgeon. No one ever thinks about . . .*

"Difficult," Ellie finished softly.

Huh? "Most people think it's exciting," Hunter repeated her inner thoughts.

"Well, I'm sure it can be. But, the patients that you see are in dire need of someone who can make critical decisions in seconds. That can't be easy for you."

Mo sat up, her jaw slacked. Women came on to Hunter for three reasons. First, she was extremely attractive. Second, she was a doctor. And, third, they all thought she was an adrenaline junkie because she was in the trauma field. None of them knew the real Hunter, and they never would. But, Ellie? Maybe, just maybe, she could be the one that could keep Hunter from her self-destructive behavior.

"It's not," Hunter confirmed sadly. "Not all of my patients understand that."

Ellie laid a hand on Hunter's shoulder. "I'm sorry. I didn't mean to upset you."

The feel of Ellie's hand on her nearly made Hunter forget what she was sad about. "No, it's okay. I had to make one of those difficult decisions last night. I altered a young girl's life indefinitely, and I don't know how to make her understand that it was the only choice." *Jesus. I'm spilling my guts to this woman like I've known her forever.* A glance at Mo's shocked face showed just how unusual that was.

"I'm sure she'll come around, Hunter." Ellie squeezed Hunter's shoulder, then slipped her hand away, immediately missing the warmth of the contact. This time she didn't want to ignore the tremble she had felt when she called Hunter by name. She just didn't know which one of them it came from.

Mo decided it was time to get them back on track. All this melancholy shit wasn't going to get Hunter any closer to finding out if Ellie even played for the same team.

"Ahem," Mo cleared her throat. Once she was sure she got both of their attention, she continued. "This is all fascinating, but I need to get home soon. And, if my wife finds out that I came here, and didn't bring anything back for her, I'm sleeping on the couch." She made sure to emphasize 'wife,' and watched Ellie's reaction. Mo knew Hunter would be watching, too. *If* her brain was functioning at all.

"We wouldn't want that, now would we?" Ellie responded evenly. She knew Mo was fishing, but Ellie refused to take the bait. "I'm sure you keep yourself in enough trouble as it is."

"Ooh!" Hunter laughed at her best friend's expense. "She has you pegged!"

"Whatever," Mo mumbled. "Can I get a chocolate pie to go?"

Ellie chuckled at Mo's surly mood. "Of course. Just one slice?"

"Oh no!" Mo perked up again. "I need a whole pie! Patty will never give me a bite if I just get one slice!"

Ellie gasped playfully. "That's terrible!" She gave Hunter a mischievous wink. "I'll go get your pie."

Hunter snuck a peek at the retreating Ellie and smiled widely. *Perfect. Beautiful, funny, caring.*

"Well, she didn't freak out when I said 'wife'," Mo recapped unnecessarily.

"Doesn't mean anything," Hunter muttered, but still had hope.

"Yeah, I know. But, maybe you should rethink your age restriction. She may be under your thirty-year-old cut-off," Mo teased.

"Mmm, I'll be right back." Hunter took her wallet out and made her way to the counter with a "good luck" from Mo at her back.

Ellie came through the door at the same time Hunter made it to the counter and barely managed to hold back a moan. *Of course, she's tall.*

"I could have brought this over to your table," Ellie said with a smile.

"I, um, I just wanted to thank you." She had actually come up here to gauge the situation and see if Ellie would be open to Hunter asking her out. However, from her table to the counter, she concluded that she didn't want to go in for the 'quick kill' so to speak. No, Hunter wanted to get to know everything about this woman.

Ellie tilted her head in question. "Thank me?"

"Yeah, for taking the time to help us, and, um, for listening." Hunter – highly successful trauma surgeon - somehow resisted shuffling her feet like some awkward teenager.

"It was my pleasure." Ellie set the pie on the counter, not ready to let the tall brunette go yet. *You're playing with fire, Ellie.* "It's hard when your life changes so suddenly. Give your patient some time." Her eyes never left Hunter's.

Hunter nodded and wondered whether there was a hidden message in there somewhere about Ellie, herself. *Wishful thinking, Hunter?* She wasn't sure. She *was* sure, however, that she would be returning to the diner as often as she could to get to know more about this woman.

"I will. Um, how much?"

"This one is on me. Just," she continued, cutting off Hunter's refusal. "Just leave Charity a nice tip for having to put up with Mo," she teased.

Hunter laughed heartily. "I don't think I have enough for *that*! We've been best friends for years, and I'm still not used to her weirdness. Thank you," she added sincerely, then thrust her hand out towards Ellie. "Hunter Vale."

Ellie slipped her smaller hand into Hunter's. *Strong.* "Ellie Montgomery."

"I'm, um, sorry for being so scatter-brained. I'm not normally like this," Hunter apologized sheepishly and forced herself to let go of Ellie's warm hand. *Soft.*

That's too bad. I like goofy Hunter. Ellie gave her a charming smile and called out to the brunette as she turned to walk away. When Hunter turned back, Ellie held up the forgotten pie to a much-chagrined Hunter. "Be careful going home."

Chapter Three

An excessively frustrated Ellie sat up in bed. Sleep eluded her. Or perhaps it was more accurate to say that Ellie avoided sleep. Every time she closed her eyes, she would see Hunter, and that wasn't something she was prepared for. No one had ever made her feel this way. And she was scared.

"*This cannot be happening,*" she whispered to an empty room. She had always been alone, but this is the first time she had ever felt lonely. A glance at her alarm clock made Ellie flop back on the bed with an irritated groan. Four o'clock in the morning, and no real sleep to speak of. And, since it didn't look like she would be getting any, there was only one thing she could do to rid herself of this frustration.

HUNTER WAS FRUSTRATED as hell. A certain blonde kept occupying her dreams, so she hadn't slept much at all. Actually, that was the good part of her 'night'. The *very* good part. It was the phone call she received from someone she was trying to put behind her that had ruined her mood. How many ways could she say she was done with that part of her life? She had tried being polite. She had tried avoiding. Hell, she had tried being the biggest prick she could be. Nothing seemed to be working. It was the only thing she was dreading about going home to see her parents. *She* would be there. And she obviously wasn't getting the hint that Hunter was no longer interested.

Sleep had been forgotten, and Hunter was running on piss and vinegar. It worked when she had a trauma, but seriously damaged her social skills. The nurses were pissed at her attitude — including Mo. Her patient still wasn't talking to her. Not even after Hunter had spent the morning trying to find out any information about family, or anyone else who could be there for the young girl.

Hunter grumpily looked at her watch. *Three more hours. Then I get to get out of here, and see Ellie. God, I hope she's there.*

DRESSED IN HER running gear, Ellie scribbled a quick note for Jessie and left quietly. Running had always been Ellie's outlet. Whenever she felt stressed, she ran. Frustrated? She ran. Happy? She ran. It didn't matter what the situation was, running had always helped. It had started when Ellie was a teenager. She would use running as an excuse to get out from under her parents' thumbs. And when things began feeling different for Ellie, she ran to think.

Thinking was exactly what she needed to do now. Had it just been two days ago during girls' night when she had thought how content she was? *My, how things can change so quickly.* Ellie wasn't sure what to do with those changes. She had made a decision long ago, and it had been easy to live with that decision. Until now.

Honestly, Ellie never thought she would have to deal with this. *I made it nearly seventeen years. I guess I'm not as immune as I thought I was. Or maybe I'm just feeling melancholy after talking about my past the other night. This feeling of instant attraction deep down in your soul doesn't happen in real life. Does it?*

Her feet pounded faster on the ground as anxiety pushed her to her limit. This wasn't something she could do when Blaise would accompany her on runs. Her best friend *hated* the sport. She didn't understand why anyone would want to do it. Ellie had tried to get her to appreciate the exhilaration the body feels afterward, but Blaise was never convinced. In fact, Blaise had been elated when her pregnancy prevented her from coming out with Ellie anymore. She remembered the utter joy on Blaise's face when she told Ellie, in no uncertain terms, that she would no longer be getting up at the "butt crack of no-one-should-be-up-now".

The thought made Ellie want to laugh, and she would have if she could breathe. *Damn. It's been a long time since I've tired myself out.* She slowed until she came to a complete stop, and bent over at the waist. Sweat dripped from her forehead as she took long, deep breaths. *Ten miles in an hour. And, not one thought, Ellie. You've accomplished* nothing.

"You're probably making a mountain out of a molehill," she wheezed to herself, then looked around to make sure she was alone. "So, she was flustered around you. That doesn't mean she's interested. And, just because you felt . . . *something* doesn't mean you have to act on it."

It was a weak, *weak* argument, but it was all Ellie had. She wasn't even going to think about the promise she made herself. What was the point? The most likely scenario would be; she would see Hunter one more time when she came in for her mom's pie. After that, life for Ellie would get back to normal. Maybe one day she'd actually believe that.

"MOM?"

Jessie dragged her pajama-clad butt into the kitchen. Her hair, that fell just below her shoulders, was sticking up in all different directions, and she had pillow-face.

"Yes, dear?" Ellie smiled lovingly at her adorable daughter.

"Why are you always so awake this early in the morning?" Jessie grumbled. "It's not normal."

The fact was, Ellie had been up for hours. After her run, she had come home, taken a shower, and began preparing the list of ingredients she would need for the pies she wanted to make today. Of course, she had also started breakfast for Jessie who should have been in and out of the shower by now.

"I don't know. Guess I'm a morning person," Ellie shrugged with a smirk. As much as she and Jessie looked alike, they were distinctly different in most aspects of their lives. Actually, when Ellie thought about it, Jessie was more like Blaise.

Jessie glanced past her mom to the hurried note on the whiteboard that hung next to the refrigerator. There were usually notes of positivity or love left by both of them that were slightly more legible than what was there now.

"You went running this morning?" Ellie nodded and flipped pancakes with practiced finesse. "But, you ran yesterday."

Ellie raised her eyes to study her daughter. "So?"

"So, you never run two days in a row. Unless something is wrong. What's wrong?" Jessie plopped herself down on one of the barstools and focused on her mom.

"Nothing is . . ." Jessie gave her a look. *Yep, she really is my daughter.* "I was a little restless, and couldn't sleep. I thought a run would help."

"Why are you restless?" She leaned in further. "Does this have anything to do with Frank leaving?"

"What? No, honey." Ellie plated the pancakes and slid them in front of Jessie. "Jessie, you know that there was nothing going on between me and Frank, right?"

Frank had been Ellie's and Jessie's reluctant roommate up until a month ago. He had been in desperate need of a place to stay, and Ellie – having known him since they'd met in college – couldn't say no. Of course, she had to put up with questions from Jessie and Blaise about the arrangement, but she endured that for her own personal reasons. Having Frank here did one good thing for Ellie. Her parents had stopped asking about her dating life. *Oh, shit. When they find out Frank left, it's going to start all over.*

"Yeah, I know." Jessie spread a healthy amount of butter on her pancakes before drowning them in syrup. "I'm sure you would have told me if you were seeing him. Or were even interested."

Ellie lowered her eyes. She almost wished Dr. Hunter Vale had never walked into her diner. If she hadn't, Ellie wouldn't feel as though she was doing something wrong. *I haven't done* anything!

"So, we're not having money problems?" Jessie asked with a mouth full of pancakes.

"Don't talk with your mouth full," Ellie automatically mothered. "And, of course not. Frank wasn't staying here because we needed money. We're totally comfortable, sweetie. And, even if we weren't, you know Blaise wouldn't let us suffer."

"Oh yeah. Blaise is richer than God."

Ellie laughed at Jessie's snort-giggle. "I don't know about that, but there's nothing to worry about."

Jessie seemed to contemplate Ellie's answer as she chewed her food. *At least she's chewing.*

"I suggested to Piper that she see a therapist," Jessie announced suddenly.

Ellie's eyebrows shot up. Part of her was grateful that questions concerning her restlessness were forgotten about. At least for now. The other part was concerned about Jessie's announcement.

"Okay. Did you discuss that with Blaise?"

Jessie crinkled her nose. "No, because it's not Blaise's decision.

It's Piper's. I would think that if I made the choice to see a shrink, you would support me."

"I . . . of course, I would," Ellie answered, perplexed. "Jessie, do you need a therapist?" she asked, wondering if this was Jessie's way of bringing the subject up.

"No, mom. But, I didn't grow up with people who told me my mother was dead, then found out she wasn't, then had to leave my country to begin life with a whole new family." Jessie took the last bite of her food. "My life is pretty drama free."

How can I possibly change that because I feel something for someone I just met, Ellie thought miserably?

"How did Piper react to your suggestion?"

Jessie shrugged. "She said she'd think about it. And, just so you don't worry so much about it, she said she would talk to Blaise." She gave her mom a smile and hopped up from her stool. Apparently, good food went a long way to perking up tired teenagers. "Gotta get ready for school. Piper will be here soon." Jessie got to the hallway, then turned back to her mom. "You would tell me if something important was going on, right?"

Ellie's smile was tremulous, and she nodded once. It wasn't a lie, right? Nothing had happened, yet. There was no point of bringing drama into Jessie's life for something that would probably never go further than one more meeting.

"HOW ARE YOU this morning, Big Al?"

Ellie smiled at the older gentleman and received a grunt in return. That was their morning routine. Big Al – aptly named - was tall, black, sixty-ish-year-old man that stood at maybe six foot five if Ellie judged correctly. That was an entire foot taller than her, and with muscles as big as her head, he was definitely formidable.

He rarely spoke, but Ellie knew he paid attention to everything thing around him. Occasionally, he would ask her a question or listen as she spoke about her day. And he was always gracious to Jessie. For that reason alone, Ellie sincerely liked the man.

His taste in beverages, however, was almost as terrible as Blaise's. Where Blaise enjoyed whiskey in her hot tea – a practice that had been put on hold during her pregnancy – Big Al insisted on drinking something that Ellie couldn't imagine being good. But she made it for him every day and served it with a smile. She filled his glass with the thick, brown liquid and set it in front of him.

"Enjoy." She had long since schooled herself not to grimace as he drank when she received Big Al's equivalent of a tongue-lashing. 'Don't knock it, girlie!' he had snarled. She was never afraid of him, not even then. Just learned not to "knock it". Though she would never try it, either.

The bell above the entrance rang out, and Ellie looked up to welcome her new customer. Her grip tightened around the handle of the pitcher she held. Good thing, otherwise she would have dropped it when she saw Hunter saunter through the door. *Be cool, Ellie. Do* not *make a fool out of yourself.*

Hunter's smile was wide and happy when she saw Ellie behind the counter. *Try to act like an adult this time.* She was insanely pleased that the beautiful blonde was here, her green eyes sparkling. *My mood has miraculously gotten a thousand times better.*

"Hunter," Ellie smiled a smile that challenged Hunter's. "Good morning."

"Morning, Ellie." Hunter gestured to the barstool. "Is it all right to sit here?"

"Of course." *Why must I be so damned happy to see her?* "Did you decide to visit your mom early?"

"Huh?" *Shit. Don't start, Hunter.* Once her brain caught on, she realized Ellie must have thought she was here to pick up the pie for her mother's birthday. "Oh! No. I'm, um, hungry," she answered with a shy smile. *I haven't felt this nervous since I was a teenager! Maybe not even then.* "I didn't get to eat at the hospital. Thought I'd come in and try some actual food."

"Ah. Coffee?" Hunter nodded enthusiastically. "You really should take better care of yourself. You're a doctor, you should know this," Ellie teased.

Touched, Hunter raised her coffee in a salute. She was sure Ellie was just being nice, but Hunter didn't mind pretending that Ellie actually cared about her.

"I know, I know. Trauma doesn't always allow for time. Besides, don't you know that hospital food sucks?"

"So, *that's* what keeps me in business," Ellie laughed.

A grunt caught both of their attention, and Big Al wiggled his empty glass with what Blaise would call 'old-timer irritability'.

"You grunted?" Ellie grinned and brought out the pitcher. *That you can drink this stuff without gagging is quite impressive.* Again, she filled his glass with the dense stuff while she kept an eye on Hunter's wide-eyed reaction. *This should be interesting.*

"I don't mean to be rude, but what exactly *is* that?"

"Don't knock it, girlie!" Big Al grumbled.

Hunter held her hands up and chuckled. "No offense! It just looks . . . refreshing."

"Would you like to try some?" Ellie couldn't resist the offering since the look on Hunter's face clearly showed horror.

"No, no! I wouldn't want to deprive Mr . . .?" Hunter paused and looked to Ellie for help.

"This is Big Al."

"Big Al," Hunter repeated slowly. "Right, well, I'll just stick with coffee." She stressed her point by taking a sip of the just hot enough beverage.

"Your loss," Big Al rasped, then abruptly got up, and headed for the restrooms.

Ellie snickered and indicated the pitcher. "Ovaltine and cold coffee," she explained with a shudder. "I don't know how he drinks it all the time, but he does. He also spends a lot of time in there," she gestured towards the bathrooms.

Hunter laughed out loud. "That's quite, um, disgusting."

"Yes, it is," Ellie agreed laughingly. "So? How hungry are you?"

"After *that?*" Hunter exaggerated a shiver. "I may never eat again."

Funny Hunter is just as charming as goofy Hunter. Shit, I am in so much trouble. "I'm sure your tummy is tough enough to handle it." *I wonder how tough it is. Ugh, Ellie, stop.*

Just then, Hunter's stomach growled loudly, causing the brunette to blush. *Thank God Mo isn't here to see this.* "I guess you're right," she grinned.

"That sounded pancake worthy. Does that work for you?"

"If they're stacked about this high," Hunter answered, holding a hand a few inches off the counter. "Then it sounds perfect."

Ellie beamed a megawatt smile. "Not a problem." She then turned to do something she rarely did for anyone other than Blaise and Jessie while here at the diner. She was going to cook the meal herself. She paused when Hunter called her name.

"Could I just ask one thing?"

"Sure."

"What's curmudgeon's story?"

"Curmudgeon?" She tsked with feigned disapproval. "Big Al has been coming here for years. Though, he used to sit at the booth over there," Ellie gestured to one of the front booths by the large window. "With his wife. They would come in, eat, drink, laugh, talk. His wife passed away a little over a year ago, but Big Al still comes in every day. Except he can't bring himself to sit at that booth anymore. So, he sits up here, drinks this concoction, doesn't laugh, grunts, and that's about it."

"Wow. That's sad," Hunter acknowledged with a pitiful peek at the empty stool down the bar from her.

"Mmhmm. Or, he's just a curmudgeonly old man with the social skills of a crocodile." Ellie had seen Big Al making his way back to the counter, and decided to have some fun with Hunter. "You decide," she said with a quick, mischievous grin, and hurried away.

"Wait, what?" Hunter's mouth hung open in surprise. She heard Big Al's distinctive grunt next to her, saw Ellie's laughing face pop up through the window separating the kitchen from the eating area, and knew she had been had. *Cute. Very cute.*

31

Chapter Four

Hunter happily chowed down on the breakfast that Ellie had brought her. She didn't think she had ever tasted food this good. *Sorry, mom.* The pancakes were fluffy, the eggs were perfectly cooked, the bacon was crispy, and the hash browns were a flawless combination of crusty on the outside, and soft on the inside. She took another bite and finally understood Mo's thorough concentration on her food yesterday.

"This is absolutely amazing, Ellie." Hunter tried to keep her enthusiasm under control, but as soon as the diner owner got back behind the counter, the words wanted to pour out. So, she stuffed her face again.

"I'm glad you're enjoying it." Ellie struggled to restrain her smile, but Hunter's obvious delight made her feel giddy. *Giddy? Come on, Ellie. You're an adult, and there are too many reasons this can't happen.* It didn't help that Ellie's eyes followed the fork to Hunter's full lips. *Oh, my.* She averted her eyes quickly when she realized she was staring.

Was she just checking out my mouth? Maybe she is . . .

"I hope I'm not prying." Ellie unwittingly interrupted Hunter's optimism. She needed to get her mind off the thoughts that Hunter's lips were making her think. "But have things gotten any better with your patient?" She immediately regretted the question when she saw Hunter's brilliant blue eyes cloud over.

Of all the things Hunter was thinking that Ellie could ask, that wasn't even on the list. She was touched that Ellie remembered their conversation, especially considering how many people she must talk with every day. Unfortunately, the subject depressed her.

"I'm sorry. I didn't mean to make you feel . . ."

"No, it's okay," Hunter was quick to relieve Ellie's noticeable remorse at bringing the mood down. She pushed around some eggs on her plate, then remembered how good they were, and ate them. "She's still not talking. Not to me, not to counselors. I don't know what else to do. She won't even look at me when I come in to do her checkups."

Ellie felt sorry for the doctor. It couldn't be easy to be condemned for doing her job. "Do you mind, or can you, tell me what happened?" she asked carefully.

Hunter sighed softly and pushed her almost empty plate to the side. "Her name is Dani." She thanked Ellie for refilling her coffee. "She came in with injuries from being hit by a vehicle."

"Oh no."

"The asshole was going too fast, and not paying attention." Hunter peered up through dark lashes, chagrined by her outburst. "Sorry."

"Don't be." Ellie tried to reserve her judgments about the driver that hit the young girl. Who was probably texting, or taking selfies. *So much for not judging.*

Hunter gave her a brief smile, then lowered her eyes. "It was bad, Ellie. In order to save her life, I had to amputate both of her legs." Her voice cracked at having to say the words to Ellie. She was sure Ellie would hate her as much as Dani does.

"Oh, God." Ellie's hand fluttered to her heart as it broke for Hunter, and a girl she didn't even know. "How old is she?"

"Eighteen," Hunter replied miserably. *Just a child and I've ruined her life.*

"How horrible. For both of you." Ellie longed to reach out to Hunter but resisted.

34

"I still have my legs."

The self-deprecation in Hunter's voice pained Ellie.

"Are they strong enough to carry the guilt you so obviously bear?" Ellie's voice held no reproach. She only wanted Hunter to see that what she was doing to herself was needless.

"I took her legs, Ellie."

"You saved her life, Hunter," Ellie countered. "She is still breathing."

"Sometimes that's not enough." Hunter hung her head under the weight of the guilt Ellie spoke of. She shook it off the best she could and tried to remind herself that what she did was necessary. "She'll stay in the hospital for at least a couple more weeks. If we can't get her to talk before then, we can't release her."

"Does that mean she'll be moved to the psych ward?"

Hunter winced. "I don't like calling it that, but yes. If we feel she's a danger to herself." She let the sentence linger there.

"What about her parents?"

Hunter scoffed with disgust. "From what I've learned from the cops, she's been on her own for some time now. I, um, wasn't able to sleep yesterday when I got home. Too restless." She missed the stunned look on Ellie's face. "So, I went to the place where she was hit. There's a strong homeless presence there, and I thought if I could find someone who knew her, or cared about her, they could come see her."

Ellie forced herself to ignore the fact that Hunter had been restless as well. *Don't be ridiculous. It had nothing to do with you, Ellie. It was about Dani, and rightly so.*

"Were you able to find anyone?"

"No," Hunter sighed. "They were quick to talk about her, but not *to* her." She sipped her coffee. "Apparently, her family kicked her out because they didn't approve of her . . . lifestyle."

"Jesus." Ellie shook her head in detestation. "What kind of parent?"

She didn't get the chance to finish her question, as Blaise burst into the diner just then. She rushed – or waddled – up to the counter, a look of such panic upon her face, that Ellie began to panic herself.

"Blaise?" She took the pregnant woman's hands. "What's wrong?"

Hunter watched the exchange with interest. And perhaps a bit of jealousy. Who was this pregnant – beautiful – woman to Ellie?

"It broke!"

Ellie's eyes widened and glanced down. She frowned when she saw no evidence of Blaise's water breaking. "What broke, sweetie?"

"My beloved Keurig! I have clients coming who completely stress me out, so I went to make some tea. You know how tea calms me, especially these days . . ."

"Blaise? Focus."

"Right, well, not so long story even shorter, I tried everything. The machine is dead." Blaise shook Ellie by the shoulders. "I need . . ."

"Tea?" Ellie laughed. "Is chamomile good?"

"Perfect!" Blaise rubbed her belly as she felt flutters from the baby's kicks.

Hunter stood, and offered her seat to Blaise. "Please, sit here." She moved her coffee over with her, strangely glad that Big Al had left earlier. *I can't believe I've been here for nearly two hours. Talking with Ellie is easy and comfortable. Something I've never felt before.*

"Thank you." Blaise smiled at the tall stranger for her thoughtfulness. Of course, getting up on the stool in her condition was not an easy task.

"Blaise, this is Dr. Hunter Vale. Hunter, this is Blaise Knight. She owns the flower shop a couple of doors down." Ellie grinned as the two shook hands. "Blaise is my Mo," she explained. She received a knowing look from Hunter and a scowl from Blaise.

"Did you just call me a Stooge?"

Hunter wished she hadn't just taken a drink of hot coffee, as it found its way out her nose. Not only was it embarrassing, but it hurt like hell!

"Oh, Hunter!" Ellie couldn't quite hold in her laugh. "Are you all right?" She gave Hunter napkins that Blaise was continually plucking out of the napkin holder.

"Hot. Coffee. Nostrils. Not good," Hunter managed between coughs. "Ow."

Oh, God. That pout! Ellie cleared her throat and turned to her best friend. "Blaise, I wasn't calling you a Stooge. Mo is Hunter's best friend."

"Oh!" Blaise chuckled. "Well, that's acceptable. Mo is a strange name."

Ellie's eyebrows raised in surprise. "Says the woman named Blaise," she teased. To her relief both Hunter and Blaise laughed.

"I meant no offense."

Blaise's contrition was sincere, and Hunter was quick to ease her mind. "Please. No offense taken. Her name is Maureen, but she, odd duck that she is, prefers Mo," she told Blaise with mirth.

Blaise gave Hunter a brilliant smile, then checked her watch. "Um, Ellie?"

"Tea and a slice of red velvet to go coming up." Ellie's body shook with laughter as she went to retrieve Blaise's items.

"SHE'S SOMETHING ELSE." Hunter watched the flower shop owner walk away, a lot happier than when she came in.

"Yes. No one quite like her," Ellie agreed with a smile.

"When is she due?"

Ellie's smile faded. "Oh, thank God you didn't ask her that! She has been trying to lose the weight, but hasn't been quite successful."

"W-what?" Hunter's head swiveled back and forth between the door that Blaise just walked out of and Ellie. "She's not, um, she's not pregnant?"

A slow smile began to form on Ellie's lips. "Gotcha! She's due any minute now." She laughed heartily as Hunter's jaw dropped in astonishment.

"That was not nice. First Big Al, now this. You, my friend, are naughty." She was mesmerized by the attractive blush that graced Ellie's exquisite face and wondered if she was blushing as well. What in the hell had possessed her to say *that*? "Um, could I ask you something?"

Please don't ask me out. Please. I don't know if I can say yes. And, I don't know if I can say no. "Sure." Ellie was grateful that her voice was strong.

"It's a favor, actually." *God, I want to ask you out. But, I can't be sure if you would be offended or not.* "Would you try talking to Dani?"

It was Ellie's turn to be astonished. Her eyes rounded as big as saucers. "Me? But, I'm not a psychiatrist or a doctor! Hunter, I'm just the owner of a small diner."

You're much more than that. "Maybe that's what she needs, Ellie. Someone who isn't paid to be there, but wants to be. Look," Hunter's eyes pleaded with Ellie. "You don't have to answer now, but think about it? Please? I can't explain it, but I've only known you for four hours, tops, and I've opened up to you more than I have my own friends. You're easy to talk to. I think that's what Dani needs."

"I don't know, Hunter. What if I say the wrong thing and make it worse?" Talking to a young girl who just lost her legs and hates the world is a lot of pressure. Hell, whenever Jessie is in a bad mood, Ellie struggles to say the right thing.

"I know I'm asking a lot, especially since we've just met." Hunter shrugged a shoulder apologetically. "I'm sorry about that. But, this is killing me. Not to mention, if I don't change my surly attitude at work, the nurses are going to lynch me."

Hunter tried a little comedy to lighten the mood and received the desired smile from Ellie.

"I'll think about it," Ellie promised.

Hunter beamed. "That's all I ask." She requested a pen and something to write on so she could leave instructions 'just in case'. "Thank you."

"HEY, PATTY." MO'S wife – and actual boss – was a strong, take-no-shit, black woman that didn't let anyone get away with anything. Especially her wife or Hunter. In fact, if Hunter was completely honest, she was a little intimidated by Patty, even though she towered over her five foot two frame.

Hunter gave her a small smile, hoping it would somehow make up for being such a bitch the past couple of days. She had just come from Dani's room with the same miserable results. Frustration was quickly becoming Hunter's constant attitude, much to the dismay of those around her.

"Dr. Vale."

Oh, shit. She's pissed at me. Hunter hung her head. "I'm sorry for being an ass."

Patty studied Hunter with a critical eye. "I understand you're having a difficult time with this, sugar, but taking it out on everyone else is not right."

Hunter sighed and leaned against the nurses' desk. "I know. I just don't know what else to do."

"Hunter, don't take this the wrong way, but you've been a little weird lately. You've never let your emotions get the best of you before."

"Maybe trauma isn't for me anymore." The words were barely audible, and Hunter knew that Patty was as surprised as she was.

"It's not just that," Patty said carefully. "When you came in today, you were the happiest I'd ever seen you. Then it changes at a moment's notice. Then you get this faraway look in your eye, and a wistful smile appears." She leaned closer and lowered her voice. Hospital gossip spread faster than any disease known to man. "Does this have anything to do with the woman Mo mentioned? I swear, if I didn't know how scared she was of me, I'd think *she* liked this woman."

Hunter raised an eyebrow. "Mo told you about Ellie?"

"Mo tells me everything, sugar. Haven't you figured that out by now? But, she also exaggerates. So, why don't *you* tell me about her."

Out of the corner of her eye, Hunter noticed the young nurse that had made no secret about her interest in Hunter. Unfortunately, even though Hunter was looking to turn over a new leaf in her life, Iris was *not* that leaf. She was too young, too eager, too . . . just too much.

"Can we talk about this later?" Hunter tilted her head to indicate that they had an audience.

"Sure. But, I want details. And, not the sordid details you know Mo gives me. According to her, you're already looking for U-Hauls."

Hunter laughed. "I need to gather up the nerve to ask her out first. Listen, I asked Ellie to stop by and try to talk to Dani. *If* she does, please don't say anything. I'm not even sure she's . . ." Her eyes tracked to Iris again who seemed like she was hanging on every word she could make out. "*You know,*" she whispered.

"Gotcha. You know me, I won't say anything."

Hunter tossed her a skeptical look. "Mmmhmm. I *do* know you. That's why I'm begging you."

Patty gave her a sly grin, and mimicked locking her lips, and throwing away the key.

"EXCUSE ME?" ELLIE glanced around the hospital corridor. She had triple checked the information Hunter had written down for her, refusing to believe it was because she wanted to study the confident handwriting. That had surprised Ellie. She was used to doctors having barely legible handwriting, but Hunter's was even, neat, and as intriguing as the woman herself.

"How can I help you?"

The blue scrubs-clad woman behind the desk was attractive with her chocolate skin and light brown eyes. Those eyes, however, looked as though they could see inside your soul, and burn it if they didn't like what they saw. *Intense. And, just a little scary.*

Ellie placed the items she held on the counter. "I'm a . . ." A what? Are Hunter and I friends? "I'm a friend of Dr. Vale's. She asked me . . ."

"You must be Ellie!" The nurse exclaimed excitedly.

"Um, yes." Ellie was momentarily surprised that Hunter would have spoken about her. It then dawned on her that Hunter must have notified the nurses about Ellie's possible visit.

"Hunter and Mo have told me about you." The nurse stood, though there wasn't much of a difference in her height from sitting to standing. "I'm Patty."

Recognition had Ellie smiling involuntarily. "Mo's wife. She did bring you the pie, yes?"

"Oh, you better believe she did." Patty's laugh was enthusiastic. *So, this is the object of Hunter's affection. I can see why Mo was so enchanted. Very nice.* "She knows better than to keep anything sweet from me. Especially from your diner. I've always wanted to compliment the baker when I've come in, but my mouth was too busy having delicious food shoveled in it."

Ellie chuckled modestly. "Well, I thank you for the compliment."

"Child, you are too young to be able to bake like that."

Ellie shook her head with levity. "I'm older than I look."

Patty tsked. At forty-eight, she was the oldest of their tight-knit group, and therefore dubbed herself the 'mama'. To Patty, the diner owner didn't look more than mid-twenties, which surprised her. She knew Hunter was looking for something different, just not so young.

"Ellie?"

Ellie's pulse kicked into high gear when she heard the alluring timbre of Hunter's voice. *Really gotta get that in control.* She took half a second to control herself and turned with a smile.

"Hey."

"You made it." As Hunter rounded the corner, she could have

sworn she heard Ellie's voice. She chalked it up to an active imagination that Ellie had been headlining all night. Then she saw the silken, blonde hair, and immediately felt exhilaration. *Calm down, Hunt. Still, doesn't mean anything.*

Ellie shrugged. "I had some time." It was true. Jessie was spending the night with Piper so they could work on a school project. Ellie had the choice of coming here or sitting alone at home. And though she had no idea what she could possibly say to the young patient to make a difference, Ellie would give it a go. "I also brought the pie for the nurses that you requested." She scooted one of the items closer to Patty.

Hunter frowned. "I . . ."

Ellie turned her attention to Patty who was watching them intently. "Dr. Vale wanted to do something for you nurses to apologize for her recent behavior," she explained. "She thought something sweet would help."

"Uh, yeah." Hunter scrambled to catch up with Ellie's game plan. *Damn, I should have thought of that. Thank you, Ellie!* "Least I could do," she added with humility.

"How sweet! Literally!" Patty laughed at her own pun, delighted when the others joined in. "You are forgiven, Dr. Vale."

"Thank God!" Hunter wiped a hand across her forehead. "I was afraid I'd be getting an enema soon."

"Still could happen," Patty muttered playfully.

"Um, that's my cue to leave. Are you ready, El?" *Shit. Tell me I did not just call her El.*

Did she just call me El? "As I'll ever be," Ellie answered with a deep breath. She walked beside Hunter down the long, sterile hall. "I'm a little nervous," she confessed.

Hunter captured Ellie by the elbow and tugged her to a stop. "You don't have to do this. I wouldn't blame you for saying no."

The sincerity behind the words gave Ellie a burst of courage. "No, let's do this. If there's a chance I can say or do anything to help, I'll do it. Oh!" Ellie held up the bag in her hand. "I brought you something to eat. I figured if it was something you wanted, you would take the time."

Deeply moved, Hunter carefully took the bag from Ellie as though it were filled with the most important item in the world. "Th-thank you. I don't know what to say."

"You just said it." Ellie touched Hunter's forearm briefly. *I hope you know what you're doing, Ellie. And, are ready for the consequences.* Truth was, Ellie wasn't sure she had the power to stop the force that drove her to be here, or to bring Hunter food. She was afraid that the situation was already out of her hands. "Come on. Take me to Dani, and then you can go eat that while it's still warm."

Chapter Five

"Dani? There's someone I'd like you to meet."

Per usual, Hunter was met with complete silence. The young girl never even took her eyes off the TV, even though it showed commercials at the moment. Hunter sighed, and nearly gasped out loud when she felt Ellie's hand on her shoulder.

Ellie noticed multiple empty pudding cups surrounding the girl and had an idea. She stood on her tiptoes. *"Give me the piece of pie from your bag,"* she whispered close to Hunter's ear.

Hunter fought to control the shudder that rushed through her body when she felt Ellie's warm breath on her sensitive ear. *Good God. Do as she asked quickly before all of your blood travels south, and you have no brain function.* Her hands shook as she fumbled with the sack. *Some surgeon. What happened to those famously steady hands?*

Ellie observed the slight tremor when she took the apple pie from Hunter. *She's just as affected as I am.* Ellie filed that away for another, more appropriate time. Right now, she had to concentrate on Dani.

"Thanks. Give me some time. I'll come and find you later."

Hunter nodded, and with a quick glance at Dani, left the two of them alone. Silently, Ellie studied the girl. She had been afraid that she would be reminded of her own daughter, but the two of them couldn't have been more different. She wasn't a classic beauty, but Ellie could see girls being attracted to the cute boyishness. Sadly, that cute, chubby face was marred with bruises and cuts from the accident.

Her dark hair was shaved on the sides, and long on top, somewhat forming a messy Mohawk. Olive skin contrasted drastically with the clinical white sheets of the hospital bed, as well as the bandages that Dani was currently sporting. A full cast covered Dani's left arm, and though Ellie was no doctor, she would bet there were more broken bones than she could detect. Not wanting to distress the young girl, even more, Ellie made it a point not to stare at the obvious emptiness at the end of the bed.

"If you're a shrink, I ain't interested." The teen still did not offer any eye contact.

The contempt in Dani's voice caused Ellie to flinch. But she made it this far. Too late to turn back now.

"I'm not a shrink, Dani. My name is Ellie Montgomery. I'm a friend of Hun – Dr. Vale's."

"Then I'm definitely not interested."

Ellie noted the slight change in Dani's tone. There was a sadness there. *I can probably work with that better than contempt.*

"Well, okay. If you don't want this apple pie . . ."

Eye contact. Interest. *Gotcha.*

"With ice cream?"

There's the young, insecure girl. "The ice cream would have melted by the time I got here, but I'm sure we could rustle some up." Ellie eased her way to the bed. "I have friends in high places, you know." She whispered conspiratorially.

"Nurse Patty?" A small smile played at Dani's lips.

"Ah, so you know who the real bosses are here, huh?" Ellie gave her a playful grin. She pressed the call button and hoped just dropping Patty's name gave her enough clout to get the ice cream for Dani.

"What do you need?"

Dani's demeanor instantly changed, and Ellie completely

understood why. The attitude of the young nurse was uncaring and bothered. With every auburn hair perfectly in place and the over-the-top yet flawless makeup, Ellie guessed that the nurse put more thought into her appearance than her patients. Ellie had always been a good judge of character. It came from years of serving many different people. This nurse? She did *not* like.

"We need some ice cream," Ellie said pleasantly.

"Yeah, it's too late for that." The rude nurse turned to leave.

"That's okay. I guess I'll just call Patty and see if she can bring us some." The mention of the older nurse's name had the redhead stopping abruptly. Ellie pulled out her iPhone for effect.

"I'll be back. We only have vanilla left," the young nurse snapped.

"Well, she's pleasant." Ellie made a face at Dani. "Glad she didn't call my bluff."

"I thought you said you and Nurse Patty were friends," Dani said suspiciously.

"Oh, we are. But we just met about five minutes ago." Ellie shrugged nonchalantly. "I'm sure if I had a few more minutes, we would have exchanged numbers and become besties." She flashed a cheeky grin and got a reluctant chuckle from the teen.

Dani sobered quickly. "What are you doing here?"

"Dr. Vale asked me to come and talk to you. I said okay."

"Why?"

"Why did she ask, or why did I say okay?" Ellie sat down in the chair next to the bed. At least she had the girl talking.

Dani contemplated the question for a moment. "Both, I guess."

Ellie's answer was interrupted by Nurse Ruderton (her nickname for the bad-tempered woman).

"Here." She put two small containers on the tray in front of Dani with a small thud. "Next time you use the call button, make sure it's for a good reason."

"Oh, I can assure you, ice cream is a *very* good reason," Ellie returned with total seriousness. "How else can we have apple pie à la mode?"

Nurse Ruderton's eyes narrowed to an annoyed squint. Ellie

thought she saw recognition reflected back, but she was quite sure she had never met the rude woman before. She would remember someone like her, and not for a good reason.

"Toodles," Ellie muttered and wiggled her fingers as the nurse stomped out. "Do you have to put up with her every night?"

Dani shrugged. "She doesn't say anything to me and I try not to bother anyone for anything." Her mouth snapped closed as though she surprised herself by saying anything at all.

"I don't know," Ellie said quietly. "That's the answer to your question. I don't know why Hunter – Dr. Vale – asked *me* to come here. She's worried about you and I guess that makes her desperate enough to try anything." *Honesty is the best policy, right? Hypocrite.*

"What do you get out of this?" Dani asked cynically.

Ellie raised an eyebrow the way she would if Jessie was getting too mouthy. "The joy of your pleasant company." She opened both ice creams and scooped them onto the pie. *At least Nurse Ruderton remembered spoons.* "I hope you like apple."

Dani nodded, shoveling a large bite into her mouth. Her eyes widened as she looked at Ellie.

"Brain freeze?"

Dani shook her head.

"Toothache?"

Another negative response.

Ellie smiled. "Good?"

Dani nodded vigorously, adding another bite to the one she had not quite finished.

"I'm here, Dani, because I wanted to help. Not just you, but Hunter, too. She feels such guilt for what she had to do, and you're not making it any easier."

"She took my legs." Dani's voice cracked with anger and sorrow.

"She saved your life," Ellie countered.

"It would have been better if she had let me die," Dani argued.

But there was no fire in the statement, and that told Ellie that Dani didn't really want to die. *Tread lightly, Ellie.* "How long have you been on your own?"

Dani's head shot up. "How did you?"

48

"Hunter told me. She cares, Dani. Enough to find out about you in order to help you. How long?"

"A little over a year." Dani frowned again and looked at Ellie with confusion.

"People tell me I'm easy to talk to. Maybe it's because I'm not threatening," Ellie suggested.

"Maybe it's the pie," Dani muttered. "You put something in here?"

"You caught me. It's called sugar," the diner owner confessed with a straight-face.

Dani fought to keep her scowl but failed miserably. "You're crazy."

"Ha! I'm actually the sane one." Tentatively, she put her hand over Dani's. "Talk to me. I promise you'll feel better. Keeping it all inside only creates a burden. But you don't have to carry it alone, Dani." When Dani stayed silent, Ellie made the decision to reveal something about herself, hoping it would help Dani open up. "I know what it's like to feel alone, Dani. To not have your parents on your side. I'm almost thirty-three years old and I'm still afraid, every day, that my parents could destroy me just because they don't understand me."

It broke Ellie's heart when a tear rolled down Dani's cheek. Without thought, she reached up and brushed it away, the same way she would for Jessie.

"My mom," Dani paused to clear her throat.

Ellie could practically feel the fear radiating from Dani. It was an emotion she knew all too well.

"It's okay. Look at me, Dani." She waited until the teen's tear-filled eyes lifted to hers. "I'm not a doctor, I'm not a psychiatrist, I'm not your parents. I'm just Ellie. And, believe me, I'm in no position to judge you at all."

There was a subtle change in Dani. Fear mixed with a tiny bit of hope and trust. Ellie knew it was a big step for the young woman and hoped she wouldn't disappoint her.

"*I-I'm gay*," Dani whispered, then hesitated as though she was waiting for Ellie to recoil in disgust and leave.

"Okay."

"You don't think I'm disgusting?"

"Oh, sweetheart, of course, I don't." Ellie's heart ached for the pain that Dani was in. Pain that was deeper than just the loss of her legs.

"My mom does." Dani lowered her head. "After she saw me kissing my best friend . . . Claire, she gave me ten minutes to get out of her house. Told me that if my father was still alive, surely what I was would kill him. I was seventeen, Ms. Montgomery." She looked up with her big, brown eyes. "I didn't have anywhere to go."

Ellie swallowed the lump in her throat and pushed down the familiar pain. "My friends call me Ellie," she offered gently and squeezed the smaller hand in hers. *She's malnourished. I could really hurt that bitch of a mother.* She almost scoffed at using that word for the woman. "I'm so sorry that happened to you. What happened to Claire? Couldn't you stay with her?"

Dani shook her head. "I loved her too much to put her through that. She offered, even begged me to stay with her, but I had – *have* – nothing to offer her. Especially now." She gestured miserably to her missing legs.

"So, you made the decision for her." Ellie kept her tone gentle, not wanting to reprimand the girl.

"I did what was best for her," Dani defended her decision defiantly.

"Sweetheart, you took her choice away." Just like your mother did to you, she added silently. "Did Claire love you back?"

"I have no legs!" Dani shouted, avoiding the question.

"Is that the part of your body that meant the most to Claire?" She knew she was pushing Dani, but it was needed. Dani was stuck in this loop of feeling unlovable and unworthy. That needed to stop before Dani could move forward.

"You don't understand! Just go away!" Dani angrily pushed the tray away from her and tried to jerk her hand away from Ellie.

"I understand more than you realize." She held Dani's hand firmly.

"Oh really?" Dani made a show of sitting up as much as she

could to look at Ellie's legs. "Looks like you still have your legs. Stick with Dr. Vale, though. That could change!"

"That's enough!" Ellie leaned closer. "You want to blame someone for the loss of your legs, blame the driver that hit you. Or, blame your mother for kicking you out when she should have hugged you closer." She put her hand over Dani's furiously beating heart. "But, *this* still beats, still lives, and can still love because Hunter made the *only* decision she could. The decision to save your life! This?" Ellie placed her hand on what was left of the girl's leg. "There is amazing technology out there that can help you walk again. You have that chance because of Dr. Vale. You have the chance to make things right with Claire because of Dr. Vale. And, you have the chance to prove to your mother that no matter what she does, she can't break you, because of Dr. Vale."

Dani dropped her head and sobbed. Ellie sat on the edge of the bed and took the girl in her arms. She rocked the teen back and forth, cooing soothing words as only a mother could do.

"I-I'm homeless, Ellie." Dani hiccupped. "How am I supposed to support Claire? What if I'm too late, and she found someone else?" She cried even harder.

"Oh, Dani." Ellie cupped Dani's face in her palms. "Reach out to her. If it's too late, you do your best to move on. As far as supporting her, mutual love means mutual support. Claire wanted to help you before. Let her if she's willing. Needing help does not mean you're weak."

"Sure you're not a shrink?" Dani sniffled, causing Ellie to laugh.

"I'm sure." She dried more tears on Dani's cheeks. "Just a diner owner."

"And a baker." Dani reached around Ellie to get another bite of pie. The ice cream was melted, but she didn't seem to care about that. "Ellie?" She looked up at Ellie through her long dark lashes. "I can't afford new legs."

Dani looked so young and scared at that moment, that Ellie's motherly instincts kicked in. "Didn't I mention that I have friends in high places?"

"HEY, PATTY." ELLIE flashed a sweet smile at the nurse that had just put a large forkful of pie in her mouth.

Patty covered her mouth and blushed. "Mmm." She held up a finger while she chewed quickly. "Child!" she complained when she finally swallowed. "You weren't supposed to see that. I don't normally eat like I've been starving for a month, but that damn pie of yours does it to me. Every. Time."

Ellie chuckled. "I'll take that as a compliment."

"You better!" Patty scrutinized the young woman. "You've been crying. Are you all right?"

"Mmhmm. It's a cleansing cry, I assure you."

"You got her to talk." Patty's eyes were wide with wonder. "How did you do that?"

Ellie gave her a small shrug. "Must've been the pie," she answered evasively. She didn't want to take credit for something she knew Dani wanted to do anyway. Ellie was just an outlet. "Is Hunter around?"

"You just missed her," Patty told her apologetically. "She's been pacing around here like a caged animal wondering what was going on in that room. Fortunately for all of us out here, she was called into surgery."

"Oh. That's okay. Could you just, um." *Just what, Ellie? Have her call you, and risk Jessie answering? I'm not ready for* that *talk, yet.* "Could you tell her that I did my best with Dani. Maybe Hunter could try talking with her again."

"I surely will. Thank you, Ellie, for coming down here, and helping with that young girl. I've known Hunter for a long time. I've never seen her this affected before."

"I just hope I helped. For both of their sakes."

Patty tapped her pen on the desktop. *Let's see what you're all about, Miss Ellie.* "She likes you, you know."

Ellie frowned. "Dani?"

"Hunter."

Ellie's pulse tripled. *What has Hunter told them?* "Um."

She's terrified, Patty observed with interest. *Terrified and interested. There's no mistaking that much. What has you running scared, child?* "It's just that Hunter doesn't make friends too easy."

Ellie let go of the breath she was holding. *Friend.* She felt twin pangs of disappointment and relief inside. "I can't imagine that. She's so goofy and personable."

Patty guffawed. "No one has *ever* described our resident, unflappable trauma surgeon that way. You must bring it out in her." She carefully watched Ellie's reaction to that news and was rewarded with a delighted smile.

"Well, I don't know if I can take credit for that, but I like her, too." She leaned in closer. "She's not crazy, is she?"

"Certifiable!" Patty cackled at herself.

Ellie couldn't help but laugh with the older woman. She liked Patty, she realized, hoping they would get a chance to know each other better. "I think I can handle that." She didn't think about the words, or what impression they would give Patty. Ellie was, for once, just being honest.

An exaggerated sigh and files being slammed on the counter behind Patty caught Ellie's attention. Nurse Ruderton gave her a scathing look before walking away.

"Oh, child, you have made an enemy," Patty snickered.

"What is her problem? You know, all I asked for was ice cream." Ellie looked over her shoulder at the rude nurse. "If she hates her job so much, perhaps she should find another line of work."

Patty laughed. "She has her sights set on Hunter. Has since she started here." Patty noted the frown on Ellie's pretty face. *Getting a little green there, child?* "Hunter, of course, has no interest in her. Pisses little miss bitchy pants off something good."

"I see." *I knew I didn't like her.* "That doesn't excuse her attitude with Dani." *That* got Patty's attention. "I may be overstepping my boundaries, but I don't want that woman on Dani's rotation anymore. Dani is going through enough without having to deal with an uncaring 'nurse'."

Patty was livid. "That young woman is already skating on thin ice. The only one she gives sweetness to is Hunter." She shook her head with disgust. "Don't you worry about overstepping, child. I see it as caring for a little girl's wellbeing. I'll make sure she's no longer Dani's nurse."

ELLIE CLOSED THE door of her apartment and leaned back with a deep, sad sigh.

"Jessie?" Her voice echoed in the empty home, and Ellie desperately wished for her daughter's presence. She slid down until she was sitting on the floor, and sobbed. The familiarity she felt with Dani was overwhelming. More than once, Ellie found herself wondering if she would have been homeless had she not made the decisions she made. *Stop feeling sorry for yourself, Ellie. You did what you had to do. And, you'll do it again if you have to.*

She shook off the depression and focused on the promises she made Dani. Ellie wiped away the tears and slipped a piece of paper out of her back pocket. Claire's number.

"Maybe I shouldn't have told her to reach out," Ellie said aloud. "If this goes badly, I'm to blame." With a deep breath and a prayer, Ellie took out her phone and dialed the number. She cursed when the 'out of service' sounded in her ear. "Damn! Damn, damn, damn! Now, what?"

She tapped her phone on her chin. "If I want to find someone, how do I go about it? And, why the hell am I talking to myself? Am I *that* lonely?" Ellie rolled her eyes at herself. "Yes, you are that lonely, and you know exactly who you need to find someone." She pushed herself off the floor and paced. Decisions. *You promised. And, it's not the only promise you need to honor.* Decision made, she typed out the text.

I need to see you. Will you meet me tomorrow? – Ellie

She didn't need to wait long for the response. *Oh, boy,* she sighed wearily.

Of course, darlin'. Name the place and the time. I'm there. – Cade

She texted back to meet her at the back door of the diner after the lunch rush. That would give Ellie time to see Hunter (*if* she comes in), talk to Cade to see if he could help her, and then go and see Dani – hopefully with good news. Now that that task was done, the silence was getting to Ellie, so she hit the speed dial for Jessie.

"Hey, mom!"

Ellie heard giggles in the background and wished she could be there with her daughter and best friend.

"Hey, sweetie! Having fun?"

"Yeah, we just finished a huge bowl of popcorn."

"I thought you were going to work on your project," Ellie reminded her in a motherly tone.

"Mom, we did. But, it's like past ten o'clock."

"Oh. Right." Ellie rubbed her temple as she tried to stem a headache that was coming on.

"Are you okay?"

"Hmm? Yes, of course. Just a little tired."

"Mom," Ellie heard the sounds in the background get quieter, and she knew Jessie was moving somewhere more private. "Something is going on with you, and I'm starting to get worried."

"Jessie, nothing . . ." she heard Jessie sigh dramatically. Decisions. *As much of the truth as possible for now.* "Okay, okay. I met a young girl recently that is going through some really bad times right now. She's only about a year older than you, and it breaks my heart to see her suffering."

"Oh," Jessie replied quietly. Ellie knew the question of where she met the girl would never be asked. It was a perk, she supposed, of owning a diner. "Will she be okay?"

"I hope so."

"Do you want me to come home?"

"No, sweetie. It's too late for you to be out, especially in your jammies." Ellie achieved the desired effect when she heard Jessie laugh.

"You sure?"

"Yes, sweetums. I'm just going to take a bath, and maybe read a little before going to sleep."

"Okay. Oh, Blaise is either trying to take off by flapping her arms, or she wants to talk to you."

Ellie snorted with laughter. She could see Blaise doing that with her big belly bouncing along.

"Give her the phone before she hurts herself!"

"I heard that," Blaise scoffed playfully. "Was whatever you had to do successful?"

"Are you still upset with me that I couldn't come over tonight?"

"No, I'm not upset that you didn't come over. Just that you didn't tell me what you had to do."

The annoyance in Blaise's voice was real, Ellie knew. There wasn't much Ellie kept from Blaise, save for one — or two — things. She was sure Blaise was feeling a bit left out.

"I went to the hospital, Blaise."

"What!" Blaise lowered her voice to a whisper. "What's wrong? Are you sick?"

"No, I'm not sick. I was visiting someone," Ellie explained. "A young girl who lost her legs."

"Oh, my God. Ellie, that's horrible. How did you? Wait, that doctor you introduced me to. Is that how you met this girl?"

"Yes." Ellie gave Blaise the condensed version of what transpired, leaving out some of the pertinent details. She just wasn't ready for that conversation.

"Well, she chose the right person to talk to this girl," Blaise lauded. "You could get a monk to talk to you."

"Ha! I still haven't gotten Big Al to do much more than grunt, so don't give me too much credit," Ellie chuckled.

"Hmm, that's true. I take it back."

"You're a brat, you know that, right?"

"Yep." Blaise let out a pained groan. "Ugh, I am so ready for this baby to pop out, and say hello to the world."

Ellie laughed softly once she knew Blaise was all right. "Don't worry. He'll be making his debut soon."

"He?"

"Mmhmm. I figured Greyson needed some reinforcements, so work on that, yeah?"

Blaise snickered. "I've been working on it for eight months. Greyson will be happy with whatever he gets, or he can try next," she quipped. "Oh, have you read your emails? See, I knew there was a reason I needed to talk to you."

"Oh, so it wasn't to nag about me not telling you everything? And, no, I haven't been able to read them, yet. Why?"

Blaise mocked Ellie facetiously. "Eve wrote. Basically, it says that the grand opening of her gallery is in about a month."

"That's quick after quite the delay."

"Yeah, apparently she's been out of the country looking for artists. But, she's back now, and will be in town this weekend to go over everything with us."

Well, maybe it'll keep me occupied enough not to miss Hunter since she is going to see her mom this weekend.

"I guess I know what I'll be working on after my bath," Ellie murmured.

"Use extra bubbles," Blaise suggested.

"Is there any other way to take a bath? I'll talk to you later, babe. Tell my daughter to go to bed. Love all around."

"Goodnight, honey. Kisses!"

The sound of Blaise's laughter kept Ellie from her morose thoughts for the remainder of the night.

Chapter Six

"Good morning, Big Al." Ellie filled a glass with the muddy looking mixture and set it in front of him.

"You look tired."

Ellie's eyebrows shot up in surprise. "Three actual words! And, an insult to boot. How lucky am I?"

"Not an insult, girl. An observation."

"Drink your drink, *old man*," she goaded. "Go back to grunting. I have other customers to tend to." She winked at him and grinned to take the sting out of her words.

Truth was, she was exhausted. Sleep did not come easy for Ellie the night before, and she was paying for it this morning. Even her run this morning had been sluggish, which never happened. She couldn't even make it this morning to the yoga class she taught. *Oh, to just stay in the corpse pose for the rest of the day.* She smiled distractedly at her customers. *Don't mess up the orders, Ellie. Wake up and get your head in the game.*

"Ellie?"

Ellie had just turned from the table when she heard Hunter call out her name. *Amazing how a shot of emotional adrenaline can wake you right up.*

"Hey. I was wondering . . . oomph." Shock, arousal (which she absolutely did *not* want to think about), and embarrassment besieged Ellie as Hunter enveloped her into a tight hug.

"*Thank you*," Hunter whispered as she tried not think about how good holding Ellie felt. *Oh, shit! I'm holding Ellie!* "Um, sorry." Hunter let go and awkwardly stepped back. "I just, uh, whatever you said to Dani, thank you."

The heartfelt words mixed with a healthy dose of bashfulness pulled on Ellie's heartstrings. They also made her forget being uncomfortable.

"Come sit down," she gestured to what was becoming Hunter's usual spot. *Big Al has some company now.* "I take it she talked to you?"

"Yes. I couldn't believe it." Hunter nodded when Ellie held up the coffee pot. "Patty told me you had been successful in getting Dani to talk. Sorry, I missed saying goodnight to you, by the way. Anyway, I didn't want to get my hopes up, you know? But, when I went in there to do her checkup, she said 'hi', and even smiled a little!" She knew she was babbling, but couldn't help it. The weight that was on her shoulders since the fateful night Dani was brought into her ER had been lifted. And it was all because of this beautiful woman standing in front of her.

"Progress!" Ellie smiled. "I'm really glad I could help, Hunter."

Hunter shook her head. "You didn't just help, Ellie. You performed a miracle. What did you say to her?"

Ellie colored slightly at the exaggerated compliment. "I basically just let her talk. I think you were right when you said maybe she just needed someone who didn't *have* to be there." She paused when a customer came in. Once they were taken care of, she turned her attention back to Hunter. "I think she understands now that you aren't to blame for the loss of her legs."

"But, I am," Hunter confessed sadly.

"Hunter, you need to let go of this guilt. Dani doesn't blame you. You shouldn't blame yourself."

Hunter nodded reluctantly. "I suppose. Is there anything I should know? Anything I can help her with?"

Ellie shook her head. "I can't answer that. I'm sure she'll come to you when she's ready."

Hunter readily agreed, not wanting to damage the obvious bond between Ellie and Dani. While Ellie excused herself to take care of another customer, Hunter studied the diner owner. She noted the faint circles under green eyes that Hunter hadn't noticed before.

"Are you okay, Ellie?" Hunter asked when Ellie joined her again. "You look a little tired."

Ellie's eyes slanted towards Big Al. "So I've been told." She managed to temper her annoyance. A little. Ellie turned back to Hunter with a wry smile. "I'm fine. I didn't sleep very well last night, so I'm a little tired. Nothing that a good nap won't fix."

Guilt burned in Hunter's gut. Was Ellie not sleeping because Hunter was selfish? "It's because of me, isn't it?" she asked regretfully.

Ellie was speechless. She opened her mouth, but immediately closed it. How the hell was she supposed to answer that?

Hunter continued, oblivious of Ellie's internal crisis. "I know I should be sorry for asking you to talk to Dani, but I can't argue with the results. Somehow I just knew you'd be able to get her to talk. But, I *am* sorry that you're suffering for it. I should have known how difficult this would be for someone not in the medical field."

Whew! "No, don't be sorry. Of course, it's a difficult situation, but I wouldn't change what I did. Especially since it helped." Ellie debated whether to tell Hunter about Claire, but thought better of it. *Maybe if I find Claire, I'll discuss the best course of action with Hunter.* Until then, it was time to change the subject. "Are you hungry?"

Hunter smiled at the obvious change in subject. "Yeah, a little. But, that lunch you brought me last night filled me up pretty good, so I'm not 'pancake-hungry'."

She flashed a lopsided grin that Ellie found incredibly endearing. An answering grin involuntarily formed on Ellie's lips. "Toast?"

"Perfect." *Like you.* "Like the burger," she said aloud. "I'm pretty sure that was the best burger I've ever eaten."

Big Al grunted something that sounded like an agreement, causing laughter from the two women.

Not normally one to get flustered by compliments, Ellie was stunned to feel a blush creeping up. "Well, I'm glad you enjoyed it. Now let me go get your breakfast." She hurried off with a small smile plastered on her flushed face.

HUNTER, AT ELLIE'S insistence, left soon after she finished her breakfast. Ellie knew that Hunter was reluctant to leave before her usual three hours were up. *Usual?* But the woman was exhausted, and Ellie worried about her making it home in one piece. It also worked out well since Cade was due to be at the diner any minute, and she didn't want to have to miss out on time with Hunter. *Oh, good Lord.* Ellie rolled her eyes at her decidedly adolescent reaction to the doctor.

"Ellie? You have a visitor." Rosa jerked her thumb towards the back with a scowl. She was worse than Ellie when it came to strangers in her kitchen. Rosa didn't even like when Blaise was back there. Of course, Ellie's word trumped everyone else's, so Rosa's annoyance didn't keep Blaise away.

"I'll be right there." Unwilling to compromise her customer service, Ellie took her time with her current patron. She gave the elderly lady a bright smile along with her change, and the hope for a great day before she headed to the back. "Cade?"

Cade Drake was a tall, attractive, ex-Marine, and Greyson Steele's best friend. With his black hair – still with a military cut – and gentle brown eyes, he was the perfect catch. Ellie found him to be a bit too Neanderthal and alpha, but underneath it all, he really was a great guy. She knew Blaise *and* Greyson hoped she and Cade would end up together. Unfortunately for them, that wasn't going to happen. But Ellie needed his help now. More specifically, she needed the services that Drake & Associates – Cade's security firm – could provide.

Cade turned to Ellie with a charming smile. And an arm full of orchids. *Crap.*

"Hey, darlin'. I'm glad you finally came to your senses. These are for you." He presented the flowers with a genial bow.

It was that combination of arrogance and sweetness that always threw Ellie for a loop. She was annoyed with the one side and charmed by the other. She took the orchids and thanked him accordingly.

"You saw Blaise." That was the only way Cade would know Ellie's favorite flowers.

He shrugged. "Thought I'd stop by there so I wouldn't be empty-handed when I picked you up."

"Wait, you think this is a date? Oh, God, does Blaise think we have a date?" As soon as the words were out of her mouth, she received a text from none other than her best friend.

I want details!

Shit. "Follow me," she ordered testily and led a confused Cade to her office. "Please have a seat." She gestured to the guest chair in front of her desk, purposefully avoiding the couch that adorned the small area.

"I don't get it. You asked me, no you *told* me you needed to see me. Now you're upset with me because I brought you flowers?" Cade crossed his ankle over his knee. It was a relaxed pose, but Ellie knew him well enough after nearly a year to know he was poised for anything at any time.

"I'm not upset about the flowers, Cade. I'm upset that you went to Blaise and told her this was a date. Or did you go to Greyson first, and then ask him to ask Blaise about the flowers?" The dig referred to the time she was basically tricked into going out with Cade on a double date with Blaise and Greyson. Only it was Blaise that asked Ellie, not Cade himself. She shouldn't be antagonizing him when she needed his help, but this seemed to be their habit when they were around each other.

Cade's nostrils flared with irritation. "Woman, you are the most exasperating . . ."

Ellie narrowed her eyes dangerously but held up her hands to call for a truce. This was about Dani, not her.

"I apologize for that; it was uncalled for." *That's it, Ellie, swallow your pride.* "I should have come to your office," she said softly.

"This is business?" Ellie nodded, and Cade dropped his foot back down with a distinct thump. "Then, yeah, you should have come to the office." Cade scoffed as he stood up. "Can't believe I thought you had thawed out."

Okay, *that* hurt. And pissed her off. "Cade, wait." She met him at the door. "I never meant to hurt you or lead you on. But, I didn't deserve that sexist remark just because your ego is hurt."

Cade shut his eyes and drew in a long, deep breath. "You're right, I'm sorry," he admitted quietly. "You just frustrate the hell out of me. For the life of me, I can't understand what it is about me that repulses you."

"Cade, I'm not repulsed by you," Ellie sighed and led him back to his seat. "You're just . . ."

"Not your type," he finished gruffly. "Yeah, I got that message from Greyson *and* Blaise." Cade spread his arms, flexing his muscles a tad. "How am I not your type?"

"I see your ego is alive and well," Ellie muttered. "Look, Cade, you're a great guy." He groaned. "What's wrong with being a great guy?"

"That's what women tell you when they're trying to let you down easy."

"When have I ever been easy on you?" Ellie jested. "It's the truth. You're handsome, successful, have a great sense of humor most of the time. You can be infuriating, but you're charismatic enough to get away with it."

"You make me sound like someone one would like to date. And, yet, you have no interest. Why? I don't even mind that you have a kid. That's major growth for me."

Definitely infuriating. "You continue on that path of growth. You'll make someone a great husband one day," Ellie informed him.

"Just not you."

Ellie was surprised by that statement. She didn't think Cade had anywhere near those kinds of feelings for her. She had always believed that he kept trying with her out of pride, or just the love of the chase.

"No. Not me. But, that is not a reflection on the man that you are, Cade."

"It's you, not me. Is that what you're telling me?" He barked out a sarcastic laugh.

Jesus. This was not *what I was expecting when I asked Cade to meet me. Decisions. How do I know what the right decision is? And, will I be able to survive the wrong one?*

"Yes."

"Come on, Ellie. Don't I deserve better than that old cliché? You know how I feel about you. If you just give me a chance, I can prove to you that I can be the man you need. The man you want."

Ellie stood abruptly and paced. "That's the problem, Cade." Ellie heard herself saying. It was like being outside her body, and not having the ability to stop the words from spilling out. "I don't want a man."

"Say again?"

It had been more than sixteen years since she last uttered the words. Words that she never imagined she would say again. Terrified didn't even begin to explain how she felt inside.

"I'm gay."

CADE LAUGHED UNTIL he saw the seriousness on Ellie's face and the trembling of her hands.

"You're not just saying that to get me to stop asking you out, are you?"

"No, Cade."

"But, Blaise . . ."

"Blaise doesn't know!" Ellie turned to Cade to plead with him. "Please. I haven't told her or Jessie. You can't say anything to anyone. Especially not to Greyson. At least not until I've had time to talk to them."

"You haven't . . . Blaise is your best friend. Jessie is your daughter," he stated unnecessarily. "Why would you keep this from them? And, why tell me?"

Her mind was spinning. She felt a sense of freedom, but the fear was overpowering. "My story is a long one and not one I want to get into right now. As for telling you? No offense, but I had nothing to lose. If you decided to hate me because of who I am, it would not hurt as much as it would if Jessie or Blaise did."

"Ouch." He held his hand up to forestall any further clarification. "I get it. Doesn't mean it doesn't hurt. If it's any consolation, I don't hate you." He studied her for a moment. "You're sure? Maybe you need . . ."

"Do not even finish that ridiculous statement," Ellie warned. Her temper cooled off a bit when she saw the twinkle in his eye. "You're an ass. You know that, right?"

"So I've been told." He reached out, and carefully took Ellie in his arms, hugging her to him. "I know you probably didn't want or plan to tell me, but I'm glad you did."

"So your pride can stand tall again knowing that it wasn't you failing at getting the girl?" she razzed with a nudge. She felt the rumble of laughter in his chest. "I know everyone thinks we should be together. And, God, that would be so easy." She looked up at him. "But . . ."

"But, you would be unhappy." He pushed her bangs out of her eyes. "Never compromise, Ellie. I could turn all of the compliments you gave me back around to you, and they still wouldn't be enough to describe how wonderful you are."

"Goddammit, Cade!" Ellie wiped a tear from her cheek. "If you dropped the Neanderthal act, and let people see how sweet you are, you'd be married by now."

He chuckled. "Well, my dream woman is not available. At least not to me, so what's the point? Besides, my sweet side wouldn't bode well for my business."

"Hmm. True." Ellie extracted herself from Cade's arms. Speaking of his business reminded her of why he was there in the first place. "I did ask you to see me for a reason. I need your help with finding someone."

"You want me to run a search for eligible lesbians in the area?" he grinned mischievously.

She flipped him off. "No, I've got that covered," she said cryptically, then sobered. "This is serious, Cade. I met a young girl recently who's going through a rough time. She needs her friend, but I can't find her."

"Does she want to be found?"

"I don't know. The two of them haven't spoken in a while, but I can't imagine she wouldn't want to know what's going on."

Cade nodded. "What information do you have?"

"A name, a disconnected phone number, and an old address."

"My team can work with that." Ellie handed over the information, and he immediately texted it to his team. "I should have an answer for you within the hour whether she can be located or not."

"Thank you. Of course, I'll pay."

Cade waved off the offer. "You'll do no such thing. Now, let's go back to you having things 'covered'. Give me a name. I'll run every search there is on her."

"You'll do no such thing!"

"I'm just looking out for you. Gotta make sure she's good enough for you."

Ellie met his gaze. "She makes me feel worthy enough to take a chance, Cade. That's good enough for me."

HUNTER'S EYES WERE wide open, as she stared at her ceiling. No matter how exhausted she was, sleep eluded her. Not even the sound of the ocean outside of her beach house could lull her to sleep this time. A certain blonde had taken up residence in her head, causing her body to remain in a constantly enticed state. It wasn't that she was complaining. Not at all. But, for once in her life, she didn't want to take matters into her own hands. Literally.

If only she could figure out if Ellie was gay. Hunter was about sixty percent sure Ellie would be receptive to an invitation to dinner. Okay, maybe it was more like fifty percent. Ellie Montgomery was an enigma. Even Mo and Patty, who bragged about their unfailing "gaydar" couldn't be sure.

Hunter blinked, losing the tiny spot she had focused on for what seemed like the past hour. "Ugh! You have *got* to get some sleep, Hunter. A tired surgeon is no good to anyone."

The ringing of her cell phone interrupted her one-sided conversation, and Hunter groaned again. *Don't be work!*

"Dr. Vale."

"I can't wait for you to get here this weekend, sexy."

Hunter cursed herself for not checking the display on the phone and cringed at the voice on the other end. She knew it was supposed to have come across as sultry, but the only reaction Hunter had was a sick feeling in her stomach. *Funny how things change*, she thought disgustedly.

"I won't be there to see you, Susan," Hunter answered coldly. "Do *not* show up at my mom's doorstep."

Susan laughed making Hunter's skin crawl. "Now don't play hard to get. We haven't been together in a long time. I need my Hunter fix."

"I told you I'm done. Find yourself another lesbian lackey."

"We've been over this, *Hunter*."

Susan's normally annoyingly high pitched voice turned dangerously low. It was a tactic that Hunter knew terribly well. Susan had always been able to manipulate her with a single change in octave. *Not anymore.*

"Yes, we have, *Susan*. And, I told you I'm done. Lose my

number." Hunter could play the dangerous bitch, too. She wasn't a young, naïve kid anymore. "Do not call me again. Do not show up at my parents when I'm there. Do not talk to my mother about me 'helping' you around the house."

"You *will* be in my bedroom this weekend, and you *will* do everything I tell you to do!" Susan screamed, then took a deep, calming breath. "You know you want me. You always have, you always will. You can't resist what we have between us."

"I have for over six months," Hunter reminded her cruelly. "And, believe me, the cleanse has been fucking amazing. You wouldn't believe how freeing it is to be rid of you."

Susan's breath came in angry pants. "Listen, you little bitch, if you don't want your parents to know what — or *who* — you've been fucking all these years, you *will* be at my home this weekend *fucking* me!"

Her traitorous body involuntarily responded to the demand, making her hate herself even more. *No more, Hunter!* As much as Hunter despised herself for the things she had done, she hated Susan more. "Are you going to include yourself in that confession, Susan?"

She didn't think Susan would be stupid enough to tell Hunter's parents about their sexual history. *God, I hope she's not.* Her mom and dad were completely supportive of Hunter's lifestyle, but Hunter didn't want them to know the sordid details of her less than respectable past. She was too ashamed. "Because I would be glad to let Paul in on your little side activities."

"You leave my husband out of this!"

"Then leave *me* the fuck alone!" Hunter hung up the phone, missing the good ol' days she could slam the receiver down with some satisfaction. She barely resisted throwing her phone across the room.

Hunter growled in frustration, her body tuned for *some* kind of release. Instead of making her hot, it pissed her off. She couldn't understand why that bitch of a woman had a hold on her. *What would Ellie think of your past?* Hunter scoffed with self-loathing. *Past. You just came to your fucking senses six months ago.* She picked up the phone again and dialed a number she hadn't wanted to dial. At least not for this reason.

It rang a few times before a breathless voice finally answered. "Hello?"

"Rebecca? It's Hunter. Did I catch you at a bad time?"

Hunter had met Rebecca years ago when the woman had come through Hunter's ER battered and broken. Her long, blonde hair had been matted to her head with blood, and her face bruised and swollen, her silver eyes dull. Delicate wrists were marred with welts from where Rebecca had been tied up. It was Hunter who mended the shattered woman, and she remembered that day as though it happened just yesterday. That was the day she could no longer ignore the agony of her job.

When Hunter found out that the woman's girlfriend had been the one that did the damage, she knew Rebecca would need a friend. It had been an easy friendship for them both, and they could talk about things that Hunter couldn't even tell Mo. As close as they were, and as attractive as Rebecca is, there was never anything more between them than a close friendship. One that Hunter was grateful for.

"Um, kinda." Rebecca's voice became distant as she spoke to the company she obviously had. "It's Hunter, baby. Give me a minute?"

"Hey, Hunter!"

Hunter laughed at the loud, quick hello. "Hey, Cass." She heard a smack, and knowing what she knew about Rebecca, she blushed. *Thank God they can't see me.*

"Okay, what's up, hon?"

"Sorry to interrupt. You didn't have to stop whatever you, um, were, you know," Hunter stuttered. Rebecca was the only woman other than Ellie that tongue-tied her. But for completely different reasons. Rebecca could be intimidating.

Rebecca laughed softly. "Hunter, we weren't doing 'you know'. Cassidy is training me."

"I thought that worked the other way around," Hunter teased. "Aren't you the Mist . . ."

"Stop!" Rebecca scolded with mirth. "Did you call to pick on me, or did you actually need something?"

Hunter remembered the reason and stopped laughing. "She called me."

"Oh, Hunter. I thought we agreed you wouldn't speak with her anymore." Rebecca knew all about Hunter's past with Susan. And the others that came after.

"I didn't check who was calling," Hunter said lamely. "Becca, my mind and heart are there. They want nothing to do with her. It's my body."

"I know, hon. Believe me. I still feel the effects of what Samantha did to me. My body became so used to the abuse, that I craved it in a sick way."

"How do you make it go away?" Even to Hunter's ears, she sounded like an insecure little girl, not the forty-one-year-old, successful surgeon she was.

"I'm still in therapy, Hunter. And, Cassidy helps. I trust her implicitly to give me what I need without hurting me." Rebecca paused for a moment. "Have you met someone, Hunter?"

Hunter was stunned at her friend's intuition. "How – how did you know?"

"I've never heard you quite this desperate. You've always been sorry for ever getting involved with Susan, but this sounds different."

"It is," Hunter confessed. "And, yes. I've met someone. I – I haven't, um, asked her out, yet."

"Is she gay?"

"I think so."

"You're not sure?" Rebecca asked, surprised. "I thought you were going to be careful this time."

"I am! I mean, I'm not sure, but I am being careful." Hunter sighed. "She's amazing, Rebecca. Beautiful, funny, smart, and she can cook better than anyone I know."

"She definitely sounds like a keeper," Rebecca chuckled. "Have Mo and Patty met her?" At Hunter's positive response, Rebecca continued. "What do their superpower gaydars say?"

"They're not sure either," Hunter answered quietly.

"Wow! Now I'm intrigued with this woman. Where did you meet her?"

"She owns a diner not far from the hospital. Mo took me there to cheer me up after what happened with Dani." Rebecca had been one of the first people Hunter had called the night she changed Dani's life forever.

"I guess it worked. What is this place called?"

Hunter readily gave Rebecca the information thinking maybe she could determine Ellie's preferences. If nothing else, Rebecca would at least be able to meet the woman that made Hunter's heart beat faster.

"Ellie's Diner?" Rebecca asked for reconfirmation. "I've been there. Actually, that's where Cassidy and I went for our first *real* date."

"*The appetizers were awesome!*" Hunter heard from Cass in the background. She was pretty sure Cass wasn't talking about food when Rebecca giggled like a young girl. The sound of a giggling Rebecca was something Hunter cherished, and she loved Cass for bringing it out. She hadn't been sure it would be possible after everything Rebecca had gone through.

"So, you know her?" Hunter asked excitedly.

Rebecca thought for a moment, trying to recall the staff at the diner. "Hmm, I'm not sure. I always imagined Ellie being a little, silver-haired old lady. Who else makes pies *that* good?"

"Right? They're amazing," Hunter laughed. "And, I thought that, too, about the little old lady. But, no, that definitely does not describe Ellie."

"Then describe her for me," Rebecca requested.

"Oh, um, she's . . . her hair . . ." Hunter stumbled over her words. How do you describe someone like Ellie? How do you put that beauty into words? "Her hair isn't as blonde as yours. It's more, um, the color of honey. It's wavy and long, past her shoulders, and looks so soft. Her eyes. Oh, God, Rebecca, her eyes. So expressive. They're, um, hazel, I think. But, I would say more green. Her body."

A strangled moan came from Hunter making Rebecca laugh

silently. "Her body?" The question got Cassidy's attention, and Rebecca soon found herself practically being smothered by her tall, slender lover. *Mmm. If she keeps breathing on my neck like that, this conversation with Hunter is going to have to continue later.*

"Well, um, please don't take this the wrong way, but I've always thought you had a great body."

Cass's eyebrows shot up. "You hitting on my girl, Hunt?"

"Shit! Rebecca! You didn't tell me Cass was listening!"

Rebecca burst out laughing. "She heard the word body, and that was all it took to get her attention."

"I – I'm not hitting on Rebecca, Cass. Just stating the obvious."

"True. Carry on."

Luckily, Hunter heard the smile in Cass's voice. She knew that Cass and Rebecca were solid in their relationship, and would never want to be a reason that changed.

"Well, uh, Ellie's body is similar to yours, Rebecca. Maybe a little less, um, endowed, but perfectly proportioned. Her legs, though, mmm. Even in jeans, I can tell she has muscular thighs. I can just imagine those legs." She clamped her mouth shut as she realized what she was saying, and who was listening.

"Go on!" Cass teased.

Hunter heard rustling on the other end of the phone and shook her head. "Forget it. I'm not going to be your foreplay!"

"Stop it!" Rebecca laughed and slapped playfully at Cass's wandering hands. "Go away. You'll get your turn in a minute. Let me finish up with Hunter."

"Kinky. Hunter, if I didn't trust my girl so much, I'd be jealous!" Cass gave Rebecca a wink and quick kiss before leaving them alone.

"She's a goof." Rebecca sighed happily.

"She's good for you. I'm so happy for you," Hunter stated sincerely.

"Thank you. Now, back to Ellie. I don't think I've seen her there. Maybe I'm not going at the right times," she chuckled. "Though, that description sounds familiar. I just can't put my finger on why." Hunter muttered something about fingers and Ellie, and Rebecca tsked. "You're bad."

"I want to be good for her, Rebecca," Hunter said with quiet seriousness.

Rebecca could hear the utter sadness and apprehension in her friend's words, and her heart broke. *It's time to start getting past this, my friend and start living.*

"Are you ready now, Hunter?"

Rebecca had been wanting Hunter to see a therapist for a while now. Hunter's knee-jerk reaction had always been to say she didn't need to see a shrink. She couldn't do that this time. Hunter wanted to be the kind of woman Ellie would be proud of. She couldn't change the past, and if she and Ellie had a chance, she would hope Ellie understood that. But Hunter could change how she acted now. She couldn't let the thought of Susan and the others keep her from opening up to someone like Ellie.

It helped that the therapist was Rebecca's aunt, and she was located in New York. Using modern technology to have their sessions gave Hunter control over the situation by being able to dictate when and where they would happen. Not being cooped up in an office with a virtual stranger while she told them all of her secrets, was also a plus.

"Yes."

Chapter Seven

"Hey, Ellie!"

Ellie smiled at Blaise's young employee. Mer was exuberant as ever. An excessively bouncy, unusually blonde, happy girl. Ellie often wondered if Mer held any dark secrets like she did herself. She hoped not, and that the girl's cheerfulness was genuine.

"Hey, Mer. She back there?" Mer nodded. "Good, could you not interrupt us unless it's an emergency?"

"Sure, no problem!"

Do you ever have a problem? Ellie scolded herself for being so petty. It was childish to be upset with the girl's zest for life just because Ellie's own life had somehow fallen through some bizarre portal. She headed straight back to Blaise's back room where she found the pregnant woman standing at a large table working on a bouquet. Blaise glanced up when Ellie cleared her throat.

"Hey!" Her smile was big, and she wiggled her eyebrows. "So? How did it go? Details!"

"You have to stop, Blaise."

The smile disappeared. "What do you mean?"

"This obsession you have with getting me and Cade together has to stop." Ellie struggled to keep her anger in check. She didn't want to be mad at Blaise. She knew her best friend only had Ellie's best interest at heart, but constantly having to dodge Blaise's attempts at matchmaking was getting to be too much. Especially now, when all of Ellie's emotions – and hormones – were in chaos.

Blaise sighed and forgot about the arrangement she was working on to give Ellie her full attention. She eased her pregnant self into the chair behind her desk. "That bad?"

"It wasn't a date!" She was rarely exasperated enough with her best friend to yell at her. "I asked to meet Cade because I needed information. *Not* a man!"

Blaise's eyebrows furrowed at Ellie's anger. Of course, she had seen it before but never directed towards her. At least not like this.

"What happened to you, Ellie?" Blaise asked softly. "In the fourteen years I've known you, I have never once seen you date. I know you said that Jessie's father didn't hurt you, but *something* happened."

Ellie stared at her. She could see the loving concern in Blaise's eyes, but how long would that love last if Blaise knew the truth?

"Why can't you just leave it alone?" The fight had gone out of Ellie. All that was left was an overwhelming ache in her heart. Decisions. The decision she made years ago has now come full circle. She couldn't ignore the feelings that Hunter ignited in her. Hadn't she just told Cade that Hunter made her feel worthy enough to take a chance? But the fears from so long ago came back in full force as she faced Blaise.

"Because I love you, Ellie, and I want to see you as happy as I am with Greyson. Cade is a good man, and he cares for you." Blaise leaned forward as much as her tummy would allow. Something was holding Ellie back, and she was determined to figure out what it was. "I know you keep saying he's not your type, but for the life of me, I don't understand how that's possible. He's *almost* as perfect as Greyson."

"You love me," Ellie repeated, ignoring everything else Blaise said. "Until I do something that changes that," she murmured.

Blaise raised a brow. "You could never do anything to change the way I feel about you."

"How can you say that? What if I killed someone?"

"Then I would help bury the body, and provide your alibi," Blaise answered seriously. She had never seen Ellie so vulnerable. One of the things she admired most about her best friend was the strength Ellie possessed. Becoming a mother at sixteen could have broken Ellie's spirit, but she flourished instead. "You and Jessie are my family."

Ellie lowered her eyes. "When you grow up the way I did, being family doesn't mean unconditional. You're only loved if you're perfect. Once you step across that line into imperfection that love is gone," she shrugged sadly.

"You love Jessie, flaws and all. You love me, and Lord knows I'm not perfect. Your parents are arseholes, Ellie." Blaise stood, and made her way over to Ellie. She took Ellie's trembling hands in hers, squeezing them gently. "And, if they're the reason you're not letting love into your life, they're not worth it."

Decisions. Cade knew about her now, and he assured Ellie he wouldn't say anything. But was it fair to *anyone* in Ellie's life — including herself — for her to keep lying?

"Do you remember the woman I introduced you to when you came into the diner a couple of days ago?" *God, has it only been a couple of days?* "Dr. Hunter Vale?"

Blaise's eyebrows furrowed in concentration as she thought of that day. "The one that gave me her seat?" Ellie nodded. "How could I not remember her? She was quite tall. And striking. Why?" Her eyes widened, and she squeezed Ellie's hands even harder. "No. Don't you dare tell me that! No! I refuse to hear that!"

So much for unconditional, Ellie thought miserably.

Blaise caught on to Ellie's anguish and her stomach dropped. "I swear, Ellie if you tell me you're sick, I'm going to kill you! You better not be dying!"

What? Ellie tried to wrap her mind around what Blaise was saying. It wasn't often the two of them were so far off mentally. "Blaise, I'm fine. I'm not dying." She couldn't help but laugh at the absurdity of the situation. "Hunter is a trauma surgeon."

"Oh." Blaise blew out a stressed breath. "Sweet Jesus, woman! Don't scare me like that. I thought I was going to go into labor."

"*You* jumped to your own conclusions!"

"Don't use your logic on me!" Blaise grinned. "Wait, does this have anything to do with that young girl you met?"

"Dani," Ellie offered absently. This was Blaise, God love her. Always so impatient. "No, this has nothing to do with Dani, no, I'm not sick, and no, I'm not dying," she held her finger up when Blaise opened her mouth again. "You asked me – many times – what my type is." Ellie took a deep breath. "Now you know."

Blaise's face was the picture of confusion, but Ellie was determined to let Blaise work it out in her head. She would get it eventually.

"I don't under . . ." Blaise's eyes widened with shock and disbelief. "Are you? You're . . . are you trying to tell me you're . . . that you're . . ."

"Gay, Blaise. The word is gay." Ellie paid close attention to her friend's reaction. So far it hadn't changed from confused disbelief.

"Since when?"

"Since forever," Ellie answered seriously.

"No." Blaise shook her head and walked away.

Instead of sitting back down, she paced, and this was when Ellie began to worry. Blaise pacing was equivalent to Ellie running. Okay, technically, Blaise eating red velvet cake was equivalent to Ellie running. Pacing was a close second.

"No," Blaise repeated adamantly. "You would have told me something like that." She looked up at Ellie who hadn't moved, a stony expression on her face. "Fourteen years, Ellie. How could you lie to me for *that* long? You *should* have told me!" Her voice continued to raise the more she spoke.

"Like you told me about Piper?" Ellie retorted angrily. "And, how you're an heiress?"

"That's different!"

"How?"

"First, I didn't even know Piper was alive! It hurt too much to talk about her." Pregnant hormones and Ellie's overwhelming confession caused tears to pool in Blaise's eyes. "Second, I didn't want anything to do with that money."

"I know," Ellie said softly. "I know. My point was, we each had something significant we felt we couldn't talk about."

"But why couldn't you talk to me about this, Ellie? This isn't a little thing. This is *who* you are. The stuff I kept from you was just a part of me."

Ellie sighed. She sat down in the chair and folded her hands in her lap. When Blaise sat as well, Ellie continued. "Blaise, when I was young I knew that I felt different than other girls. I didn't know exactly what was different, but I realized that I didn't want what my parents wanted for me. Up until that point, I had been the model daughter. I excelled in school, excelled in sports – ones that my father approved of, of course – never got in trouble. My parents bragged about me every chance they got. Because of that, I made the decision to trust them with what I was feeling."

Blaise swiveled in her chair to grab two bottles of water out of the small refrigerator hidden under the counter behind her. She handed one over to Ellie, then opened her own.

"Thank you." Ellie drained half of the bottle.

"So, you told your parents that you're . . ."

"Why can't you say the word, Blaise?" Ellie's tone was a bit harsher than she intended.

"Cut me some slack, Ellie." Blaise shot back. "You come in here and completely change everything. Give me some time to catch up."

"That's the thing. *Nothing* has changed. I certainly haven't." Ellie's features softened as she tried to understand Blaise's side. It wasn't as though Blaise was being antagonistic towards her, just a bit flustered. For as long as she had known Blaise, Ellie never knew her to be homophobic. She just hoped that extended towards her. "The only thing that has changed is now you know."

Blaise closed her eyes and breathed deeply. As a yoga instructor who had taught Blaise the technique, Ellie recognized the practice for what it was, and let Blaise have her moment.

"What happened when you told your parents you're a lesbian?" Blaise asked evenly, eyes still closed.

"Oh, so you can say it?"

Blaise's eyes flashed open, and she was ready for a fight until she saw the smirk on Ellie's face. "It's not nice to tease the pregnant lady." She smiled, glad that they could still be silly with each other.

"I'll be glad when you can't use that excuse anymore," Ellie laughed, equally as happy that their playful banter hadn't changed.

"You and me both, sister." Blaise groaned a little as she changed her position in her seat. "Are you going to answer?"

"Yeah," Ellie sighed. "It's the typical story, really. Highly religious parents, gay kid. Obviously, they didn't take it well. In fact, they tried everything they could to change my mind." Ellie scoffed. "Like it's a choice. But I did make a choice. I *chose* to deny who I was."

Blaise stayed silent for once and waited for Ellie to collect her thoughts. Her heart hurt for Ellie. She couldn't even begin to imagine how hard it would be to have to reject who you are inside. Yes, she was upset that Ellie kept it from her, but perhaps there was a good reason. There was always a good reason, right?

"I did everything my parents asked me to do. I never spoke of my feelings again. I dated the boy they chose for me." It was definitely the condensed version. However, with the threat of being interrupted, Ellie didn't feel right talking about *everything* while they were at Blaise's shop. She made a mental note to have a 'bestie's night' where she could tell Blaise the entire story without censoring anything.

"Jessie's father?"

Ellie nodded. "I slept with him hoping that maybe I was wrong about myself. I didn't have any other experiences, certainly not with girls, so maybe I just didn't know." She shrugged with a sorrowful smile. "I wasn't wrong. But, it was too late. I was pregnant. And, my parents spent every moment they could stilling being with me promising me that if I *ever* spoke of being gay again, they would take my baby away from me. They would find a way to make me out to be an unfit mother, and if they couldn't do that, they would make sure that my baby would grow up hating who I was. That scared me more than anything. So, I suppressed everything I felt. I lived for my baby, not me."

"My God, Ellie." Tears streamed down Blaise's face. What Ellie sacrificed for Jessie was tremendous. "Would they really have taken Jessie away from you?"

"Yes, they would have found a way. Even before they had Jessie to use against me, they threatened to kick me out of the house. I was fifteen, Blaise. I had nowhere to go." Dani's words. That's why she felt such a connection with the teen. "Dani is like me," she said quietly.

"Dani? The girl who lost her legs?"

"Yes. Her mother caught her kissing her girlfriend. Kicked her out with only ten minutes to grab what she could. She had nowhere to go." Ellie shuddered. "That could have been me, Blaise."

Blaise shook her head in disbelief. "How could a mother do that to her child?" It was a rhetorical question, but still, Ellie shrugged with sadness. "Couldn't Dani's girlfriend help?"

"Claire. She wanted to, but Dani was too proud. She didn't think she had anything to offer Claire, so Dani pushed her away."

"That's why you needed to see Cade? You're going to help Dani find Claire, aren't you?"

"I'm going to try."

"And, you're doing all of this for this doctor?"

"Hunter. And, no, it's not just for her. I want to do this for Dani. I understand all too well what she's feeling." She closed her eyes and took a breath. When she opened them back up, they were clear. Intense. "She shouldn't have to do this alone."

"I want to help if I can," Blaise offered sincerely.

Ellie smiled. "I was hoping you'd say that."

"May I ask you something?"

"I'm thinking at this point, Blaise, there's nothing else that we could keep from each other."

Blaise chuckled. "True. Why now?"

Ellie knew Blaise was asking why she was choosing to come out now, and she gave her a small smile. "Because of Hunter," she answered simply. "When I made my decision to hide so long ago, I also made myself a promise. I vowed that if ever there was a time when *someone* made me feel . . ." she paused, searching for the right words to express herself. "*Anything*. Who made me feel worthy, I would make an effort to be true to myself."

"And, Hunter makes you . . . feel?"

A faint blush graced Ellie's features, which annoyed her. She hated blushing. *I'm too damn old to feel like a teenager with a crush.* But she knew it was more than just a crush. "Yes. When you came to me and told me how Greyson made you feel, I listened, but I couldn't really understand. Now I do. I *feel* what those chick flicks are all about. What romance novels boast."

"I didn't think you read those," Blaise laughed.

"I don't. I can't. That doesn't mean I don't know what they're about," Ellie smirked.

Blaise's head tilted to the side in question. "What do you mean you can't? Why?"

"For the same reason I can't talk to you about, um . . ."

"Sex?"

Stupid blushing. "Yes. I didn't want it. No, that's not quite right. I didn't *want* to want it. I had repressed my feelings for so long that I thought they had just disappeared." The last word was spoken so low that she wondered if Blaise even heard her. "It was easier that way, and I didn't want to chance it by reading about it, watching it, or talking about it."

"I guess I can understand that." Blaise didn't sound quite so convinced, but at least she was trying. "Were you, um." Blaise shifted awkwardly in her chair. "Was there ever a time when you, uh, were attracted to me?"

Ellie burst out laughing. Not only was Blaise stuttering as much as Hunter did, she was also blushing furiously. The blush didn't hide Blaise's scowl, though. "I'm sorry, I'm not laughing at you. I just wasn't expecting that question or your bashfulness." Blaise stuck her tongue out at Ellie, making her laugh even harder. *Now, what do I say without hurting her feelings? Have to go with the truth.* "No, sweetie. I've never felt that way about you."

Surprise flashed in Blaise's eyes. "Why? What's wrong with me? I'm hot, damn it!"

Ellie snorted with laughter. "You're really upset about this? First of all, you're straight."

"Like that's ever stopped anyone," Blaise muttered grumpily.

"True," Ellie snickered. "But when we met, I was in no position to be attracted to anyone. And, you became my best friend. The sister I never had. At that point, it would've just been awkward to have any feelings of attraction."

"I guess," Blaise pouted.

"Aww. Blaise, you're a remarkably beautiful woman, and perhaps if things had been different," Ellie shrugged.

That seemed to brighten the Kiwi up. *She's so weird*, Ellie thought humorously.

"Tell me more about your doctor."

My doctor. I hope one day that will be true. "Not much to tell since I just met her." This time it was Ellie who shifted uncomfortably. "Um, I know that she's a doctor. I know that she's cute when she can't find her words around me. I know that she's sensitive. I know that she enjoys my pies." Her eyes dropped from Blaise's intense stare. "I know that she's incredibly beautiful. I know that she has the bluest eyes, I could drown in them. And, that when she's around me my heart races, and I forget who I am sometimes."

Blaise was shocked. She had *never* heard Ellie speak of anyone with such reverence other than Jessie. She really hoped this woman was worth what Ellie was going through right now. "And, she's a *lesbian*?" she asked, emphasizing the word playfully.

Ellie rolled her eyes. "I'm ninety-nine percent sure she is, yes." When Blaise lifted a brow, she chuckled. "It's not like we have neon lights that only blink for each other. But, if the way she acts around me is any indication, then I'd say yes."

Blaise nodded. "Have you told Jessie?"

Ellie slumped down in her chair with an anguished groan. "No, and I don't know how I'm going to. What if she hates me, Blaise?"

"Oh, Ellie, she's not going to hate you. That girl worships you."

A small smile formed at the corners of her mouth at that. Then she frowned thinking of her parents' threat. One they made sure to reiterate every time Ellie saw them. "What if my parents got to her?"

"Ellie, sweetie, *you* raised Jessie to be a kind, open-minded, open-hearted young woman. Trust her and yourself. And, stop letting her visit your goddamn parents!"

Ellie smiled at Blaise's fervor. "Jessie *is* a beautiful, caring young woman," she agreed. "But, it's different when it's your mom, don't you think? Even *you* had a problem with hearing it."

"Wait just a minute. I didn't have a problem with you being gay. Not really. That just surprised me. My issue was with you keeping such a huge secret from me."

"Same difference," Ellie teased. "And, I can't forbid Jessie from seeing her grandparents. They dote on her, and even though we don't get along, I can't keep them from their granddaughter."

"You can if it's detrimental to you," Blaise argued with a sour look on her face.

Blaise mumbled something that Ellie didn't quite catch, but she was sure it was quite colorful. A smile stretched across Ellie's face, lighting it up. Blaise was defending her. She didn't hate her. Maybe she would survive this after all. Jessie would be the biggest test of all.

"Do you want me to be there with you when you tell her?" Blaise asked interrupting Ellie's internal happy dance.

"I would love that, but I think I need to do this myself. I'm sure she's already not going to be happy that I've told two people before her." She snapped her mouth shut as she realized her mistake a bit too late.

"*Two*!? You told someone *before* me? Who?"

Ellie shrank further into her chair and mumbled.

"I'm sorry, I didn't quite catch that. Who?" Blaise snarled.

Geez. Pregnant Blaise has a short temper. "Cade."

"Cade!!"

"Wait! It wasn't because I wanted to! It was a necessity, Blaise. I needed him to know, in no uncertain terms, that we would never happen."

Temper quashed marginally, Blaise blew out a breath. "I can't believe you told that Neanderthal before you told me."

Ellie laughed heartily. "First he's *almost* as perfect as Greyson, now he's a Neanderthal. Which is it?"

Blaise blinked at her. "Both," she said dryly. "Just like Greyson. Though I do like when Greyson gets dominant . . ."

"Blaise! I'm still not there, yet." She flipped Blaise the bird when she laughed at Ellie's discomfort. "Anyway, if it makes you feel any better, I told Cade that the reason I came out to him was because it didn't matter if I lost his friendship because of it."

"Ouch."

"Yeah, that's what he said," she grinned mischievously. "But it's true. I had nothing to lose by telling him unless he blabbed it to everyone else. I have *everything* to lose by telling you and Jessie."

"You're not going to lose anything, sweetie. I promise."

God, I hope you're right. "Well, we'll know for sure this weekend."

"Is that when you're going to tell her?"

Ellie nodded. "Hunter is going to visit her parents this weekend. I'm banking on the fact that she probably won't attempt to ask me out – *if* she even does - and *then* go out of town. So, it gives me a little time," she reasoned.

"Does Hunter know about Jessie?"

"No. I haven't really had an opportunity to tell her. Besides, I wanted to be sure what was happening between us before bringing my daughter into it."

"Understandable. More understandable than me being the second to know this news."

"Well, third technically, but who's counting?" Ellie laughed.

Blaise threw her hands in the air in exasperation. "Don't tell me, Frank came on to you so you had to tell him so he'd keep it in his pants."

Ellie belly-laughed until her insides hurt. "Sweetie, Frank is gay. There's no way he would come on to me. And, I haven't told him."

"Frank was gay?"

"I suspect he still is since he moved in with his boyfriend," Ellie quipped. She could practically see the questions churning in Blaise's head. "Frank ran into some money slash housing problems. He has no family, so I offered to let him stay with me until he got back on his feet."

"I always thought that was nice of you," Blaise acknowledged. She always *knew* Frank wasn't Ellie's type. Now she knew the feeling was mutual.

"Not really. He served a purpose for me." She smiled when both of Blaise's eyebrows shot up. "Get your head out of the gutter, Kiwi. I just meant that with him around, my parents left me alone. I guess that's not going to matter soon, huh?"

"Your parents can suck it."

"Blaise."

"What? They can! After everything they put you through, why would you even *think* of defending them?"

"They're my family, Blaise. They may not love me unconditionally, but I'm not like that."

Blaise slowly shook her head. "You are such a good person. Much better than I am, since I had what's left of my family arrested."

Ellie scoffed. "That's different."

"Not really." Blaise sipped her water. "My family wanted me to be someone I wasn't and kept my daughter from me. Yours forced you to be someone you aren't, and threatened to take your daughter away from you unless you complied."

Ellie blinked, startled at how similar their stories were. "Well, when you say it like that."

"Only way *to* say it," Blaise chuckled. "They don't deserve your unconditional love if they can't return it, sweetie." She let her best friend ponder that. Blaise, herself, had no problem hating Ellie's parents. Had since she met them years ago. But Ellie had to have been born with a huge heart to still find love and forgiveness for such hateful people.

Ellie drew in a deep breath. She knew Blaise was right. She had given up way too much for her parents, and Ellie couldn't do it anymore. Did she still love them? Of course. But it was time to love herself more.

"Like I said before, I won't forbid Jessie from seeing them. She's old enough now to make her own decisions." Ellie straightened in her chair with a defiant look. "And, I'm old enough to stop being afraid of them."

"Good for you! Now, let's get to the good stuff."

An elegant, blonde eyebrow raised. "Excuse me? I just told you a shit load of 'good stuff'. What more do you need?"

Blaise clicked her tongue. "That was like the news. Now I want more of the reality TV stuff. Like the fact that you're a virgin," she smirked.

"Blaise!" More blushing ensued. "I am *not* a virgin. I have a daughter for crying out loud."

"Eh." Blaise waved her hand dismissively. "That doesn't count. It's been so long that you can reclaim your virginity. So, tell me. What are you going to do to get ready for *the* moment?"

"We are *not* having this discussion here. I don't even know if Hunter is interested."

Blaise laughed at Ellie's uneasiness. "I think you *do* know. And, I think you've already been thinking of *that* moment."

Blaise squealed when a delicate flower came sailing through the air at her. *Where the hell did she get that from?* "Don't ruin my bouquet just because you're horny!"

"I hate you," Ellie glared.

"You love me," Blaise singsonged, pleased with herself that she can *finally* get Ellie Montgomery back for all those times she teased Blaise about her dating life.

Chapter Eight

Hunter sat back and blew out a frustrated breath. She had just finished a preliminary chat with Rebecca's therapist aunt. *Post-Traumatic Stress Disorder.* That was Dr. Willamena Woodrow's first impression. Of course, Hunter didn't want to believe it. But she promised Rebecca she would give her "Aunt Wills" a chance, and she intended to do just that.

"You okay?" Rebecca asked softly. At Hunter's request, she had stayed for the initial meeting, even listening in on some of the things Hunter had revealed. *No wonder she's unhappy.*

"Yeah. No. I don't know, Becca. Maybe I should just leave Ellie alone. Who needs this shit?" Hunter scrubbed her face with frustration. The last thing she wanted to do was give up on her hope that the diner owner would be interested in going out with her. But how fair was it for Ellie to have to deal with Hunter's baggage?

"Hunter, don't do that. First of all, you deserve to be happy, and I have never seen you act like this about anyone. Ever."

An unbidden smile came to Hunter's face. Her head was still leaning on the back of the couch, and her eyes were still closed, yet there was no denying what just thinking about Ellie did for the doctor.

"Ah, ah!" Rebecca saw the frown forming and knew Hunter was about to say something Rebecca wasn't going to like. "I'm not finished. Second, you're not going to let someone like Susan keep you from a *normal* relationship."

"What if I'm unable to have a *'normal'* relationship?" Hunter asked weakly.

"I don't believe that. You want it too badly. You know you're ready, Hunter. You've already made the first steps."

"But . . ."

"Stop trying to talk yourself out of this." Rebecca studied her friend, amazed by their similarities. *Probably the reason nothing ever happened between us. Lord knows she's a beautiful woman, but we would never have made it.* "Do you think I don't deserve a normal relationship with Cassidy?"

Hunter shot up. "Of course I don't think that! You deserve all the best in the world." Her voice trailed off as she realized what Rebecca was doing.

Rebecca smirked, satisfied that she had gotten her point across. "So, you're going to pursue diner chick, yes?"

"Diner chick?" Hunter chuckled. "Honestly, I don't think I could stay away. I just wish I knew if she was family."

"Take me there to eat. We'll see if we can figure it out," Rebecca suggested with a shrug.

"You just want to scope her out."

"And? I'll have Cassidy meet us there. She seems to be pretty good at picking out the lesbians." Rebecca smirked, before becoming serious. "So, you're going to visit your mom this weekend?"

"Yeah. Actually, I was thinking about leaving tonight and making a long weekend of it. I'm due some time off." Hunter caught Rebecca's skeptical look. "I'm *not* going to see *her.*"

"Are you sure it's a good idea to spend more time around temptation?"

"Susan is not a temptation for me. Not anymore," Hunter insisted.

"Babe, it's been how long?"

"Six months," she muttered. Rebecca shook her head. "I can do this, Becca. I have a reason now not to fuck up."

Rebecca contemplated that for a moment. "Okay, how about this. You go there, spend time with your family, avoid Susan at all costs, come back and ask Ellie out." Rebecca was sorry she was going to have to erase the happy grin that graced Hunter's beautiful face. "But, if you go there and fuck up, you leave Ellie alone."

Hunter's eyes widened. "But . . ."

"Honey, I'm sorry, but if you're with Susan this weekend, you're not ready for a real relationship with Ellie. What if there comes a time when you *are* with Ellie, and temptation happens again? Make sure you can resist the past before you move on to the future."

Tears pooled in Hunter's eyes at the thought of screwing up a future with Ellie. One she wasn't even sure was possible in the first place. Since when did anyone affect her like this? *Getting soft in my old age*, Hunter thought bitingly. But if she really thought about it, she was ready to be soft now. She was ready to find love, as scary as that was to her.

It all started the night Rebecca was brought into her ER. She felt an immediate kinship with the woman and knew they both deserved more. It took them a long time to actually get to the point where they were ready for that change. Then again, it could have been as simple as meeting someone who made them feel . . . worthy.

Maybe that's what was different about Ellie. Even though Hunter barely knew the woman, *something* about Ellie made Hunter feel worthy of believing she deserved better. As close as she was to Mo and Patty, or Rebecca and Cass, that feeling had always eluded her. Until now. No. She *wasn't* going to screw this up. Hunter had allowed Susan to manipulate her for far too long. No more.

"Hungry?" Hunter asked Rebecca, whose face blossomed into a huge smile.

"Thought you'd never ask!" She typed out a quick text to Cassidy to meet them at Ellie's Diner and bounced up. "Lead on, my friend. I'm so excited!"

"Don't embarrass me like Mo did."

Rebecca laughed wickedly. "Would I do that? Besides, Mo has her own special way of just being embarrassing."

Hunter snickered. "True. But, I'm still telling Patty you said that about her woman."

Rebecca raised a brow with a smirk. "Do you think I'm afraid of Patty? Have you forgotten who I am?"

Hunter looked Rebecca up and down. "No, ma'am, I sure haven't." She tucked a strand of hair behind Rebecca's ear. "Why didn't we ever get together?"

Rebecca looked up at Hunter in surprise. "What made you ask that?"

Hunter shrugged self-consciously. "I don't know. I was just wondering, I guess."

Rebecca cupped Hunter's cheeks with both of her hands. "Because neither of us was ready for each other when we met. And, when we were ready, someone else called to our hearts. But, I wouldn't change what we have for the world, Hunter. Besides Cassidy, you're one of my best friends, and someone I trust with my life. I'm glad we didn't do anything to ruin that."

Hunter smiled brilliantly. "I feel the same way. Thank you for always being there for me." She leaned down slightly and brushed Rebecca's lips lightly with hers. It was a chaste kiss and confirmed that the only feelings they had for each other was a close friendship. "Let's go. I miss seeing Ellie's face."

GOT THE INFORMATION you need. Sending to your email now. – Cade

Ellie read over the simple text five times before her fingers were able to stop shaking enough to respond. Cade certainly was good at what he did. It didn't even take him a full twenty-four hours to gather the info. Now all she needed was the courage to contact

Claire. She hoped Dani was ready for this. Hell, she hoped *Claire* was ready!

I could kiss you! I won't, but I could. I don't know how to thank you. Name your price. Be reasonable! :P – El

She knew her text would put a smile on Cade's face. As much as the man frustrated her, she was happy that they were able to still remain friends. Ellie had actually been surprised by Cade's reaction to her news, but grateful nonetheless.

I work for kisses from beautiful women. But I'll settle for dinner and a smile next time I come into the diner. ;)

That she could do and texted him as much. Ellie slipped her phone into her back pocket and wondered – not for the first time – if Hunter would be in today. It was silly. Did she really expect the doctor to come in every day? Just because Ellie wanted to see *her* didn't mean the feelings were mutual. Shaking those thoughts out of her head, she checked her email. Sure enough, all of Claire's current data was sitting right in front of her. *She's still here in LA. That's a plus. I hope.* Personal information like; Did she have a girlfriend? Was she living with someone she was committed to? was omitted, of course. That was something Ellie would have to find out for herself. She printed the email out and folded it carefully. *Maybe I'll go see Dani tonight if Jessie will be out again.*

"Miss Ellie?"

She had been so absorbed in her thoughts, that she hadn't heard the knock on her office door. She looked up to see fresh-faced Charity poking her head in.

"Yes?"

"There's a lady asking if you're working today."

Hunter. Ellie smiled. "Thank you. Is she at the counter?"

"No, ma'am. They're at table one." With that, Charity was gone. Ellie found herself wondering if that was just the way of young people these days. Always in a hurry. Wait. *They? Hmm, maybe Mo is here, too.*

Ellie closed her office door and straightened her shirt. *Silly.* At least she stopped at fixing her hair. Great. Now she wondered if her hair looked okay. Chuckling at herself, she pushed her way through to the dining area and stopped in her tracks. *That is* definitely *not Mo. Shit. Maybe she's already seeing someone. But, why would she come here every day if she had someone waiting for her?* Ellie decided that wondering about these questions was *not* going to get them answered. She grabbed a couple of cups and a pot of coffee, straightened her shoulders, plastered on a smile, and made her way to Hunter.

"*HERE SHE COMES!*" Hunter whispered excitedly. "*Don't look!*"

Rebecca couldn't help but chuckle. "Well, if I ever missed being in high school, this certainly helps."

"*Shut up.*" Hunter barely resisted sticking her tongue out at her friend just as Ellie made it to their table. *God, she's beautiful.* She was wearing what Hunter had come to know as the 'uniform' of Ellie's Diner. Only today the jeans were dark, and the green shirt brought out the amazing green in Ellie's eyes. "Hey!"

"Good morning, Hunter," Ellie responded with a smile. Knowing Hunter's love of caffeine – one that rivaled Blaise's before she became pregnant – Ellie automatically poured a cup of coffee, and set it in front of Hunter. She lost herself in the bright blue eyes for a moment before remembering Hunter wasn't alone.

Rebecca used the moment that Ellie was talking to Hunter to check the woman out. Intrigued by Hunter's description of Ellie's body, she started there and was *not* disappointed. *Hunter was not joking about those thighs! Wow!* Her eyes traveled up until they were caught by a familiar green.

"Ellie?"

Ellie's eyebrows rose in surprise. "Rebecca!"

Hunter looked from Ellie, to Rebecca, and back again. She wasn't sure how she felt about the familiarity between the two. *Surely Ellie doesn't know Rebecca's alter-ego.* She pleaded for that to be true.

"You two know each other?" To hide her nervousness, she lifted her cup to her lips.

Rebecca caught the gesture and knew exactly what Hunter was thinking. She toyed with the idea of teasing her friend but thought better of it. This thing with Ellie was too important.

"Ellie is my yoga instructor."

The sip of hot coffee came right back out of Hunter's mouth – and nose – as she coughed. *Goddamn it! Again!*

Ellie immediately patted Hunter on the back as she reached for napkins. Rebecca, on the other hand, was busy laughing her ass off. *She's as bad as Cassidy!*

"Are you okay?" Ellie tried desperately not to laugh. *Poor thing. That has to hurt.*

"Yeah." Hunter cleared her throat, embarrassed. "Um, you're a — you do?" *Shit! Stop thinking about Ellie bending over in yoga pants!* "Yoga?"

She's so damned cute when she's flustered. Ellie chuckled. "Yes, yoga. Though I've been a little remiss this week." She smiled apologetically to Rebecca. "Sorry about that. I'll definitely be there tomorrow."

"Ugh, I hope so! I do not like Amy!" Rebecca laughed. "Way too bubbly." *And, so not gay. But, are you?*

"She's not that bad," Ellie admonished jokingly. "So, how do you two know each other?"

Rebecca grinned. "I had the unfortunate need for Dr. Vale's expertise years ago." She winked at a blushing Hunter. "But, it all worked out pretty well." Rebecca hadn't meant to insinuate anything other than friendship, but she saw the flash of something in Ellie's eyes. *Hmm. Is that jealousy I detect?*

Oh. Ellie mustered up a small smile. "I'm not sure whether to say sorry or be happy for you." Rebecca tilted her head in a way Ellie found charming. *Well, if they are together, at least Rebecca is a nice person.* "Sorry because if you needed 'Dr. Vale', it must have been bad. But, I'm happy for you that everything turned out for the best."

Wow, Hunter. You've picked a beautiful person inside and out, Rebecca thought in awe.

Hunter was thinking along the same lines, grinning goofily as Ellie poured coffee in Rebecca's cup. *Please be gay.*

The bell on the door sounded, and Ellie glanced up to see an extremely handsome, androgynous woman come in.

"Hey, baby!"

Ellie stepped to the side – confused - when the woman moved to Rebecca, bending to give her a quick kiss. *Wait, Hunter and Rebecca are not together?* She wasn't even going to question being insanely happy about that.

"Sorry, I'm late. So, where's the . . ."

"Babe!" Rebecca abruptly stood, and hooked her arm through Cassidy's. "This is Hunter's friend Ellie. Ellie, this is my lover Cassidy."

"Cass." Cass's response was automatic as she took in the sight before her. *Nice. Real nice. Good job, Hunter! Now, let's see if she's gay.* She lifted her sunglasses, settling them on the top of her head, and gave Ellie a charming grin. "Nice to meet you."

Interesting eyes, was Ellie's first thought when she came into contact with Cass's two-toned eyes – one an unreal blue, and one amber. "You, too." There was an awkward moment of silence before Cass shrugged, and slid into the booth after Rebecca. When Cass was settled, the diner owner in Ellie took over. "Would you like some coffee, Cass?"

"Could I get some chocolate milk instead?" Cass shrugged her shoulders when Rebecca groaned. "What, babe? It's good for me! *Does the body good,*" she whispered close to a flustered Rebecca's ear.

Ellie laughed quietly at the couple. *That's what I want.* Her eyes went to Hunter who was watching her intently. She cleared her throat. "Are you hungry?"

Oh, yeah. For you. "Yeah, um, I thought maybe I'd get that breakfast platter. But, I don't think I'm pancake-hungry," she paused. "Though I'm a little hungrier than toast." Hunter gave Ellie a lopsided grin.

Oh, my. "Got it." Ellie turned her attention to the couple who were still cooing at each other. "And, you two?" she asked with a smirk.

"Babe?" Cass deferred to Rebecca.

"Go ahead. I'm still trying to decide." *Haven't even looked at the menu, especially since you got here.*

"'Kay. I'll have what Hunter's having, but with the pancakes. No, wait, French toast. No, um, pancakes."

"Cassidy, make a decision." Rebecca chuckled at Cassidy who looked seriously torn.

"How about both?" Ellie suggested helpfully.

"Ooh! Yeah, that!" Cass sat back, satisfied, and gave her lover a smug grin.

Ellie snickered. "Rebecca?"

Rebecca tore her amazed gaze away from Cass. "Well, since I wasn't blessed with the metabolism these two obviously have, I'm going to need something a little lighter. What would you suggest?"

"Hmm." Ellie tapped her chin with a manicured nail. "I have the perfect thing. Are you allergic to anything?" Rebecca shook her head. "Good. Leave it to me. I'll be right back."

All three women watched Ellie walk away. Then Rebecca leaned close to Cass. "You know you're going to be punished for looking at her like that, right?"

Hunter laughed at Cass's wide eyes.

"But, baby! You, I – I didn't . . ." Cass sighed. "Yes, ma'am."

The provocative smile that curved Cass's lips told Hunter the punishment would be more than welcome.

"Okay, you two, focus!" Hunter leaned forward and lowered her voice. "So? Is she?"

Cass shrugged. "She didn't bat an eye at my charm."

Hunter rolled her eyes. "Rebecca?"

Rebecca shook her head at her girlfriend. "Your ego is certainly healthy, baby. But, rightfully so." She looked over at Hunter who was *not* waiting patiently. "I don't know, hon. I've been trying to figure that out for months, actually."

That got Cass's attention. "What now?"

Hunter couldn't help but laugh. "Did we not tell you? Ellie is Rebecca's yoga teacher."

Rebecca moaned and slid down in the booth, much to Hunter's

enjoyment. They were of no help to her when it came to Ellie's sexuality. Teasing was now fair game.

"Yoga! Holy shit." Cass looked back towards the kitchen, then focused on her girlfriend. "How did I not know you did yoga? Explains so much," she muttered happily. "Hunter, for your sake, I hope she's gay because . . ."

Rebecca slapped a hand over Cass's mouth. "Too much information, sweetheart."

"No, it's not," Hunter reassured helpfully. "Tell me more."

"She will not."

Cass mumbled something behind the hand currently attached to her face.

Rebecca tentatively moved her hand. "What was that?"

"I was just wondering why you've been wondering about Ellie's sexuality," Cass answered moodily.

"Oh, baby." Rebecca was genuinely sorry for making Cass feel less than confident with her. "I didn't mean for it to sound like that. I'm not interested in her. I just saw her with another woman, and I was curious."

Hunter sat up straight. "What woman?"

Rebecca was now sorry she said anything at all. "I don't know. Some pretty brunette that she seemed close with. I thought maybe they were together, but then the brunette turned up pregnant, so I don't know."

"Did she have an accent?" Hunter asked hopefully, blowing out a relieved breath when Rebecca nodded. "That's her *married* best friend, Blaise."

"So, we still don't know?" Cass threw out there as she grumpily tore up a napkin. She felt Rebecca's hand squeeze her thigh and glanced over. The remorse in her woman's eyes made all of Cass's insecurities disappear. She leaned over and kissed Rebecca on the cheek. "*I love you.*"

Rebecca's frown turned into a brilliant smile. "I love you, too."

Hunter watched her friends get all googly-eyed over each other with a bittersweet feeling. Of course, she was happy for them, but that kind of love is what she wanted. She lifted her eyes in time to see Ellie come out of the kitchen. Yes, Hunter was definitely ready to find out what love truly was.

HUNTER WAS THOROUGHLY enjoying herself. Rebecca and Cass were certainly entertaining breakfast companions. And, Ellie spent as much time talking with them as her other customers permitted. Unfortunately, time was moving quickly, and Hunter had things to take care of before beginning her long weekend. She saw Ellie heading back towards the kitchen and excused herself even though Rebecca and Cass probably wouldn't even know she was gone.

"Ellie?"

Ellie stopped abruptly at the sound of Hunter's voice, causing the bigger woman to run into her. "Oh!" Strong hands on her hips steadied her, and she fought to keep her blush at bay.

"Sorry," Hunter grinned sheepishly.

Ellie smiled. "Is everything," she looked past Hunter's shoulder to see Rebecca and Cass staring at them, "all right?"

Hunter followed Ellie's line of sight and turned her head to see the same scene. She tossed them a nasty look, and they immediately turned back around laughing. Only then did she realize her hands were still on Ellie's hips. Hunter promptly dropped them.

"Yeah, everything was great." She rubbed her neck, embarrassed by her breach of Ellie's personal space. *But, God, it felt good to touch her.* "Um, I wondered if I could get that sampler pie now."

"So soon?" Ellie was surprised, and a bit saddened. That meant she wouldn't be seeing Hunter again before she left.

Hunter shrugged. "It's been a while since I've seen my folks."

More than six months, she thought miserably. "I thought I would make a long weekend out of it, so I took a couple of days off, and I'm going to drive up tonight. Plus, I could use those few days to recharge, you know?"

"Good for you," Ellie smiled sweetly. "Wait, didn't you work last night?" Hunter nodded. "Then I hope you're going to get some sleep before you make the drive."

Touched that Ellie cared, Hunter grinned. "Yes, ma'am. My plan is to go home, throw a couple things in my duffel, and sleep until it's time to hit the road. I promise I'll get a few hours."

"Good," Ellie approved. "I guess that means I'll be missing you." *Oh, shit. Did I just say that?* Judging by the look on Hunter's face, she totally did. "Um, I meant at the hospital. I'm going to visit Dani tonight."

Damn. Hunter was disappointed that she'd miss seeing Ellie outside of the diner again. Okay, so they were playing musical workplaces, but whatever. "I wish I'd known. I would've been there in case you or Dani needed me."

Now Hunter felt like shit. She had been worried about her own problems and her feelings for Ellie to think more about Dani's needs. Obviously, Ellie wasn't having the same issues. Thankfully, *Someone* needed to be there for Dani.

"Don't be silly. No offense, Hunter, but you look pretty exhausted."

"Hey! I just got off a twelve-hour shift!"

"Hang on," Ellie chuckled. "I didn't mean that in a bad way, but I think it's good for you to get away for a bit. And, honestly, I think it will be good for Dani. Let her miss you," she grinned to take any sting away from her words. "Besides, we're just going to be hanging for a bit. She called me earlier to tell me that they're trying to kill her over there with what the hospital calls food. So, I'm bringing her some real food."

"Well, now I'm jealous." *In more ways than one*, Hunter mused. *She* wanted to be the one that Ellie hung out with. *She* wanted to have Ellie's phone number and be able to call her when she needed to see her. She shook off the selfish thoughts, knowing that Dani needed Ellie more. *Not by much, though.*

Ellie laughed softly. A magical sound to Hunter's ears. In the days she'd known Ellie, Hunter found herself trying to hear that sound as often as she could.

"I've been cooking for you for the past few days. It's Dani's turn now."

Hunter pouted playfully. "Fine. As long as when I come back, you'll cook for me again?" It was as close to asking Ellie out as she could come right now. She was determined to make it through this weekend without incident. Then she would come back, and ask Ellie out for real. And hope for the best.

Ellie's heart rate spiked. Did Hunter just ask her out, or was that just Ellie's wishful thinking? "You know where to find me," Ellie drawled and winked mischievously. She turned on her heel and left a highly confused — highly *hopeful* — Hunter with her jaw on the floor.

"MOM! I'M HOME!"

"No need to yell, sweets. I'm right here," Ellie called from the kitchen. Jessie came in and flopped her backpack on the counter with a grin. "How was school?"

"One day closer to being over." Jessie reached over and plucked an olive out of a bowl in front of Ellie. "Smells good in here."

"Hey! Leave my olives alone." She snapped the tongs she was holding at Jessie's hand. "I thought you liked school."

Jessie snuck another olive, holding it between her teeth before eating it. She laughed at her mother calling her a brat. "I do like school." Jessie chanced another olive but snatched her hand away before her mom could whack her. "But I'm ready to get out of the drama of high school and learn things that I'm actually going to use in life."

Ellie looked up from chopping vegetables. "Have you been sending out your applications?"

Jessie rolled her eyes. "Yes, mother. Don't chop your fingers off."

This time Ellie rolled her eyes. "I know what I'm doing. Have you made any decisions between UCLA and Berkeley?" Mother and daughter had spent many long nights discussing college. Ellie was surprised, yet particularly happy, that Jessie wanted to stay close by going to a local college.

Jessie was glad when Ellie went back to chopping, so she didn't have to look her in the eye. "No, not really. I sent applications to both, so we'll see," she answered evasively. "So, um, I'm going over to Piper's. We're going to work on our project tonight."

Chopping stopped. "Again?"

"It's, like, ten percent of our grade, mom."

"Why does Blaise get to know what this project is, and I'm left in the dark?" Ellie wasn't normally a jealous person, but this particular project was keeping Jessie away from her way too much. She couldn't help but wonder if it was really the project, or being with a family that kept Jessie at Blaise's.

"She doesn't know," Jessie explained patiently, unwittingly cutting into her mother's pity party. "The only reason we do it over there is because Blaise has that space where she does all those flower experiments. If we were doing a cooking project, we'd be here."

"Cooking is a science, too, you know," Ellie argued.

Jessie laughed. "Yes, but not the way you do it. You're like some kind of cooking guru who doesn't need recipes or measuring cups."

Ellie smiled. "That's not exactly true, but it's good enough to get me to stop grilling you. Are you eating there?" Jessie nodded. "Okay, well, don't be too late. It's a school night."

"Are you going to be okay here by yourself?"

Ellie raised an eyebrow. "I'm perfectly capable of taking care of myself," she replied dryly. "Besides, I'll be going to the hospital to visit Dani."

Jessie stopped her retreat into her bedroom at that. "The girl who lost her legs?"

"Yes." Ellie had told Jessie a little about her visit with Dani, leaving out information she wasn't ready to discuss yet.

Jessie found it incredibly sad that someone around her age had been living on the street and something this tragic had happened. She had wanted to know more, but her mom was reluctant to betray Dani's confidence. Jessie could understand that, but it didn't stop her curiosity.

"Do you think I could go with you one night? I'd like to meet her."

Surprised, Ellie stared at her daughter. Jessie wasn't exactly the outgoing type. That's not to say she wasn't friendly with everyone, she absolutely was. But she had a small core group of 'real' friends, always telling Ellie that it was quality, not quantity that mattered more to her. Jessie never *actively* sought out meeting others. She was truly like her mother that way.

"I'm not sure if she's up for that," Ellie answered quietly. "She's still trying to get used to all of this, and isn't exactly open to seeing people, yet."

Jessie pondered that for a moment and then nodded. "I can understand that, I guess. Will you at least ask her?"

"Of course, I will." Ellie gave her daughter a sweet smile. She knew that exposing Jessie to Dani meant exposing Jessie to Hunter and her friends. She needed to talk to Jessie before that happened. "Jessie?"

Once again, Jessie stopped and barely resisted groaning in exasperation. She was going to be late if her mom didn't let her go soon. "Yeah?"

"I need you to be home Saturday. All day."

"All day? But, mom, my project!"

"No buts, please? There's something I . . . I need to talk to you about. Besides, I miss you. You can work on your assignment tomorrow night, and Sunday morning while Blaise and I meet with Eve. Then we'll have girls' night like every other Sunday. But, Saturday, it's just you and me. Please?"

Jessie didn't know what it was about the look her mother was giving her. Was it fear? Sorrow? Whatever it was, it made it impossible to refuse her plea.

"Sure, mom." She walked back to the counter. "Does this have anything to do with why you've been stressed?"

"Restless," Ellie corrected automatically.

"Same difference."

"Not really," Ellie muttered laughingly. Though she did have to admit that what had been 'just restlessness' at the beginning was quickly turning into stress. It was certainly not going to be easy coming out to her daughter. "But, yes."

"And, it's not money," Jessie reiterated for her own sake.

Ellie rolled her eyes playfully at her daughter. "You know, I'm actually surprisingly good at managing our money," she said drolly. "I even have a hefty college fund saved up for you, so you can choose where you want to go. Money is not a problem, Jess. I promise."

Jessie definitely didn't want to talk about college right now. Maybe Saturday. Maybe. "Okay, so what is it?"

"Nope." Ellie pointed at her daughter who looked so much like her. *God, I hope you don't end up hating me.* "You need to go to Piper's and get to work so you can get home at a decent time. I need to finish these fajitas and get to the hospital. So, we'll talk on Saturday."

"Argh! Wait. Fajitas?"

Chapter Nine

The fajitas, thankfully, kept Jessie distracted enough to stop questioning Ellie. They also made both of them late to their respective destinations. Ellie wasn't sorry for that, however. She got to spend a little more quality time with her daughter, even if talk was minimal because Jessie was too busy stuffing her face. Much like Dani was doing now.

"Ohmygodthisissogood."

Ellie was pretty sure she understood what Dani had said, and smiled. "I'm glad you're enjoying it. But, don't talk with your mouth full, and wipe your chin."

Dani stopped chewing and gawked at Ellie. "You sound like a mother," she mumbled around the food.

Ellie wasn't sure if that was a good thing or a bad thing with Dani. "Sorry."

Dani swallowed, and dutifully wiped her mouth. "No, don't be. It was nice being mothered again," she said quietly.

Ellie reached over and gently squeezed Dani's casted hand. Not wanting to ruin Dani's appetite, Ellie had purposefully waited until the fajitas were all but destroyed to bring up Claire.

"Did you have enough?"

"Mmm, yeah. I'm stuffed!" Dani let out a small burp and apologized with a bashful grin. "Thank you, again, for bringing me food. And, um, for, you know, visiting me and stuff."

"It's my pleasure, Dani." Ellie stood and began cleaning the remnants of food. "Are you tired, or would you like to talk for a bit?"

"Um, talk maybe?" Dani picked at her cast nervously.

Ellie smiled sweetly. "You got it." She sat back down in the cushioned chair and tucked her feet under her in an attempt to get comfortable. *Here goes nothing.* "I found Claire."

HUNTER YAWNED AND tossed her duffel in the back seat of her RAM 1500 Crew Cab. Anxious to see her folks, she was glad the drive was only about an hour long. Not to mention, Hunter was tired as hell, not having slept well at all. Of course, if she really thought about it, she hadn't had a restful sleep since she met a certain blonde diner owner. This time, however, it wasn't about Ellie, much to her dismay.

Hunter was apprehensive. She hadn't been back home since she broke things off with Susan, and resentment for that left a bitter taste in Hunter's mouth. She had allowed Susan to take so much from her already. She wouldn't give up her family. And she sure as hell wouldn't give up a chance with a woman like Ellie. Hunter smiled when she thought of the conversation she had earlier with her best friends.

"What do you think it means?" Hunter paced around her living room as Mo, Patty, Rebecca, and Cass watched her with amusement.

"What exactly did she say again?" Mo smirked at the others. Hunter had gone over this five times already, but each time they asked, she giddily related the story once again.

"She said she was going to miss me tonight because she was going to visit Dani and take her some food." Hunter missed the snickering coming from her friends. "I said I was jealous, and then told her it'd be fine if she cooked for me again when I got back. I wanted so badly to ask her out, but . . ." Hunter shrugged off the bad thoughts that wanted to sneak in. "Anyway, she said; 'You know where to find me' and winked! She winked at me! That has to mean something, right?"

"Some people just like to wink," Rebecca reasoned. She didn't want to deflate Hunter's hope, but she did want Hunter to be careful.

"That's true, sugar," Patty agreed.

Mo tsked. "It's all about how she winked. Did she lick her lips and wink? Maybe she put an extra sway into her hips when she walked away?"

"You're making fun of me," Hunter grumped, throwing herself on the couch.

"You make it so easy," Mo laughed. "I've known you most of my life, and I've never seen you so hung up on a chick." Mo cried out when Patty slapped her on the back of the head. "Ow, babe. That hurt!"

"That was the point. You leave Hunter alone now. I'd rather see her like this than . . ." Patty's voice trailed off.

"It's okay, mama Patty," Hunter reassured her quietly. "I know how I was when I was with . . . her."

"And, the others," Mo chimed in, earning another smack from Patty.

"And, the others," Hunter agreed. "Maybe that's why I want this so much with Ellie."

"I don't believe that." Rebecca tucked her legs up under her and leaned into her girlfriend. "You want this with Ellie because you feel something with her you've never felt before. Don't diminish that."

Cass wrapped her arm around Rebecca, drawing her closer. "I know that feeling, Hunt. I'm rooting for Ellie to be gay."

The others laughed and agreed wholeheartedly.

"Okay, here's the deal," Mo began. "None of our gaydars are working with this chick." She ducked another whack from her wife. She knew Patty hated it when she called women chicks and sent her an apologetic look. "Ellie. So, why don't you just ask her?"

Hunter blinked at her childhood friend. "You want me to walk into her diner, go up to the counter, and say 'could I get a coffee? Oh and by the way, are you gay?'"

Mo shrugged. "Why not?"

"And, if I end up wearing that coffee?"

"Then you know she isn't gay." Mo chuckled, stopping abruptly at Patty's menacing glare. "Oh, come on, mama! That was funny! Fine," she sighed when there was no change in the look. "But, who you really need to be hitting right now is Hunter."

Hunter's eyes went wide. "What did I do?"

"You're leaving early to go back home. What are you thinking?" Mo had been irate when she found out Hunter had changed her plans. She wasn't sure Hunter had enough willpower to stay away from Susan. Hell, even Mo had been tempted with Susan once. Only once, thank all that was holy. Though she would never tell Hunter that. Or Patty. She shivered at the thought.

"I'm not going to let her keep me away from my family anymore, Mo."

"That's a bullshit answer. You're not over her!"

"Yes, I am!"

"Enough!" The absolute authority in Rebecca's voice stunned everyone except Cass, who sat back with a smirk. "Mo, you are being unfair. Hunter wanted out of the situation she was in, so she got out. You questioning her at every turn is not helping." Mo dropped her head with guilt. "Besides, Hunter knows that if she fucks up this weekend, she leaves Ellie alone for good. Right, Hunter?" Hunter winced but nodded obediently.

"That's harsh, babe," Cass muttered.

"Maybe. However, both Ellie and Hunter deserve to go into this — if there is a this — knowing that they're both ready."

"She's right, Cass." Hunter stood up and paced. "I'm, uh." She glanced at Rebecca who gave her a reassuring smile. "I'm seeing a therapist. I really do want this, Mo. I want to be rid of Susan, and what all of that entails. I want to find out if Ellie is someone I can be with. But, whatever happens with Ellie, this thing with Susan is over. I just can't do it anymore. It's – it hurts too much."

Mo rarely saw Hunter this emotional. She got up and interrupted Hunter's pacing. "I'm sorry. I've been trying to get you out of this for a long time."

"I know. And, I know I've screwed up many times before." She took ahold of Mo's shoulders. "I'm ready now, Mo. But, I need you to believe in me."

"You know I do." She hugged Hunter briefly, embarrassed by the emotions she was showing in front of the others. *"Anyway, I don't think you'll do anything when you have a hot piece . . ."* Patty cleared her throat loudly. *"Of pie waiting for you when you get back."*

Hunter's chuckle filled the silence inside the cab of the truck. Good ol' Mo. If Hunter ever needed to step out of the seriousness of life, Mo was the one she wanted around. Of course, being as close as sisters also meant the occasional fights that could get out of hand. Since Patty, the two of them had settled down a bit, but that didn't stop Mo from teasing Hunter relentlessly for anything and everything she could.

I wonder if Ellie is at the hospital, yet. She knew what she was about to do would get her ribbed for months by Mo, but that didn't stop Hunter from making the call.

"Nursing station, this is Patty."

"Is she there?"

"Hunter? My goodness, sugar, you are really hung up, aren't you?" Patty chuckled at her enamored friend. *Good lord, I hope Ellie is gay. Otherwise, Hunter is going to be devastated.*

"Come on, Patty. Just tell me if she's there. Please? And, don't tell Mo about this?"

Patty shook her head with a smile. "Yes, doctor, she's here. And, she was carrying something that smelled like heaven. If she hadn't stopped to give me some pie, I would have been extremely envious."

Hunter remembered that Ellie was taking Dani some food, and wondered what the delicacy would be. She wanted to be able to smell the scents. Not only of Ellie's delicious food but of Ellie herself. Hunter often found herself wondering if Ellie always smelled as sweet as her pies. *Damn, you have it bad.*

"What is she wearing?"

"Oh, for crying out loud, Hunter. You can't be serious!"

"Patty," Hunter whined. *Shit. Next thing you know I'll be stomping my feet.*

"Just so you know," Patty began with hilarity. "I *will* be blackmailing you with this for the rest of your life." She laughed out loud at Hunter's groan. "Okay, your lover-to-be had that great ass of hers covered in dark, tight jeans, and an over-sized Henley shirt that looked like it could be one of yours. And, she had it unbuttoned enough to show some awfully nice . . ."

"Uh, Patty? Were you really checking out Ellie's, um, assets?" Hunter was shocked. She didn't think Ellie was Patty's type. Though in Hunter's opinion Ellie was everyone's type.

"You will not tell Mo I said that."

"Hey, I'll keep it quiet if you promise not to blackmail me with this," Hunter pledged with a laugh. "Just stop looking at my girl's . . . stuff." *My girl?*

"Your girl? Hunter, I think maybe you need to slow down a bit with this. What do you even know about her? I mean, you don't even know if she'll be interested. Though I can't imagine anyone not being interested in you."

Hunter blushed at the compliment but opted to ignore it. "Patty, I know that when I'm around her I feel like a giddy teenager. Something I haven't felt in a long time. If ever." She swallowed the lump that began to form in her throat. It had been so long since she felt a guiltless, innocent attraction to someone. Someone she truly wanted to *date*, and get to know instead of it being just about sex. "I know that she has a wicked sense of humor. I know she has a good heart. You can see that by what she's doing there at the hospital for Dani. I know that I want to know much more." She sighed heavily. "Even so, I didn't mean to say that. She's *not* mine, yet. It just sorta popped out."

Patty listened carefully as Hunter spoke of Ellie. She could clearly hear the emotion, something she never thought would happen for Hunter with the kind of women she usually ended up with. "Well, my mama always told me that the truth always comes out when you're not thinking enough to censor yourself." She paused to sign a chart that was handed to her. "But, sugar, you need to focus on getting through this weekend before you start thinking that way about Ellie."

"Yeah." Hunter tried not to sound as defeated as she felt right then. Her friends had their doubts that she could do this. She honestly couldn't blame them since they had all been through this before. Hunter had said many times that she was done with Susan, only to fall back into the trap once again.

Patty heard the frustration and knew exactly what Hunter was thinking. "Sugar, we believe in you. This phone call proves that you're ready. Don't let that bitch hurt you anymore."

"Yes, ma'am."

"And, you tell that mama of yours that we all said Happy Birthday."

"Will do. Thank you for everything, Patty." *Especially for the visual I now have of Ellie.*

"DANI? ARE YOU all right?" Ellie was concerned with how pale Dani had gotten. The teenager hadn't spoken a word since Ellie mentioned Claire's name. In fact, she looked positively ill. "Are you going to get sick?"

Dani shook her head weakly. "Is . . . is she?" Dani couldn't get her brain to work. Just hearing Claire's name made her heart race. She felt Ellie's fingers brush her hair out of her eyes, and Dani leaned into the motherly touch. If she were thinking clearly, maybe she would have wondered if Ellie was a mother.

"She's still here in L.A.," Ellie answered, guessing Dani's question. "She's living in an apartment not too far from here." Dani closed her eyes, and Ellie wondered if she had made the right decision in finding Claire. Naturally, she had discussed it with Dani that first night, but maybe Ellie should have been more thoughtful about Dani's mental state. Or consulted a psychiatrist first.

"*Does she have someone,*" Dani whispered as though the words physically hurt her to say.

"I don't know, sweets." Ellie eased herself onto the edge of

Dani's bed. "I wanted to talk to you before I called her. I want you to make sure this is really what you want."

"What if – if she hates me? Or if she's in love with someone else?" Dani's head fell back onto her pillow. *Please don't let her be in love with someone else.*

"Do you want my opinion?" Ellie asked softly. Dani closed her eyes and nodded. "I think you owe it to *both* of you to see her again. She wanted to help you, and your pride kept you from letting her." Dani's eyes popped open, and Ellie raised a finger to keep Dani from interrupting. "*If* she's with someone, or decides she doesn't want to see you, at least both of you will have closure. I think if you don't do this, each of you will live with the 'what-ifs' for the rest of your lives."

"Do you think she even remembers me?"

Oh, Dani. You're so young, so vulnerable. "From the stories you've told me, I don't see how she could forget you." Ellie got a small smile from the teen. "Give her a chance, Dani. It may not turn out the way you want, but at least you'll know."

Dani was silent, and for a moment Ellie thought she wasn't going to answer.

"Okay."

The anxiety in Dani's voice broke Ellie's heart. "Hey. No matter what happens, I'm here. I'm not going anywhere."

"Promise?"

Ellie graced her with a bright smile. "I promise."

"MA?" HUNTER LET herself in her childhood home. She had made good time on the road, thanking all that was holy for the unusually light traffic. Dropping her duffle near the front door, Hunter tossed her keys on the little table that had been in the foyer for as long as she could remember. *Home.*

She had always loved this place. Her family wasn't rich by any means, but the single-story ranch style house was well maintained by her parents. Her father, Alton, was an avid gardener, taking up the hobby after getting out of the construction world. His expertise had kept the house in great shape all of these years.

Her mother, Cecilia, had been a homemaker all of Hunter's life. In fact, she couldn't remember a time when her mother wasn't there with a hot meal or a bedtime story. The inside of the house was impeccably kept and always smelled of cinnamon. That had always baffled Hunter since her mother couldn't bake to save her life. She had yet to find the source of that particular scent.

"I know you're not bellowing in the house. And, you best be taking that ratty old bag up to your room." Cecilia smiled at her tall daughter. At five foot six, Cece had been looking *up* to Hunter since the girl turned sixteen. "I've missed you."

Hunter wrapped her mom into a warm embrace with her free arm. "I've missed you, too. Sorry I haven't been around lately."

"I understand that you're busy, honey."

"That's not an excuse, ma."

"Maybe not, but if what you have in your hand tastes as good as it smells, I'll forgive you for almost anything."

Hunter reluctantly let her mom go and gave her a toothy grin. "Happy birthday!" She handed over her treasure, excited to see her reaction.

Cece greedily took the box and quickly headed towards the kitchen. "Are you hungry? I could fix you up some leftovers."

"Nah, I'm good. Maybe just some coffee?" She knew as soon as the words left her mouth, she'd get a look from her mother. Cecilia Vale did not allow coffee to be brewed in her house after a certain time. 'Too much temptation for your father' she would say. And that wasn't good for his high blood pressure.

"You can have some tea." Cece lifted the lid of the pie box. "Oh, my!"

"It's a sampler of eight different types of pie," Hunter explained with a proud grin. "I couldn't decide which one to get you, so Ellie suggested this. That way you could try a little bit of everything."

It wasn't lost on Cece the way Hunter's tone changed when she said the name. *Interesting.* "Ellie?"

"Hmm?" Hunter was lost in thoughts of the diner owner and missed the odd look her mother gave her. "Oh, she's the one who baked all of that." She made a sweeping gesture towards the desserts, making her mother laugh.

"Mmhmm. Anything else I should know about this Ellie?" Cece turned away to get a couple of plates, smirking at her surprised daughter.

"Um, where's pop?"

"It's Friday, dear. You know exactly where he is. His weekly poker game with the guys. Nice try, though. Spill it." She used the highly scientific method of eeny, meeny, miny, moe to choose which slice she would try first. It was either that or take a bite of each. Though that was certainly a viable option.

Hunter watched her mother with delight. She couldn't believe how long it had been since she last sat here with her mom. Normally, Hunter would be here every other week having dinner with her family. Six months in between visits would not be acceptable any longer. Bitterness filled her when she thought about how her stupidity, and Susan's manipulation, kept her away for way too long.

"Ellie is just a friend, ma."

"But? You want more?"

"How in the hell do you do that?"

"Language. And, I'm a mother. We just know things." Cece scooped up a bite of the pie she selected. "Oh!"

"Amazing, right?"

Her mother held a finger to her lips, telling Hunter to be quiet. That hand fell to her chest, resting over her heart, and she closed her eyes reverently. It took all of Hunter's willpower not to laugh. Cece had a weakness for sweets, namely baked goods. No matter where they went, Cece inevitably found a bakery. It was a mystery how she stayed so thin. Good genes, Hunter supposed.

"You better marry this woman," Cece demanded once she finished the bite.

Hunter laughed to cover up her true yearning for the baker. "I have to find out if she's gay first, ma."

"I don't care if she is or not. You will marry this woman, and bring her into our family. I'm going to need her to supply this regularly." She looked up at Hunter, whose eyes were sparkling. *She's smitten with this woman, whoever she is. I've never seen her like this. Heck, we've never met any of her girlfriends. I need to know who this Ellie person is.*

"You're crazy, you know that?" Hunter hugged her mom once again. She thought of Dani, and how she was shunned by her mother for who she was. It made Hunter even more grateful to have such understanding parents that loved her unconditionally. Though it always scared her to wonder if that would change if they knew about Susan.

"Ha! If I am, you and your father made me that way."

"The excess sugar you eat made you that way!" Hunter teased.

"Preposterous!" Her motherly instinct was telling her there was something more to Hunter's early visit. "Sit down and talk to me. Tell me about this Ellie woman, and everything else that has been happening with you."

Hunter obliged, and spilled her guts about Dani, including all of her troubles. Cece teared up at the young girl's emotional pain, as well as Hunter's. It was clear that the young girl had affected Hunter immeasurably. As did this diner owner that Hunter spoke so highly about.

When Hunter told Cece about Ellie, and what the woman had done for Dani and Hunter, Cece was even more impressed. It wasn't often that you met a person who would help someone they barely knew in such a selfless way. And the way her daughter lit up whenever she spoke of Ellie was particularly interesting to Cece.

"I can't believe a mother would do that to her child," Cece spat disgustedly once Hunter finished. "Putting that poor child out on the streets is abuse if I've ever seen it! Why, I have half a mind to find that, that *woman* and . . . and . . ."

"Calm down, ma. She isn't worth it." Hunter patted her mom's hand.

"She may not be, but that young girl certainly is. I'm just thankful that Ellie could get her to open up." *Yep. Every time the name is spoken, Hunter glows.*

"Yeah, she was amazing."

I wonder if she knows she has a dreamy look on her face, Cece wondered happily. Finally, her daughter had found someone that makes her feel this way. She just hoped it worked out for them both. She wanted what all mothers – or *most* mothers – wanted for their kids. Happiness. She had a feeling that this Ellie woman was "The One" for her daughter.

"WAIT!"

Ellie's thumb moved away from the green call button. Dani was panicking. They had been doing this back and forth for the past ten minutes. Call. Don't call. Call. Don't call. And each time, Ellie patiently waited for Dani to come to her decision.

"Sorry," Dani muttered miserably.

"It's okay. Take your time. If you decide you can't do this now, we can try another time."

"No! I mean, um, I want you to call. I need to know." Dani sighed. "Maybe you could, uh . . ." Her eyes tracked to the door, then back to Ellie again.

"You want me to step out to call her?" Ellie guessed.

Dani nodded. "Then maybe if she doesn't want to see me, you could break it to me gently? You seem like you'd be good at that."

Ellie chuckled. "Do I? Okay, if it makes you feel better, I'll go out into the hall. Don't go anywhere, I'll be right back."

Dani snorted with laughter. She appreciated having someone

around that treated her like she was a normal person. Ellie's teasing was gentle, yet fun and Dani found herself really warming up to the woman. She may have lost the love of her mother, and her legs. But talking to Ellie these past couple of days has helped a lot. And now there was even a small chance of getting Claire back. "Well, I was thinking about going for a stroll, but I guess I can stick around for a while."

"You do that." Ellie gave her a wink and stepped out of the room. She took a deep breath, trying to psych herself up for this call. *Come on, Claire, be available. Dani needs you.* She pressed the little green button and hoped for the best.

Chapter Ten

"Hello?"

"Hello, I'm looking for Claire Oliver." There was a noticeable pause before the female voice answered.

"This is she."

Don't screw this up, El. "My name is Ellie Montgomery." *Crap. This is harder than I thought.* "I'm calling to speak to you about Dani Reed. Please hear me out before you hang up," Ellie rushed when she heard the surprised gasp.

"I — I'm not going to hang up. Is Dani okay?" Claire's voice wavered when she said Dani's name. "Do you know where she is? Have you seen her?"

She still loves her. Whether that's enough remains to be seen. "She's . . . yes, I've seen her. She gave me your name, and asked me to call you."

"How? I haven't heard from her in so long, I thought she had forgotten about me." There was bitterness in her tone now. "Everything has changed."

"Have your feelings changed?" Ellie asked carefully.

"Who the hell are you? What do you know about my feelings!"

Okay, now Claire was getting mad, and Ellie needed to work fast before she lost any hope she had of getting Claire here.

"Claire, Dani is in the hospital." She heard a quiet 'oh my God' from the other end and continued. "I can't tell you she's okay, but she's alive. And, she has asked for you."

"Why me?"

"Because her feelings haven't changed, Claire. She still loves you." Ellie was taking a chance by disclosing that information, and she hoped it was worth it.

"Did she love me when she told me to get away from her?" Claire cried. "Did she love me when she pushed me away as I begged her to let me help?"

"Yes," Ellie answered firmly. "She thought she was doing the right thing. She felt she had nothing to offer you, and thought you needed more than a failure like her."

"She is *not* a failure!" Claire declared vehemently. "It wasn't her fault her mother was a fucking bitch!"

Ellie suppressed the motherly urge to reprimand Claire about her language. This was a horrible situation, and she couldn't blame the girl for being upset.

"Claire," Ellie prompted quietly. "I agree with you. And, I've told Dani the same thing, in less colorful language." She smiled at Claire's soft giggle. Taking a breath, she went on. "Her situation has gotten worse, and she could use a friend."

"Worse how?" Claire asked timidly.

"I'd rather tell you that face to face," Ellie suggested carefully.

"I don't know. It took me a really long time to get over Dani pushing me away. I don't know if I can go through that again. I barely survived the first time."

Ellie clearly heard the crying, and her heart went out to both of the girls. *They're so young and have been through so much already.*

"Do you still love her, Claire?" Ellie's tone was soft and caring. She knew she wouldn't judge this girl no matter what her answer was. But the intense emotion in Claire's words gave Ellie hope that she could bring them back together.

"I – I never stopped. I tried. God, I tried, but I couldn't get her out of my heart." Claire sniffed. "*I looked for her.*"

"She wasn't ready to be found, sweetheart. The rejection from her mother destroyed her." Ellie didn't think she was betraying Dani's confidence by telling Claire what Dani had said to her. Surely Dani would understand that Claire had the right to know why her life had turned upside down that fateful night. "I don't agree with what she did to you, and I've told her that. I think she understands now. Claire, she needs you."

"Who are you to Dani? Why is she opening up to you? Are you a doctor?"

Ellie detected the note of jealousy. "No, I'm not a doctor. Actually, I'm a friend of Dani's doctor who asked me to come in and speak to Dani. She just needed a friend. But now she needs someone more."

"But, you must be someone special if Dani opened up to you." Claire tried again.

"It was the pie," Ellie said with a chuckle. "I brought her pie, and I guess she felt like she could trust me."

To Ellie's surprise, Claire laughed. "That would do it. Dani has always been a sucker for sweets." She let out a long, weary sigh. "Where is she?"

"You'll come see her?" Ellie asked anxiously.

"Yes. How can I stay away? She still owns my heart."

Ellie teared up at the admission. This was more than young love. This was strong and true. She gave Claire the information and told her she would meet her outside. She would need to prepare Claire for what she was in for. They hung up after Claire promised she would be there in thirty minutes.

ELLIE PACED OUTSIDE the front doors of the hospital. Claire was late, but Ellie had to believe she would be there any minute. And she was nervous. Dani was a basket case. It took all of Ellie's motherly skills to keep Dani from changing her mind about seeing Claire. For both of their sakes, Ellie decided to go for a walk while waiting for Claire. Dani needed time to prepare herself, and Ellie needed to not pull out her hair in response to Dani's stubbornness.

She had stopped by the nurse's station to let Patty know what was going on, and was rewarded with the message that Hunter had called and said 'hello'. It surprised Ellie how much that little gesture meant to her. It frightened her how quickly she stopped listening to the little voice that told her she couldn't pursue anything with Hunter. She tried justifying the turnaround by telling herself she was just keeping her promise to herself. Whatever the case, she still had to get through her talk with Jessie. And just the thought of that conversation made Ellie's stomach ache.

"Excuse me?"

Ellie spun around at the nervous voice behind her. A young woman, no more than twenty years old, stood before her. Her soft, brown eyes were rimmed red, no doubt from crying. She was a petite girl, cute with her strawberry blonde pixie cut, and heart-shaped face.

"Claire?"

The girl nodded. "Miss Montgomery?"

"Ellie." Ellie held her hand out, and Claire took it anxiously. "How are you?"

"Nervous as hell," Claire answered honestly with a tremulous smile.

"So is Dani." Ellie smiled charmingly, trying to calm the girl's nerves.

Claire's smile turned into a grin. She released Ellie's hand and ran both of hers through her short hair. "I'm sorry I'm late. I – I couldn't quite make my legs work. I hope you haven't been waiting out here long."

Ellie forced herself not to react to Claire's choice of words. "It's okay. I used the time to take a walk. Dani was about to drive me crazy," she laughed and was glad when Claire laughed with her.

"She can be headstrong, that's for sure," Claire agreed.

"Oh, you're being nice!" Now came the part that Ellie had been dreading. "Claire, there's something you should know before we go up to see Dani."

"Whatever it is, I don't care. I just want her in my life again." Claire paused. "Wait. Please tell me she's not dying. I figured she's been on the streets for a while. Did she – has she had to do things?"

"She's not dying," Ellie assured immediately. "Anything else you need to know about her time out there, she'll have to tell you." Claire nodded in understanding. "And, I know you're anxious to see her, but you need to hear me out. Okay?"

"Okay."

"Dani was involved in an accident." Ellie reached out to Claire who began to cry again. "She was hit while crossing the street. I won't lie to you, Claire, it's bad."

"W-what happened to her?"

Ellie pulled the sobbing girl close and held her as she told her the news of Dani's legs. She led Claire to a nearby bench and rocked her gently as she broke down.

"Can I see her now?" Claire asked softly.

"Of course. Why don't you go and splash some water on your face, and then I'll take you up to see her."

IF IT HAD BEEN possible, Dani would be pacing in her room like a caged animal. *What the hell is taking so long?* She was scared out of her ever-loving mind, and she wanted the moment to just get here already. Would Claire be pissed at her? Would she pity her? Hell, did Claire even love her anymore?

"*Closure,*" Dani whispered in the empty room, trying to keep what Ellie said in mind. If nothing else, at least Dani would know where she stood with Claire after the night was over. She laughed sarcastically at the thought of her standing at all. A light knock on the door caused Dani to gasp, and practically choke on her own spit. "Yeah?"

Ellie poked her head in, immediately noticing Dani's angst. "Are you ready for some company," she asked brightly. Dani nodded weakly. "*It's okay,*" Ellie mouthed and opened the door wider.

The moment Claire walked in that room, time seemed to stop. Both girls began to cry immediately, and Ellie had a hard time keeping her own emotions in check. Claire ran to Dani's bedside, and after a split-second hesitation, she launched herself at Dani.

"Why didn't you let me help you? Why didn't you stay with me?" Claire sobbed while kissing Dani's stunned face.

Dani used her good arm to hold Claire tightly. "I was stupid," she readily confessed. "Forgive me, baby. Please? I have nothing to offer you . . ."

"You!" Claire stated angrily. "All I ever needed was you!"

Dani tenderly wiped tears from Claire's cheek. "*I need you,*" she whispered.

At that admission, Ellie felt the two needed some time alone, so she quietly stepped out, and closed the door behind her. She wiped her tears and wished she could talk to Hunter about what was happening right now. *Maybe I could have Patty tell her. Or give me her number.* She wondered if she would have the courage to call Hunter, and realized that hearing Hunter's voice is exactly what Ellie needed right now.

A certain rude nurse caught Ellie's attention as the short, redhead made her way to Dani's room. Ellie moved in front of the door, cutting Nurse Ruderton off.

"Where are you going?"

Iris stopped abruptly, giving Ellie a dirty look. "Visiting hours are over. You and your friend need to go." She made a move to go around Ellie but was cut off once again.

"Leave them alone." Ellie crossed her arms defensively, refusing to let Dani and Claire's reunion get ruined.

"Listen, lady, I don't know who you think you are, but around here *I'm* the boss."

Ellie raised a brow and smiled. "Hmm. Someone should really tell Patty that. And, while we're bothering Patty, maybe she could explain to me why you're anywhere near Dani's room."

Iris cackled. That's how Ellie heard it when it came out of Iris's mouth. Maybe it was because Ellie thought of her as a witch . . . with a b.

"Did you really think Hunter would take me off her patient? She *wants* me around."

The smile that Iris gave Ellie was ugly. Normally Ellie wouldn't be so judgmental, but the damned woman got on her last nerve.

"You're either delusional or stupid." Ellie tilted her head, pretending to study the nurse. "Or both." She stood her ground when Iris stepped into Ellie's personal space.

"Listen, bitch, Hunter is mine. Don't get in my way, or you'll be sorry."

Trying to hold in laughter is like trying to hold in a sneeze. Eventually, it was going to explode, and it did. Right in Iris's face.

"Oh my God." Ellie wiped tears of a different sort this time. "Did you really just threaten me?" She lost her smile and took her own step forward. "*You* listen, Regina George, you may have been head mean girl in high school, but you're in the real world now. You don't scare me. Back off. Hunter doesn't want you. And, *I* don't want you near Dani." *Oh my God, is this what jealousy feels like? I've felt like a teenager ever since I met Hunter, and now I'm acting like one.* Not *a good look on me, I'm sure.*

"Is there a problem here?" Patty had gone on break and decided to see how the reconciliation was going. What she didn't count on was a faceoff between one of her nurses and the diner owner.

"No, ma'am," Iris said immediately, backing away from Ellie.

"Nope, no problem," Ellie reiterated. "Except that Nurse Iris here wants to kick Claire out of Dani's room." Was it petty to 'tattle' on Nurse Ruderton? Maybe. Did Ellie care? Not a damn bit. Not when it came to giving Dani the break she needed.

Patty placed her hands on her flared hips and stared down the nurse. "Now I know I removed you from this rotation. What are you doing over here?"

Iris opened her mouth to say something but quickly closed it again. "Visitation hours are over. Rules are rules," she finally muttered.

"That is not the question I asked you, but we'll get to that later. In my office." Patty strategically stepped beside Ellie. It wasn't often when she didn't have her nurses' backs, but Iris had rubbed her the wrong way the first day she came to this hospital. "Dani is a special case, and Dr. Vale has asked Ellie for her help. The rules do not apply here. Understood?"

"Yes, ma'am," Iris muttered with a slight attitude.

"Good. Go on break. I'll see you in my office in an hour." Both women watched the redhead storm away. "That girl has got a bad attitude."

"She's young and entitled," Ellie reasoned with a shrug. "She'll learn one day that the world doesn't spin for her."

"You sound pretty knowledgeable."

Shit. Stop sounding like a parent, Ellie! "Oh, um, it's years of being in the restaurant business. When you see different types of people every day, you learn how to read people." *Sounds reasonable enough.*

"I imagine so," Patty laughed, and lifted her chin towards Dani's door. "How's it going in there?"

"It seemed to be going well when I left them alone. And, I haven't heard anything breaking. So far, so good," Ellie beamed.

"Good job, Ellie!"

Ellie blushed slightly, groaning internally. She couldn't remember a time when she had blushed *this* much.

"I didn't do much. It's all about who you know in this world." Ellie grinned slyly.

"Nonsense. You have gone above and beyond for this young girl, and it has helped Dani *and* Hunter exceedingly. I can't wait until she hears about this!"

Here's your chance, El. Don't blow it. "About that. I was wondering if I could possibly get Hunter's number from you. If you can't give it to me, I totally understand," she said quickly. "I thought maybe I could tell her about Claire myself, but I don't want you getting in trouble with her."

Patty snorted. "*I* don't get in trouble with Hunter. *She* gets in trouble with *me*. Of course, I'll give you her number. I think hearing from you will help her a lot."

Ellie frowned. "Is there something wrong?"

Patty winced inwardly. *Shit!* "No, no! I just meant that she's still worried about Dani. It'll be nice for her to hear that things may be looking up." *That works,* Patty thought when Ellie nodded. She rattled off Hunter's number as Ellie programmed it into her phone. *Hunter is going to owe me big time for this one.*

HUNTER GROWLED AT the sound of her phone going off. She had *just* fallen asleep and was having an extremely good dream. Irked that that dream was interrupted, she snatched up her phone. *This better be good.*

"Dr. Vale," she snarled. There was a hesitation on the other end, which only served to annoy Hunter even more. The sudden thought that it could be Susan made her regret not checking the damn display before answering.

"Oh, God, you were sleeping. I'm so sorry! I'll call back at a more decent time."

That voice. Hunter knew that voice. It was as sweet as the pies she had sampled tonight. She sat up abruptly, sleep completely forgotten. "Ellie?"

"Yeah, I'll call back . . ."

"No, I'm up! I'm awake. Please don't hang up." *Could you sound more desperate?*

"Are you sure?" Ellie asked hesitantly.

"Absolutely. Is everything okay?" Hunter wasn't quite sure what to think about Ellie calling. On the one hand, she was ecstatic that she was hearing from her. On the other hand, what if something was wrong with Dani?

"Yes," Ellie answered hastily. She hadn't wanted to worry Hunter. She also hadn't wanted to find Hunter's sleepy voice so damned sexy. "Everything is great. I hope you don't mind that I asked Patty for your number."

"Of course not. I should have thought about giving it to you myself." *And why would you have done that, Hunter?* "You know, in case something happened with Dani."

Ellie smiled at the hurried explanation. "Well, actually, Dani is why I'm calling." *And, I wanted to hear your voice.* "I found Claire," she continued before Hunter could begin to worry about her patient.

"No shit?" Hunter cringed at her use of language.

"No shit," Ellie repeated with a chuckle.

Hunter grinned. *Oh yeah, I like her.* "So? Was it a good idea? Or should I come back just in case of an emergency?"

"I don't think your services will be needed tonight." Ellie blushed and laughed to hide her embarrassment.

I would love to service you tonight, Hunter thought. "So," Hunter cleared her throat. "Wanna tell me about it?" She leaned back against the headboard and settled in.

Ellie relaxed in the waiting room - grateful for the comfortable loungers – and related the entire story to an acutely attentive Hunter.

"I left them alone so they could get reacquainted. Seems to be going well since Claire is still in there," Ellie finished.

"Wow. You're amazing," Hunter gushed. She couldn't believe that in such an abbreviated period of time, Ellie had managed to do what professionals were incapable of. She brought Dani out of her misery. Not only that, she also brought back the one person Hunter believed could help Dani the most.

Ellie blushed again. *I'm so glad no one else is in here.* "I had some assistance in finding Claire," she said demurely.

"Help or not, Claire is there at that hospital because of you. This is wonderful for Dani. A fresh start." Hunter took a deep breath. "Now all I have to do is convince the hospital to forgive her bills."

"No insurance," Ellie guessed.

"Exactly. I've already forfeited my pay. They wanted to transfer her to Community Hospital, but I threatened to quit if they did." Hunter sighed with frustration. Bureaucracy was a bunch of shit.

Wow. "Can you do that?"

"Nah, not without breaching my contract. But, I would if it meant keeping Dani in a better hospital than Community."

"And, you say I'm amazing." Ellie wondered how many doctors would give up their pay *and* fight the system for a homeless girl with no insurance.

"I – it's not anything anyone else wouldn't do," Hunter stammered with embarrassment.

"Bullshit," Ellie laughed softly.

"Yeah, well." Hunter fidgeted uneasily. "I can do what I can with the hospital, but rehab will be a bit harder. I'll call around, see if I can set something up for Dani."

"Why don't you let me take care of that, Hunter. You're putting yourself out there already."

The suggestion warmed Hunter's heart. She had already concluded that Ellie had a big heart, but this was above and beyond. "I can't ask you to do that, Ellie."

"Good thing I offered then, huh?" Ellie checked her watch and was surprised that she had been on the phone with Hunter for almost forty-five minutes. *Time flies.* "I have friends that would like to help Dani. If you can't get anywhere with the hospital administration, let me know. I'm sure between the two of us we can figure something out."

"You're too good to be true, Miss Ellie," Hunter teased gently.

"Right back at ya, doc." Ellie stifled a yawn. "I should let you go back to sleep, and check on the girls."

"I'm sure Patty wouldn't mind if Claire wanted to stay with Dani," Hunter suggested, disappointed that her time with Ellie was ending.

"As long as Nurse Iris leaves them alone, they should be fine." If she hadn't been so tired, she would never have mentioned the nurse. Apparently, her judgment was severely compromised, and Ellie couldn't help the bite in her tone. Just thinking of the rude woman infuriated her.

"Iris? She's not on Dani's rotation anymore."

"She must not have gotten the memo. But, I think Patty has another one written out for her." Maybe it was wrong to be so callous, but whatever.

"Hmm. Well, I'm happy to let Patty take care of that. The less I see of that woman, the better." Hunter grimaced at the thought of Iris, and how aggressive she was.

Good to know, Ellie thought with a smile. "Well . . ."

"Oh!" Hunter interrupted, knowing that Ellie was about to say goodnight. "I meant to tell you that ma fell in love with the pie, and she's only tried one so far." Hunter chuckled.

Ellie grinned at Hunter's exuberance when talking about her mother. *They must have a great relationship. Must be nice.* "I'm so glad. I hope you have a good visit. And, happy birthday to your . . . ma."

"Thanks, Ellie. And, thank you for calling to let me know about Dani."

"Of course. Sleep well, Hunter. I expect you to be well rested when you get back." She covered her eyes with her free hand when she thought about how that sounded.

"Yes, ma'am." Hunter was grinning ear to ear. *She cares!* "Goodnight, Ellie," she said softly. She listened as Ellie said her goodbyes and waited until she hung up. With a happy sigh, Hunter settled back into bed. *She cares.* Those were the last words in Hunter's head before she let sleep take her over.

Chapter Eleven

For the first time in a long time, Hunter Vale woke up with a smile on her face. She felt refreshed and ready for what the day had in store for her. It amazed her that a simple phone call could work wonders. She was more determined than ever to get past this weekend without incident. Then she would be free. Free of Susan. And free to ask a beautiful woman out on an honest to God date.

After a quick, invigorating shower, Hunter dressed in a comfortable pair of lounge pants, and a tank top. This trip was going to be all about rest, relaxation, and quality time with two of the most important people in Hunter's life. She bounded down the stairs, grinning when she smelled the aromas of breakfast.

"Smells great, ma! I'm starving . . ." Hunter stopped short when she saw Susan sitting at the breakfast bar, casually sipping coffee.

"Good morning, Hunter."

Susan's dark eyes peered at her over the rim of the cup. Hunter hadn't known what emotion to expect if she ran into the older woman, but anger was first and foremost. Anger, nausea, unhappiness. The one thing she *didn't* feel was arousal. *Step forward.*

Hunter ignored the woman and walked around the opposite side of the kitchen island to get to her mom who was standing at the stove. She kissed her mom on the cheek, murmuring a good morning. The good mood she was in had been seriously deflated.

"Now, Hunter, I'm sure your mother has taught you better than to be rude," Susan chastised.

Hunter actually felt her mother's shoulders stiffen underneath her hands. She gave them a quick squeeze, knowing her mother hated when someone else tried to mother her. *What a fucking mess.*

"Susan." Hunter busied herself by getting down a mug and pouring herself some coffee.

"I could use a warm up."

Hunter could feel Susan's eyes on her and hated it. It no longer made her feel wanted and sexy. She wasn't sure it ever did, or if she just wanted it to. But, now, it made her feel dirty. Without a word, Hunter topped off Susan's mostly filled cup. She jerked her arm away, sloshing the hot liquid onto her hand when Susan touched her.

"Shit!"

Cece turned from the stove at Hunter's expletive. "Oh, sweetheart. Are you okay?"

"I'm fine, ma." She put the carafe down and strode to the sink to run cold water over the burn. "No big deal," she smiled down at her mother, giving her a quick wink. "Breakfast almost done?"

"Few more minutes." Cece took Hunter's hand in hers, checking the damage herself. Hunter may be a doctor, but Cece was Hunter's mother. Nothing heals a child's boo boos more than a mother's kiss. That's exactly what she did, much to Hunter's chagrin if the slight blush was anything to go by. "All better."

"Thanks, ma."

"It's my job," Cece smirked. "Will you set the table, please?"

"How many plates?" Hunter asked warily. Oh, how she hoped Susan wasn't staying. Hungry or not, Hunter didn't think she would be able to eat with the woman there.

"Three. Your father will be in shortly. You know he's been up for hours tinkering out in the garden." Cece glanced at Susan. She didn't know why exactly, but the woman made her feel uneasy. Nevertheless, they were neighbors, and Cece didn't have it in her to be impolite when Susan showed up at her door. "Susan just came over to see if you were available to help her this morning."

"No," Hunter answered abruptly.

"I assure you, it's nothing too difficult," Susan smiled wickedly behind Cece's back. "Though you might get a little sweaty."

Hunter glared at Susan. *You're pushing it, bitch.* "I'm here to visit my parents and rest. I'm sure whatever you need to be done, your husband can do it."

"Paul is out of town, unfortunately," Susan answered saccharine sweetly. "And, this job needs to be taken care of this weekend."

"Then I'm sure you can find some teenager that needs a little extra money to do the work for you. Sorry, Mrs. Hinde, my time here is all planned out." Hunter smiled at Susan's outraged face. She was sure the woman wanted nothing more than to scream obscenities at her but was stifled because Hunter's mom was in the room.

"Hunter? You've always helped out Susan. I'm sure we can spare you for an hour or so," Cece reasoned, unsure of why Hunter was being so boorish.

"No, ma. I came here to visit and rest. It's been a tough few months."

"May I speak to you for a moment?" Cece grabbed Hunter's arm and pulled her into the next room. "What is going on?" she whispered harshly. "She's right, I did not raise you to be rude!"

"I'm not trying to be rude, ma. I'm just tired of having to do *stuff* for Mrs. Hinde every time I'm here." She sighed, running her hand through her hair. "She just . . . she makes me feel uncomfortable." That was as honest as she could get with her mother.

Cece frowned. "Why?"

Hunter shrugged. "I don't know. Just something about her . . ."

"Makes you uneasy?" Cece finished for her. Hunter nodded. "Me, too. Why didn't you tell me this before?"

Hunter shrugged again, looking very much like a surly teenager.

Cece sighed. "Okay, why don't you go out and collect your father. I'll let Susan know that you're unavailable."

Hunter gave her mother a lopsided grin. "Thanks, ma." She kissed her again on the cheek, then scooted her happy ass out the door. One day down, two to go. That was easier than she thought it would be. But she also knew that Susan wasn't going to give up. *Just don't answer the damn phone if it's her,* Hunter reminded herself.

AS PROMISED, ELLIE returned to the hospital the next morning after her yoga class. Patty had arranged for another bed to be brought into Dani's room for Claire since the young woman refused to leave her girlfriend's side. And that's where Ellie had found Claire when she arrived. Laying in the beds that had been pushed close together, with Claire's hand protectively resting on Dani's arm. Now, the three of them were chowing down on the breakfast that Ellie brought in.

"So, what now?" Claire asked before taking a bite of her pancakes.

Ellie secretly smiled when Dani reached over to wipe syrup from Claire's chin. "According to Hunter, Dr. Vale," she explained for Claire's benefit. "Dani will have to stay here for another couple of weeks. In the meantime, we'll look into prosthetics and physical therapists."

Dani dropped her fork with a loud clank. "And, just how am I supposed to pay for all this shit? If you haven't noticed, I'm homeless."

"Dani!" Claire scolded before Ellie could say anything. "We talked about this last night. You're not homeless anymore, you're coming home with me."

"I agreed to that, but I didn't agree with you paying my bills, Claire!"

Claire's eyes flashed with anger, and Dani's were defiant.

"Girls!" *This is going to be fun,* Ellie thought irritably. She was surrounded by stubbornness. "Let's be adults about this, shall we?" Both girls had the decency to look abashed. "Dani, you're going to have to accept the fact that you are cared for, and that means accepting help. Hunter is already working on getting your hospital bills forgiven. Claire has offered you a home and love. I, along with a friend of mine, want to help with the rehab and prosthetics."

Tears pooled in Dani's eyes. "Why is everyone doing this for me? I'm a nobody."

"Baby, you're not a nobody." Claire moved closer to Dani, lifting her chin until they were eye to eye. "Face it, you're worth it. Just go with it," Claire grinned, giving Dani a quick kiss.

They spent the rest of the morning hashing out details and conditions – which Dani had a lot of. She didn't want to be a burden or a charity case. So, she insisted that she would work off the debt when she was physically able to. Once everything was agreed to, Ellie got back to her own life at the diner.

"HEY, SWEETS!"

Ellie glanced up from pouring Big Al his second cup of gunk to see Blaise toddling into the diner.

"Hey, momma," Ellie grinned. "Still baking, I see."

"Ugh, don't remind me." Blaise hoisted herself up onto a seat at the counter. "Good morning, Big Al," she greeted with a bright smile. As usual, Big Al grunted his response, amusing both women.

"Grunt, grumble, grumble, grunt. Ungh," Blaise responded good-naturedly.

Big Al just grunted once again before getting up and heading towards the bathroom.

"Good talk!" Blaise called after him. "Was it something I said?" she asked Ellie innocently.

Ellie chuckled. "You shouldn't tease him like that."

"Oh, come on! He totally smiled. I saw it!"

"I think that was the Ovaltine," Ellie teased.

"Whatever. I was just trying to speak his language. At least it's not as complicated as 'teen speak'." Blaise studied her best friend. She was still reeling from what Ellie revealed to her. But she loved Ellie, and nothing would change that. It may take her a minute to get used to this new Ellie — no, new information, not new Ellie — but that's to be expected, right? "Have you had the talk with Jessie yet?"

Ellie felt Blaise's scrutiny but stayed quiet. She suspected there would be a period of "getting used" to things, and she was willing to give Blaise and Jessie that time. At least Blaise was here talking to her. That was a plus, right?

"When?" Ellie snorted. "You keep monopolizing my daughter!" She grinned to take the sting out of her words, even though she was only half-joking.

"Hey! I barely see them. They're locked in that room working on that damned project they won't even tell me about."

Blaise's pout rivaled a toddler's, but it did make Ellie feel a little better. At least she wasn't the only one being left out.

"I know. It's just . . ."

Blaise reached out to cover Ellie's hand with hers. Well, that had been the intent, but her big belly stopped much of her forward motion.

"Help a pregnant sister out, and meet me halfway here!"

Ellie laughed, and leaned over the counter, taking Blaise's hand. "Better?"

"Shut up. This is me comforting you, and asking you what's wrong." Blaise squeezed Ellie's fingers. "Are you afraid of what Jessie is going to say when you talk to her?"

"Yes, of course."

"But?" Blaise asked, clearly hearing Ellie's hesitation.

"I can't help but think I screwed up with Jessie," Ellie confessed quietly.

"Oh, Ellie. How could you think that? Jessie is a loved, happy, healthy, intelligent, caring, beautiful, young woman. You've been an amazing mother."

"But, I never gave her a real family. And, I never will. At least not in the traditional sense."

"Wait, is that what you're thinking? That's she's been coming over to our house because she wants a family?" Blaise asked incredulously.

Ellie shrugged. *Yes*. That's exactly what she thought, and it made her miserable.

"Sweetie, she talks about you constantly. Whenever I make dinner, she'll tell me how yours is so much better," Blaise laughed at Ellie's proud smile. "I don't even think she realizes she's doing it, and she's not mean about it. I actually think it's funny. Everything you do is amazing, and that's unheard of for teenagers." She paused. "But, she's also worried about you."

Ellie frowned. "Worried? Why?"

"She says you've been stressed, and running a lot."

Ellie rolled her eyes. "Restless!" she corrected. "And, I run. That's what I do, you know that."

"I know," Blaise conceded. "But, from what she's told me, you've been getting up pretty early. I'm guessing it has something to do with . . . you know."

"Yes," Ellie admitted. "But, it really was a restlessness in the beginning. Hunter . . . I . . . ." She groaned with frustration. *This is what happens when you avoid talking about this your whole life.*

"Your body came to life?" Blaise guessed with a smirk.

"Don't laugh at me."

"I'm not, sweetie. I'm actually really glad this is finally happening. I'll have someone to talk to about *sex* now." Blaise stage-whispered the taboo word, intrigued by the blush that formed on Ellie's face. *Wow, I don't think I've ever seen her blush so much in all the years we've known each other.*

"I still can't, Blaise," Ellie said softly. "It's bad enough I'm going to have to talk to Jessie about my sexuality, and possibly my feelings for Hunter. Just *feeling* them is driving me crazy. Why the hell do you think I'm running so much?"

"I don't see why you have to run." Blaise shivered with disgust at the word. "Just take care of that 'restlessness' like every other woman. With B.O.B. Wait, would it be a B.O.G. for you?"

Ellie exploded with laughter. "I cannot believe you just said that!" she managed to get out between breaths. "I'll stick with running, thanks."

"Whatever pops your popcorn, sweets. Personally, I would be staying in bed, and giving myself a nice, big . . ."

"Stop it!" Ellie contemplated stuffing Blaise's mouth just to get her to shut up. Especially since Big Al finally made it back. She didn't want to think about B.O.B.s or B.O.G.s or nice, big whatevers. What she needed was to know how Jessie was going to react to her news, and where she stood with Hunter. *Then* maybe she could focus on . . . whatevers.

Blaise sighed and leaned close to Big Al. "Perhaps you could talk some sense into her." Big Al gave her a bemused look, grunted, and went back to reading his book, and drinking his gross drink. "Or not."

"Leave the old man alone," Ellie laughed. "Now, did you come in here to badger me, or do you want food?" She snickered at Blaise's look and held her hands up. "Sorry I even asked! I should have had the food ready for you even though I didn't know you would be here."

"That's more like it," Blaise grinned. "So? Is you-know-who going to be here today?"

Ellie shook her head, glancing at Big Al. *What does it matter if he knows? What's he going to do? Blab it to everyone?* "She's taking a long weekend to visit her parents for her mom's birthday." She allowed herself a wistful moment to think about the doctor, and hoped she was having a wonderful time.

"Well, at least that gives you the time to talk to Jessie," Blaise reasoned. She saw the wistfulness and hoped Ellie wasn't going to get hurt by this woman. Otherwise, the doctor is going to need a doctor.

"Yep." *Good times.* There was a definite need for a change in subject. "Hey, you were serious when you said you wanted to help Dani, right?"

Whew, whiplash! Blaise accepted that Ellie needed some reprieve from thinking about Hunter, and having the talk with Jessie. "Of course."

"She has nothing, Blaise. No insurance, no money." Ellie thought of the short-lived argument where Dani refused financial help from anyone. Claire and Ellie had tried to talk the teen into not letting her pride get in the way again. It was a hard sell for someone who hadn't had anyone caring for her in the past two years. That time on the street had made it difficult for Dani to believe that anyone would help her for nothing in return. That argument lasted all of one minute as Claire furiously reminded Dani that *she* had wanted to help out of pure love. And, if Dani wanted to keep Claire in her life this time, she would have to let go of her ego and accept assistance from people who cared. "Hunter has already forfeited her fee for the surgery, and she's working on getting the hospital to forgive Dani's bills."

"Good luck with that," Blaise muttered.

"I know. I don't see the hospital higher-ups caring about someone like Dani."

"What do you need me to do?"

"You have so many connections through your shop. Do you have any connections on the hospital board?"

"Hmm. Let me check. If I don't personally, I'm sure someone I know does. Maybe the Gallos," she wondered thoughtfully. "I'll think of someone, and if I don't, we'll just take care of it ourselves."

"I knew you were my bestie for a reason," Ellie grinned. "But, I'm going to need us to take care of the physical therapy part. And, new legs."

"You're really serious about helping this young girl, aren't you?" Blaise asked sincerely.

"Yeah. I know it would be impossible for me to help everyone like this, but I feel a connection with Dani. Like I told you before, this could have been my story if I did things differently back then." Ellie shook her head. "In a way, she's much stronger than I was.

She's been through so much, Blaise, and she's only eighteen. She just needs a break."

"So we'll give her one," Blaise smiled. "It'll give me something good to do with this money I never wanted."

A relieved smile graced Ellie's face. "Thank you. Sometimes I don't know what I would do without you."

"Just sometimes?!" Blaise clucked her tongue. "You know what I've noticed? I still don't have food in front of me."

HUNTER STRETCHED HER long, muscular body out on the lounge chair. *This is exactly what I needed*, she thought happily. Complete relaxation was on the agenda today. Her folks were out shopping for the barbecue her dad wanted to have, and Hunter decided it was the perfect time to sit out by the pool, soaking up the sun. Even with the chill in the air as winter tried to make its presence known, the warmth from the sun made it comfortable enough for Hunter to lay out in her bathing suit.

She had already braved the cool water to get in a few laps - which had actually been refreshing after her morning workout - and now it was time to just let it all go. Of course, these days when she let her mind wander, it almost always ended up wandering towards Ellie. What was it about the woman that captivated Hunter so much? The beauty was obvious, but it was more than that. Beautiful women were a dime a dozen in Los Angeles. Innately good women? Now those were harder to find.

There was nothing for Ellie to gain by helping Dani. She certainly didn't have to do it to get Hunter's attention. It was done out of the goodness of Ellie's heart, and that's one thing that held Hunter's attention. She wasn't used to being around women like that — excluding her friends, of course.

Still, there was something . . . more about Ellie that intrigued the doctor. She hoped to be able to explore that. Very soon. She closed her eyes and shook her head. A small smile formed on her full lips as she allowed her mind to completely immerse itself in thoughts of the beautiful blonde.

Hunter jumped out of the lounge chair — not to mention out of her skin — when she felt a touch on her inner thigh. *Goddamn it! I should have known she would try something!*

"Stay away from me, Susan," Hunter sneered.

"Not going to happen, sexy." Susan didn't bother hiding the lust in her eyes as she looked Hunter up and down. "You need to be punished for yesterday."

Hunter snatched up a towel, wrapping it securely around her, and hating that her traitorous body responded to Susan's words. Her only solace was that she felt no desire for the woman at all. *It's all physical*, Hunter thought with relief. *She has no hold over me anymore.*

"Stop," she snarled when Susan took a step towards her. "I told you I'm done with you. No more, Susan."

"*I* will say when we're done, Hunter." Susan tossed a manila envelope onto the chair Hunter just vacated.

"What the hell is that?"

"Insurance," Susan smirked grimly. "You think you can just toss me aside?"

Gingerly, Hunter picked up the envelope and opened it. Her stomach dropped when she saw herself — naked — servicing one of Susan's 'friends'.

"You would throw her under the bus?" Hunter asked miserably. "I thought she was your friend."

Susan shrugged with indifference. "Collateral damage. Besides, it keeps her in line." She skirted the lounge chair. "Do you know how convenient it is to have a councilwoman in your back pocket?"

Stepping back, Hunter shook her head. "No, I wouldn't know. I'm not a devious bitch like you."

"Now, now. Is that any way to talk to your lover?"

"Believe me, that was the tame version of what I wanted to call you. And, you are *not* my lover."

Rage filled Susan's eyes. "Do not test me, Hunter. Unless you want these photos to get out, you *will* be at my house in less than ten minutes. You *will* be strapped! And, you *will* fuck me until I say I've had enough!"

Her body betrayed her once again as she felt the heat between her legs. She fought to keep Dr. Woodrow's words in her head about how it was a natural reaction. It didn't mean she wanted Susan, only that her body was used to responding to Susan's demands.

Hunter tossed the envelope at a stunned Susan. "Go ahead and release those. I want to be away from you so badly that I don't care." There. She had called Susan's bluff. Now she could only wait for the repercussions.

"Do you think I believe you!" Susan shrieked. "This would *ruin* you!"

Hunter shrugged nonchalantly. "I don't think you've thought this through, Susan. It would ruin you more than me." She smiled. "Have you considered what destroying the council woman's life will do to you? You'd lose whatever advantage you think you have with her in your 'back pocket', and I highly doubt she'll keep your part in this quiet. What do you think Paul would say about your little 'sex ring' of desperate housewives looking for some lesbian love?"

She couldn't help the feeling of satisfaction as Susan's face turned a deep shade of red.

"If you care about your career, you'll do what I tell you. None of this has to get out, Hunter. All you have to do is be a good girl."

Hunter clenched her hands into fists. *What would the repercussions be if I hit her?* "You're banking on the fact that I would be devastated if the hospital got rid of me." She grinned. "I could use a vacation. Maybe even a career change. Hell, I may even open up a small clinic for the underprivileged. Go ahead, Susan. Give it your best shot."

"And your parents? Do you want them to know who you really are? *What* you really are? Or what about that little whore you seem to be interested in. Do you think she'll still want you if she knew about your pastime?"

Hunter barely schooled her reaction. *What the hell does she know?* "I don't know what the hell you're talking about."

"You think I don't know about your daily visits to that trashy little diner?"

Fuck. Now she's a goddamn stalker! "I don't know what you think is going on, but I have a friend there that's helping with a patient of mine." Hunter lifted an eyebrow suggestively. "Besides, I have all I need at the hospital. You know how nurses can be. Thank God for on-call rooms, right?" *Let's hope that gets her off Ellie's back. All I need is for this witch to start talking to Ellie about me.* When Susan frowned, Hunter smirked. "What's wrong? Can't believe you paid for bad intel?"

Susan started towards Hunter, the intent to cause harm clearly written all over her face.

"Hunter?" Cece called from the front of the house. "Could you come out and help us unload the truck?"

"Duty calls," Hunter smirked. "You better slither on out of here the way you came in. Unless you really want to let my parents know that you're trying to blackmail their little girl into sleeping with you. Pathetic," Hunter scolded with a shake of the head. It felt amazing to be able to face Susan without feeling the overwhelming need to do as she asked. She didn't allow Susan to win this time. And that was a huge step for Hunter.

"You'll regret this, Hunter."

"I regretted it the moment I got involved with you, Susan." Though proud of herself for standing up to Susan, and resisting the manipulation, Hunter wanted her body to stop reacting. A call to Dr. Woodrow was in store, if just for Hunter's peace of mind.

Chapter Twelve

Ellie was overwhelmed by the scents of breakfast as she walked into the apartment. Another ten-miler this morning left her famished, and her stomach immediately growled at the aroma of bacon.

"Hello?" she called out carefully.

"Hey, mom. How was your run?"

Jessie's hair was mussed from sleep, her pajamas were covered by an apron, and she had flour . . . everywhere. There was also the weird phenomena of not only Jessie being awake before noon on a Saturday, but also being in a good mood.

"Good," Ellie answered cautiously, looking around suspiciously. "You look like my daughter. You sound like her. But, *my* daughter would still be in bed. So, who are you, and what have you done with Jessie?"

"Ha. Ha." Jessie was clearly unamused by her mother's attempt at humor. "I wake up early to try to do something nice for you, and this is how you repay me," she pouted.

"Aww, poor baby," Ellie laughed. She made her way to Jessie and went in for a hug.

Jessie stepped back, waving the spatula she held at Ellie. "Eww, mom! You're all sweaty!"

"Yes, that's usually what happens when you work out," Ellie said dryly. "Imagine that."

"Go shower before you start overpowering the smell of bacon," Jessie teased. She encased her hands in oven mitts and began pushing her mom towards her bedroom. "Shoo!"

"Keep it up, kid. You're about to get a great big, *long* hug, and like it."

"Mom! You're going to make me burn . . . stuff."

"Stuff? Do you even know what you're cooking? Will *I* know what you're cooking?"

Jessie rolled her eyes. "Yes and yes. Now go get cleaned up so I can cook in peace."

"Fine. Try not to burn down the place."

"*Try not to burn down the place,*" Jessie mocked good-naturedly. "You're such a comedian. I have learned a few things from you, you know."

Ellie's eyes went wide, and she clutched her chest over her heart. "Are you telling me that all that time you spent complaining about having to learn how to cook, you actually learned something?!"

"Bricks. That's what you're getting for breakfast. Bricks as hard as your teasing heart."

Ellie let out a loud belly laugh. "All right, I'm going. But, if you don't take those biscuits out of the oven in," she sniffed the air, "six and a half minutes, we really will be eating bricks."

Jessie glanced at the timer on the oven and shook her head. "It's not even right that you can do that!" she yelled after her snickering mother.

"THIS IS REALLY good, sweetie!" Ellie gushed, taking another bite of her eggs. "I don't know why you don't have more of an interest in cooking. You're good at it."

Jessie shrugged. "I like cooking sometimes, but I'll never be as good as you. It's not what I love or want to do."

"And what *do* you love and want to do?" This was the area that Jessie had always avoided in their recent talks. It was easier when all she wanted to be was a princess or a superhero. But now that the time had come to be serious about it, Jessie was keeping her thoughts to herself, much to Ellie's dismay.

"I don't know, mom. I think I'm still working things out in my head." She pushed her leftover food around on her plate, avoiding eye contact with her mother.

"Fair enough," Ellie agreed, taking a sip of her coffee. She could always tell when Jessie was lying, or at least telling half-truths. This was one of those times. But, she would let Jessie "work things out" without too much pressure. For now.

"Are you ready to tell me what's going on?" Jessie had had trouble sleeping the night before, knowing instinctively that whatever her mother said to her today was bound to change their lives. She didn't know why she thought that way, but the feeling was so strong it kept her tossing and turning for most of the night. When she heard her mom getting up early this morning for her run, Jessie made the decision to cook breakfast and try to make this as easy as possible for Ellie.

Truth be told, Jessie was scared. There had never been much drama in their lives, besides what happened with Blaise. That had devastated the both of them. But when it came to Ellie and Jessie personally, it had always been easy. Yes, there were the typical mother/daughter disagreements, but they never escalated to much more than a slam of a door before an apology.

Ellie took a deep breath. "Let's clean this up, and then move into the living room."

"You're avoiding," Jessie accused.

"No, I'm . . . stalling." She ignored Jessie's mutter of "same difference" because she knew it was true. "Come on. Act like I'm the mother, and do as I say." Ellie tweaked Jessie's nose and gave her a wink.

They worked quickly . . . mostly due to Jessie's impatience . . . cleaning up the kitchen and then made themselves comfortable on the couch. Jessie was way past nervous, with her leg bouncing, and fingers tapping the back of the sofa as she waited for Ellie to say *something*. Ellie — although hiding it much better — fought to keep her food down.

"I — I don't know where to start," Ellie stammered. She had never been so nervous in her life. This conversation could ruin her life, and that was something she didn't think she was ready for. But it was time. Jessie deserved to know the truth, and Ellie deserved to live it.

"The beginning?" Jessie suggested.

Ellie sighed. "You know that your grandparents and I don't exactly get along."

"Yeah, I always wondered about that. I mean, you're like the perfect daughter." Jessie waited for a beat. "You're like the *perfect* daughter," she reiterated with feeling.

Ellie blinked at her. "No, no. *You* are the perfect daughter," she said dryly, laughing when Jessie grinned. "I need to start limiting your time with Blaise."

"Ha! I'm definitely my mother's daughter." Jessie stuck her tongue out at her mom.

I hope that's the way it stays. The humor was bittersweet for Ellie. She didn't want her relationship with her daughter to change. The one constant in her life was her great rapport with Jessie. She didn't think she'd be able to survive if Jessie ended up hating her. Ellie's mood darkened at that thought.

"The thing is, my parents were never affectionate. They never told me they loved me, but I would hear them talking about me — bragging — to their friends. They would say how proud they were of my grades, of how I was never any trouble. In my mind, that meant love. What else could it be, right?" Jessie nodded. "When I was a little younger than you, I — I . . ."

Jessie reached over and put her hand on Ellie's arm. She

wasn't used to seeing her mom so flustered. One of the things Jessie loved the most about Ellie was her strength. She spent many nights hoping she would grow up to be half the woman her mother is.

Ellie gave Jessie a sad smile. "I'm having a difficult time with this, Jessie."

"Why?"

"Because if I'm completely honest with you, it could change your relationship with your grandparents." *And me.*

"Mom, I know how they can be. I'm not sure you could say anything that would surprise me."

"Oh, sweetie. I wish that were true. They're so much different with you." *Being a mother is hard! Please let me be doing the right thing.* Ellie blew out a frustrated breath. "I would hope that you trust me enough to come to me with *anything.*"

"I know," Jessie said sincerely.

"I felt that way with my parents once," Ellie continued. "No matter how distant they were emotionally, I trusted their love in me. With that trust in my heart, I went to them when I felt . . . when I knew for sure . . ."

In the moments Ellie took to find her words, something in Jessie clicked. It was almost as if a movie went off in her head; all sixteen years of her life right there on display. The way her mother was acting now, the way she was uncomfortable in front of her parents, the way Jessie's grandparents spoke when they had Jessie alone, the way Ellie never dated, or how she never spoke of being attracted to anyone.

"Mom?" Jessie interrupted Ellie's stuttering. "Are you gay?"

Ellie's jaw dropped and her heart stopped. Every time she tried to answer, she felt sick to her stomach. *Decisions,* she thought. The only decision she had now was being honest with her daughter.

"*Yes,*" Ellie affirmed in a whisper.

Jessie shot up off the couch and began pacing. "You've been lying to me my whole life?!"

"No, Jessie. I never lied."

"Never lied?" Jessie yelled. "You told me we had no secrets! You *told* me you would always tell me the important things! That we were a *team!*"

"We are!" Ellie got up and stood in front of a crying Jessie. Her own tears streamed unchecked down her face as she searched for the right words to explain her decision to her daughter. "Sweetie, I never lied to you. I lied to myself."

Those last four words stopped Jessie's retort cold. "I don't understand," she sniffed.

"I know, honey. And, I will tell you whatever you need to know to help you."

"Everything," Jessie demanded. "I want to know everything. I *deserve* that, don't I?"

"Yes, of course." Ellie guided Jessie back to the couch. "But, if you want everything, Jessie, you have to understand that it won't be pretty."

"One question." Jessie was angry. For the first time in her life, she didn't feel important enough in her mother's life to know the truth. "Does Blaise know?"

Ellie closed her eyes. *Shit.* Locking eyes with Jessie, she told the truth. "I told her a couple of days ago. Only," she continued quickly, "because she was hounding me about Cade."

The corner of Jessie's mouth twitched, but she refused to smile. Thing is, she could totally see Blaise doing that, and Ellie getting annoyed. But that didn't make Jessie feel any better.

"Okay," Ellie sighed. "You wanted me to start from the beginning, so let's try this again." She was almost relieved that the hardest part was over. Now all she had to do was explain her decision to her profoundly hurt daughter and hope Jessie forgave her. "I was fifteen when I told my parents I was gay. It was the late nineties, so I wasn't naïve about what that could mean for me. What I *was* naïve about was my parents' ability to love me no matter what."

Ellie fought the urge to get up and pace herself. This was the part she didn't tell Blaise. The part she never imagined telling Jessie. Nevertheless, she promised everything. No matter how much it hurt, that's exactly what Ellie would give. She prayed, once again, that she was doing the right thing.

"I know grandmother and grandfather are religious," Jessie said carefully. So many things were beginning to make sense now, and she wasn't liking what they were adding up to.

"Yes, extremely. And, me being gay was *not* acceptable." She glanced at the teenager who looked so much like her. "Jessie, I don't want to come between you and your grandparents."

"Mom, all you need to do is tell me the truth, and trust that I'm old enough to make my own decisions about how I handle it."

"God, when did you get so grown-up?" Ellie shook her head in wonder — and a bit of sadness. "Truth. The truth is, when I told them, that was the first time my father hit me." She painfully swallowed past the lump in her throat. "After that, I was basically a prisoner in my own home. I was only allowed to go to school or church, and church was *all* the time. If I wasn't there for service, it was to be counseled by the pastor. That counseling consisted of the pastor touching me in places he shouldn't be touching, and telling me that it was only appropriate for a man like him to do that to me. Anything else was a sin." She wiped a tear from Jessie's cheek. "At first, I rebelled. I wouldn't allow them to dictate who I was, refusing to say I was 'cured' each time they asked. Then I overheard the pastor talking to my parents about conversion therapy. I didn't know what it was, but I was afraid it meant being institutionalized. When I looked it up, it scared the hell out of me. I made the difficult decision to suppress that part of me, and just do what they demanded."

Jessie couldn't believe what she was hearing. How could her grandfather *hit* her mother and try to force her to deny who she was? *Try? He eventually won,* she thought miserably. Knowing her mom suffered from that treatment, and the disgusting treatment by their pastor, inevitably made a horrendous situation even worse. She wiped tears away with the back of her hand.

"What they demanded?" Jessie repeated carefully. "Did that include going out with my father?"

Ellie hesitated for a split second. "Yes. They chose him, but I chose to sleep with him. I was hoping it really would change me. I didn't have experience with guys or girls, so I tried telling myself that maybe I was wrong. Maybe I wasn't gay at all, just confused." She took Jessie's hands in hers. "Jessie, I can't regret anything that happened back then, because it gave me you. But, finding out that I was pregnant with you was the most amazing, yet the most terrifying thing for me."

Jessie's heart pounded painfully. Part of her wanted to stop this conversation. Part of her wanted to go back to earlier this morning when she didn't know any of this. But the biggest part of her still wanted to know everything.

"Why terrifying?" she asked quietly.

"If being gay set my parents off, just imagine what would happen when I told them I was an unwed teenage mother-to-be. I was already attached to you." She gave Jessie a small smile. "I was so afraid they'd make good on their threat to kick me out. Or worse."

"What could be worse than throwing you out on the street?"

"Forcing me to have an abortion," Ellie answered as tears pooled in her eyes.

Jessie sat back, blowing out a gust of breath. She stared up at the ceiling as she thought about everything. "Obviously neither happened," she prompted.

Ellie snorted mirthlessly. She mirrored her daughter's position. "Nope. Apparently being pregnant proved that I couldn't possibly be gay, and that overruled everything. They were ecstatic. Of course, they tried to get your father to marry me, but his parents put a stop to that."

"Would you have? Married him, I mean?"

"Let's just say I'm very glad that was one thing my parents didn't insist on. I definitely didn't love him, and I didn't want him to have to endure a life with me just because I used him."

Jessie rolled her head towards Ellie. "Oh yeah, you're just a terrible person. I can't believe *I* have to 'endure' a life with you," she said sarcastically.

Ellie playfully smacked Jessie's pajama-clad leg. "What I meant by that was, he would be stuck with me instead of out there finding real love. I had already given up that dream for myself. I didn't want that for him. He's a good guy, Jessie."

"How good can he be? He didn't want anything to do with me." Jessie picked at invisible fuzz on her polka dot pants.

Ellie sighed. "His parents were as overbearing as mine are, sweetie. They had plans for him, and him being a father at that time was not it. He knew they could make my life miserable if we pursued it, so he gave up his parental rights. His father . . . was our pastor."

Jessie sat up quickly. "So, both of my grandfathers are abusers?!"

"Honey . . ."

"No, mom! It's true! Grandfather *hit* you. And, the other one? Ugh! I can't even!"

Ellie grabbed Jessie's arm before she could get up again. "I am, by no means, excusing what *either* man did. But, after I became pregnant, the pastor told my parents to find another church. I knew it was to keep them — and me — away from their son, but it also kept me away from him. As for my parents, they did a one-eighty. They took me to every doctor's appointment, bought me all the supplements I needed. Basically, they were the parents I needed them to be when I told them I was gay. I couldn't do it on my own, sweetie. I *needed* them."

"They still treat you like crap!"

Ellie shrugged. "I'm damaged. The 'gay thing', and even getting pregnant, tainted me."

"Then why did they help you? Why do they insist on having a relationship with me? Why do you allow it?" Jessie wasn't understanding any of this. She just couldn't imagine the woman who raised her bending for anyone. No, not just bending, breaking. Totally giving up who she was.

"I imagine they helped me so they could have another chance at a perfect child. Or grandchild. I allowed them to spend time with you because I felt I owed it to them. And, I owed it to you to know who your grandparents were. If you had ever come to me saying they had upset you or hurt you in any way, I would have put an end to it immediately."

Jessie turned to her mother. "It wasn't me they wanted to hurt." She saw Ellie's confusion, and though she didn't want to, she explained. "It all makes sense now. They've always been a bit prejudiced."

"A bit?"

"Well, I *thought* I was getting through to them by *debating* their views. Respectfully, of course."

"Of course," Ellie smiled.

Jessie stuck her tongue out at her mom, then frowned. "But, they were always adamant about one thing."

"Homosexuality being a sin?" Ellie guessed.

"Yes. I didn't know what they were doing before, but now?"

"Now you know they were trying to make sure you would hate me if I decided to 'be gay' again." Ellie was fuming, but she kept her composure. "When I was pregnant, they would make remarks here and there. More like threats. They wanted me to know that if I ever reverted to my 'perverted' way of thinking, you would hate me. They would somehow make me look like a bad mother, and take you away from me."

"And, yet, you owed them a relationship with me," Jessie repeated bitingly.

"Hey! I was young, pregnant, and scared. Then I was young, with a tiny baby, and scared. I had no idea what I was doing, Jessie. I never left you with them by yourself until you were old enough to tell me if I was making the wrong decision. I did my best, and did what I thought was best."

Jessie felt awful for upsetting Ellie even more. She had been through — and given up — too much to have her daughter bitching at her. "I'm sorry, mommy," she sniffed.

"Come here." Ellie pulled her daughter close, holding her as they both let the tears flow freely. "*I don't want you to hate me,*" she whispered.

Jessie pulled back a little so she could look her mother in the eye.

"I could never hate you. I wish you knew you could have trusted me enough to tell me anything."

"Oh, sweetie. It had nothing to do with trusting you. I buried that part of me so deeply that I just . . . well, I thought," Ellie blew out a frustrated breath, and chuckled. "This is something I never thought I'd be telling my daughter, but I had no feelings at all."

Jessie contemplated that for a moment. "Like, asexual?"

Ellie laughed a little. "You're way too smart for *my* own good. But, yes. Which I found to be comforting in a way."

"Because it meant you wouldn't have to face the possibility of rejection from me?" Jessie surmised.

"Too smart," Ellie reiterated.

"What changed?"

Oh boy. "Um, I — I met someone and figured out that those feelings were not gone, just dormant," she answered honestly.

Jessie's eyebrows shot up to her hairline. "You met someone? A woman, I'm guessing."

"Yes."

"Are you dating her?" Jessie asked, trying not to feel betrayed.

"No, of course not. I wouldn't do that without talking to you first. I'm not even one-hundred percent sure she's interested in dating me." *Ninety-five percent, maybe,* Ellie mused with a little too much exhilaration.

It may have been wrong, but Jessie felt relieved by that. Yes, it was weird to know that her mother was having *feelings* for someone. But Jessie told herself she would feel that way no matter *who* — man or woman — Ellie was into.

"Will you tell me about her? Wait, is she why you've been running a lot lately?"

Ellie fought the blush she felt creeping up her neck as she remembered how Blaise told her she should handle her restlessness.

"Yes. I didn't know how to deal with what I was feeling." Ellie answered with absolute honesty. "Running helps me think, you know that."

"And, expends all of that, um, energy," Jessie teased.

"Jessie! I am *seriously* limiting your time with Blaise. She is a bad influence on you!"

Jessie laughed. "You're probably right, but you love us both, anyway."

"Most of the time," Ellie mumbled grumpily.

"Tell me about her," Jessie requested once again.

Ellie told Jessie all she knew about Dr. Hunter Vale, grinning when Jessie would laugh at Hunter's goofiness. It was what Ellie had hoped for. The rapport between her and Jessie was still there. She knew Jessie would probably have questions, and that it wasn't guaranteed to be smooth sailing from here on out. But it was a great start and took a heavy burden off Ellie's shoulders.

As promised, the entire Saturday was devoted to mother and daughter spending quality time together. They talked, laughed, joked, cooked (which even Jessie found to be more fun than before), watched movies, and painted each other's nails. She could sense a shift in her mom — a peace of mind that hadn't been there before — and Jessie was proud of Ellie for keeping the promise she made to herself all those years ago. It took a lot of courage to risk the love of those around you. Especially when the fear of losing that love is what kept you hidden for so long.

Ellie had never felt so free in her life. Not even when running. There was nothing like being true to yourself, and to your family without being hated for it. Fear kept her from living a genuine life. In fact, it almost made her forget who she was. Until Hunter. Whatever happened with the beautiful doctor, it would be worth it just for this opportunity to have Jessie know the real Ellie.

Chapter Thirteen

"Fuck!" Hunter growled with frustration and threw the covers off her overheated body. She sat up and scrubbed her head as she contemplated pulling her hair out. Everything was going great. She was resting, spending time with her parents, talking to them about Ellie. So, what the hell was wrong with her? Why did her body refuse to keep up with her heart and mind? "Why can't Susan just leave me alone?"

She had finally blocked the older woman's number, but that didn't stop the texts or calls. They would come from different numbers, and Hunter realized she would have to change her own damn number to stop them.

She was most embarrassed by the way her body kept reacting to this fucking messed up situation. Susan's demands and filthy words caused a craving in Hunter that made her hate herself almost more than she hated Susan. She snatched up her phone and made the call she wished she didn't have to make.

"Dr. Woodrow," a sleepy voice answered.

"Um, hi. This is, uh, Hunter Vale. I'm so sorry to bother you . . ."

Dr. Woodrow interrupted Hunter's stammering. "Hunter, I gave you this number for a reason. Please feel free to call me whenever you need to. Is there something I can help you with?"

"I — I need to understand," Hunter said quietly.

"Understand what?"

"Why my body reacts to her. To Susan. I don't want her; I swear I don't! I know you said it was normal, but this doesn't feel normal to me." This was only the third conversation Hunter had with the psychiatrist, but for some reason, she felt comfortable. Perhaps it was the unconventional way they had their sessions. Or maybe it was because of the woman's relationship with Rebecca. Whatever the reason, Hunter was thankful for the guidance she had been given so far. Dr. Woodrow had a way of explaining things to Hunter that made her feel . . . sane.

"Hunter, have you had a lot of contact with Susan while being there?" Dr. Woodrow asked, her once-sleepy voice now clear and concise.

"She won't leave me alone. She showed up here at the house twice and keeps texting and calling," Hunter confessed.

"And in these, let's call them confrontations, has she been forceful with you?"

"Yes."

Dr. Woodrow paused for a moment, and Hunter thought she could hear the scratching of pen to paper. She wondered if the doc kept an endless supply of notebooks and pens wherever she was.

"Hunter, I want you to listen to what I'm saying, okay?" Hunter agreed, and the doctor continued. "Just because your body reacts, it does not mean you desire Susan. Your body has been conditioned to respond to her demands. From what I've learned during our previous conversations, whenever Susan wanted you, you were expected to perform. *That* is what your body is responding to. The demand, not the woman."

"Conditioned," Hunter repeated slowly.

"I can tell you're having trouble comprehending that, so let me ask you another question. Have you had any recent interaction with any of your other affairs?"

Hunter tried not to let the word Dr. Woodrow chose bother her.

The truth hurts. But that's exactly what they were, and that was something Hunter was not proud of.

"Yes. I, uh, contacted one of them because Susan has photos of us, and is threatening to expose us."

"Oh, my. We'll get back to that in a moment. First I would like you to tell me, did you have any kind of reaction when speaking with her?"

Hunter thought about it and frowned. She had felt absolutely nothing. Was that wrong? They had slept together. Shouldn't Hunter have felt *some* kind of connection?

"No, nothing. So, why Susan?"

"Because Susan is the one who got to you when you were vulnerable. She began to manipulate and control you when you were naïve and confused. That is why your body responds to her," Dr. Woodrow explained.

"But, I'm forty-one now. How the fuck long is she going to have this hold over me?" Hunter demanded angrily.

"I imagine that's why you're talking with me now, Hunter. You're ready to let her go. It's not an easy thing, which I'm sure Rebecca has told you."

"But, Rebecca was abused by that bitch for a long time. I wasn't abused."

"Oh, Hunter. If this is going to work, you're going to have to come to terms with the fact that what Susan did to you *was* abuse," Dr. Woodrow said kindly.

"I didn't refuse her," Hunter argued.

"From what you've told me, she didn't give you a chance to refuse. She manipulated you, Hunter. And, she was able to continue that manipulation throughout these years because she was already in your head."

"I want her out!"

"And, that's why we're talking now. Have you given in to these cravings?"

"No. I can't. I won't." *I will not ruin my chances with Ellie.* "Do you . . . Will I be able to have a normal relationship?"

"I don't see why not. You've told me about Ellie, and while I think she could be good for you, I believe you need to be honest with her about everything."

"You mean tell her about Susan? I'm trying to date her, not push her away."

"If honesty pushes her away, Hunter, perhaps she's not the one. Besides, secrets have a way of coming out. Wouldn't you rather she hears everything from you?"

Hunter heard tapping on the other end as she contemplated what the doctor was saying. Maybe she was right. Susan has already threatened to talk to Ellie.

"Why don't you tell me about the blackmail," Dr. Woodrow suggested, interrupting Hunter's musings. Hunter explained everything that had happened since coming home to see her parents. "And, how does that make you feel?"

Hunter chuckled. "You really are a shrink."

The psychiatrist tsked. "You've been hanging out with Rebecca too much. This is what I get the big bucks for. Getting you to face your own feelings," she teased Hunter.

"I should have thought of that when I was deciding my specialty," Hunter teased back.

"I'm sure you're doing just fine as a trauma surgeon," Dr. Woodrow laughed. "Speaking of, do you think if Susan made good on her threat your job would suffer?"

Hunter sighed. "Maybe a couple of years ago, I would be more worried about it. But, I'm just not anymore. I'm out at the hospital, and while it would be embarrassing, it won't ruin me."

"And, your family and friends?"

"The friends that matter already know. It's my family that I'm worried about. And, Ellie. But, I can't do it anymore, doc. I feel like a part of me died a little every time I was with her, and the others."

"That's understandable, Hunter. And, we'll delve into that more as our sessions continue. For now, is there anything you can do to stop her from releasing the photos?"

"The councilwoman is looking into that. Susan likes having a politician in her pocket, but let's see how she feels about having one against her. I don't think Susan expected me to warn her."

"Hunter, I'm not sure Susan is altogether sane. I know it's not ethical of me to make that diagnosis without an evaluation, but I can't help it. What she did to you . . ." Dr. Woodrow made a sound of disgust. "Forgive me for being unprofessional, but I feel a bit protective over you."

Hunter was surprised. She had never met the woman before, why would she possibly feel protective of Hunter?

"You're probably wondering why," Dr. Woodrow correctly presumed. "And, it's because you helped my niece when she needed you the most. She's told me all about you, and your friendship. I'm sorry it took us this long, and under this circumstance to meet. And, I'm sorry it took me so long to thank you."

Hunter blushed uncomfortably with the praise. "I was just doing my job," she mumbled.

"Maybe that's how it was for you, but for me, you saved my family. And, not just in the OR. You've been a good friend to Rebecca." Dr. Woodrow exhaled. "And, now that we've completely gotten off subject . . ."

Hunter laughed. "It's fine. Actually, it got my mind off of everything else, so your form of therapy has worked pretty well, Doctor."

Willamena laughed as well. "That's why I get the big bucks," she restated. "In all seriousness, Hunter, you should think about telling your parents the truth. Don't let Susan have anything to hold over your head."

"They're going to hate me," Hunter said sadly.

"No, they're going to hate her. Susan preyed upon you, Hunter. And, if I were you, I would tell your parents in a place where they are far, far away from Susan. Especially if your father has a shotgun."

They talked for a little while longer, and after the phone call ended, Hunter had a myriad of thoughts running through her head. She had never thought of herself as Susan's prey before, and she sure as hell didn't appreciate it now. She couldn't deny the sense of reprieve in being told that everything she was feeling was natural, but she didn't like feeling like a victim. Hunter shook off the morose mood.

"One more day," she sighed into the quiet of her childhood bedroom. One more day and she'd be away from Susan again. But more importantly, she'd be able to focus on asking Ellie Montgomery out. *I can do this. I can have a normal relationship. That's all I want.*

"WHAT TIME IS she supposed to be here?" Ellie asked a distracted Blaise. "Hey, preggo, the cake isn't going anywhere. Slow down."

"Of course, it's going somewhere. In my belly to feed this kid. I swear he's got a sweet-tooth," Blaise said around a mouthful.

"Honey, he doesn't *have* teeth. That's you," Ellie smirked. "Stop blaming your kid for how much red velvet you eat, and tell me when Eve is supposed to be here."

"*If you read your email, you'd know,*" Blaise muttered before taking another bite.

Ellie lifted an arched brow and snatched the plate out from under Blaise's nose.

"Okay, okay! I'm sorry. She's supposed to be here in," Blaise checked her watch, "ten minutes. Can I have my cake back, now, please?"

Ellie slid the plate back in front of Blaise and was glad they were secluded in her office. *No one needs to see a pregnant Blaise murdering that poor piece of cake.*

Blaise smirked around her fork as Ellie shook her head. "How did your talk with Jessie go?"

"Much better than I expected." She noted the time and decided to tell Blaise the condensed version for now. "She still has questions, which she asks at the oddest times, but that's understandable. She actually woke me up in the middle of the night just to ask me more about Hunter."

"How does she feel about there being a woman you're interested in?" Blaise asked delicately.

Ellie looked up from doodling on a napkin when she heard the hesitation in Blaise's voice. "How do *you* feel about it?"

"I'm still getting used to it," Blaise answered honestly. "But, really, I'm just jealous that you never saw me that way." She grinned and winked.

"You're such a brat!" Ellie chuckled. "Now wipe your mouth, and let's go. Eve will be here soon."

"Ooo, what about Eve?"

Ellie frowned. "What about her?"

"Any kind of, you know, tingle with her?"

"Tingle?" Ellie rolled her eyes. She stood up and headed for the door. "You're a nut, and the answer is no."

"Impossible!" Blaise disputed. "Eve Sumptor-Riley is hot!"

Ellie's eyebrows shot up. Blaise had never been one to shy away from complimenting another woman, but never quite like this. "I agree, but she's just not my type."

Blaise snorted. "Eve is *everyone's* type. Hell, *I* would change my status for Eve for one night."

"Blaise!" Ellie picked her jaw up off the floor, then smacked her friend on the arm. "Apparently, I'm not as easy as you are." She stuck her tongue out at her best friend. They headed out of the kitchen into the dining area. The aforementioned Eve Sumptor-Riley, and her friend and business associate, Lainey Stanton, were already waiting at a table.

Ellie couldn't refuse that *both* women were incredibly attractive. But even with her newfound emotions, Ellie never felt a 'tingle'. That's why her reaction to Hunter baffled her so much. There was just something more *chemical* when it came to Hunter. That was the only explanation Ellie could come up with.

"Would you like me to be your wing-woman with Eve?" Ellie teased.

"Shut up." Blaise bumped Ellie's hip with hers, sending the smaller woman into the counter. "Oops, sorry. Anyway, she's married, and as straight as I am. Sad day for you, I know."

"Devastating," Ellie groused cheekily. She noted the subtle closeness of Eve and Lainey as they approached the table. Most people would see best friends enjoying a private chat. Ellie's many years of experience in a highly people-oriented business had her seeing something more, even though she knew both women were married. *Hmm, maybe not as straight as we thought,* she mused with interest. "Ladies," she said with a bright smile.

Eve stood and hugged Ellie and Blaise briefly. "I bet you thought I was never going to open the gallery," she joked. Her smoky, alto voice always took Ellie a little by surprise.

"It crossed my mind," Ellie grinned. "Hi, Lainey, it's great to see you again."

"Likewise," Lainey smiled up at them. "And, *I* was beginning to wonder if we were going to open as well." She rolled her eyes playfully at Eve, who scowled at her.

"Whose fault was it that we had to get a new artist?" Eve slid back into the booth.

Lainey addressed Ellie and Blaise as they sat across from her. "He was a horrible person. He was condescending, and I will not apologize for kicking him to the curb."

"This is why she's my right hand," Eve said with a proud smile. "She takes shit from no one. It all turned out for the best. We found another local artist that is extremely talented *and* nice, and we just returned from Paris."

"I take it Paris was successful?" Blaise asked.

"Yes, it was very . . . enlightening," Eve smiled.

Ellie noticed Lainey's soft blush, as well as Eve's impish grin. *Oh, yeah. There is definitely something more between them,* Ellie concluded. She caught Eve's stare and raised an eyebrow. "Sounds wonderful. I can't wait to see how everything comes together."

For the next thirty minutes, they discussed what Eve expected for opening night. She gave Ellie the number of people she would be catering for and a broad idea of the kinds of food she preferred.

Finger food should be easy enough, Ellie thought as she ran through recipes in her head while listening. *A bit of sweet and savory. I wonder if Hunter would be interested in going.* That thought brought everything else to an abrupt halt. Did she really just contemplate asking Dr. Hunter Vale out on a date?

"El?" Blaise waved her hand in front of Ellie's face.

"Hmm? Oh, I'm so sorry! I, um, got caught up thinking about the menu," she lied with a sheepish smile.

"No problem," Eve said with her customary wink. "I was just asking if you had a designer picked out already. If not, I have someone coming in from Germany whose help would be perfect for the occasion."

"There hasn't been much time to shop for anything yet, so that sounds great, actually. Thank you." Ellie was no stranger to designer clothes. Not with Blaise as a best friend. However, she had never worked directly with someone to design a dress just for her. Could be fun.

"I'm just hoping either this baby stays put until after the opening, or comes out tomorrow," Blaise whined, only half kidding. "I hope your designer can work with this." She rubbed her belly lovingly.

"Kiara actually works with many different designers," Eve explained with a chuckle. "She found someone for me when I was pregnant with Bella, so you're good."

"Miss Ellie?" Charity interrupted timidly. "I'm so sorry, but you're needed in the kitchen."

Ellie gave her a gentle smile. "I'll be right there." She shrugged apologetically. "Duty calls. Eve, I should have a preliminary menu with samples for you by mid-week."

"Sounds good," Eve agreed. Ellie wasn't sure, but she thought she felt a cooling in Eve's attitude towards her.

Ellie acknowledged Eve's answer before turning her smile up. "Lainey, it's always a pleasure. Blaise, I'll see you later tonight." She got up and made her way to the back.

"Ellie?"

Ellie winced at Eve's smooth voice. Something was definitely wrong. She turned back with what she hoped was a relaxed, happy look. "Yes?"

"Whatever it is you think you see between me and Lainey . . ." Eve began icily.

"Is none of my business," Ellie finished evenly. "Eve, believe me, you have nothing to worry about."

Eve's face softened, and she stepped closer. "Lainey is incredibly important to me. I don't want her hurt."

"I understand that," Ellie granted. *What I don't understand is why you're both married to other people.* "Look, I've just spent the week coming out to Blaise and my daughter. I think I've had enough drama to last me a while," she smiled at the shocked look Eve gave her. "Like I said, you have nothing to worry about. I like Lainey. And, you. I have no desire to cause anyone any pain."

"You're?" Eve hesitated. "I apologize for the way I approached you. I guess you've noticed that I'm particularly protective of Lainey."

Ellie gave her a reassuring smile. "No harm done. Eve?" she called out as the other woman turned away. "May I ask a question?" Eve nodded warily. "If I wanted to invite someone to the opening?"

Eve chuckled with relief. "Invite whomever you want. Just let me know the final count." With a wink, she left Ellie.

"SO, BLAISE?" JESSIE could only move her eyes since her mom was currently slathering a mask all over her face. "Have you met this Hunter person, yet?"

Ellie froze. *Oh, shit.*

"Yes, I've met her." Blaise completely missed Ellie's panicked look, as she scooped up another blob of the green mask, and plopped it onto Piper's face. When she finally looked up, she saw

Ellie's face. "She seems pretty nice," she offered, thinking Ellie needed her to talk the doctor up.

Ellie rolled her eyes. "Hunter comes into the diner to eat breakfast after her shift," she explained to a frowning Jessie. "Blaise met her when she came in, panicking about her coffee maker breaking."

"Keurig," Blaise corrected dourly.

"I'm surprised she remembered meeting anyone that day. She was in mourning until Greyson and I promised to get her a new one." Piper giggled, cracking her already drying face mask.

Blaise covered Piper's laughing mouth. "Hey! Whose side are you on?"

"Clearly she's on mine," Ellie snickered. "And, since she's not asking who Hunter is, I'm guessing you two talked?"

"Yes, ma'am." This came from the shy Piper.

Ellie took a deep breath. If Piper knew, that meant Greyson knew, too. Part of her was relieved. The other part, the one that was still scared of her parents, was overwhelmed. If news traveled this fast, how long would it be before she heard from her father?

Blaise leaned close to Ellie. "It was just Greyson and Piper, El. You know I wouldn't tell anyone else."

"I know. I just wonder if I'm in over my head." Ellie tapped Jessie's shoulder to let her know she was done. "Since I've met Hunter, I've come out, felt jealousy for the first time, I'm pretty sure I've made an enemy and was trusted to get a young girl who needs a lot of help to open up. My considerably tidy life has become pretty messy."

Jessie sat next to her mom and took her hand. "What I'm hearing is, you're finally being true to yourself, you're feeling a totally normal emotion, and you were the perfect choice to help Dani. That enemy, whoever they are, doesn't stand a chance against you, so don't waste time thinking about that." She grinned at Ellie. "Mom, you may think your life is now messy, but to me, you finally started living."

Ellie hugged her daughter close, not caring about the goop on her face. "You're growing up too fast," she whispered close to her ear. She pushed her back a bit to look her in the eye. "I don't want you to ever feel like I wasn't happy before all of this. It's always been just you and me, and that has been perfectly imperfect." She laughed at Jessie's mock glare.

"Whatever," Jessie grumbled. But she knew exactly what her mother was saying. Their relationship has had its difficulties, as all mother/daughter relationships do. But there was never a time when Ellie wasn't there for her. That was one of the things Jessie feared the most. Losing the closeness they had because someone else was occupying her mom's time.

"You've given up so much for me," she held up her finger, cutting off Ellie's rebuttal. "You have. You've lived your life for me. But, I'm getting older now and will be going to college soon. It's time for you to live for you now."

"I love you. You know that, right?"

Jessie smiled. "Of course I do. I love you, too. Now, we should probably stop all of this emotional talk before Blaise floods the place." She gestured towards the crying, pregnant woman with her chin.

"Oh, God!" Ellie laughed. "Come here, you big ball of hormones!" She pulled Blaise into a hug with Jessie, then reached over for Piper. "Ah, yes. Girls' night. Facials, deep discussions, and blubbering messes. What more could we ask for?"

"MA, DON'T CRY, please?" Hunter pleaded as they stood at the front door. "You know I hate it when you cry."

"Well, if I knew it wouldn't be so long in between visits, your leaving wouldn't bother me so much."

No one dishes out guilt quite like a mother. Hunter hugged Cece – again – and discreetly rolled her eyes at her father over her head. "I'll be back soon, I promise."

"I'll hold you to that. But, I'll also be expecting more of that pie." Cece looked up at her daughter with a wicked smirk. "Or Ellie."

"Ma!"

"Best you just do as she says, Hunt." Alton gave his daughter an indulgent smile and a wink.

"Pie I can do. I can't promise Ellie." *Though I'm going to try my hardest to make it happen.*

"I doubt she'll be able to resist your charm." Cece patted her daughter on the stomach.

"Of course not," Alton chimed in. "She takes after her pop."

It was Cece's turn to roll her eyes. "Without a doubt, dear."

Alton brushed past his wife to hug his daughter. "Don't you listen to her sarcasm. I got her, didn't I?"

"That you did, pop. That you did." Hunter laughed at her parents' playfulness. This was the kind of relationship she wanted. They obviously loved each other immensely, but they also never let life get too serious. That passion and friskiness kept the couple happily married for over forty-five years.

"I felt sorry for you," Cece teased her husband before addressing her daughter again. "Don't wait another six months, Hunter." The seriousness almost made Hunter wince.

"You know, the road goes both ways." Hunter moved swiftly to avoid getting smacked by her mom. "Come on, ma. I already said I'd do better."

"It's a mother's right to dish on as much guilt as possible." Cece stood on her tiptoes and kissed Hunter's cheek. "Go on now so you can get home at a decent time. Be careful, and let me know when you get there."

"Yes, ma'am." She took her duffle from her father. "Love you both."

"We love you." Not comfortable with showing a lot of emotion, Alton hugged his daughter again briefly. "Good luck with that young lady."

Hunter chuckled. "Thanks, pop. I may need it."

Chapter Fourteen

Hunter walked meekly towards the diner, muttering to herself. "I'm just going to walk in there, and ask her out." She stopped and turned back the other way. "No, I will walk in there, be charming, and *then* I'll ask her out." She started back towards Ellie's just to pace away again. "No, I will go in there, have breakfast, hope I can keep it down, be charming, and *then* ask her out." With a definitive nod, Hunter squared her shoulders, took a deep breath, and headed for her uncertain, but hopeful future with Ellie.

"WHAT ARE YOU watching, doll?"

Blaise leaned back into the solid chest of her husband. She smiled when Greyson wrapped his arms around her belly in a protective embrace. "I'm watching someone either working herself up to do something wonderful or have a nervous breakdown," she chuckled.

Greyson's chest rumbled with silent laughter. "Someone you know?"

Blaise tilted her head back, giving Greyson a quick kiss on the cheek before she answered. "That's Hunter."

Greyson's eyebrows shot up. "Ellie's Hunter?"

"I'm sure they're both hoping that," Blaise smiled.

"Wow. Good for you, Ellie," Greyson murmured. He saw Blaise's raised eyebrow. "You are carrying our child. No one is more incredible than you, doll." He kissed her smirking lips.

"And, if I weren't carrying 'our' child?"

"*No one* is more incredible than you, baby." Greyson nuzzled Blaise's fragrant neck. He peeked out the window at the dark-haired beauty currently talking to herself. Ellie certainly had good taste. "I hope she doesn't hurt Ellie."

Blaise sighed. "Me, too. I've never seen Ellie so vulnerable. That woman out there could destroy her."

"Or, she could make Ellie happier than she's ever been," Greyson countered.

She turned in her husband's arms and wrapped her arms around his neck. "When did you become such an optimist?"

"When I met you." Greyson bent his head and kissed Blaise gently, but passionately. "I wish you weren't working, doll. You should be resting so close to your due date."

"I arrange flowers, stud. I'm not doing any deliveries, and I've already promised I would stay away from chemicals. I'm fine. Women have been doing this for centuries, you know," she grinned.

"None of those women were my wife carrying *our* child." He sighed. "Be careful, yeah?"

"Yeah." Blaise raised up on her tiptoes – not an easy task for a largely pregnant woman – and kissed Greyson. He wasted no time deepening the kiss and she moaned. "Whoa there, stud. Keep that up and you'll send me into labor." She thought about that for a split second, gave him a wicked grin, and then kissed him again with even more fervor.

ELLIE SLID A plate full of an egg white omelet, wheat toast, and fruit in front of Big Al. She expected an argument and was not disappointed.

"Didn't order this, girl."

"Nope, you sure didn't. Eat up."

"Don't want it. Got what I need." To emphasize his point, he took a large gulp of his weird concoction.

"That's *not* what you need. What you need is a well-balanced meal. Like this. Big Al, you know this is what your wife wanted for you. If you're not going to do it for yourself, do it for her."

Big Al grunted something unintelligible, and Ellie was pretty sure she wouldn't want to know anyway. Nevertheless, he picked up his fork and began eating. She smirked. *Score one for me!* When the bell sounded from above the door, Ellie beamed as Hunter walked in.

Hunter's gaze immediately found Ellie's, and her mouth went dry. She didn't even try dimming her responding smile. *God, she's beautiful. Don't screw this up, Vale.*

"Hey! I didn't think I'd see you today." Ellie winced inwardly. *Ugh, could you be any more enthusiastically awkward? Be cool. She's just another customer.* She inwardly rolled her eyes at herself. *Yeah right.* "Surely you didn't work last night."

Hunter hoisted herself onto the barstool. Her heart was pounding, but she was encouraged by Ellie's reaction to seeing her. "Nah, I just got home last night. Mornin', Big Al," she greeted before turning her attention back to the charming blonde. "It's shift rotation time at the hospital, so I thought I'd stop by *before* I have to go in," She gave Ellie her lopsided grin.

"Ah. Well, you certainly look well-rested." It was true. Hunter looked good. *Very good.* Well-worn jeans and a light hoodie over a t-shirt gave Hunter a relaxed, comfortable — extremely sexy — look.

Hunter caught the subtle once-over Ellie gave her, and the blood started pumping double time. She just hoped she wouldn't blush. "Yeah, um, I always have a great time visiting my folks." *Except when I had to deal with Susan.* "I didn't do much." She thanked Ellie when a cup of coffee was placed in front of her. "Except a little gardening with pop and some pie tasting with my ma. She loved everything, by the way."

The image of Hunter gardening amused Ellie and she smiled. "Good. I'm so happy she enjoyed it."

Hunter shook her head. "Enjoyed is not the word. I don't think I'm allowed home again unless I bring you . . . er, your pies." She chuckled despite her near flub.

Ellie's eyes widened with feigned anguish. "We wouldn't want that. I'll be sure to supply you with whatever you need," she winked playfully. "So? Are you hungry?"

Hunter had to shake herself out of the temporary shock of Ellie's words and impish wink. *Oh, yeah, I'm hungry.* "Um, I am. I kinda missed dinner last night."

Ellie tsked. "You should know to take better care of yourself, Dr. Vale."

Hunter shrugged sheepishly. "I know. But I crashed when I got home last night. Besides, I'm not the greatest cook, and fast-food isn't exactly healthy, and didn't appeal to me."

"So . . . diner food it is," Ellie teased.

"I know the owner," Hunter's eyes twinkled. "I trust she uses nothing but quality ingredients."

Do not blush! "How hungry are you?" Ellie asked, willing herself not to embarrass herself. The best way to keep herself in check was to get out of there and cook.

"Hmm," Hunter tapped her chin in thought. "Empty stomach, more than twelve hours since it's had food, I'd say pancakes *and* French toast." *You better be sure you can keep that down when you stop being a coward and ask her out.*

Ellie gave her an amused smile. "I'll be right back."

Hunter allowed her eyes to stray to Ellie's blue-jean clad ass. Never had a pair of Levi's looked so enticing.

"Grow a pair."

The gruff words startled the still-staring Hunter, causing her to slosh her hot coffee on her hand. "Ow!" She shot a look at Big Al and grabbed a napkin. *Maybe I should stop drinking coffee here.* "Excuse me?"

"Grow a pair," Big Al repeated. "Ask the woman out already." He scraped up the last of his food and crammed it in his mouth.

Hunter's eyes just about popped out of her head. Not only was the man talking in full, coherent sentences. But, obviously, he was picking up on Hunter's feelings for Ellie. "Wha? How? How did you know I . .?"

"Got eyes, don't I?"

Hunter was dumbfounded. She glanced nervously towards the kitchen, hoping Ellie wouldn't be coming out right away.

"Do you, um, think she'll say yes?"

"Only one way to find out," Big Al rasped. "Grow a pair."

"Yeah, got it." She stared as Big Al got up, threw down some money, and walked out. "Thanks," she muttered, not feeling any more self-assured. Her legs bounced nervously as she went over what she would say in her head. *Try not tripping over your own tongue,* she thought tensely. She imagined confidently asking Ellie for dinner and a movie, and the response being another beautiful smile. And, of course, a yes.

"Everything okay?"

Hunter jumped. *At least I wasn't holding any coffee this time.* "Oh! Um, yeah. I was just, um, daydreaming I guess." She gave Ellie a small smile.

Ellie arched her brow. "Was it good?" She moved a plate of steaming, delectable food in front of Hunter.

She stalled by inhaling the savory aroma. *Just do it, Hunter. The worst she can say is no. Well, the worst she can do is throw coffee in your face, and yell that she's not gay.* Hunter silently scolded herself. Ellie was too polite to do anything that drastic. She hoped. "Very," she said absently, then realized what she said. "Um, Ellie?"

"Hmm?" Ellie kept an eye on Hunter as she refilled her coffee cup.

"Would you? I mean, um," she swallowed, then took a drink of her coffee to wet her parched throat. After she cleared her throat, she tried again. "Ellie, would you . . ."

"Hey, mom!"

Ellie's heart — which had just been racing at the realization that Hunter was about to ask her out — stopped. She sent Hunter an apologetic look and hoped the doctor would give her the chance to explain.

"Hey, sweetie. Why aren't you in school?"

Hunter's stomach dropped, and she was suddenly glad she hadn't started eating yet. *No.* Slowly, she turned towards the young voice, and what she saw floored her. There was no doubt that this teenager was Ellie's. *How is that possible? Shit, that means . . .*

"Free first period," Jessie answered, glancing at the woman sitting at the bar. *Is that her?* "And, I need a few pastries for a bake sale."

"I — I have to go." Hunter numbly stood and brought out some money.

"Hunter, wait."

"Work," she replied coolly. Without another word, she turned her back on the scene that caused her confused heart to ache. She only faltered when Ellie called out to her again, but she couldn't allow herself to turn back. *No more.*

"Shit." Ellie leaned against the counter, pinching the bridge of her nose.

"I take it that was her," Jessie said softly.

Ellie laughed bitterly. "Yeah. Guess she doesn't want a woman with a kid."

"She looked kinda surprised, mom. She didn't know about me, did she?" Jessie tried to sort out her feelings. She felt guilty for driving Hunter away, disappointed that the woman just walked out, and resentful that her mom hadn't thought to mention her. It was all jumbled in her mind.

"I wasn't going to tell her about you before I told you about her.

Or me," Ellie explained heatedly. "She went away for the weekend, and this is the first I've seen her since our talk, Jessie."

"Okay, I'm sorry." Jessie tentatively touched her mom's shoulder. "Seriously, mom, I'm sorry about this. I just wanted to see if she was here. I wanted to know what she was like."

"Do you really have a free period?" Ellie asked sharply, immediately regretting it when she saw the sadness in Jessie's eyes. She was angry at Hunter's reaction, but she shouldn't be taking it out on her daughter. Ellie could hardly blame Jessie for being curious. "I'm sorry," she sighed, pulling her daughter in for a hug.

"Go talk to her," Jessie suggested.

"No. I think she made it abundantly clear how she feels."

"Mom, I've never known you to back down from anything."

"I'm not backing down. But, I'm not going to chase someone who wouldn't even give me a chance to explain," Ellie argued stubbornly.

Jessie rolled her eyes, then peeked at her mom, hoping Ellie hadn't seen that. "She was probably shocked and didn't know how to respond. People sometimes run when they're scared. I mean, we're like doppelgängers, mom, and you don't look old enough to have a daughter my age. Maybe she just doesn't know what to think?"

Ellie raised her eyebrow. "Flattery will get you everywhere."

Jessie giggled. "It's the truth, but I'll take whatever you're handing out. Go talk to her, mom," she said in all seriousness. "I think you'll regret it if you don't. Besides, how else can you give her a dose of the famous Montgomery ire?"

Ellie snorted. "Montgomery ire? Did Blaise teach you that?"

"Um, Greyson, actually. He's kinda scared of you."

Ellie laughed fully at that. "Good. Make sure you practice that skill for the future."

"I learn by example," Jessie said cheekily.

Ellie shook her head and sighed. "Fine, I'll go talk to her. But, I am *not* going to make it easy for her."

"That's my mom!"

"WHERE IS SHE?" Ellie was annoyed — and beyond being polite — so, she was minimally glad that it was Patty manning the nurse's station. Unfortunately, Mo was also there giving Ellie the evil eye.

"What did you do to her?" Mo blustered.

"What makes you think *I* did something to her?" Ellie took a breath to calm herself. This was Hunter's best friend, and she couldn't blame Mo for sticking up for Hunter.

"Obviously you did something to upset her . . ."

"Mo," Patty, who was watching Ellie intently, gently warned her wife. "What happened?"

"That's between me and Hunter." Ellie leaned into the desk. "She should have stayed to talk to me. That's all she needed to do to understand everything. But, she chose to run away."

Patty raised a finger to keep Mo quiet. She knew Mo could get nasty when she was upset and Patty didn't want the wedge between Ellie and Hunter to get deeper. Not if there were a chance things could be worked out. "She's been through a lot, Ellie."

"Haven't we *all*?" Ellie said irritably. "Look, no offense, but I don't owe you two an explanation. Hell, I don't even owe Hunter an explanation, but I'm here to do exactly that. Now, are you going to tell me where she is, or do I have to march up and down these halls calling out her name?" She was so far out of her element with these feelings, that Ellie wasn't sure if that was an empty threat or not. Surely she wouldn't do something that silly, would she?

"Can you answer me one question?" Patty said.

Ellie fought to keep her patience and nodded.

"Are you gay?"

Of all the possible questions Ellie could imagine, she wasn't expecting *that* one. She laughed mirthlessly. "I don't know why that matters to you, but yes. I am."

Patty gave her a small smile. "She's in the doctor's lounge."

"Patty!"

"Hush, Mo. Whatever happened, it's between Ellie and Hunter. And, I refuse to let Hunter's stubbornness — or yours — prevent them from talking." She handed Ellie a keycard. "You'll need that to get in. It's down the hall on the left." Patty winked, mouthing "good luck" when Ellie thanked her.

"You're too late," Mo muttered. It wasn't that she didn't like Ellie. She did. But if the woman did something to hurt her best friend, she would always have Hunter's back. Even if she thought Hunter was making a huge mistake.

Ellie ignored the comment and concentrated on keeping calm as she walked down the hallway. Stopping in front of the lounge, she inhaled deeply. What would happen when she opened this door was anyone's guess, and Ellie contemplated just walking away. *No, that's what Hunter did. Besides, you told Jessie you would do this, so get your ass in there.* With a quick swipe of the card, she heard the lock disengage.

Ellie pushed open the door and froze. She couldn't believe her eyes. Across the room, seated on one of the beds that decorated the room, was Hunter. Only Hunter wasn't alone. Iris – Nurse Ruderton – sat on Hunter's lap, happily gyrating her hips as she kissed Hunter's neck. Ellie swallowed down the intense disappointment and wondered why – even now – she didn't just walk away.

"Occupied," Iris giggled.

"Get out." Ellie hadn't even realized she had spoken out loud until Hunter jumped up, effectively dumping the young nurse off her perch, and onto the floor on her ass.

"Ellie!" Hunter flushed with embarrassment, confusion, and anger. Having Ellie catch her with Iris was the worst possible scenario. Ever.

"Ow." Iris scowled at Hunter, who did nothing to help her up. To hide her embarrassment, she smirked at Ellie as she struggled to pull herself up off the floor. "We're a little busy. Perhaps you can find another doctor to help you."

Since Hunter refused to look at her, Ellie turned her heated gaze on Iris. "Get. Out. Now."

"Hunter." The smirk didn't leave Iris's face. "Could you tell this . . ."

"Go," Hunter ordered, her eyes cold and emotionless as she looked at Iris. *What the hell was I thinking?*

"Wait, me? But!" The nurse wasn't smiling anymore.

Hunter finally brought her gaze to Ellie's. The disappointment in Ellie's eyes felt like a punch in the gut. A punch she rightly deserved. "Leave, Iris."

Iris huffed, and both Hunter and Ellie wondered if she would start stomping her feet. "Fine!" She gave Hunter a saucy smile. "I'll be back to finish what we started." Iris stormed towards Ellie with a glare. "Told you she wanted me."

Ellie saw it coming and braced herself for the impact. As expected, Iris shoulder checked Ellie but stumbled back a couple of steps with another 'ow'. She wished she could take more pleasure in the fact that Iris walked away rubbing her shoulder, but her focus right now was Hunter.

"Is this who you are?" Ellie asked Hunter once they were alone. "Instead of talking things out, you go and find someone to *screw?*" The words *"dodged a bullet"* ran through Ellie's mind. Yet, even with what she had just walked in on, she couldn't believe that. She didn't know why, but this didn't feel right.

"That's none of your business." It wasn't what Hunter wanted to say. She wanted to apologize for what Ellie had walked in on. She wanted to apologize for walking out of the diner. She wanted to know why it hurt so much thinking Ellie could be like all the others. None of that happened because her ego put her on the defensive. Yet, as soon as the words were out of her mouth, she regretted them immensely. Especially when the shutters came down in Ellie's usually expressive eyes.

She stared at Hunter, struggling to keep her anger in check. *Forget the anger, Ellie, keep your damn feelings in check. Obviously, she's not interested in you. Or, she was just interested in one thing, and you having a kid ruined those plans.* "You're right, it's not." She turned on her heel and reached for the door.

Hunter panicked. She knew if she let Ellie leave like this, it would be the end. Even believing Ellie had lied to her, knowing she was probably just another straight woman wanting to use her, Hunter couldn't let her go.

"Ellie, wait." Hunter was grateful when Ellie paused. "Why did you lie to me?"

Ellie spun back around, resentment written all over her face. *Montgomery ire*, she thought fleetingly. "I didn't lie to you!"

Hunter sneered as thoughts of Susan and all the lies she ever told Hunter were prevalent in Hunter's mind. "A lie by omission is still a lie."

"Are you kidding me?" Ellie stormed towards Hunter. "I've known you for a week! A *week*, Hunter! And, half of that time you've been gone! We haven't even begun to get to know each other, and because I didn't tell you I have a kid, you call me a liar? You never asked me if I had children. And, I certainly wasn't going to tell you about her before I told her about me!" she yelled, not realizing that she echoed what she had told Jessie.

Everything Ellie said resonated with Hunter. Behind all the pain and insecurity Susan caused her was actual sanity. She *knew* she was overreacting. She *knew* what she said and did after finding out about Ellie's daughter was beyond wrong. Ellie was *not* Susan. She was not any of the women that Hunter had been with. She couldn't be. So, what was it that was making Hunter react so dreadfully?

"You're in the closet?"

Ellie threw her hands up in frustration. As angry as she was that Hunter didn't seem to be listening, there was a vulnerability in Hunter's eyes that made her stay.

"No."

Hunter frowned in confusion. "Are you gay?"

"Yes."

Hunter growled with frustration of her own. "I don't understand!"

"You're right, you don't. You know why? Because you didn't

want to stick around and *ask* me about it. Instead, you came here, and." *Ugh. Enough of this! If all these* feelings *only bring drama, I don't need it.* Ellie made her way to the door again.

"I'm here now," Hunter said.

"No, Hunter. *I'm* here. You ran away, I ran *here.*"

"You're right." Hunter's quiet admission stopped Ellie's retreat once more. "You're right and I don't know how to apologize for how I reacted. I want to understand and I want us both to try to understand why I did what I did."

Ellie was surprised by the agonizing honesty of Hunter's words. She realized at that moment that Hunter was just as confused by her attitude as Ellie was. "I . . ."

Hunter's pager sounded and she murmured an apology before checking it. "They need me in surgery," she said abjectly. "I'm really sorry, Ellie." *For everything.*

Though she understood, Ellie was disappointed. She took a business card she had written on before leaving the diner out of her back pocket. "If you want to get to know me, Hunter, show up here after your shift." She handed the tall doctor the card. "We'll talk, get to know each other, and hopefully come to an understanding." Once again, she made her way to the door. "But, if you decide to finish what you started before I walked in, don't bother showing up. I don't play games, Hunter, and I refuse to let them be played with me."

Chapter Fifteen

Ellie sat back with her glass of wine and propped her feet up on the coffee table. After she left Hunter, she stopped by Dani's room for a quick visit. This time when she walked in and found two women together, it filled her heart instead of breaking it. She had been delighted to see Claire with Dani, kissing, giggling, and happy. Not wanting to intrude for long, Ellie spoke briefly about plans for when Dani was released and promised to be back soon. No matter what happened between her and Hunter, Ellie wouldn't let Dani down. She would do whatever she could to help the girl.

"Mom?"

Ellie checked her watch. She had been under the assumption that Jessie would be going over to Piper's to finish their project. It was one of the reasons she felt comfortable enough to invite Hunter over to talk. "I'm in here, sweets," she called out from her perch on the couch.

"Hey, I . . ." Jessie's eyes fell to the glass of wine in Ellie's hand. "I went to the diner, but you weren't there. You're here. Drinking."

Ellie frowned. "Jessie, this is my first glass of wine. And, technically, I'm not drinking since I have yet to take a sip." She didn't understand Jessie's concern. Ellie had never been one to overindulge in drinking. Even when Blaise could still have alcohol, Ellie never drank enough to get more than a buzz.

"Okay, so why are you here, and not at the diner?"

Ellie placed her glass on the table and motioned for Jessie to join her. She smiled when her daughter chose to sit on the table in front of her. "I'm working on a few ideas for the menu for the gallery opening. It's easier for me to do that here, instead of getting in everyone's way at the diner."

"Oh. So, that's what smells so good." Jessie sniffed the air. "Smells like, um, beef Wellington."

Ellie proudly grinned. "That's my girl. I know that cooking isn't your passion, but I'm glad you've picked up a thing or two." Jessie shrugged bashfully. "Don't worry, I'm not going to motherly ask you what your passion is. I will wait patiently until you're ready to share."

Jessie snorted humorously. "Thanks." Concerned eyes slid towards the glass of wine again. "So, how did your talk with Hunter go?"

"She was called into surgery, so it was cut short. Hopefully, we'll be able to continue soon," Ellie explained evasively. She was more concerned by Jessie's obvious unease with Ellie's untouched wine. "Does that really bother you?" she asked gesturing towards the glass.

Jessie shrugged again. "You — you've been under a lot of stress recently. I just don't want you relying on this."

"I'm not relying on anything, sweetie," Ellie interrupted. "It's one glass. You know me. You know that I've never used alcohol as a crutch. Running, maybe," she smiled. "But, not alcohol. So, what is this all about?"

With a heavy sigh, Jessie had to admit her mom was right. She had never seen Ellie even close to being drunk. Blaise? Yes. Mom, no. "Grandmother drinks a lot. I figure it's to deal with grandfather all the time, but still."

"Mom drinks?" Jessie nodded. "She never did before. At least not that I noticed." Ellie leaned forward and took Jessie's hands in hers. "You don't have to worry, Jessie. Lord knows I am nothing like my mother. And, yes, I've had some overwhelming moments this past week. But, knowing you still love me after everything I've told you? I don't need anything except that to get me through."

"*Still?* Mom, there is nothing that could make me stop loving you. What grandmother and grandfather did to you was awful, but I'm not them."

"I know you're not." She pulled Jessie in for a hug. "I still can't believe they really make you call them that."

Jessie laughed. "Right? It's so pretentious. My kid is going to call you something fun. Like granny."

Ellie pulled a face. "Like hell, they will. I'll accept grandma. *Maybe* grams or gramma. That's it. As long as you remember that I will *never* be old enough to be a granny."

"I'll keep that in mind *if* I decide to have kids." Jessie slapped her hands on her knees. "Well, now that I know you're not going to turn into a lush, I gotta go finish this project. Thank God it's almost done." She stood, and headed for her room to change. "Oh! Do you think I could meet Dani soon?"

Ellie smiled. "Sure, I don't see why not. She seems to be in a much better mood now that Claire is with her. I'll ask if she's okay with it."

"Claire?"

"Dani's girlfriend."

"Oh. Is that why you're helping her? Because she's gay?"

Ellie was taken aback by the question, and how nonchalantly Jessie asked it. "I'm helping her because she needs it. Because she was discarded when she needed love the most," she said softly.

"Because that could've been you?" Ellie nodded. "Now I understand. And, now I want to meet her even more." She went back to her mom and hugged her again. "You're a great person. I'm lucky to have you as my mom. I love you." She rushed off then, not wanting to get caught up in an emotional outburst.

"I love you, too," Ellie whispered, tears pooling in her eyes. In her mind, *she* was the lucky one to have such a wonderful daughter. The oven sounded, breaking the poignant moment, and Ellie wiped the tears away. *Back to work.* She picked up her forgotten glass of wine and chuckled thinking how Blaise would be so disappointed by what she was about to do. With that in mind, she walked into the kitchen and poured the wine down the drain.

"OW." ELLIE WINCED as she gingerly raised her head from the back of the couch. She massaged the crick, slowly stretching her head side to side. With a sigh, she picked up her phone. No calls, no texts. No Hunter. It was six in the morning – *I must have been more tired than I thought* – and Ellie had fallen asleep waiting for the doctor to show up. Hunter's shift must have ended hours ago. Hell, she should be getting ready to go *back* to work by now.

"That's exactly what I should be doing," Ellie told herself firmly. "Get ready for work and forget Hunter and all this drama. If she doesn't care to get to know me, I shouldn't either." She shook her head and laughed at herself. "Is this what happens? The woman you like doesn't come over to talk to you, so you start talking to yourself?" *Get over it. Go for a run, go to work, and get on with your life. This isn't the end of the world.* It was a nice little speech. Too bad it didn't stop her heart from hurting. Which was absurd since she barely knew Hunter other than her name, profession, and that she ran away from difficult situations.

Ellie pushed herself off the couch with a grunt and headed for her bedroom. She froze when a knock sounded at the door. *Who the hell is here this early,* she wondered, even knowing it could only be one person. Jessie had a key, and Blaise sure as hell wouldn't be up before she absolutely had to. If Hunter thought she could just show up now, Ellie was not in the mood. It was early, she was tired and supremely annoyed. She needed to run. She needed to clear her head. But the damn knock persisted.

Ellie stormed over to the door and wrenched it open. The

absolute weariness that greeted her, stopped her from saying anything rude. "Hunter?"

Hunter had a hand on the wall, propping herself up. The sound of Ellie's voice forced her to bring her head up to look directly into Ellie's angry eyes.

"I wasn't with her. I swear I wasn't with her." Without a thought of what she was doing, Hunter cupped Ellie's cheek and kissed her.

"Mmph!" Startled by the action, Ellie's hands gripped Hunter's arms. What was it that Blaise said about a tingle? This was more than that. This was more like an electrical shock. Before she could react, the kiss was over, and Hunter looked as stunned as Ellie.

Hunter stumbled back. "I – I'm sorry. I . . ." She turned to leave but was stopped by Ellie's soft hand on her arm.

"Hunter, wait." When Ellie was sure she could breathe again, she studied Hunter's face. She detected no deceit, just utter fatigue. "You look exhausted."

"Yeah." Hunter scrubbed her face, wondering if it was as red as she felt it was. *Tell me I did not just kiss Ellie.* "I've been in surgery all night. That's why I couldn't be here. I needed you to know that. I needed you to know that I *wanted* to be here."

The sincerity in the words touched Ellie. "Come in."

"I should go. I'm, um . . ." Hunter took a step back.

"You are far too tired to drive, Hunter. I'm surprised you made it here without killing yourself or someone else." Ellie opened the door wider. "Come in and rest for a bit."

"I guess I could use a cup of coffee," Hunter agreed reluctantly and followed Ellie inside. She wished she was lucid enough to take in the vision of Ellie's home. When Hunter followed the address and noticed it was an apartment building, she had been surprised. Even in her exhausted state, she knew how much it meant that Ellie trusted her with her home address. Especially after what had happened . . . Jesus, was that yesterday?

"Coffee is not going to cut it," Ellie said as she led Hunter across the expansive apartment.

They trekked down a short hallway, and Hunter stopped

abruptly when she saw a bed through the doorway. "Um, Ellie? What?"

"You're going to sleep." She pulled Hunter into the room. "I would put you in the guestroom, but I haven't made it up, yet." She shook her head when Hunter jerked to a stop, eyes widened.

"This is your room!"

"I'm aware. Sit." Ellie nudged a bewildered Hunter until she sat down on the bed. She knelt and began removing Hunter's shoes.

"You don't have to do this," Hunter said quietly. She couldn't figure out why Ellie was being so nice after what she did with Iris.

"I know." Ellie stood up again. "But, you came here in person to tell me what happened. I appreciate that." She took a deep breath. She could still see the scene she walked in on, and it still pissed her off. But she had already made the decision to give Hunter a chance to explain, so that's what she would do. "The bathroom is right through there, and anything you need will be in the linen closet on the left when you walk in. I think there are even a couple of new toothbrushes. If you need anything else, I'll be right out there." She gestured behind her. "Sleep as long as you need to. I don't need to be anywhere today."

"Ellie?" Hunter watched as Ellie paused, turning towards her with a passive expression. "Thank you." Her heart leaped to her throat when Ellie smiled at her before closing the door.

THE TAP, TAP, tap of her pen on the pad of paper was somehow calming to Ellie. She was finding it difficult to concentrate with Hunter sleeping in her bed. She had been sitting there for the past two and a half hours trying to work, but ultimately thinking about what had happened that morning. Absently, she touched her lips, still feeling the thrill of the unexpected kiss. It was her first kiss with a woman. Yes, it was over as quickly as it began. Yes, it was completely unexpected. And, oh God, yes, it was exhilarating. It made her wonder how it would be when Hunter *really* kissed her.

Focus! She had less than three weeks to come up with an amazing menu for Eve. She should be working on that instead of thinking about whether she would get kissed by Hunter in the future. She shook those thoughts out of her head, put pen to paper again, and lost herself in what she did best. Food.

"YOU'RE LEFT-HANDED."

Ellie, completely absorbed in her work, flinched at the sound of Hunter's voice. "Only when I write," she answered, glancing up at her guest. Hunter's hair was damp, and Ellie tried not to think about Hunter being in her shower. *Whew! Not ready for that, yet.*

"You're ambidextrous?" Hunter mentally slapped herself. *What the hell, Hunter? Could you be more awkward? This woman has graciously offered her hospitality, and all you can do is talk about which hand is dominant?*

"Mmhmm. Did you sleep okay?"

"Yeah, I did. Thank you, again." Hunter rubbed the back of her neck and shuffled her feet. She didn't know what to say or do. Hell, she could barely look at Ellie without feeling terrible. "I, um, took you up on your offer to use the shower."

"So I see." *She can't even look at me.* "Would you like some coffee?"

Hunter was so uncomfortable, she contemplated just hightailing it out of there — with her tail between her legs. But she owed Ellie more than that. She owed her an explanation. "Um, yes, please. That would be great." *Smooth.* Hunter mentally rolled her eyes at her ineptitude.

Ellie took a cup down from the cabinet and filled it. "You know," she slid the cup in front of Hunter as she finally took a seat at the counter. "It's going to be really difficult having a meaningful conversation if you can't even look at me. I know you're upset with me."

"No!" Hunter's eyes met Ellie's for a fraction of a second before she lowered her head again. "I'm not upset with you. I'm angry with myself. You were right, I never asked you if you had kids. I should have stayed to talk to you instead of . . . doing what I did."

"Why did you? Why her, Hunter?" That was what hurt the most. "Are you attracted to her?" She hated asking the question. Did she really want to know that the woman she thought Hunter was could truly be interested in someone like Iris? And, then, Ellie silently chastised herself for judging a person she didn't know. *Hypocrite.*

Hunter snorted miserably. "Not even a little."

Ellie shook her head. "Then I don't understand."

"I, um, I know she's gay. At that moment, that was the only thing I needed."

"*I'm* gay, Hunter."

Hunter stood abruptly and started pacing. "I didn't know that! I thought . . . I thought you were just another straight woman trying to use me to get her kicks!"

"You could have stayed," Ellie countered hotly. "You could have *asked* me instead of doing what you did."

"I know! I fucked up," she said quietly, suddenly losing all of her fight. She lowered her head in shame. "I'm sorry, Ellie."

Ellie's anger evaporated with a heavy sigh. *What the hell am I doing?* She didn't want to see Hunter so defeated. She had no hold over the woman. They weren't even dating. Hell, they didn't even know each other. "You don't owe me an apology, Hunter." She held up her hand, cutting off Hunter's rebuttal. "I have no right to be upset. You're an adult and you don't belong to me." *No matter how much I wish you did.*

I wish I did, Hunter thought miserably. "I *do* owe you an apology. I think we both know what I was going for with you, and to leave like that, and then use that poor, young woman." Hunter's voice trailed off as she shook her head.

"I somehow doubt Iris minded being used by you," Ellie

muttered quietly. It was childish and made Ellie wonder when she had become such a teenager. *Guess I'm making up for missing this kind of stuff while in high school.*

"*I* minded, Ellie," Hunter said just as quietly.

Ellie searched Hunter's eyes for . . . for what? *What are you looking for, Ellie? The better question is, what is Hunter looking for?* "What is it that you want, Hunter? You said we both knew what you were going for with me, but after what I saw, I *don't* know. Are you looking for some fun? A one-night stand? Friends with benefits? Am I a conquest? What do you want?" she asked again.

Hunter couldn't admonish Ellie for thinking the worst of her. Not after what she did. "I want something real," she whispered.

"And, you thought you'd find that in the call room with Iris?" Ellie asked, unconvinced.

"No." Hunter leaned wearily on the counter.

Ellie softened, her heart hurting at seeing Hunter weighed down with what she could plainly see was guilt. "Can you help me understand?" she asked gently.

Hunter paled. She knew she had to tell Ellie the truth. Dr. Woodrow had prepared her for that. She just didn't think it would be so soon. Hunter had hoped she could convince Ellie to go out with her, they'd go on a few dates, Hunter could show Ellie the person she really was inside, and *then* she'd tell her. Maybe that wasn't fair, but it was the best plan Hunter had for getting Ellie to . . . to what? Date her? Fall for her?

"I want to," Hunter ground out, her throat suddenly dry. "I — I . . ."

"Are you hungry?" Ellie asked suddenly, sensing Hunter's uneasiness.

"Um." The question caught her off guard, causing her brain to spin. One minute she was trying to find the words to explain to Ellie, and the next she wondered if her stomach could hold down any food. "You don't have to cook for me, you've done so much already."

"It's no trouble, Hunter. I held off on eating until you woke up, anyway, because I thought maybe you'd be hungry. I could make us some sandwiches. Nothing too heavy," Ellie added as though she sensed Hunter's dilemma. When Hunter nodded, Ellie put the menu she had been agonizing over aside — something she probably shouldn't be doing since the opening was coming up way too soon — and got to work.

"Why didn't you walk out?" Hunter asked as she watched Ellie's skilled hands create an extraordinarily appealing sandwich. *Why don't my sandwiches ever look that good?* She glanced up to see Ellie's questioning look. "At the hospital. Why didn't you just tell me to go to hell and walk out? I deserved that." *Thank you for not doing that. Like I did.*

Ellie thought about the question and how she felt at that moment. "I'm not sure," she answered sincerely. "I don't know you that well, but I'm usually a good judge of character. What I walked in on just didn't feel right. It didn't feel like you."

Hunter stared at the woman. *Scary.* "It's not," she whispered. Unnerved by Ellie's intuitiveness, Hunter scrambled to change the subject. "Tell me about your daughter."

Ellie picked up a large knife, hiding a smirk at Hunter's widened eyes and obvious shift in topics. She cut the sandwiches in half and placed one of the plates in front of her guest. "Jessie." A spontaneous smile formed at just saying her daughter's name. "She's sixteen going on forty."

Hunter chuckled at Ellie's description. The love that this woman felt for her child was unmistakable. And quite beautiful to witness.

"She's caring, funny, and smart. Too smart for my own good," Ellie laughed.

"Sounds like she takes after you," Hunter offered.

Ellie passed a bag of chips over to Hunter and gave her a small smile. "I'm not so sure that's a good thing. I know how stubborn I am. And, with Blaise as a Godmother, I knew Jessie was going to be a handful."

Hunter took a healthy bite of her sandwich – after she realized just how hungry she was while watching Ellie prepare the food — and almost groaned out loud. "How do you do this? It's bread, lunchmeat, and veggies. I have all that stuff, but when I put it together, it doesn't taste half as amazing as this does."

Ellie let out a pleased laugh. "I'm glad you like it. I make the bread from scratch, and the mayonnaise is my own recipe. I try not to use store bought if I can help it. Too many ingredients that I can't pronounce."

"That sounds healthier. Doctors must love you." Hunter choked as she realized what she just said. Red-faced, she graciously accepted a glass of water from her hostess.

"I don't know about the doctors, but Jessie and Blaise enjoy it, as do my customers."

Hunter cleared her throat, thankful that Ellie glossed over Hunter's bout of embarrassment. *Why am I always choking around her? Would I have been this awkward if things had been normal for me?* "You and Blaise, uh?"

Ellie shook her head with laughter, knowing exactly what Hunter was asking. "No. Much to Blaise's consternation, I never felt that way about her. Hurts her ego," Ellie explained.

I don't blame her, Hunter thought with a grin. "Why not?"

Ellie wasn't surprised by the question. Hunter met Blaise and knows how beautiful she is. She obviously witnessed Ellie and Blaise's closeness. "Besides the fact that she's straight?" Curiously she watched as Hunter lowered her gaze. *There is definitely something with Hunter and straight women.* "When I met Blaise, I was eighteen with a two-year-old. I needed a friend, and Blaise became more of a sister. I also . . ."

"Also?" Hunter prompted when Ellie hesitated. At Ellie's continued silence, Hunter gently probed further. "Does this have to do with why you were, um, why you didn't tell Jessie about you?"

Ellie wiped her mouth and took a sip of her water before answering. She did invite Hunter over to talk, so she couldn't back down now. Maybe by opening up, Hunter will feel comfortable enough to open up herself. "Yes."

Chapter Sixteen

The two women agreed to finish lunch before getting into the deep conversations. To keep it light, Hunter eagerly asked more about Jessie, and Ellie was more than happy to recount some of her most precious memories with her daughter. Eventually, the two moved to the living room to get more comfortable.

"Is Jessie's father in the picture?" Hunter asked carefully. She sincerely hoped that it wasn't a question that would hurt Ellie.

"No." Ellie settled back onto the couch, pulling her feet up under her. She saw Hunter wince, and instinctively knew what she was thinking. "I wasn't raped, Hunter. I knew what I was doing. It was stupid and selfish, but I would do it all over again if the outcome remained the same. I can't imagine life without Jessie. She's been my salvation."

"What happened, Ellie?"

There was nothing but sincere curiosity in Hunter's question. This was the woman Ellie believed Hunter to be. Not the one she saw in that on-call room. That awareness made it easier for Ellie to talk more openly. So, she told Hunter everything. About the abuse, the threats, the decisions, all of it. To Hunter's credit, she listened quietly, and intently. At one point, taking Ellie's hand to offer support and comfort.

By the end of Ellie's story, Hunter was fuming inside. How could parents treat their child that way? How could they threaten a kid with things like homelessness and conversion therapy? Hunter couldn't imagine the pain Ellie went through and now had a deeper understanding — not to mention a deeper respect — for the diner owner. She certainly didn't think she would have been strong enough to deny who she was for so long.

"I'm so sorry, Ellie. I feel like those are such empty words, but I mean them."

"I believe you," Ellie smiled. "But, please don't feel sorry for me. I made my decisions, and I can't regret them. Just as I've made my decision now to be who I really am."

I wish I had made decisions I didn't have to regret. "How did Jessie take it?" Hunter asked, too chicken shit to ask the question she *really* wanted to know. Perhaps it was her ego talking, but she would rather keep hoping *she* was the one who inspired Ellie to "come out". Her heart skipped a beat when Ellie smiled brightly. *She's so incredibly beautiful*, Hunter thought not for the first time.

"Better than I expected. Of course, she was upset about me keeping it from her, but she supports me."

"Good. I know how important that must be to you. Especially after everything you went through."

"It is. Honestly, I never thought I would have to tell her, or Blaise, so it's been an overwhelming week."

Hunter arched a perfect brow. "Even being out from under your parents, you didn't think about living for yourself?"

Ellie's first instinct was to be angered by Hunter's question, thinking Hunter obviously didn't understand what she had gone through over the years. Yet, she heard no judgment in Hunter's tone, so she tempered her irritation, and answered honestly. "My parents did a good job at making me believe that Jessie would hate me if I told her. I guess that was their form of conversion therapy. I spent so long suppressing what was inside me that I . . . well, I thought it had just gone away." She could tell Hunter didn't understand. Not that she blamed her. Ellie wasn't sure *she* fully understood how the feelings seemed to have just disappeared. "I felt nothing, Hunter. I had no desires, no longing to be with anyone. In fact, I began to think that I was asexual." She finished shyly.

Wow. Everything Ellie had told her up to this point had been a surprise. But this? Hearing a woman as beautiful and vibrant as Ellie describe herself as asexual was unfathomable. "What changed?"

Ellie could feel the warmth in her cheeks, and let out a nervous chuckle. "You walked in my diner," she confessed demurely. "The moment I saw you, I realized the feelings were still there."

A full, toothy grin blossomed on Hunter's face. She wouldn't have been able to stop it if she tried. *She has feelings for me!* Outside, Hunter tried to keep her composure. Inside, she was doing a victory dance to end all victory dances.

"Don't let that go to your head, doc. We still have a lot to talk about," Ellie warned playfully.

"I know," Hunter acknowledged, still smiling. "But, you have no idea how happy what you just said makes me." She looked up at Ellie through hooded, shy eyes. "You should know that I felt — *feel* — it, too."

Ellie smiled. "I kinda figured that out by the way you acted around me. It was cute."

"Ugh," Hunter rolled her eyes dramatically and collapsed back against the cushions. "I'm too old to be cute!"

Ellie laughed at Hunter's antics. "To be honest, Hunter, you being awkward is what won me over."

"So, clumsiness and stuttering are what turns you on?"

Ellie barked out laughter as Hunter's hand flew to her mouth. Her eyes were wide and apologetic, and she stuttered muffled apologies behind her hand.

"It would seem so," Ellie teased with a wink.

"Oh my God, I can't believe I said that." Hunter crossed her arm over her face, trying to hide her blush. She peeked out from the crook of her elbow and saw Ellie grinning at her. "You're enjoying this way too much."

Ellie shrugged. "Of course, I am. It's not every day I get to see a beautiful trauma surgeon blush." *Good Lord, I'm flirting with her!* Ellie wasn't sure what had gotten into her, but she had a feeling she was going to like getting to know this side of herself.

She's flirting with me! Hunter flushed, even more, this time from pleasure as much as embarrassment. She took a breath and sat up straight to face Ellie. "Okay, well, I guess it's my turn to tell you about me. Might as well get all of the embarrassing, terrible stuff out now. Um, before you showed up at the table, Mo and I were talking about me getting back into the game. Or, if I'm being honest, just getting me *in* the game."

Sure looked like you were in the game in that on-call room. Ellie kept the petty comment to herself. *No need to bring that up again.* "I don't understand."

Hunter stood up and started to pace. *Just tell her!* "I don't know where to start, Ellie," she confessed softly. "I'm afraid."

"What are you afraid of?"

"Losing you before I even have a chance at being with you."

The admission stunned Ellie. The vulnerability she had witnessed in Hunter the morning before was there once again. Ellie stood up, blocking Hunter's path. She took Hunter's hands in hers, marveling at how soft they were.

"Hunter, nothing in this world is guaranteed. Sometimes, you just need to take the chance and hope for the best."

"Like you did with Jessie?" Hunter asked, her query almost childlike.

This woman standing before her was a mystery to Ellie. She was obviously a successful trauma surgeon, well liked if her friends were any indication, evidently loved by her family. And, yet, there was just something so incredibly naïve about her. "Yes. I took the risk. My faith in Jessie made it easier. Marginally easier, but still," she smiled, trying to lighten the mood.

"Are you trying to say I can trust you, Miss Montgomery?" Hunter wanted to do just that, but past experiences held her back.

"I'm saying you can trust me to listen without judgment, and then determine how to move forward," Ellie answered.

ELLIE HANDED HUNTER a steaming mug of tea. "Chamomile," she murmured.

"Thank you." Hunter took a careful sip of the hot liquid, relishing the slight burn as it slid down her throat. "I'm seeing a therapist," she blurted out, immediately humiliated by the admission.

Ellie caught the slight flush and contrition in Hunter's expression. She was never one to find getting outside help as a bad thing and was quick to let Hunter know that. "Okay. Hunter, that's not something to be ashamed of."

Hunter nodded skeptically. She knew better than to look at seeing a shrink as a stigma. There was just something about it being *her* that made it feel shameful. With everything she had accomplished in her life, she felt she should be strong enough to get over this Susan thing on her own. Perhaps it was a pompous way to think, in fact, she was sure it was. She just couldn't help wanting to feel perfect for Ellie.

"I guess." Hunter braced her elbows on her knees, tapping the mug with her fingernails. "I asked her if I would be able to have a normal relationship. She said yes, but that I needed to be open with you."

Ellie's eyebrows rose with surprise. So many questions from one simple statement. She went with the first one that sprang to mind. "You told her about me?"

Hunter glanced up. "Yes. Does that scare you?"

"No," Ellie grinned. "It makes me happy, actually. I told Jessie and Blaise about you. Does that scare you, Dr. Vale?"

Hunter shook her head. "I'm honored and humbled," she answered sincerely, receiving another beautiful smile as a reward.

Ellie cleared her throat, not accustomed to blushing so much.

I'm not sure I regret missing this in high school. "May I ask what you meant about having a 'normal relationship'?"

"You may ask whatever you want," Hunter answered seriously. She took a deep breath. "Bear with me, please. This isn't something I talk about, nor am I proud of it."

"Take your time, Hunter."

Shit, this is harder than I thought it would be. Please don't hate me. "All right, um, I'm a bit older than you, so when I started to realize that I wasn't boy crazy, I didn't really know what to think of it. I just knew wasn't like my other friends. Except for Mo," she snickered. "We both just thought we were tomboys, you know? It didn't actually hit me *how* I was different until . . ."

"Until?" Ellie prompted gently.

Hunter sipped her tea, trying to calm her hammering heart. "Okay," she blew out a breath. "We had this neighbor who used to come over a lot. Her husband would go out of town on business, or whatever, so I guess she came over to have some company and to hang out by the pool." She scrubbed her hands over her face, wanting to be talking about *anything* but this with Ellie. "I, um, began to notice what her body looked like in her bikini."

"How old were you?"

"Almost fifteen, and confused as hell as to why *my* body was feeling that way when I looked at her when it didn't do that with guys." Hunter shook her head, cheeks coloring with chagrin. "I became well acquainted with myself that summer."

Ellie smirked at Hunter's admission. "I think that's normal, Hunter." At least she thought it was. In reality, it wasn't something she had ever done, but then nothing about her childhood seemed normal. And, of course, Ellie couldn't think about Jessie doing that, so she didn't. However, she assumed that most kids at that age were discovering their body, their feelings, and all that entailed.

"Yeah, I suppose. But, man, I was so naïve. I couldn't even talk to Mo about what I was feeling. She may have acted like me, but I couldn't take the risk, you know? If only I'd known that she was going through the same thing at the time."

Too restless to stay seated, Hunter got up, taking a moment to actually look at Ellie's apartment. It was exactly how she thought it should be. The focal point was most certainly the modern, chef's kitchen. But, the high ceilings, subtle paint color, and comfortable furniture made for a truly inviting atmosphere. Comfortable enough for Hunter to relax a little more. "I tried not to stare at her," she began again, scanning photos of Ellie and Jessie together settled upon the mantel. "I just didn't know how to stop."

When Hunter glanced over her shoulder, Ellie gave her an encouraging smile. She was having trouble not staring at Hunter's backside at the moment. She could hardly fault a teenager for not being able to control her hormones.

"Anyway," Hunter made her way back to the couch, forcing herself to face Ellie. "While other kids were excited about summer, I dreaded it. I dreaded seeing her and feeling the way I felt."

"Why?" It was natural to have an innocent crush, wasn't it?

Hunter shrugged. "It felt wrong. She was married, older than me, and she had always made me feel uncomfortable."

Ellie's brows furrowed. She was beginning to not like where she assumed this story was going. "Did she say something to you?"

Hunter hesitated. "It was just a vibe I got when she was around. I used to think that she came over to flirt with my dad. But, my pop is so single-mindedly in love with ma that even if she had come over naked, he wouldn't have noticed."

Ellie chuckled softly. "That's certainly an interesting way to put it. They sound like they have a great relationship."

A crooked grin enhanced Hunter's already charming face. "They do. Their relationship is what I long for," she confided shyly. "I just don't know if anyone would want that with me."

"Why would you think that?" Ellie was astonished that a beautiful, successful, charismatic woman like Hunter would think no one would want a loving, lasting relationship with her.

Hunter scoffed self-deprecatingly. "I've done things, Ellie. Despicable things. Things that would make even my parents disappointed in me. And, that's saying quite a bit."

"Have you killed someone?" Ellie asked deliberately.

"No, of course not."

"Hit a kid or an elderly person?"

Hunter blinked at Ellie. "No."

"Then nothing you've done is unforgivable," Ellie opined with finality.

"How can you possibly say that? There are more things out there that are terrible things to do."

"Sure there are. But, unless they resulted in someone getting killed, maimed, or physically hurt, Hunter, anything can be forgiven."

Hunter shook her head. "Her name is Susan. My parents' neighbor. And, up until about six months ago, I had been sleeping with her," she divulged bluntly. Maybe she should have been more tactful, but Hunter needed Ellie to see who she really was. She needed Ellie to decide whether she could be with someone like Hunter, knowing the whole truth.

The shock wasn't that Hunter slept with an older, married woman. It was that it had lasted up until recently. "When did it start?" She struggled to keep her voice even, and constantly reminded herself that she had no right to be jealous.

Hunter marveled at Ellie's composure. If it hadn't been for the slight twitch in the younger woman's eye, Hunter would have thought her revelation didn't faze Ellie at all. "I — I should have kept going from the beginning instead of just blurting that out," Hunter acknowledged, effectively skipping over Ellie's question.

"Yes, you should have. But, you wanted to test me. To see if I believed my theory that almost anything is forgivable." Hunter lowered her head, weakening Ellie's indignation. "I'm not perfect, Hunter. I've learned recently that I can be pretty judgmental at times. Not something I'm proud of," she muttered, "but, I'm human. So are you. I told you I would listen without judgment, so this is me doing exactly that. If you're feeling up to it, you can tell me what happened."

You're pretty perfect to me, Hunter thought with admiration. *Though, you're a little scary with how perceptive you are.* She shook off the shock from that perception and struggled with where to pick up the story. *Back to the beginning.*

"That next summer," Hunter began, wringing her hands together nervously. She marveled at how they shook. Of course, it wasn't the first time they trembled while she was near Ellie. *Good thing I'm not performing surgery on her.* She cleared her throat and tried again. "That next summer, I had somewhat of a growth spurt. I'd always been kinda tall and lanky, but with the help of athletics, and the need to release a bunch of pent-up energy, I sort of, um, filled out.

"Of course, that meant more attention from the boys in my class. It felt like every time I turned around, someone was asking me out." She eyed Ellie briefly and saw a slight smirk. She supposed it sounded a bit egotistical, but it was true. "Problem was, I wasn't interested in them at all."

"You were interested in . . . Susan?"

The minor hitch in Ellie's voice when she said Susan's name did not escape Hunter's notice. Was it jealousy or disgust that caused it? Hunter wasn't sure she wanted to know. Rather than think of that, she contemplated the question and analyzed her teenage feelings. "No," she answered finally. "She had a nice body and I enjoyed looking at it. But, Susan as a person? As I said before, she made me feel uncomfortable."

Even though she had questions, Ellie kept her mouth shut. She would let Hunter relate her story however she needed to.

"I know it doesn't make sense," Hunter said, sensing Ellie's bemusement. "If I didn't like her, why would I sleep with her? That's something I've been trying to figure out for years. Hopefully, with the help of Dr. Woodrow — my psychiatrist — I'll finally understand."

"Would you like to stop?" Ellie asked when Hunter paused. The trauma surgeon had a far-off look on her face, and Ellie worried that talking about this with anyone besides her therapist may not be a good idea.

Hunter shook her head. "I want to finish. Maybe it'll shed some light on why I screwed up so royally yesterday."

Oh, right. Iris. Ellie had almost forgotten about the scene she walked in on. "All right. Before you say anything else, I have the feeling that you need this. I forgive you. You didn't do anything wrong," she added quickly. "We aren't together, and you're free to do as you wish. But, since you're being so hard on yourself about what happened, I forgive you. Hopefully, you can forgive me for not being forthcoming about Jessie."

Hunter was stunned. Those three words were exactly what she needed. She didn't know how much until she heard them coming out of Ellie's mouth. "Thank you. I, um, you didn't do anything to warrant forgiveness." Ellie just raised an eyebrow, and Hunter reluctantly relented. "Deal." She couldn't bring herself to say the words because they felt wrong.

"I know what you did there, but I'll let it go."

Hunter grinned sheepishly, then sobered again. She took a deep breath. This was the hard part. The only thing that made it somewhat easier is the fact that she just recounted this story to Dr. Woodrow – the only other person that knew the details. She had never been able to tell Mo or Rebecca everything. Yet, here she sat in front of the woman she wished to seek a future with and considered telling all.

"My sixteenth birthday was coming up, and being an only child, ma wanted to throw a big surprise bash. She was never great at keeping things from me, though." Hunter chuckled a little at the memory. "She was insistent that I not know *everything* she was planning. That's where Susan came in."

No. Ellie didn't like where she thought this was going. She forced herself to stay impassive, even though she felt like weeping.

"She told my mom that she would take me over to her house, and keep me occupied."

"I bet," Ellie scoffed, slapping her hand over her mouth when she realized she said that out loud. "Sorry."

Hunter gave her a small smile. She detected a fierce protectiveness radiating from the small blonde and it gave her a warm, pleasant feeling. As well as the courage to continue.

"Do you want me to go on?" Hunter asked politely, and Ellie gave her a curt nod. "I wanted to refuse, but I didn't want to disappoint ma. When we got over there, Susan started in on how she was glad we had a little time alone together. Said she had a gift for me that she'd rather give me without an audience. That's when my anxiety got really bad."

Oh, Hunter. The ache in Ellie's stomach became more prominent.

"She guided me to this room, telling me how she had seen how I looked at her. And, that she knew what I was doing to myself in my room while I watched her. I was mortified." Hunter covered her flushed face with her hands. Just the memory of that day brought back all of the terrible, awkward feelings. "I thought for sure she was going to tell my parents, and I would get in trouble."

God, how I hope that's what happened, Ellie thought in vain. Of course, she knew that's not what transpired and it hurt her heart. If anything like this had happened to Jessie . . . Ellie couldn't even finish that thought without feeling nauseous.

"She would touch me gently, talk to me like she cared. I begged her not to tell on me, and she hugged me. Telling me she didn't want to get me in trouble, she wanted to help me. She wanted to teach me how to treat a real woman."

"Oh, God, Hunter."

"I didn't want to, Ellie! I — I didn't know anything about sex. I mean, I masturbated," she mumbled the word, oddly embarrassed even though she was a doctor. She had talked to patients about this kind of thing multiple times, but that was vastly different than confessing her own . . . stuff. "But, other than that, all I had was, you know, teenaged fantasies and what you hear at school."

Ugh, I feel sick! Hunter swallowed back the bile that threatened to come up. *Ellie is going to hate me. She's going to think I'm a terrible person. Fuck, she's probably right.*

"I didn't know what to do. When I told her that I didn't think it was right, she started telling me that she would be forced to go to my parents. That she couldn't allow me to be how I was without her guidance." Hunter snorted mirthlessly. "God I was so naïve and stupid. She made me believe every fucking thing she said. She went from kind and understanding to demanding. She was harsh with me. Of course, she would never hit me, but if I made the mistake of telling her I didn't think what we were doing was right, I'd be punished."

She laid her throbbing head on the back of the couch, willing her stomach to stop churning. "Oh, and the gift she wanted to give me? It was a fucking strap-on with condoms, dental dams, and surgical gloves. She told me that 'people like me carry diseases'. But that didn't stop her from wanting to help me, teach me. It didn't stop her from wanting me to fuck her. And, when I say fuck her, that's exactly what I mean. She never touched me. She said real women wanted to be treated as princesses, not the sex slaves their husbands treated them as. When her husband was in town, she would 'loan' me out to her other married friends. I needed 'practice and research' so when I was able to be with her again, I could show her what I learned. I learned to be grateful for the protection she insisted on. I began insisting on it myself. If those women could be with me like that, they could be with anyone." Hunter bowed her head in shame.

Jesus. "Hunter?" Ellie waited until Hunter lifted her eyes. She wanted to reach out to her but wasn't sure if it would be welcomed.

For some reason, the compassion in Ellie's eyes made Hunter feel guilty. "I didn't want to do it, Ellie! But, I couldn't let my parents find out. I thought that when I left for college it would stop. But whenever I came home to see my parents it started all over. I was in so deep, I didn't know how to quit. It was all I knew! She held it over my head, and I didn't know how to get out."

Hunter's agitation spurred Ellie into motion. She stepped between Hunter's legs and pulled her into her arms. Ellie held on as Hunter wept, muttering over and over how she hadn't known how to stop.

"It's okay," Ellie murmured. "Let it go."

"It's not okay!" Hunter tried pushing away, but Ellie held on tighter. "Did you hear what I told you? What I've done? I'm not a good person!" Hunter said with self-loathing. "I'm forty-one, Ellie. After all these years, why couldn't I stop? I should have been stronger." She sniffled. "I've never had a real relationship because

I'm afraid I don't know how. What if I'm too weak? I told her I didn't want to do it . . ."

"Exactly." Ellie cupped Hunter's face in her hands, tilting her chin up until they were eye to eye. "You said no. She manipulated you, Hunter. She used your naiveté and fear against you. *None* of what happened to you was your fault." *It was that bitch's fault,* Ellie thought angrily. She wanted so much to find this Susan person and hurt her. "She knows what you're afraid of, and that's how she kept you all these years." She brushed a tear from Hunter's cheek with the pad of her thumb. "Hey, you got away from her."

"Have I?"

Ellie silently sighed at the pain and uncertainty she heard coming from Hunter. She pulled Hunter back to her, closing her eyes when Hunter wrapped her arms around her waist. "Yes, you have. You acknowledge that you needed help and sought out a therapist. But, more than that, look at what you've become, Hunter. You didn't let her break you. You're a surgeon, you're successful, caring, sweet, beautiful." Ellie felt Hunter squeeze her tighter. "She can't hurt you anymore."

"She can," Hunter mumbled. She allowed herself one selfish moment to revel in the sensation of being held in Ellie's strong, safe arms. *Safe. That's exactly what I feel here.* Of course, she knew that wasn't all she was feeling being pressed against Ellie's body. Hell, her face was practically buried in Ellie's breasts. *God, I hope to be back in this exact position when I can enjoy it more. And explore.* Much to Hunter's disappointment, Ellie released her hold a bit and stepped back.

"What do you mean 'she can'?"

Involuntarily — at least, that's what she would say if asked — Hunter's hands rested on Ellie's hips. She craved the connection and couldn't bring herself to let go. It was inordinately pleasing that Ellie kept the connection as well by keeping her hands on Hunter's shoulders.

"Susan has photos," Hunter confided.

"Of the two of you together?" That sick feeling Ellie had before just tripled.

Hunter scoffed. "Nah, she would never expose herself like that.

Instead, she'll throw one of her 'friends' under the bus with me. A councilwoman no less."

"To what end? What does she want from you, Hunter?"

Hunter's fingers inadvertently dug into Ellie's hips. Whether it was to steady herself or keep Ellie from going away, she didn't know.

"Me."

Chapter Seventeen

"You?"

Hunter nodded. "If I don't go back to her, play her games again, she'll release the photos. To my work, to my parents. To you," she finished with a flinch.

"Me? What does she know about me?" Ellie did move now. She was disturbed that a woman who would prey on children would know anything about her. "Does she know about Jessie? I swear, Hunter, if she comes near Jessie I will kill her."

Hunter sprang up from the couch, turning an extremely furious Ellie towards her. "I would *never* let her near Jessie! That woman would have to get through me first and, being a doctor, I know how to make it look like natural causes."

That got Ellie's attention. Her head snapped up and she saw that Hunter was undoubtedly serious. "You mean that."

"Yes. I swear to you, she will never hurt Jessie. Or you."

"Don't worry about me." As Ellie turned away, she thought she heard Hunter mutter "impossible". "Can I ask you something?"

"As I said before, you can ask me anything you want."

"Was she there when you went to visit your parents last weekend?"

Shit. "Y-yes. But, nothing happened, I swear!"

"This is when she told you about the photo?" Ellie went on, deciding she believed Hunter's vow.

"Yes. And, in case you were wondering if she was bluffing, she showed it to me." Hunter shivered when she thought about how Susan had pornographic photos of her. *I don't even want to know what she does with those when she's not trying to blackmail me.* She was going to have to be more conscientious about her surroundings when she and Ellie were together. She'd be damned if she would let Susan disrupt Ellie's life. *That's if Ellie wants anything to do with me after all this shit.* It was undoubtedly in Ellie's best interest to stay away from Hunter, but the surgeon didn't know if she had the strength to walk away. Just the thought depressed Hunter more than she expected.

"Well, isn't she delightful," Ellie hissed with disgust.

Hunter watched helplessly as Ellie angrily moved around the living room. If the situation weren't so serious, she would have laughed at the flailing arms and heated mumblings. "I — I should go."

Ellie's mini rant fizzled at Hunter's faint suggestion. "Is that what you want to do?"

"No!" She cleared her throat. "No, Ellie, it's not what I want. But, you don't deserve this. Susan wants to ruin me. I won't allow that to happen to you."

"That bitch can't hurt me, Hunter."

"She has connections."

"So do I," Ellie told her matter-of-factly. She chuckled at Hunter's surprise. "Nothing illegal, Hunter, but just as effective. Greyson, Blaise's husband, and his best friend are both military special ops. They also happen to own an elite security firm. If that's not enough, Blaise has plenty of money to 'make it look like natural causes' if that *woman* ever came anywhere near someone I care about again." She took a step towards Hunter. "She's a fool if she thinks her 'connections' will trust her when she's willing to betray them so easily. And, she's a fool if she thinks she can keep manipulating you for her sick perversions."

Hunter grinned at Ellie's fierceness. "Has anyone ever told you that you're a little scary?"

"More often than you can imagine," Ellie laughed. She reached her hand out — delighted when Hunter didn't hesitate to take it — and guided them back to the couch. "How much damage can she cause you? Could you lose your job?"

Hunter let the warmth of Ellie's grip pacify her anxious heart. "I don't think so. I've never made my preferences a secret at work. I may get a mild reprimand for causing embarrassment to myself and the hospital, but I doubt they'd fire me."

"You don't sound like you'd care either way," Ellie inferred.

Hunter shrugged. "I certainly don't care enough to go back to Susan. The only thing that scares me is my parents finding out."

"Why?" She held on firmly when Hunter tried pulling away. "Why are you scared of that, Hunter?"

"How do you think they're going to feel about me when they find out what I've been doing?"

"They're going to love you."

Hunter snorted. "Right. Their daughter has been having sex with *married* women since she was fifteen! They're proud of me now, but when this comes out that pride will disappear!"

"They're going to love you," Ellie repeated with conviction.

"You don't know that," Hunter mumbled.

"Hunter, I'm a mother. If Jessie ever came to me with the story you just told me, the first thing I would do is hug her and tell her it wasn't her fault. The second thing I'd do is most likely try to murder the bitch that hurt my daughter." Ellie inhaled deeply and let it out as she silently counted to ten. "They're going to love you because they will know what happened was not your fault. They'll love you because you're their daughter and no matter how perfect they *think* you are, they *know* you're imperfect." She squeezed Hunter's hand. "You should be the one to tell them. Don't let them find out by a photo. And, you should probably make sure the bitch isn't around when you do tell them."

A huge, toothy grin spread across Hunter's face. "Were you a therapist in a past life? Dr. Woodrow said practically the same thing," she explained.

Ellie smiled. "Never a therapist. Just a mother."

HUNTER'S EYELIDS SLOWLY fluttered open. Momentarily confused, she stayed still until she was able to determine where she was and what was weighing her down. It wasn't until Ellie's hair tickled her nose that she realized the blonde was sleeping in her arms. She couldn't help herself from breathing in Ellie's scent. *Oh, God! This feels so right. Please, Ellie, please feel the same way.* As though Ellie could hear her thoughts, she began to stir in Hunter's arms. The taller woman held her breath, hoping Ellie wouldn't flip out finding herself in Hunter's embrace.

Ellie felt arms around her and a firmness beneath her that she certainly wasn't accustomed to. Even so, she felt comfortable right where she was. *I'll have to analyze that later. For now, I should probably find out how this came about.*

She cleared her throat, leaving her head on a very cozy shoulder. "I seem to have fallen asleep on you. Literally. Sorry about that."

"Don't be," Hunter murmured against Ellie's silken hair. "I'm quite comfortable."

Ellie smiled. "How did we end up like this anyway?"

"Not sure. But, I'm certainly not going to complain."

Ellie lifted her head finally, still grinning. "I have to admit it feels good. Feels . . ."

"Right?" Hunter offered, her heart soaring with Ellie's admission. Ellie nodded and Hunter went with her instincts, hoping she wasn't about to blow everything.

She knew Hunter was going to kiss her and Ellie wanted it. God, how she wanted it. But she found herself placing her fingers over

Hunter's descending lips. "Hunter, as much as I would love to kiss you — and believe me I do — we're both vulnerable right now. You especially." She moved her hand to caress Hunter's cheek. "The one thing I don't want is for this to be all about sex. Besides, I'm not sure I'm ready for this yet." Hunter grinned that lopsided grin Ellie was quickly coming to adore.

Well, it wasn't a no and she didn't run away. I can work with this. "Okay. We'll take it slow."

Ellie laughed and put her head back on Hunter's shoulder. "You know when people say that it never happens. When Blaise and Greyson met, they said they were going to take it slow. They've been together less than a year and they're married and have a kid on the way."

A chuckle rumbled through Hunter's chest. "How about this, then? We'll go at your pace."

Ellie traced imaginary figure eights on Hunter's firm tummy, completely unaware of the havoc she was causing inside the doctor. "I'm not sure I trust myself either," Ellie professed with an amused sigh. "Look at where I am? And, I don't even remember how we got here."

Hunter closed her eyes when Ellie snuggled even closer. "Doesn't seem like you're complaining either," Hunter laughed.

"I'm not. However," she checked her watch. "It's getting late and I have a menu to finish." She began to roll on her back, misjudging her position on the couch. Strong arms tightened around her and it wasn't just a tingle, but an electric charge she felt throughout her body. "Ahem. Maybe I should invest in a bigger couch."

"I don't know, I kinda like this one," Hunter grinned, holding Ellie close.

Her lips look so soft. If you just leaned in, Ellie, you could know what it's like to kiss her for real. She could feel herself leaning in. "Ugh. Menu. Work." Ellie reluctantly pushed herself up to a sitting position.

Hunter immediately felt the chill as Ellie's warm body left hers. *We're in trouble,* she smirked. "New menu, huh?" She scooted herself up, swinging her long legs above Ellie's slumped-over position.

"You changing things up at Ellie's, because I may need to approve first."

An amused eyeball peeked through fingers. "Oh yeah?"

"Mmhmm. That menu is perfect as is. How do I know you're not going to put some crap like wheatgrass on the menu? Or that weird stuff Big Al drinks?"

Ellie burst out laughing. "First of all, you've only had breakfast and pie. You don't even know what else I serve. Second, you're a doctor. How could you not endorse something as healthy as wheatgrass? Third, I would never put Big Al's drink on the menu. It would scare everyone away." She sat up straight, bumping Hunter's shoulder. "Relax, doc. I'm working on the catering menu for the Sumptor Gallery opening."

"No way!" Hunter had no idea Ellie did catering. *It's going to be interesting getting to know everything about her.* "Cass is showing there."

Ellie's eyes widened. "Cass is an artist?"

"Yep. Really good, too. Eve is a friend of Rebecca's, and she put in a good word. Not that Cass needed it. Her work speaks for itself."

The pride in Hunter's voice made Ellie smile. "I have no doubt it does if Eve offered her a showing." She fidgeted a bit. Never in her life had she contemplated asking someone out. With talk of the opening on the table, Ellie saw an opportunity she couldn't pass up. No matter how anxious it made her. "So, um, does that mean you're going to the opening?"

Oblivious to Ellie's predicament, Hunter grinned with delight. "Yeah, Cass scored me an invite as soon as she was confirmed."

"That's good." *Are you going with anyone?* Of course, she didn't have the guts to ask that out loud.

"Are you, uh, going to be working all night?"

"No," Ellie grinned. "I'm just making the food. I don't serve it." *Do it, woman!* "I had actually thought about asking if you would like to go. With me." Ellie watched Hunter expectantly.

"You — you did? Really? Yeah, um, yes! I mean, I would love to. Go with you. If you're asking, of course." Hunter's face broke out into a goofy grin. She couldn't help being a bit inelegant with all of this.

She didn't have any experience *truly* dating. Hunter was extremely grateful that Ellie found her awkwardness refreshing. "But, um, we can still go out before that, right? I was hoping you would honor me by having dinner with me this weekend." She gave a little shrug. "Saturday is my next day off. I'd like to spend the night with you."

Ellie's eyebrow shot up. "What happened to taking it slow?"

"Huh? Oh, shit! That's not, oh man! That's not what I meant!" Hunter hid her burning face behind her hands. "That didn't come out right."

Ellie couldn't hold back the smirk any longer. "I'm teasing you, Hunter. I know what you meant."

"You're rotten!" Hunter let out an embarrassed chuckle. "So? Will you have dinner with me?"

"Yes, I'd love to," Ellie answered, echoing Hunter from earlier.

Yes! "Thank you. I, uh, guess I should probably get out of your hair." In reality, Hunter was disappointed that the time had come for her to go home. *It's going to be really lonely there.* She stood up, helping Ellie up as well.

"You haven't been 'in my hair' as you put it. I'm glad you came over to talk." Ellie made no effort to remove her hand from Hunter's as they made their way to the door.

"Me, too. I know it wasn't pretty, but . . ."

"We said what we needed to say to get through this part, Hunter." She gripped Hunter's larger hand. "Nothing is always sugar and spice, but if we can make it through these talks without falling apart, that's a good thing."

"Yeah. You didn't run screaming, so I'll count that as a win."

Ellie tsked and mumbled a "whatever" before cringing. "Wow. Can you tell I have a teenager?" she laughed.

"Would never have believed it if I hadn't seen her with my own eyes," Hunter confessed kindly.

Ellie peered up at Hunter through her lashes. "Are you always this sweet?"

"Nah. I'm pretty sure the residents at the hospital think I'm an ogre."

"Right." She gave Hunter a once over. "I can see that. You're tall enough," she teased.

"Hey! Just because you're vertically challenged . . ."

"I am no such thing!" Ellie pushed Hunter away from her with feigned irritation. "I will have you know, *doctor*, that I am the average height for a woman. Just because *you* are freakishly tall doesn't mean I'm short."

"Okay, okay." Hunter held her hands up in surrender. "I was just kidding. Don't kick me with those legs of yours!"

Ellie glanced down at her legs then up at Hunter again. "What's wrong with my legs?"

"Not a damn thing," Hunter answered reverently. When she caught herself staring at said legs, she blushed furiously. *Good lord, I feel like such a teenager with her!* "I, uh, they just look nice."

A fair eyebrow raised. "You've never seen them." *Teasing her is fun*, Ellie thought with beguilement.

"Well, I . . . no, I haven't. But, I can just imagine that they're nice. You know, because you do yoga." *Ugh. I'm so lame.*

Ellie chuckled lightly. *She's so cute when she's flustered.* "Yes, I do. Though my students are going to forget about being Zen with me if I keep missing classes."

"I could always be your student," Hunter shrugged, trying to sound nonchalant. *Hell, sign me up for hot yoga if it means seeing you in yoga pants.* "I'll bring Mo, Patty, and Cass. Rebecca is already a student. There you go! Instant class." Hunter smiled smugly.

"Ha! You, Mo, and Cass will only be there to watch me, Patty, and Rebecca in our yoga pants."

"And?" Hunter laughed out loud when Ellie slapped her playfully on the stomach.

Just then, the front door opened and though the two women were a respectable distance from each other, they each took a step back.

"Mom! I'm . . . oh." Jessie stopped short, eyeing the tall woman who looked a tad panicky.

Shit. You're an adult, Hunter. Try acting like one. Hunter cleared her throat, discreetly wiping her suddenly damp hands on her jeans and waited for a visibly nervous Ellie to make introductions.

"Hey, sweetie." Ellie pulled Jessie to her, giving her a quick hug. "Um, I would like you to meet someone. This is Dr. Hunter Vale. Hunter, this is my daughter Jessie." She held her breath, knowing Jessie was most likely annoyed with Hunter after the incident the day before. After all, she was her mother's daughter.

Hunter held out her hand and gave the teen her best smile. "I've heard a lot about you. It's nice to meet you."

An eyebrow — a carbon copy of her mother's — raised and she shook the larger hand. "I've heard a lot about you, too. And, you could have met me yesterday, but you seemed to be in quite a hurry."

"Jessie!" She should have known. Ellie *knew* her daughter better than anyone. Once her annoyance was piqued, it took a while to get past it.

"It's okay, El. She's right," Hunter said wistfully.

"Right or not, Jessie knows better than to be rude." Ellie gave her daughter an ultra-motherly look.

"Sorry," Jessie mumbled. The look her mother was giving her was *definitely* a warning. Unfortunately, Jessie couldn't get past the way her mother looked the day before when Dr. Vale walked out. And, it annoyed her that she found the doctor so likable and um . . . *Mom has great taste.* "So, have you been here all night?"

"N-no! Uh, I got here this morning." *Is it hot in here?* Hunter resisted the urge to stuff her hands in her pockets like a bashful fool.

"She was in surgery all night," Ellie supplied quickly. She didn't want Jessie thinking that Hunter had made her wait all night long for her to show up. Of course, that's exactly what happened, but it wasn't deliberate and Jessie didn't need to know *all* the details.

The teen's eyes widened a bit. "The big accident involving the bus?" she asked Hunter, then continued when the doctor nodded. "I saw that on the news. Looked terrible."

"It was. I was in surgery for hours. Thankfully there were no casualties." Hunter was relieved that the conversation had turned to something she could actually talk about without feeling reprimanded by a teenager. Not that she blamed Jessie. The past week or so had been filled with huge changes for all of them. "Anyway, I was, um, just heading out."

Jessie glanced down. "Without your shoes?"

Shit! Hunter looked down, saw her socked feet, and wiggled her toes. "I guess I need those," she said sheepishly and turned to Ellie. "They must still be in your room."

Hunter took off towards Ellie's bedroom leaving a very confused Jessie staring at her mom.

"Your room?"

"It's not what you think, sweetie. She was exhausted when she got here, so I let her sleep in there. *Alone.*"

"We have a guest room."

Ellie's answer was stalled as Hunter came back, hopping as she tried to put on her shoe while walking.

"Sorry," she mumbled to Ellie, sensing the tension between mother and daughter.

"Are you playing my mom?" Jessie asked abruptly.

"Jessica Anne!"

Hunter felt compelled to jump to a sufficiently chagrined Jessie's defense. "Ellie, it's okay. She's only protecting you," she said delicately. She turned kind eyes to the teenager. "No, Jessie, I'm not 'playing' Ellie. I know that my boneheaded actions," she slid an apologetic glance to Ellie knowing she knew exactly which actions Hunter was referring to, "weren't a very good first impression, and they were hurtful to your mother. That's something I don't want to do again. When I got here this morning, your mom could have told me to go to hell and I wouldn't have blamed her. But, she invited me in, gave me a place to rest, fixed me lunch, and listened as I tried to explain." She looked at Ellie again. With only a moment's hesitation, she made a heavy decision. "If you need to tell Jessie what we spoke about today so she understands, that's fine with me."

She took a deep breath and addressed Jessie once more to finish pleading her case. Hunter wasn't foolish enough to think Jessie's opinion wouldn't have any influence on Ellie's decisions. She knew that if Jessie didn't approve of her, Ellie may not give this thing between them a chance.

"People like your mom, *genuinely* nice people, are hard to find these days. I don't want to lose that. And, if you give me a chance, I will prove to you that I can be worth her . . . friendship." Hunter wasn't sure if Jessie was ready to think of her mom being in a relationship with another woman, so she censored herself.

Jessie studied the tall woman, seeing nothing but sincerity in her shockingly blue eyes and sighed. "Well, I am the one who convinced mom to go and talk to you." She noted the surprised look that Hunter gave Ellie who shrugged. "I would be somewhat of a hypocrite if I didn't give you a chance as well." Jessie held her hand out, smiling when Hunter shook it. "Hurt her and you'll have to deal with me. I know people."

To Hunter's surprise, Ellie snickered. "She's talking about the military guys, isn't she?"

"Mmhmm," Ellie confirmed with a smirk.

"Gotcha. Good thing I plan on being on my best behavior." She gave Jessie's hand a friendly squeeze before letting go. "Okay, I'm going to get out of here and let you two talk things out. Remember, El, you have my blessing to tell Jessie anything you think she needs to know." Ellie nodded. "Can I, uh, still stop by the diner for breakfast?" she asked shyly.

"How else am I going to be sure you get at least *one* good meal a day?" Ellie winked and opened the door for her guest. "Be careful going home."

"I will."

"Text me?"

Hunter gave that lopsided grin. It made her feel all warm and fuzzy inside to know that Ellie cared about her safety.

"Definitely. It was nice to officially meet you, Jessie."

"You, too," Jessie said, surprisingly meaning it.

JESSIE TURNED ON her mom as soon as the door shut behind Hunter. "Are you sleeping with her?"

"No."

"But, she was in your bed?"

"Yes."

"Why?"

Ellie raised an eyebrow at her daughter's attitude. "Not that I owe you an explanation, young lady, but the guest room isn't made up so I offered her my room."

"We have a couch," Jessie pointed out defiantly. She knew she was pushing her luck with her mom, but she couldn't help herself. It was like her mind had a mind of its own.

"I was working out here, Jessie. What is this about? *You* told me to go and talk to her and now you're giving me a hard time *because* I'm talking to her!"

"This isn't just *talking*! This is about you inviting a woman you *just* met into your bed! That's not you!"

Ellie silently counted to ten and then counted again backward. "I didn't sleep with her, Jessie," she reiterated calmly, then remembered waking up in Hunter's arms not that long ago. *That's different.* "She was exhausted when she got here and I did what I thought was right. Now, what's going on? You've never questioned my judgment like this before. And, I have to tell you, I don't like it."

"You don't like it?" Jessie scoffed. *Oh yeah, I am so grounded. But I have to be honest with her!* "For years, my life has been one way. Drama free. I knew who you were, where you were, what *we* were. In less than a week – a *week*, mom – I've found out you've been lying to me my whole life." She held up her finger, stopping Ellie's protest. "I know, okay. I know that you denied yourself, but see it from my side, mom. One day everything is the same and the next everything changed. You're gay, my grandparents are terrible people, there's a woman in your bed . . . I have to share you now and I don't know how to do that," she confessed softly.

"Jessie," Ellie sighed, taking her daughter in her arms. She guided them to the couch, pulling Jessie down on her lap as though she was still a little girl. It didn't matter to Ellie that Jessie was almost the same size as she was. Right now, Jessie *was* Ellie's little girl.

"Mom! I'm too big to sit on your lap."

"Never." She held on tight. "I understand. Everything you just said is a *lot* to deal with. Even with years of knowing, it's a lot. But, the one thing that will *always* remain the same is my love for you. I am your mother, I will always be your mother. Nothing that happens can ever change that. Not even me being gay," she teased with a playful squeeze. She got the desired response when Jessie giggled.

"I know. I mean, the smart part of me knows that. The insecure part of me can only think about losing time with you."

"Oh, *now* you want to spend time with me. For the past few weeks, you've been leaving me almost every night to work on that secret project of yours." Ellie laughed to soften the reality of her words.

Jessie rolled her eyes. "It's not secret. You're so dramatic." She squealed when Ellie tickled her and squirmed off her mother's lap. "Okay, so *I'm* being dramatic with this whole Hunter thing. You deserve to have someone – other than me and Blaise – in your life. Just give me a minute to get used to this. I really didn't expect to find her here when I got home. I guess it just threw me for a loop." She bumped Ellie's knee with hers. "So? Was her excuse for walking away good enough? Did you show her the Montgomery ire? Was it as good as mine?" She grinned cheekily.

Ellie chuckled. "You have a few more years to go before you can catch up to my temper." She patted Jessie's knee. "Come on. Let's make an elaborate dinner and we'll talk about everything."

"By elaborate you totally mean tacos, right?"

"Uh, yeah. Duh."

Ellie laughed and took off towards the kitchen with a throw pillow headed straight for her.

Chapter Eighteen

She got the evil eye with a twitch of a grin when she slid the plate of food in front of Big Al.

"You're welcome," Ellie with a grin of her own. The bell signaling someone entering the diner had Ellie glancing up. Her grin turned into a full-fledged smile when Hunter walked in dressed in pressed black slacks and a fitted, navy Oxford shirt. *Very nice.*

"Hi." Hunter's voice cracked with nervousness and she cleared her throat. She had woken up in a great mood this morning thinking of seeing Ellie. Then she let her insecurities take over. What if Ellie had thought about everything Hunter had told her and decided she didn't want to deal with the baggage? What if Jessie had talked her out of being 'out'? What if Ellie couldn't get over what she had seen in the on-call room? Fortunately, if the bright smile was anything to go by, Ellie looked nothing but happy to see her.

"Hey. You look nice." Ellie laughed softly at Hunter's slight blush as she started fidgeting with the collar of her shirt.

"Thanks."

It never ceased to amaze Ellie how shy Hunter seemed to be around her. There had been an aura of confidence surrounding the woman when she was with Mo or Rebecca and Cass. With Ellie, Hunter became a little shy, yet that confident demeanor was never far away. Ellie couldn't say she minded being the source of Hunter's imbalance. It held with it a slight pretense of control. Something Ellie rarely felt when she was near Hunter.

"Are you hungry?" she asked, hoping the familiarity of their mornings since they met would put Hunter at ease.

"Yeah, but I have to get something that's easy to eat on the run," Hunter answered apologetically.

"You can't stay?" Ellie, disappointed that her Hunter 'fix' would be short this morning, reached for a to-go coffee cup. She filled it and placed the top on it with the expert efficiency of years of practice.

"Nah, I got called in. I have to get in before my rounds. That's why I'm in this get-up."

An unbidden flash of Hunter with Nurse Ruderton in the on-call room crossed Ellie's mind.

"You're not in trouble, are you? Did Iris say something?" She didn't want to admit how much she disliked saying the nurse's name. It was such an adolescent reaction that it embarrassed Ellie.

Hunter frowned in confusion. *Iris? What would she . . . oh, shit. She thinks I'm being called in for sexual harassment. Perfect*, she thought with self-disgust. "No, no. She's never made it a secret how she, um, feels about me. Not even in front of the boss." Hunter stifled a laugh at Ellie's muttering of "charming". "I doubt she'd find sympathy in that department," she continued carefully. Truth was, she did use that young nurse and could be reprimanded for it. As luck would have it, Iris had never exactly ingratiated herself to anyone at the hospital. Hunter, on the other hand, was good friends with Mack – Dr. Mackenzie – who just happened to be the head of the emergency department. "Ahem, anyway, they said it's about some administrative stuff. Which in suit-speak means they've turned down my appeal to relieve Dani of her bills."

Ellie nodded. The idea that a hospital would have enough heart to forgive a debt – even for a homeless girl - was too much to wish for. "I see. Well, don't worry too much about it. Dani, Claire, and I have been talking about that. I'm pretty sure we've come up with a solution." As much as Dani hated it, she finally relented on letting Ellie – or Blaise rather – help her with a 'loan'.

"That's great!" Hunter took a sip of her coffee, savoring the mild bite of the caffeine. She didn't know what Ellie did differently with her coffee, but Hunter sure as hell had never had a better cup. "I hope you'll let me help out wherever I can."

"Just keep in touch with her, Hunter. She talks about you when I visit. About how you check up on her and take the time to explain what to expect to her and Claire in ways they can understand. Dani respects you."

"Even after what I did to her?"

"Save her life? Yes. In fact, I'm pretty sure Claire would kiss you for that if she didn't think Dani would get jealous."

Hunter blushed again and shook her head. "It's such a stark contrast in how Dani felt about me just two weeks ago. I don't know how to thank you for that."

"There's no need. However, if you insist, I'm sure you'll come up with something this weekend," she winked. "How about a breakfast sandwich to go?"

Hunter – who was rapidly beginning to think she would stay in constant state of blushing around Ellie - nodded enthusiastically. "Sounds portable enough," she grinned.

Ellie chuckled. "I'll be right back."

"Um, El?" Ellie looked over her shoulder and Hunter continued. "You look beautiful today," she said shyly.

Ellie looked down at her everyday attire. "Thank you, but it's just jeans and a t-shirt, Hunter."

"Yeah, but I've never seen them look better." Hunter's eyes sparkled as she wiggled her brows at the diner owner.

Ellie rolled her eyes mirthfully, turning abruptly in hopes Hunter didn't catch her reddening cheeks.

"'Bout time."

Hunter tore her gaze away from Ellie's retreating backside. "Morning to you, too, Big Al."

Big Al grunted. "She's a good woman," he said quietly, surprising Hunter with his candor.

"Yes, she is."

"Don't hurt her."

His surly demeanor seemed to have grown even surlier with his warning.

Irritation spread through her and Hunter fought to keep her cool. "Don't plan on it."

"See that you don't or you'll have to deal with me."

It was possibly the longest sentence she had ever heard from the old man. That thought along with his unveiled threat made her laugh. "Get in line. I've already been put on notice by Jessie. And, to be honest, she scares me way more than you do."

To Hunter's surprise, Big Al let out a sharp bark of laughter. "Don't blame you there. That girl has her mother's moxie."

Moxie, she snickered. "She sure does." Hunter turned to him. "I'll take care of her heart as best I can," she said frankly.

ELLIE WAS EXHAUSTED, and it had only been an hour since Ellie sent Hunter away with a breakfast sandwich, a fresh cup of coffee, and a promise for Dani that she would be by later. The breakfast crowd was particularly demanding this morning. It was either that or Ellie was just feeling particularly frazzled.

She had missed her run again this morning and was beginning to feel the effects. After all the talking she had been doing, she needed the time to run and think. Or, more importantly, to clear her head. Blaise had been texting her. Jessie constantly wanted to talk about Hunter or how Ellie was feeling. Everything that Hunter had told her kept running through her brain on an awful, endless loop. Then, of course, there was that scene she walked in on in that on-call room. Oh, how she wished she could forget that, but her mind was spinning too much to put anything into perspective.

Ellie smiled absently at the petite, elderly customer as she refilled her coffee cup. "Do you need anything else, Mrs. Odeen?"

"No, dear. Oh! Maybe another slice of that nice butterscotch pecan pie? To go, of course." Mrs. Odeen clucked with laughter, reminding Ellie of the Mallard ducks she often saw at a nearby park.

"Absolutely. I'll have one of the girls bring it out to you with your check."

Out of habit, Ellie turned towards the door with a smile and a welcome as soon as the bell sounded. She was a bit surprised to see Rebecca walk in alone. She gestured to one of the few open tables, raising the coffee pot in question. When Rebecca nodded, Ellie asked one of her passing waitresses to fetch her a coffee cup.

"Good morning, Rebecca. I'm afraid you missed Hunter this morning. She had to go in early."

Rebecca grinned charmingly. "I'm actually here to see you."

Fantastic. More talking. The young waitress sidled up to them just then, thrusting the coffee cup in Ellie's direction. Ellie fought to keep her annoyance in check. "Put it on the table, please," she said through gritted teeth and forced smile. She filled the cup and handed the pot over to the waitress. "Let Rosa know that I'm going to take a quick break."

"Yes, Miss Ellie."

Ellie slipped into the booth opposite Rebecca and rolled her eyes. "Every time they call me Miss Ellie I feel like I should be looking for bifocals and a walker."

Rebecca chuckled. "I have to admit, I thought that was exactly what you were like before I met you. Minus the walker. Your baking just reminds me of that."

"I get that a lot," Ellie smiled. Having an idea of what Rebecca was there for, she sat back and waited.

Rebecca recognized the gesture for what it was and she found her respect for Ellie increasing. *Tough cookie. Definitely something Hunter needs in a partner.*

"Is Ellie short for something?" Rebecca asked, hoping to get the diner owner to be less defensive.

"Elena."

"That's a beautiful name." Rebecca received nothing more than a polite 'thank you' and decided it was probably best to just get to the point. "So, I got a call from Hunter last night," Rebecca began and noticed an almost imperceptible flash of irritation in Ellie's beautiful features. *Interesting.* "She gave me a run-down of what's been happening the past couple of days."

Ellie raised a brow. "What exactly did she tell you?"

Hmm, she does not like that. Rebecca secretly smiled. *Hunter is going to have her hands full with this one.*

"Nothing too personal," Rebecca assured Ellie. "She would never betray you like that. However, she did mention that she told you about Susan."

Ellie heard the disdain in Rebecca's voice when she spoke of Susan, but since she had no way of knowing how much Rebecca actually knew, she remained vague. "Yes, she did."

Loyal. "I have no idea what that woman did to get Hunter in her claws, but I'm glad it's over. With that being said, Hunter is in a very vulnerable state right now."

So, Rebecca doesn't know the whole story. Ellie couldn't explain why that little tidbit pleased her. Or, rather, she didn't want to think about why it did.

"What is it you want to say, Rebecca?"

Oh, yeah, I like her. This woman is dominating for sure. Rebecca laughed soundlessly at her assessment.

"I want to know that you're not using her, Elena." Rebecca turned on her 'professional' persona which never failed at provoking some intimidation.

Ellie sat up, leaning her elbows on the table, and looked unwaveringly into Rebecca's distinctive eyes. "Are you saying this as a friend or an ex-lover?"

"Does it matter?" She watched in fascination as the muscles in Ellie's jaw bunched. "A friend," Rebecca answered quickly. The last thing she wanted to do was alienate the woman Hunter was enamored with. "Hunter and I have never been lovers."

"Why not?"

Surprised, Rebecca sipped her coffee before answering. "Because when I met Hunter, she was still mixed up with Susan, and I certainly wasn't in any shape to be with someone. Once I was ready to give my heart away, I met Cassidy. Now that Hunter is ready to move on, she has met you. Which is why I'm asking you not to hurt her, Elena."

Ellie breathed in through her nose, letting it out slowly. She understood the sentiment, she just wasn't in the mindset to deal with this right now. "I don't intend to hurt Hunter, Rebecca. Obviously, I can't predict the future, but I'm not the type to play games. You'll just have to trust me that I'm *nothing* like Susan. Hunter and I both have our vulnerabilities and we've have discussed that." Her phone buzzed in her back pocket and she pulled it free to quickly check it. Another text from Blaise. The pressure was building inside Ellie and she knew it would not be good for anyone if she let it continue this way. "I know that you're looking out for Hunter and I can appreciate that. I do the same for my best friend. But you have nothing to worry about from me." She stood up and gave Rebecca what she hoped was a friendly smile. "Thank you for stopping by, Rebecca. I hope to see you again soon. Oh, and my friends call me Ellie."

Rebecca watched in awe as the young diner owner walked away. "I have effectively been put in my place," she murmured to herself with a satisfied smile. "Cassidy is going to love this."

HER LUNGS WERE burning and she struggled to catch her breath. It was during that last mile when Ellie knew she had pushed herself too hard. But she needed to get out of her head and the only way she was able to do that was to run out of it.

"Trying to kill yourself?"

Ellie's head snapped up at the familiar voice. "What are you doing here?" Even though she was beat, she somehow managed to catch the bottle of water that came flying towards her.

"You haven't returned any of my texts. That's never happened before, so I had to drag my pregnant ass out here to this god-forsaken place to make sure you were still alive."

Unfortunately for Ellie, she had just taken a large gulp of water when Blaise started talking. Now, she was spitting water out, coughing, and laughing all at once.

"God-forsaken place?" she snorted, which didn't feel good considering there was still water up her nose. "This place is beautiful. The only reason you don't like it is because exercise is involved when you're here."

Blaise grunted, gingerly lowering herself on a nearby bench. "Whatever."

"How did you know I was here?"

"I went to the diner. Rosa told me you were upset and needed some time to yourself." She patted the space next to her. "Come over here and tell my why you're avoiding me. But, if you're too stinky, sit closer to that side."

Ellie sighed but obeyed. "I'm not avoiding you."

"I've got a handful of unanswered texts that say otherwise," Blaise said knowing full well that her pregnancy hormones were possibly helping her blow this way out of proportion.

"I'm sorry." Ellie took another gulp of water, this time managing to actually swallow it. "The past couple of weeks have been . . ." She groaned with frustration.

Fourteen years Blaise has known Ellie and it was a rare occasion when she let things get to her. Very rare. And nothing like this. Then again, Ellie had always avoided relationships and speaking of her sexuality. "I can't imagine what you're going through, sweetie." Blaise placed her hand over Ellie's. "I hope you know that I'm here to help you, not lecture you."

"I know. The problem is, I've been talking so much recently — about really heavy stuff — that it was just getting to be a little overwhelming. I didn't want to talk anymore."

"So, you came out here to run yourself to death." It wasn't a question and Ellie caught the twinkle in Blaise's whiskey colored eyes.

"No, I came out here to remember what it was like when I had no feelings. When my life was simpler." Ellie poured some of the water over her head to cool herself off from her hard run. "Feelings are overrated." She laughed at herself. "And, now I sound like a whiney child."

Blaise chuckled. "Maybe a little. Can you tell me what's bothering you the most?" Deep down she knew she should give Ellie more time to process everything, but Blaise was worried. Ellie was never one to run away from her problems. Well, she ran, but she also talked.

Ellie shrugged. "Ugh, Blaise, you know me. Normally I would be able to handle whatever is thrown at me. I've done it my entire life." Blaise nodded her agreement. "But, right at this moment, I feel like I've been living my teen years all the way up to my current age in the span of two weeks. I feel juvenile jealousy, fear, desire, excitement. Did I mention fear and desire? Oh, and anger. An anger I shouldn't feel and wish I could get over."

"Anger over what?" All the other responses to the changes Ellie was going through, Blaise understood. The anger was the odd one out, especially when it came to Ellie. Maybe it was the yoga, but Ellie was one of the most chill people she had ever met. It drove Blaise crazy sometimes. It also saved their friendship multiple times.

"It's stupid."

"So? I'm your best friend, El. That means I'm obligated to listen to you tell me stupid things and be on your side no matter what." She rubbed her belly when the baby kicked. Lately, it was as though the kid was using her stomach as a punching bag. Since it meant he – or she – was healthy she didn't mind. Much.

Ellie laughed softly. "I suppose you're right. I've listened to you tell me stupid things numerous times."

"Don't make me get this baby to kick you," Blaise warned with a glare.

"Well, he could probably do it better than you."

"I would say you suck but you're probably right at this point. Still think it's a boy, hmm?" She waved the question away and swatted Ellie playfully on the arm. "Anyway, stop stalling. Tell me why the anger."

With a deep sigh, Ellie tried to sort out everything in her head. "Okay, so the short version of the story is Hunter found out about Jessie before I could tell her. She got upset for reasons I know now. But, at the time it irked me that she would just walk away without talking to me." She twisted the cap of the bottle crankily. "Jessie convinced me to go and talk to her. When I got to the hospital, she . . . she was in the on-call room. With a nurse on her lap."

Blaise sucked in a breath. "Ouch. Sounds to me like you have a reason to be upset."

"But I don't!" Ellie said heatedly. "Hunter and I are not together. I have no claim on her and she doesn't owe me any loyalty. But that doesn't stop it from hurting. Which pisses me off."

"Sweetie," Blaise took a breath. "Do you remember when I went to that masquerade charity event the Gallos put together?"

"Mmhmm. The night you found out Greyson was engaged. At least, you thought he was."

"Right. The same night he showed up at my apartment to tell me it wasn't true and I agreed to go out with him." The baby kicked again and Blaise welcomed the jolt of discomfort. She *hated* thinking about this, but maybe it would help Ellie. Now if she could just get it all out without choking on the name of Greyson's ex. "Anyway, I found out later that Pricilla . . . serviced him in the limo on the way to the party."

"Serviced him?" Ellie had a feeling she knew what Blaise was talking about though she didn't want to believe Greyson would do something like that.

"Went down on him," Blaise explained painfully.

"I can't believe he would do that. How did you find out?"

"Pricilla told me."

"How do you know she's not lying to you? She lied about everything else. Including the engagement."

"She told me in front of Greyson. He didn't deny it. In fact, he wanted to explain. I told him exactly what you said about Hunter. We weren't together at that time. I told him to let it go."

"You haven't," Ellie guessed.

"For the most part, I have. Still, it hurts knowing he would allow that to happen when he was pursuing me." Blaise adjusted her body which was getting increasingly uncomfortable. The hard bench wasn't helping much. "Pretty silly, right? After everything I went through, that's one of the things that sticks in my mind."

"You love him," Ellie said as if that was the answer to everything.

"I do. I *try* not to think about that or bring it up very often. Maybe when he's being particularly annoying and I'm feeling bitchy." She laughed along with Ellie.

"What has he said about it?"

"He says that he was thinking about me and thought his imagination was just working overtime." Blaise rolled her eyes. "He swears that once he figured out what was going on he pushed her away."

"A man trained in special forces didn't realize that some woman was taking his dick out of his pants?" Ellie said incredulously.

It was so uncharacteristic for Ellie to use a word such as 'dick' that Blaise was momentarily taken aback. "Right? But that's his story and he's sticking to it."

"Do you believe him about pushing her away?" Ellie wanted to believe that Hunter wasn't the type to run and jump into bed with someone else when complications arose. If she couldn't, this thing between them would be over before it even began.

"Yes. I see it in his eyes. I see the regret. The truth."

Ellie popped up from the bench. "Great. What I'm hearing is this feeling will never go away?"

"It'll fade progressively each day if you don't let yourself dwell on it. It only bothers me when I think about it, and I rarely think about Pricilla these days." She studied Ellie who was currently bouncing on the balls of her feet as though she was about to take off running again. "Hunter's reason? Was it believable?"

Ellie thought of everything Hunter had told her yesterday. It still made her sick to know what Susan had done, and for that reason alone, she could believe Hunter.

"Yes."

"Good. If you want this to work with Hunter, then do your best to let the on-call scene fade from your mind. Easier said than done, I know, but no one said all this dating slash relationship stuff was easy." A devilish grin stretched across Blaise's face. "By the way, I bought some things for you. I'll bring them over on Sunday."

She looked at Blaise through narrowed eyes. "What did you buy me?"

"Just some things to help you out. You know, get you acquainted with lesbian love." Blaise grinned and wiggled her eyebrows.

"I hate you." Ellie stuck her tongue out at her best friend.

"You love me. And, I'm pretty sure the book I bought you will tell you all the things you can do with that thing," she teased.

"I'm leaving." She walked backward towards the parking lot flipping a laughing Blaise off with both hands.

"Come on, I was just kidding! Come back!" A mild case of panic bubbled up inside Blaise when Ellie refused to stop. "Seriously, El, come back! I can't get up!"

Chapter Nineteen

Nerves were a bitch. As a rule, surgeons were taught to tamp down nerves. It was something Hunter was very good at. Until now. She scanned the clothes in her closet, a towel draped around her naked body.

"I have nothing to wear."

"Damn, Hunt, you sound like a girl."

Hunter peered around the door and glowered at Mo. "I *am* a girl, you dope. You're not helping at all."

Mo laughed at a stupid video someone had posted on Facebook and glanced up at Hunter. "Just wear whatever. You look good in everything." She blushed at giving Hunter such uncharacteristic flattery. "Just get dressed," she muttered, going back to her phone.

Hunter shook her head. *Should have asked Rebecca to come over and help me.* Decision made, Hunter went for her phone.

"Yo?"

"Hey, Cass, it's Hunter."

"Hey! Aren't you supposed to be getting ready for a date?"

"Yeah, that's why I'm calling. I'm a nervous wreck and Mo is of no help to me."

"You need me to get Rebecca?"

She heard the mirth in Cass's voice, but thankfully there was no ribbing or resentment. "Nah, I thought maybe you could help me."

"Whoa! 'Kay, hang on one sec." Cass held the phone away from her and called out to her lover. "Hey, baby! Hunter is on the phone and wants *me* to help her!"

Hunter tapped her phone against her forehead. "I don't know why I bother."

"I'm just messin' with you, Hunter. What do you need?"

She had a sinking feeling that she was never going to live this down. "I – I've never been on a date before," she said quietly. "I want to impress Ellie, but I have no idea what I'm doing, Cass."

Cass didn't know everything about Hunter's past, but Rebecca had filled her in enough that she knew better than to tease her.

"Hunter, you've already impressed Ellie," Cass encouraged. "Now it's all about the courting."

Hunter laughed. "How did you court Becca?"

"Uh, let's focus on you," Cass said bashfully. "Listen, you already know that Ellie likes you. Hell, you spend every day having breakfast with her. She spends her spare time at the hospital helping you with Dani. Just be yourself. That's all she wants."

"Being myself isn't all that great," Hunter said sadly.

"Bullshit!" Mo chipped in. "Don't you let that bitch Susan ruin this with Ellie. Whatever you did, it's in the past. You said Ellie knows and she still agreed to go out with your ass. So, buck up, put on some sexy duds, and blow that woman's mind."

"I thought you said she wasn't helping you," Cass laughed.

"Yeah, well, she was looking at cat videos a minute ago," Hunter smirked at Mo who flopped back onto the bed with embarrassment. "Okay. What would you wear, Cass?"

"Are we talking casual? Formal?"

"Casual. I didn't want to overdo it and be uncomfortable."

"Good."

Hunter heard muffled, muted voices.

"Rebecca says nice jeans, a white shirt because – as my baby puts it, white is hot – and boots." There was a pause. "Hey! That's what I was wearing when we met!" Cass shouted to her lover.

"I guess it really does work then," Hunter snickered. *Sold. If I can get what Rebecca and Cass have, I'll wear that outfit for the rest of my life.*

"MOM, YOU CAN'T go on a date dressed in a towel." Jessie looked worriedly over at Blaise, who shrugged. Jessie held up a little black dress. "What about this?"

Ellie lifted her head from her prone position on the bed. "Too 'I'm-trying-to-get-laid'," she said and collapsed again, arms spread out.

"What's wrong with that?" Blaise asked.

"Last time I went on a date and got laid, I got her," she pointed at her daughter.

"Clearly that was a once in a lifetime thing," Jessie giggled.

"Besides, as virile as Hunter looks, I doubt she could recreate that." Blaise cracked up and immediately regretted it. "Damn it, I have to pee again."

Jessie shook her head and plopped down next to her mom. "Okay, out with it."

"What do you mean?"

"Mom, you've been out of the shower for, like, an hour and a half. In that time, you've been laying here rejecting every outfit Blaise and I have suggested. Did you change your mind about going out with Hunter?"

"No," Ellie sighed. "I'm scared, Jessie."

"I think that's normal. In fact, after meeting Hunter, I can probably guarantee that she's just as nervous as you are." That got a smile out of Ellie. "I know that this is your first date — we're not going to count my conception." She laughed when Ellie thwacked her leg. "You've already spent a lot of time with Hunter. This is just like that, only you'll be eating with her instead of serving her food."

"That easy, huh?"

"Why not? You consider Hunter your friend, right?" Ellie nodded. "Stick with that and don't let Blaise get into your head with all this sex stuff."

"I heard that!" Blaise yelled from the bathroom.

"Good!" Jessie jumped up and rummaged through her mom's closet. "Okay, I got it! First of all, these jeans look amazing on you. And this blouse totally brings out the color of your eyes." She held up the outfit up to herself so her mom could visualize it.

The jeans were a dark denim, and Jessie was right, they made Ellie's ass look pretty damn good if she said so herself. The blouse was an army green, long sleeve chiffon blouse that laced up in the front. It was sexy without being over-the-top. In a word, perfect.

"Good job!" Blaise praised from the doorway of the bathroom. Better to stay close to the facilities these days.

Ellie sat up. "I love it," she smiled. The nerves were still there. Now, so was the excitement. For the first time in her life, she was doing something truly for herself. "Now both of you get out of here so I can get ready. I have a date!"

HUNTER WAITED UNTIL Ellie was seated before taking a seat herself. She was having a hard time keeping her eyes from roaming over the vision before her. It only served to make her more nervous.

"Have I told you how beautiful you look?" Hunter said shyly.

Ellie grinned. "A few times. But who's counting? Thank you, again." She deliberately allowed her eyes to take a leisurely inspection of her date. The slight blush that graced Hunter's beautiful face was exactly the effect she was going for. "You don't look so bad yourself."

"Thank you." Hunter glanced around. The ambiance was

pleasant enough. She could only hope the food was up to Ellie's standards. "Um, is this okay?"

Ellie did her own scan. The light was low with a single candle casting a romantic glow across the table. The chocolate walls paired with plush white dining chairs gave the place an enchanting modern look that Ellie found welcoming. It was considerably different than the cheerful décor of her diner.

"I've never been here before, but it's beautiful."

Their conversation was interrupted when their waiter appeared with a smile to take their drink orders. Even with the nerves, both women decided to keep their heads clear by ordering iced tea.

"I read reviews," Hunter said when they were alone again. "The food here is supposed to be pretty good. You have no idea how difficult it is to plan a *dinner* date with someone like you?" she laughed.

"Someone like me?" Ellie watched, amused, as Hunter's eyes — once again — strayed to her cleavage.

Hunter lifted her gaze to Ellie's smirk and raised an eyebrow. *Shit. Caught.* "Um, yeah. A chef."

While it was true that Ellie attended the Culinary Institute of America, she didn't claim herself to be a true chef. Her master's degree was in business, but Ellie had never put much emphasis on her education. What she did at the diner, she was passionate about. It was a part of her, and in her mind, it didn't require any fancy titles.

"You sound like Greyson." She snickered, then explained further at Hunter's bemused look. "Blaise owns the flower shop a couple doors down from the diner."

"Wait, Knight in Bloom?" Ellie nodded. "That's where I got your flowers."

"I know," Ellie smiled. "I recognized Blaise's handiwork."

"She wasn't there. I had to deal with this extremely bubbly blonde."

Both women laughed at the accurate description. "That's Mel," Ellie revealed. "I don't think I've ever met anyone quite like her.

Wait, if Blaise wasn't there, how'd you know orchids were my favorite flower?"

Hunter's eyes widened. "I didn't. I just wanted to get something more unique than roses. I saw those and thought they were perfect."

"They are," Ellie agreed. They held each other's gaze for an instant before Ellie dropped hers. "Um, what were we talking about?"

"Sorry for interrupting," Hunter apologized contritely. "You were talking about me whining about how difficult it was finding a place to take you to eat."

Ellie smirked. "Ah, right. Well, Greyson always complains that he can never surprise Blaise with flowers because going to another shop is like cheating and going to hers, well, that ruins the surprise."

"That must suck when he's in the doghouse," Hunter grinned.

"He tries to stay on Blaise's good side. Especially now with the pregnancy hormones. That's where my red velvet cake usually comes in."

"I feel for the guy." Hunter shook her head with amusement. "It seriously took me two hours to find a suitable place to bring you."

"Hunter, I'm not so snobbish that I don't eat what others put in front of m – " Ellie blushed furiously at the innuendo. Her embarrassment was *not* being lessened by Hunter's sly smile. "Ahem. I eat out . . . Oh, God!" She buried her burning face in her hands. "Damn it. You know what I mean!"

Hunter smothered her laughter and reached for Ellie's hand, bringing it away from her face. "Hey, I got it. You're telling me to stop being such a worrywart, right?"

Ellie shook with silent laughter. "I would never use the word worrywart, but yeah, something like that." She reluctantly pulled her hand from Hunter's when the waiter returned with their drinks and a bread basket.

"Are you ready to order?" the young man asked pleasantly.

They hadn't even opened their menus, yet. "We're going to need another minute, please," Hunter answered amiably. The man nodded, disappearing into the dim glow of the candle light. "I'm sorry," she murmured as she picked up her menu. "I didn't mean to make you uncomfortable."

"You didn't," Ellie sighed. "Hunter? Look at me, please." She waited until Hunter's troubled eyes met hers. "You're going to have to give me a little time to get used to all of this. You've been out most of your life. It's only been a few days for me. I have to get used to not feeling guilty or wrong when we touch. It felt nice holding your hand." She smiled sadly. "I'm not ashamed to be with you, I just need to practice a bit more."

Hunter grinned at that. "Practice does make perfect." She should have known that this would be a delicate situation for Ellie. Perhaps deep down she did. As a trauma surgeon, Hunter was used to jumping into a situation with both feet. She realized now that her methods weren't going to work with Ellie. She scolded herself mentally. *You did promise to go at her speed. Remember that next time.* "How about we order before our waiter has a coronary over there." She gestured with her chin to their server who was bouncing on the balls of his feet.

"He can wait a little longer," Ellie briefly brushed Hunter's hand with her fingertips. "I'm in no rush for this night to be over."

"FAVORITE COLOR?"

The two had decided to walk off their big dinner – which Ellie had deemed excellent – by taking a short drive to a quiet beach. Hunter smiled proudly when Ellie slipped her arm in Hunter's and leaned close as they strolled barefoot in the sand.

Ellie glanced up at the question and her breath caught in her throat. The wind coming off the water whisked Hunter's dark tresses away from her angular face and her blue eyes appeared to glow in the moonlight. *Beautiful.*

"Hmm." She cleared her throat — as well as her mind from thoughts she wasn't ready for yet — and thought about Hunter's question. A slow smile formed. "Sunset and sunrise." She gripped the taller woman's hand tightly as Hunter helped her up onto the rocks near the water.

Hunter found a safe place to sit, far enough away from the spray of the waves that they wouldn't get soaked, and carefully pulled Ellie close. There was a slight chill in the air and Hunter wanted to make sure Ellie stayed warm. Of course, she couldn't fault the bonus of feeling Ellie's body against hers.

"Tell me more," she said close to Ellie's ear.

The shiver that coursed through Ellie's body had nothing to do with the cool breeze. Even so, she nestled closer to Hunter.

"When you look up at the sky at sunset, you get a beautiful display of rich oranges, pinks, reds, and purples against the deep blue of the darkening sky getting ready to slumber. Sunrise, you see that same sky awakening with equally splendid colors until the blue becomes vibrant and bright." When there was no response, Ellie turned to find a slack-jawed Hunter staring at her. "What?"

"Usually when people are asked what their favorite color is, the answer is something simple like; blue, red, green. But that? That was beautiful, Ellie. I didn't know you were so poetic." Hunter smiled when Ellie ducked her head modestly. "Now I wish I had been able to watch the sunset with you."

"There will be other nights," Ellie promised quietly. "Favorite sound?" Ellie asked, keeping with their 'getting to know each other' theme that had begun during the salad portion of their dinner.

"Mmm, this right here," Hunter answered without hesitation. "The sound of the waves crashing against the rocks, then the muted withdrawal as they give themselves back to the ocean. The distant cry of the seagulls in the background." She paused when she felt Ellie laugh.

"And you called me poetic."

Hunter humbly shrugged. "I've just always loved the ocean. When I've had a particularly hard time at the hospital, I'd go home, go out on the balcony, close my eyes, and just let the waves carry my sorrows out to sea. I learned early on that drinking only exacerbated the depression." She fidgeted a little. "Alcohol also made me not care about the other ways I dealt with things," she admitted softly. "I . . ."

"So, you live by the ocean?" Ellie interrupted. She knew Hunter was starting down an unpleasant path and didn't want this moment tainted by bad memories.

"Um." Ellie's abrupt question caught Hunter off-guard. She glanced down at the woman tucked against her side. Innocent eyes peered back, unflinchingly. In that look, she saw what Ellie was trying to do. Hunter smiled appreciatively. "Yeah. When I came back here after school, I immediately started looking for a place on the beach. I got lucky and found a great fixer-upper with its own private beach. My folks chipped in with a down-payment and the rest, as they say, is history." She shifted, bringing her arm around Ellie, but resting it on the rock behind her. "Over the years, I've built it into a place where I think I could be for the rest of my life. I couldn't imagine living anywhere else."

"It sounds divine." Ellie tried imagining the place that held Hunter's heart, wondering how the doctor would choose to decorate. Was she contemporary? Mid-century modern? Eclectic? Or perhaps, a coastal feel was more Hunter's style. *I wonder what the kitchen looks like.*

"I'd love to show you sometime. Maybe I could put the kitchen to use, finally, and cook dinner for you sometime?" Hunter laughed suddenly. "Or, maybe I'll stick to barbecuing. At least then it'd be edible. Though we'd only have steak. Maybe some chicken."

Ellie bumped Hunter with her shoulder. "Barbecue? How butch," she teased. "Tell me about your kitchen."

Hunter turned on the charming, crooked grin. "A chef's dream. I went all out on that damn kitchen."

"Why? You don't cook."

"It was my mom's idea. She swears the kitchen is where a relationship flourishes. If I found a good woman who could cook for me, I'd never be happier. I stopped listening when she started talking about how a table or counter could be used for more than, uh, food."

"Oh, God!" Ellie snorted. She could never imagine having that kind of conversation with her mother.

"Exactly! Anyway, to get her to stop talking, I agreed to whatever she wanted for the kitchen. Can't say I'm sorry. It could probably hold its own in a competition with yours. With a few minor adjustments," she added with a chuckle.

"Blaise always tells me that I'm a kitchen snob." Ellie rolled her eyes. "Like she has any room to talk. She and Greyson bought a house not too far from here. Greyson wanted to surprise her with a greenhouse. But you can't surprise Blaise with a greenhouse. She needs to be involved in *every* aspect of that thing down to which nails are used to hold the thing together."

Laughter filled the air once again and Hunter couldn't remember the last time she had enjoyed herself so much. "I'd like to get to know her better," Hunter suggested hesitantly.

"She'd like that, too. So would I."

"Good," Hunter beamed. "Maybe everyone could come to the beach house? I could barbecue. Though, I may need some help on the side dishes."

Ellie leaned her head back on Hunter's shoulder so she could look up at her. "Everyone?"

"Yeah. My friends have all met you, but they'd like to get to know you better. I thought maybe we could kill two birds with one stone. Have everyone meet?" She held her breath in anticipation. Was she going too fast for Ellie? This was only their first date and here she was throwing dinner parties like they were a couple. Is that what they were? *Shit. Dating is hard!*

"A barbecue get-together?" A small nod from Hunter. "That's one hell of a plan for a second date," Ellie joked.

"Now hold on," Hunter disputed, getting on board with Ellie's playfulness. "Good barbecue get-togethers take time to prepare. Then we have to make sure everyone can make it."

"Hmm, that's true."

"You're not really going to make me wait until whenever all that happens for a second date, are you?"

"Is this you asking me out again?"

The joy she heard in Ellie's voice incited Hunter's confidence.

"No." She moved away from Ellie, feeling the loss immediately. After making sure Ellie was secure, she jumped down off the rocks, stood in front of the diner owner, and took her hands in hers. "This is me asking you for a second date. Will you do me the honor of going out with me again, Ellie?"

Charmed, Ellie smiled. "Yes."

THEY WALKED HAND in hand down the hallway towards Ellie's apartment. Each silently reflected on their night and disappointed that it had to end. When they reached their destination, Hunter plunged her hands into her pockets as Ellie unlocked her door.

Ellie turned back to Hunter. "I would ask you in."

"It's okay," Hunter reassured. "I have to work in the morning anyway, so I should get going."

"I had a wonderful night."

"Me, too. This was . . . beyond anything I could have ever imagined. Thank you." Hunter bowed her head and took a deep breath. "Shouldn't this be easier since I already got that awkward first kiss out of the way?" Damn! Had she ever been this nervous before about *anything*?

Memories of that morning and the shock of feeling Hunter's lips on hers made Ellie chuckle. And blush. "That certainly wasn't something I had expected."

"I know. I'm sorry. About every . . ." The words were blocked by soft fingers pressed gently against her lips. Her heart pounded painfully in her chest as Ellie leaned closer.

"Don't spoil a beautiful night with bad memories," Ellie whispered close to Hunter's ear. She dropped her hand and kissed Hunter softly on the cheek. "Goodnight, Hunter."

Hunter returned the peck, marveling at how smooth Ellie's skin was under her lips. "Goodnight, El." She forced herself to step back instead of stepping forward and taking Ellie in her arms.

"Be careful driving home."

"Will do," Hunter saluted playfully.

"Text me?"

With a toothy grin, Hunter nodded. "Absolutely." When she realized Ellie was going to wait until she was gone, Hunter winked merrily. "If you're going to watch me leave, pretend you don't see me doing a little jump for joy as I skip down the hall." Ellie's laughter rang out, and Hunter knew at that moment that the melody of the ocean had been replaced as her favorite sound. And just so she could hear it again, she jumped up and clicked her heels together.

"You're a goof!"

Hunter would carry the glorious sound of Ellie's delight with her well into her dreams tonight.

Ellie was still smiling when she walked into the apartment — and right into a waiting Jessie.

"Oh! I thought you'd be asleep by now." Here Ellie was coming home from her first date and her daughter was up waiting for her. There was something so bizarre about that. Especially since Jessie stood there with a stern look on her face and her hands on her hips.

"I was waiting up." She studied her mom, noting the ear-to-ear grin and the twinkle in her eye that she had never seen before. Jessie was so happy for her mom but didn't want to give that away quite yet. "You look like you had a good time."

"I did," Ellie answered hesitantly.

Jessie couldn't stand it anymore. Her little charade was causing Ellie anxiety and all Jessie really wanted to do was gossip. She grabbed her mom's hands and literally dragged her across the apartment to the couch. "I want to hear *everything*! Where did she take you? Was she nervous? Ooo! I saw the flowers! Nice touch! Was she goofy? Wait!" Jessie pulled her phone out of the pocket of her pajamas. "I have to call Blaise. She's been waiting."

There was a millisecond of silence in which Ellie still couldn't answer anything because she was still reeling from Jessie's about-face.

"Blaise!" Ellie heard Jessie saying. "Get Piper. Mom is home from her date! I'll put you on speaker phone!"

"You're kidding," Ellie muttered. The emotional high she had been on since saying goodnight to Hunter was slowly turning into dread. All she wanted to do was go to bed and think about the wonderful night she had. Now it seemed as though she would be sharing that with her daughter, Blaise, and Piper. "This couldn't have waited until tomorrow?"

"Uh, no! This was your first date," Blaise's voice came from the phone. "We can't sleep!"

"All of you are insane," Ellie laughed. She kicked her shoes off and got comfortable. "First of all, thank you for not being here when she picked me up. If you had acted like this, Hunter would have probably run away screaming." She snickered again when Blaise mimicked her in a ridiculously childish way. "The date started when she nervously handed me orchids — from Knight in Bloom — when I opened the door . . ."

Girls' night had started early this weekend.

Chapter Twenty

"God, I'm exhausted." Ellie fumbled with the keys, trying to unlock the diner's back door. She hadn't been this tired since Jessie was a newborn. Last night was pretty much exactly like those times — only with two newborns. Jessie and Blaise — and Piper by default even though she didn't say much — kept her up way too late wanting every last detail of her date with Hunter. If she had the audacity to drift off, Jessie was there to nudge her awake. Or, Blaise's voice would pierce her pending dreams through the speaker. Then, when she finally *did* get to bed all she could do was think of the beautiful doctor. Maybe it was a bit obsessive, but you only get one first *real* date.

"Ellie?"

"Shit!" Her keys fell from her hand as she whirled around. She squinted her eyes in the low light, blowing out a relieved breath when she made out the shadowy figure. "You scared the hell out of me! What are you doing hiding in the shadows?"

"Sorry," Hunter apologized sheepishly. "I didn't mean to frighten you. I, uh, wasn't hiding, I was leaning against the wall." She stooped to pick up Ellie's keys.

Ellie reclined against the still locked door, taking in all that was

Dr. Hunter Vale. After last night, she felt her inhibitions begin to loosen considerably. She still couldn't bring herself to do anything about the feelings she was having about Hunter, but the thoughts were a good start. Running helped with the physical part. At the moment, she was thinking how incredibly sexy Hunter looked in her faded jeans and black leather jacket over a dark gray V-neck T-shirt.

"I suppose I could forgive you for taking ten years off my life," she teased.

"Ah, just means you've caught up to me, now," Hunter bantered back, thankful that Ellie wasn't upset with her.

"You're here awfully early for breakfast. If you haven't noticed, the diner isn't open yet." She took the keys from Hunter, letting her touch linger for a moment.

"Actually, I'm here to tell you I won't be in for breakfast," Hunter said, realizing at that moment how ridiculous that sounded. Obviously, Ellie was thinking the same way if the wry grin and raised eyebrow were a sign.

"You came here to tell me you wouldn't be here?" Hunter nodded. "Did you lose my number?" Ellie honestly didn't mind the visit. In fact, she found it extremely sweet. But she couldn't resist teasing the doctor. The meek blush was just too irresistible.

"No, I . . ." The cheeky grin Ellie gave her finally clued Hunter into the fact that she was being baited. "Cute." *More than cute.*

"Thanks," Ellie winked. "Another administration meeting?"

"Nah, there's a Septal Myotomy going on this morning that I wanted to watch." Hunter loved the way Ellie's nose crinkled when she was curious. "It's an operation performed on the heart to decrease the congealing of the heart muscles — and your eyes are glazing over." She laughed. "Once upon a time, before I decided on trauma, I considered cardiovascular and neurology. Couldn't decide on the heart or the brain, and with everything going on in my life at the time, I chose the adrenalin rush."

"Something you regret now?" Ellie asked carefully.

"Not regret," Hunter answered sincerely. "Maybe I'm just ready for something a little more stable. Once I get to the hospital, my day becomes unpredictable. One of the reasons I'm here now. I didn't know if I would be able to see you today if I didn't come here this morning." She shrugged.

"Then I'm glad you're here. Do you have time for me to whip you up something to eat? Or at least make some coffee?"

"Unfortunately, I don't. I should have been on my way five minutes ago," Hunter grinned. "Maybe, um, if my day doesn't get too crazy and I get out of there at a decent time, we could have dinner?" she asked hopefully.

Ellie seriously considered it. Now she knew the turmoil Blaise went through when she gave up her time with Greyson for girls' night. She shook her head sadly. "I'm sorry, I can't tonight. I already have plans."

"Oh. Okay."

"It's girls' night," Ellie explained to a dejected Hunter. "A tradition every Sunday night for me, Jessie, Blaise, and now Blaise's daughter, Piper."

"Blaise has a daughter?"

"Long story. One I'll tell you sometime."

"Sometime" means more time spent with this beautiful woman. I'll take it! Hunter spread her arms wide and gave Ellie her best smile. "I'm a girl."

No, you're definitely a woman. "I can see that. But we have rules, so I can't invite you."

"Rules?"

"Mmhmm. No one we're dating is allowed. We can't talk about you if you're there." She laughed when Hunter's eyes grew comically wide. "I've never had to adhere to that rule, until now. I'm thinking of revoking it."

"So, you're the president of this little club?" Hunter smirked. Even leaving her house early, she was so going to be late getting to the hospital. But she couldn't bring herself to leave. *Five more minutes. It'll be fine. If I miss the first cut, that's okay.* It was a strange concept for her to comprehend. Hunter Vale *never* missed the first cut. Oddly enough, she didn't mind if she missed it this time.

"Ha! No, I'd never get away with inviting you since Blaise has had to pretend to 'go get some air' too many times. She would meet

Greyson and the girls and I would bet on where the grass stains would be."

Hunter roared with laughter. "That's awesome!" She wiped tears from her eyes. "So, what does Greyson do while Blaise is at girls' night? Besides sneaking over and getting down and dirty with her." Even when she snorted, Ellie was too damned cute!

"He and Cade get together to play poker with some friends mostly. Why? Would you like me to score you an invite?"

"Well, since I can't crash girls' night, perhaps I can learn a few things about you at these poker nights." She wiggled her eyebrows.

Ellie's smile faltered slightly. "Hmm. Since Cade has been asking me out for almost a year now, he may be more interested in knowing about the person I actually said yes to." The crestfallen look on Hunter's face broke Ellie's heart, especially after seeing her so lighthearted just seconds before. She stepped closer. "I'm not interested in him, Hunter."

"He's the security guy, right?" Hunter's heart constricted when Ellie nodded. "So, he could find out things about me."

"He wouldn't do that."

Hunter scoffed. "He wants you. You don't think he would do whatever he can to get you?" *Just like Susan is doing.*

"Hunter, he was supportive when I told him. Yes, he asked me if I wanted him to do a background check," she disclosed. "But I refused. Whatever there is to learn about you, I want to learn from *you*. Cade understands that. He's not Susan." Ellie was convinced that was what Hunter was thinking.

Hunter threw her arms up, frustrated, and paced away. "If you're wrong and he does?" She faced Ellie, sadness darkening her features. "I don't want to be an embarrassment to you."

Ellie's eyebrows shot up. "Is that what you think?" She closed the distance between them and took Hunter's hands in hers. "You could never embarrass me."

"I slept with married women, Ellie!" She tried to pull away, but the younger woman was much stronger than she looked.

"We've talked about this. What you've done in the past is in the past. And, it was a product of what happened to . . ."

"No!" Hunter successfully got her hands free and balled her fists in fury. She was angry with herself for getting Ellie into a situation that could disrupt her nice, hassle-free life. "Susan is not an excuse!"

"Stop." She stood in front of Hunter once again. It was inevitable that Hunter would have doubts. Ellie had expected it. She could kick herself for mentioning Cade's interest in her. She should have known that it would be a kind of trigger for Hunter's insecurities. Wasn't that psychology 101? A damn class she'd actually taken in college. "I'm not making excuses for you, Hunter. You've made mistakes, we all have. Can I ask you something?"

The fearful nod from Hunter was almost imperceptible.

"Did you seek any of those women out? Did you ever go out for the sole purpose of finding a married woman to be with?"

"No," Hunter answered timidly.

"No. You were delivered to them. Used by them. Manipulated at a young age to think this is what you should do. Blackmailed when you were older to keep you 'in line'. Conditioned to think this was who you were." Ellie touched Hunter's cheek gently. "If anyone knows about conditioning, it's me. You made mistakes, but you're fixing them now. I'm not embarrassed by who you were. I'm proud of who you're becoming."

She leaned into Ellie's touch. Never had a simple caress felt so incredible. So safe. "What if she outs you?" she whispered.

Ellie chuckled softly. "I seem to be doing a good job of that all by myself. I may flounder at times. I may get scared. We both will. Hell, I'm scared now. But, I have nothing to hide anymore."

"And, your parents? What if they find out?"

Ellie allowed Hunter to take her hand, smiling when Hunter placed a small kiss on her palm. "My parents have nothing left to threaten me with. All who are important to me know who I am now. Susan can't hurt me. And, I'll be damned if I let her hurt you again."

"I don't know if I deserve you, Ellie Montgomery."

Not knowing quite how to respond to that, she pushed Hunter away lightly. "Go to work, Dr. Vale. You're going to be late."

"Already am," Hunter grinned. "Can I call you later?"

"Mmhmm."

She felt much lighter than she did mere moments ago. The meeting hadn't gone quite how she expected, but Ellie's compassion did wonders for her fragile spirit. "Have a good day. Tell Big Al I said hi."

Ellie rolled her eyes playfully. "I will."

"G'wan." Hunter gestured towards the diner. "I'll wait until you're safely inside."

"Yes, dear." She winked at a slightly flustered Hunter and opened the door. She was also getting a late start, but it was worth it.

"El?" Hunter waited until Ellie glanced back. "Am I going overboard? I have no clue how to do this, so I'm just following my heart."

"When given the choice, always follow your heart."

The parting smile that Ellie gave Hunter had her grinning from ear to ear. "It's going to be a good day."

MO SHOVED THROUGH the doors of the hospital cafeteria and spotted her best friend sitting alone at one of the back tables with a full plate of untouched food in front of her. Whatever was going through her mind must be more interesting than cafeteria food. *Has to be the surgery we witnessed this morning.* "Yo, Hunt! That surgery was frickin' gnarly. I can't believe you missed the first carve." Mo waved a hand in front of Hunter's face. She'd never seen such a goofy smile. Especially on the usually stoic woman. Somehow, Mo didn't think it had anything to do with the surgery. "Hello?"

"Huh? Oh, hey. Sorry, what's up?"

"What's up?" Mo repeated mockingly. "Did you not hear a word I said?"

Hunter frowned at Mo's tone. "No. I was thinking of . . ."

"Let me guess," Mo interrupted. "Ellie?"

"Do you have a problem, Mo?"

"There was a time when surgery beat everything. You would never have missed that first cut before. I guess I'm just wondering how long this is going to go on."

Hunter sat back in her chair and crossed her arms. "What happened to you being encouraging? I thought this is what you wanted for me. A normal relationship."

"I don't think I said the word relationship." Mo scooted her chair closer to the table and leaned in. "Hunt, you're free of that shit with Susan. You're hot, you're a surgeon, you can have any woman you want."

"I want Ellie," Hunter said dryly. She loved Mo. They'd been friends forever. But the shit she was spewing right now pissed the doctor off. Mo was married and happy with one woman. Why couldn't Hunter have the same thing?

"Why settle for one? The world is your oyster, Hunt! You now have free range to get down and dirty with some chick that's down and dirty."

"What is wrong with you? You've seen how I am with Ellie. I *finally* got to go out with her and now you're pushing me to move on."

"I didn't say you couldn't sleep with her. I mean, she's hot. Hit it. But you don't need to get tied down the first time out of the gate."

Hunter shook her head. "I don't even know you right now. But, what I do know is that I'm done talking to you."

Mo angrily pushed away from the table. "I'm the one who has stood beside you all these years. You didn't listen to me back then when I said lose Susan's number. If you don't listen to me now and you miss out on multiple experiences, don't come crying to me!"

Hunter watched, stunned, as Mo stormed off. "What the hell just happened?"

"Don't let her get to you." Patty squeezed Hunter's shoulder as she walked up from behind and slid into the seat Mo had just vacated. "She's just going through some kind of mid-life crisis. She thinks you should be out there sowing your oats." She smiled unhappily. "You thinking of getting serious with Ellie right off is messing with her chance to live vicariously through you."

Hunter studied a normally happy Patty's expression and she didn't like what she saw. Dark circles under her eyes, tiny frown lines, normally bright brown irises were currently dull. If Mo was the cause of Patty's unhappiness, Hunter was going to be even more pissed. "What's going on, Patty? Are you two having problems?"

Patty waved away the question. "It'll pass."

"Do you want me to kick her ass?"

Patty gave her a little laugh. "She's your best friend, Hunter."

"So are you," Hunter said sincerely. She leaned over and took Patty's hand. "She loves you. You know that, right?"

"I know. She just gets these bees in her bonnet every once in a while, and I think she gets a little sad that she didn't do more 'exploring' before we got together." Patty shrugged. "Life has its ups and downs. It just happens to be a down at the moment."

"She's never said anything to me." In fact, Hunter was shocked. Mo may have been scared of Patty's feisty side, but she always spoke of the older woman with nothing but love and respect. There was no way Mo would be unfaithful to Patty. Right?

"No, she wouldn't. Anyway, enough about that. I want to hear about your date. Don't you let Mo's attitude dampen what you feel for this young woman."

"OKAY, NOW THAT we're alone — somewhat — you can tell me the truth."

Blaise struggled to get her pregnant self up on the bar stool. Girls' night started two hours ago, and now the teen girls were watching TV and giggling while she and Ellie made snacks. Okay, Ellie was making snacks while Blaise watched. She would have loved to help Ellie, but being on her feet for more than five minutes was akin to running a marathon these days. She also knew that while she could hold her own in the kitchen, she would probably just be in Ellie's way. She smiled her thanks when Ellie came around the counter and helped her scoot her butt onto the stool.

"Either you're going to need to have this baby soon, or I'm going to need to build up my muscles." She jumped back as Blaise took a half-hearted kick at her.

"I'm keeping a list, you know. Everything that you've done and said to me throughout this pregnancy when I've been too big to retaliate, I'm keeping them all right up here." She tapped her temple with her index finger.

"Eh, you'll forget as soon as you give birth. New mom memory loss and all," Ellie teased.

"You're terrible! Wait, what were we talking about?"

Ellie laughed at her best friend. She loved Blaise dearly and *loved* teasing her. The pregnancy brain gave Ellie a ton of material, even if it was a little mean. Besides, Blaise gave as good as she got.

"You were saying something about the truth. Which makes no sense, so I thought it was just your craziness talking."

"Craziness, check." Blaise tapped her head again. "It makes perfect sense. You can now tell me what really happened on your date with Dr. Hot Stuff."

"Dr. Hot Stuff," Ellie sniggered. "You kept me up for hours last night, Blaise. You *have* all the details. Even down to the color of Hunter's socks."

"I don't mean the details that are teenaged daughter friendly. I want the good stuff. Like the color of her undies. And if she wears boxers or briefs."

Ellie stopped plating the spinach and artichoke phyllo bites and blinked at Blaise. "Boxers or briefs," she mumbled. "It was our first date."

"No offense, sweetie, but like you said, your last first date got you pregnant," Blaise grinned knowing she had gotten Ellie back for at least one of the things on the list.

"Ha, ha. That was different."

"Come on. Not even a kiss?"

The blonde shook her head. "You have no idea what it took for me to walk arm in arm with her on the beach, or lean close to her as we sat on the rocks. It's not easy to let go of years of fear and denial. A kiss might have sent me into a panic attack. I just hope she didn't notice my anxiety."

"I'm sorry, El. I guess I haven't thought about how difficult this would be for you."

"That's the thing. Being with Hunter wasn't difficult. It was wonderful. The problem is my head keeps getting in the way. Did I want to kiss Hunter last night? Absolutely. Am I ready? I don't know."

"I can understand that." Blaise grinned wickedly. "So, I guess that means I have enough time to have this baby before you start dragging me to the lesbian bars?"

It was like mental whiplash sometimes when talking to Blaise. "Why am I going to lesbian bars?"

"*We*," Blaise corrected. "Isn't that where you go to pick up women?"

Once again, Ellie's hand froze in mid-task. "Why would I go pick up women when I'm seeing Hunter?"

"You just came out, El. Don't you want to know what your options are?" Blaise had been a serial dater before meeting her husband. By the time Greyson came around, Blaise was very sure about what she wanted in a partner. As beautiful — and apparently romantic — as Hunter is, Blaise would have thought Ellie would want to play the field a bit before settling down.

Ellie finished getting the goodies ready, barely resisting throwing a buffalo chicken slider at Blaise's head. "Blaise, I'm going to explain this one time, so I want you to really listen to me, okay?"

Blaise nodded cautiously. She knew that tone. Ellie was annoyed, and when Ellie was annoyed, she got scary.

"Every day I experience many people. All different kinds. Big, small, beautiful, ordinary, successful, unlucky, mean, sweet. Thousands of people have come into my diner over the years since I opened. Do you know what I *hadn't* experienced?" Ellie waited until

Blaise shook her head. "Someone who made my heart and body wake up from its dormant state. Until Hunter walked in." She paused to let that sink in for a minute. "So, you see? I don't need to go out to bars to encounter more people to know what I want. I know that may be difficult to understand because it is for me, too. But, unless Hunter decides that she wants to see others, dating multiple people is just not for me."

"Wow."

"Get it now?"

"Yeah. I do. As much as Greyson irritated me when I first met him, I felt that, too."

"Hello!" Jessie called from the living room. "We're starving! You guys have been in there *forever!*"

Ellie rolled her eyes. "Kids are so demanding," she said loud enough for Jessie to hear.

Blaise laughed and rubbed her belly. "And, here I am having another one."

"You love it."

"You bet I do." She glanced over at Piper. "I want to be able to do it right this time."

"That wasn't your fault, Blaise. Piper knows that."

"Fooood!" Jessie and Piper sang out together, cutting off any response Blaise may have had.

Ellie picked up the tray of food. "Can you get down by yourself?"

"*Can you get down by yourself,*" Blaise mocked. "Yes, I can get . . ." she looked down at the floor which seemed to have gotten further away in the last ten seconds. "Maybe. Go!" she shooed Ellie. "I got this."

Ellie shrugged her shoulders and started making her way towards the living room. "You okay back there?" she called over her shoulder.

"Yes." Blaise finally touched her feet to the floor. *It's all downhill from here. Oh, shit!* "Um, no. I will pay to have that cleaned."

Her hands still full of a tray of food, Ellie turned back. "What?" Her eyes followed Blaise's. "Oh, shit! Okay. Stay calm." She hurriedly put the tray on the counter, careful not to slip in the puddle left by Blaise's water breaking. She took a very nervous Blaise's hands in hers. "Everything is fine. We're strong, intelligent women. We've both done this before."

"Seventeen years ago when we were kids ourselves!" Blaise whined.

Both women stood there for what seemed like an eternity. Blaise wondered if she was truly ready for this. Ellie wondered where the hell she put her keys.

"I'll get mum a change of clothes and call Greyson," Piper said decisively. "Jessie, you make sure *your* mum is ready, and get the keys because you're driving. With the state they're in, who knows where we would end up."

Ellie shook herself out of her moderate state of shock. Who knew Piper would be the one to take charge? She's always so quiet and unassuming. "Okay, we have strong, intelligent teenagers."

"Oh, Lord!" Blaise exclaimed. "Don't let them hear you say that. They'll never let us live this down."

"HUNTER."

Hunter set her phone aside, rising to meet her guests. She kissed Rebecca on the cheek and gave Cass a hug.

"Thanks for coming."

Cass pulled out Rebecca's chair for her, kissing her lovingly on the top of the head after she was settled.

"We were surprised you asked us to meet you for dinner. We thought you'd be out with Ellie," Cass grinned slyly.

"I'd love to be with Ellie right now." Hunter winced when she thought about how that sounded. "No offense."

"None was taken," Rebecca smiled sweetly. "Is everything okay?"

They paused when the waiter appeared and Hunter proceeded to order for the table. The trio had been here enough times before that Hunter knew what her companions wanted.

"Everything is fine," she said once they were left alone again. "Ellie has a standing date on Sundays with her daughter."

Cass's surprise was obvious. "Hang on, Ellie has a daughter?" She looked to Hunter, then to Rebecca who looked apologetic.

"I found out on Monday. I meant to tell you, but then we got a bit distracted." She winked at Cass. "I forgot pretty much everything after that. Sorry, baby."

Eyebrows furrowed for a millisecond before Cass's face split into a cheesy, love-struck grin. "Oh yeah. You're definitely forgiven." She leaned over and gave Rebecca a quick kiss. "So, wait. Ellie's family, right?" Hunter nodded. "But, she has . . . oh, shit. She wasn't?"

"No, no. That's a longer story. Cliff note version; she has very disapproving parents and she did things she thought was right at the time." Hunter shook her head with a smile when she thought of Ellie's gutsy teen daughter. She hoped the two of them would be able to find some common ground and get to know each other. "Can I ask you two something?"

"Bondage is fantastic when done with someone who knows what they're doing," Cass supplied with a smirk, earning a playful smack from her lover.

"Cassidy!" Rebecca scolded her girlfriend with a feigned scowl. Inside she felt the heat begin to rise. The one she always experienced when even the mere thought of being with Cassidy crossed her mind. "What's your question, Hunter?"

"Do you think I'm crazy for not wanting to date multiple women?" Her friends stared at her, bemused. "Mo seems to think I should be out there being a player," she explained. "That's not what I want. In fact, I'm pretty sure I've found what I want in Ellie. I know it hasn't been that long."

Rebecca held up her hand. "Hunter, you do realize who you're talking to, right?"

"Yeah, Hunt." Cass reached for Rebecca's hand. "I'm pretty sure I fell in love with Rebecca the first time I saw her face. And, I didn't even know her name. Just follow your heart. I promise it'll be worth it."

'When given the choice, always follow your heart.' This was the second time she had gotten that advice today. It had to be a sign, right? A glance at the two lovebirds gave her even more incentive to follow her heart. They were a great couple. She knew that the way Cass and Rebecca met was somewhat unconventional, but the love they had for each other ran deep. Something she *thought* she knew about Mo and Patty.

"Have the two of you noticed Mo acting strange?" Hunter caught the look that Rebecca gave Cass. "What?"

"Tell her, baby," Cass encouraged when Rebecca hesitated.

She sighed heavily. Rebecca took the privacy of the patrons of her club very seriously. It's what kept her successful. "Normally I would not disclose this information. But, it's Mo." She looked to Cass once more, hating the fact that she had to be the bearer of this news. "I received an inquiry for the club. It was from Mo."

"What? How?" Hunter was stunned. "Rebecca, I've never told Mo about your club. I swear!"

"I believe you. The invitation did not come from you." She held up her hand. "Don't ask me who. I will not tell you that."

Hunter nodded yieldingly. "Can you tell me if the inquiry was for a couple?"

"No, but that doesn't mean anything," Rebecca answered. It wasn't quite a lie, but she knew full well eighty percent of the time she received single inquiries from someone in a relationship meant something shady.

"Of course," Hunter scoffed. "I don't see Patty going for that kind of stuff."

"Hey! There's nothing wrong with what Rebecca and I do," Cass said quietly, but heatedly.

"No, I — I didn't mean." Hunter blew out a breath. "I have no problem with the lifestyle you choose. In fact, I find it intriguing. But I honestly don't think Patty would be drawn to it. And, if Mo is doing this to cheat on her wife, I'm going to kick her ass."

"I'll be in line behind you," Rebecca vowed. "I vet my clients as best I can, and try to bring couples together as opposed to tearing them apart. I don't like my club being used like that."

Before she could respond, Hunter's phone sounded. She apologized to her friends for the interruption before answering. "Dr. Vale." She dropped her head. "Where is Dr. Mackenzie? Right. How long? Fine, I can do that. I'll be there as soon as I can." Hunter ended the call and took out her wallet.

"We got this," Cass said, placing her hand over Hunter's. "You didn't even get to eat."

Rebecca spied the food coming their way. *Perfect timing.* "You can get the next one." She smiled charmingly at the waiter. "Could we get a box, please. One of us has to go and save some lives."

"I can just get something out of the vending machine," Hunter insisted.

"Hmm. I wonder what Ellie would think of that." Rebecca smirked and Cass snickered when Hunter's eyes got wide.

"There's no need to threaten me. I'll take a doggy bag."

"Oh, Hunt. You're a goner," Cass laughed, making a whipping sound.

"Baby, don't tease Hunter about being whipped unless you want the real thing." She laughed out loud when Cass made the whipping sound again with a brazen grin.

"On that note," Hunter laughed. "I'll call you later."

"Much later!" Cass wiggled her eyebrows. "Like tomorrow."

Chapter Twenty-One

Ellie stopped her pacing when she heard a familiar voice confidently call out medical words that Ellie didn't understand. Her eyes sought out the source until they landed on Hunter. She was wearing one of those yellow, disposable gowns, tinted with blood. Ellie was sympathetic enough to hope the patient would be all right, but she was also mesmerized enough by the pure authority in Hunter to be — dare she say — aroused.

"SHE'S STABLE, LET'S get her up to the OR." A warm feeling washed over Hunter and she lifted her head in time to see Ellie watching her. It was almost comical how the woman could look so damned adorable and sexy at the same time. She had on dark gray sweats and matching hoodie with running shoes. Hunter didn't think she had ever seen anything quite as cute. *I look like a bum when I*

wear stuff like that. Why does she still look like a goddess? "Go on, I'll be right up." Hunter removed her blood-stained gown and gloves, tossed them in the biohazardous bin, and made her way to Ellie, who was now flanked by Jessie and another young woman that looked like a younger version of Blaise.

"Hi." Ellie tucked a strand of hair behind her ear, feeling extremely adolescent at the moment. And underdressed.

"Hey. Is everything okay?"

"Hmm?" While her brain was focused on Hunter, Ellie had forgotten she was wandering around the ER. "Oh! Yes. Blaise is in labor. They took her up to get settled, so we decided to wait for Greyson down here."

Hunter beamed. "That's exciting." She turned to the girls. "It's nice to see you again, Jessie. And you must be Piper." The brunette teen nodded shyly. "It's nice to meet you. I'd shake your hand, but." She held up her hands as if they were covered with the blood that had contaminated her gloves.

"No problem. It's nice to meet you, too. I've heard a lot about you."

Great. The girl never talks, and when she does, she tattles on me, Ellie thought with a silent moan.

"All good, I hope," Hunter grinned. "I, uh, have to get up to surgery. But, I'll come back down to see how everything's going if that's okay."

"Absolutely. Only if you're not exhausted. I thought you'd be gone by now."

"I was. I was out to dinner with Rebecca and Cass when I got called in. Should only be for a couple of hours."

"Good," she smiled warmly. "Now, go do what you do best. I'm sure we'll be here for a while." *Ah, yes. There's that crooked grin.*

Hunter took a chance and reached out to touch Ellie lightly on the arm, forgetting all about needing to wash her hands. "See you, soon. Congrats on the brother or sister," she told Piper. With a wink, she disappeared into the elevator that had just opened.

"She's hot."

Mother and daughter slowly turned their heads to stare at Piper.

"What?" Piper walked away, hiding a small smile.

HUNTER PEEKED INTO the waiting room of the Labor and Delivery Unit hoping to find Ellie. No Ellie, but she did see Jessie. She considered her options. Go in and face Ellie's mini-me, or chicken out and text Ellie.

"Hunter?"

Shit. "Hey, Jessie. I, um, was just looking for your mom."

"She's in with Blaise at the moment. They kicked Greyson out." An exhausted, yet handsome, man stopped pacing for a moment to look over at them. His brown hair was disheveled and his five o'clock shadow looked a bit overgrown. His gray eyes were a combination of excitement and weariness. It was a look Hunter had seen in many fathers-to-be.

"I was just trying to help," he muttered.

Hunter chuckled. "We get that all the time here. When the women are in pain, they tend to lash out at the ones who did it to them. Don't take it personally." She walked up to Greyson and held out her hand. "I'm Hunter."

"Greyson. Nice to meet you." He shook her hand, taking note of the firm grip. The woman was even more beautiful up close, even if she still looked a bit nervous. "You work here?"

"Hunter is a trauma surgeon," Jessie answered. "Have you delivered babies before?" she asked Hunter.

Hunter could have sworn she heard a touch of pride in Jessie's voice. Of course, it was most likely wishful thinking, but it made her feel good nonetheless. "Yep. A few of them. It's nice to be able to bring a life into this world. Trauma doesn't allow that too often."

"Yo, Grey! I got here as soon as I could, brother."

Hunter eyed the tall man who gave Greyson a bro-hug. *This*

must be Cade. She tried not to dislike the man merely because he asked Ellie out. Constantly. Honestly, it wasn't easy to put on a friendly smile. But Hunter did exactly that as Greyson introduced the two.

"So, you're Hunter Vale, hmm?"

Cade squeezed her hand a little too tightly.

"*Dr.* Hunter Vale," Hunter corrected with a smirk. "Careful, I'm a surgeon," *and a lesbian,* "I'm going to need my hand back in working condition."

Cade winced and had the decency to apologize. "So, you've been a doctor for how long?"

"Long enough."

"Have you always lived in California?"

"Are you writing a book?"

"You'll have to excuse Cade." Greyson stepped in between the two, giving Cade a slight shove with his elbow. "He's always on the job. Plus, we care for Ellie and just want to make sure she doesn't get hurt."

Hunter resisted the urge to throw her arms up in frustration. Did she *look* like a player? Did she *look* like someone who was out to hurt a sweet woman? "Am I going to have to sign some kind of agreement in order to date Ellie?"

"No, you're not."

Cade, Greyson, Jessie, and Hunter all cringed at an extremely miffed Ellie standing at the door. Her arms were crossed and she the look she had was enough to make the two big special ops guys take a step back.

"I thought I made it clear that you two were *not* allowed to interrogate Hunter." Ellie spent a good part of last week's girls' night ordering Blaise to put a muzzle on Greyson and Cade. She didn't want Hunter to have to defend her intentions. She wanted Hunter to be accepted just as she accepted Greyson.

"It wasn't an interrogation, sugar," Cade began.

"Don't you sugar me. And, don't you try to tell me you were just trying to get to know Hunter." She relaxed her posture and stood next to Hunter in a show of solidarity. "I know everyone is looking out for me, but I'm fine. I'm a grown woman and experienced or not, I'm not naïve. Let me and Hunter figure this out ourselves. *Without* interference from anyone in this room." She glanced at her daughter who lowered her eyes (after rolling them, of course). "Greyson, you're up. Blaise promises to be nice this time." She grinned. "How long that lasts is anyone's guess."

Greyson sprinted out of the room with Cade hot on his heels.

"I guess I'll go keep Piper company," Jessie said, sensing she should give her mom and Hunter a bit of privacy. "Are we still going to visit Dani at some point?"

"Yes. Once we have a better idea of when Blaise is going to pop that baby out, we'll go."

Jessie nodded and gave Hunter a slight bump and smile on her way out.

"I think I might be growing on her," Hunter grinned happily.

"Well, you are quite charming," Ellie winked. She gestured to one of the plastic chairs that was bolted to the wall. "I'm sorry about all of that."

Hunter settled in next to Ellie and gave in to the urge to touch her. She laid her hand on Ellie's forearm. "Never apologize for being cared for. It's a sign of the kind of person you are." She squeezed lightly. "Even Big Al gave me a warning. Kinda makes me wonder if I look that bad," she chuckled.

Ellie's eyebrows shot up. "Big Al?" Hunter smiled and nodded. "Wow. And, to answer your question, it's not you. This is as new to everyone in my life as it is to me. I'm not sure they know how to handle it." Ellie watched as Hunter mulled that over. A slight crinkle formed between dark, arched eyebrows. Something Ellie found adorable. "I was warned as well," she revealed.

"Huh?" The crease became deeper.

"Rebecca came to see me. I'm sure Cass, Patty, and Mo are just waiting for their moments."

Hunter would have been worried by Ellie's words if she hadn't looked amused by the prospect. "Rebecca never told me you two spoke. I don't know about Mo and Cass, but you may get a question or two from Patty. I guess they're not used to this with me, either. It's good to know people have our backs, right?"

"Absolutely. It may get a little annoying, but I know their hearts are in the right place."

Hunter nodded agreeably. The realization that Ellie was out here talking to her instead of in the room with her best friend meant a lot to the doctor. "How is Blaise doing?"

"Good." Ellie hesitated, wondering how Blaise would react to what she was about to tell Hunter. Hopefully, she would understand. "She's scared."

"That's natural."

Ellie glanced at Hunter. "Perhaps. But, Blaise's reasons go deeper than just the pain of giving birth. When she had Piper, they told Blaise her baby was stillborn. She didn't find out that Piper was alive until earlier this year."

"Oh shit! Who the hell would do that to someone? Especially a young girl who was most likely already scared shitless about having a baby."

"Her grandfather. The bastard paid off the doctors to lie to Blaise so he could steal her child."

Hunter sat back with a thud. "Unbelievable." The doctors themselves were despicable. But for a grandfather to do that to his own family? That's heinous. "I feel like there's more to this story."

"Yes, there is. But right now, I'm worried about Blaise. She won't let Piper out of her sight. And, I'm afraid she'll go ballistic if some stranger takes her baby out of the room."

"I don't blame her." She took Ellie's hand in hers. "Um, if you think it would be okay, I could be in there the whole time. As soon as that baby is born, I would be its shadow. I promise, you and Blaise, that I won't let anyone do anything that isn't necessary to that baby."

"You've had such a long day, I can't ask you to do that."

"You're not. I'm volunteering. I'm fine. I'd like to be here for you and Blaise if I could."

The feel of Ellie's soft lips on hers made Hunter's heart slam against her ribs. It was fleeting, but Hunter felt it deep in her soul.

"Thank you," Ellie said softly. She caressed Hunter's cheek before she stood up and started off to Blaise's room. When she didn't hear Hunter behind her, she turned around. The stunned look on Hunter's face made her smile. "Are you coming?"

"Huh? Oh, um," Hunter touched her lips with her fingertips and smiled. "Yeah."

ELLIE SAT UP in her chair, taking Blaise's hand as her eyes fluttered open.

"Where is he?"

"He's fine, sweetie. They're getting him all set to come see you."

"I want him here!" Blaise's gaze turned wild as she searched the room. Whether she was looking for the baby or Piper, Ellie wasn't certain.

"Blaise, Greyson is with him. And, if there's somewhere Greyson can't go, Hunter is there. He won't be alone."

"I can't lose him, Ellie."

"You won't, honey. He's safe. I promise."

Blaise relaxed back onto the bed when Piper came over to hold her other hand. The teen didn't speak, but her presence spoke volumes to Blaise.

"You trust Hunter?" Blaise asked Ellie.

"Yes." There was no hesitation to Ellie's answer. She couldn't say why she knew deep down it was true, but her instincts have always served her well.

"Obviously, you're a great judge of character," Blaise smirked and Ellie shook her head with a laugh. "So, I will trust her, too." She squeezed Ellie's hand. "You were right."

"I usually am," Ellie smiled smugly. "You're going to have to a little more specific."

Blaise laughed for the first time since getting to the hospital. Her fear took away from the joy of giving birth and she would never forgive her grandfather for the damage he caused. But she wasn't going to let him ruin everything. Not for her and not for Greyson and Piper. "You knew it was a boy."

Ellie smiled broadly. "Are you happy?"

Blaise looked up at Piper, her eyes shining with unshed tears. "Very."

Ellie gave the two a moment to revel in the mother/daughter moment. "Have you thought of a name?"

"Yes. I named Piper after my mum. Greyson and I thought it only fitting to name our son after my father. Ezra Asher Steele. Asher is Greyson's middle name."

"It's beautiful, sweetie."

"So is he." Greyson's proud voice filled the room along with the coo of a newborn. A coo that abruptly turned into a sharp cry. "I think someone is hungry."

"He gets that from mum," Piper teased with a watery laugh. She stroked her brother's soft head lightly as Greyson handed him over to Blaise. "I wonder if your milk will taste like red velvet."

The room erupted in laughter and Blaise settled in to feed Ezra. Ellie quietly left the family to their privacy, taking a silent Hunter's hand as she passed by.

"Hunter," Blaise called out before the door was shut.

Hunter poked her head back in. The scene she was met with was a beautiful one. Greyson and Piper surrounded Blaise, with Ezra feeding happily. "Yes?"

"Thank you." Blaise smiled sincerely at the doctor, receiving one just as sincere back.

"You're welcome." Hunter closed the door and turned to Ellie. "Gorgeous family."

"They are. I'm so happy for them."

"Does it make you want another one? Speaking of, where is Jessie?"

Ellie laughed. "Um, no. My one and only was visiting with Dani and Claire earlier then got sleepy waiting for Blaise to have the baby. She texted me that Cade was dropping her off at home so she could sleep. She'll be back before heading off to school." She then became aware that she had no idea if Hunter wanted children. What if she did? Would that be a deal breaker? "Have you thought about having kids?"

She trusts Cade with her daughter. He can't be all that bad. Hunter coughed uncomfortably. "Nah. I, uh, it's never been something I've thought of," she said apologetically.

"That's nothing to be sorry about. Not everyone wants kids and that's fine," Ellie reassured her.

"But, you have a daughter."

"Yes, does that bother you?"

"No, of course not!"

"Then what's the problem?"

"I don't want you to think that I have an issue with kids, especially Jessie."

"Hunter." She steered them towards the waiting room. Luckily it was relatively empty at this time of the night. Ellie nudged Hunter into a chair. "If you tell Jessie what I'm about to tell you, I'll deny it. But if I hadn't gotten pregnant that one fateful night, I don't think I'd want children." She watched as Hunter's eyebrows shot up. "Don't get me wrong, I love my daughter more than life itself and I wouldn't change anything I've done. Motherhood wasn't something I thought about either until it was necessary."

"Wow. Thank you for telling me that. Fortunately for Jessie, you're a natural from what I've witnessed. I've, um, been lucky that my mom doesn't hound me about kids. Now, settling down is a whole different can of worms," she chuckled, then cleared her throat. *Don't scare her away by getting too serious.* "So, I guess Dani, Claire, and Jessie got along?"

Ellie took the segue for what it was. It was way too soon to be talking about settling down. Right? "Yep. I was a little worried how Dani would react to meeting new people, but I think with Claire there to help ground her, she's more open."

"I honestly can't thank you enough for what you've done for Dani."

"There's no need. In fact, I should be thanking you for

introducing me to her. Let's call it even," Ellie grinned, holding out her hand to shake on it.

Hunter immediately gripped Ellie's smaller hand, giving it a healthy shake. "Deal." She caught the time on her watch as they let go. A mere three hours before she had to clock back in. *Damn. I don't want to leave her.*

Accurately predicting Hunter's dilemma, Ellie apologized. "I've kept you here. I'm so sorry."

"No, please. I stayed because I wanted to. However, I *do* need to get some shuteye before my rounds."

"Are you okay to drive?"

"Not worth the drive," Hunter told her, mentally going through her schedule. She could have the surgeon she filled in for stay a little later which would give her a little more time to sleep. That would mean pushing up her rounds, but she couldn't find fault with an extra hour. Or two. "I'm just going to crash in the on-call room for a few hours."

"Oh." God how Ellie hated having that dreadful scene flash in her mind. *How annoying. Get the hell over it.* She stood. "You should go get some rest. I'm just going to say goodnight to Blaise and then head home."

Shit. I had to bring up that damn room. Maybe she's forgotten, Hunter thought hopefully. *Yeah, right.* The only thing Hunter could feel lucky about was the fact that Ellie didn't bring it up. She was already completely humiliated that she had stooped so low. She didn't need reminders from the woman she really wanted to be with.

"Are you okay to drive?" she threw the question back at Ellie. "I can drive you."

"Yes, I am. No, you can't." Ellie smiled to soften the harshness of her words. "*You* need to sleep. I'm just going to say goodnight to Blaise and then take off."

"May I at least walk you back to Blaise's room?"

Ellie agreed and they walked slowly side-by-side. "Are you sure you're going to get enough rest here?"

"Yep. I'm going to lock the door and lock the world out for at least four hours. I'm owed at least that much, I think."

Ellie shook her head. "That's not enough sleep."

"I'm a doctor. We're used to little sleep and long hours."

"Okay." Ellie was not convinced, but she was sure Hunter knew what she was doing. "I'm going to stop back by here in the morning. Maybe I'll see you?"

"Only way I'll miss that is if I'm in surgery." Hunter gave Ellie a killer grin. "Be careful going home?"

"You bet."

"Text me?"

Ellie chuckled. "Will do."

Hunter wished they were somewhere a little more private. She didn't think Ellie was ready to be kissed. Especially in front of Hunter's colleagues. "Goodnight, El."

Ellie placed her hand over Hunter's heart which caused it to stutter. It was as brief as the kiss before, but both sweet gestures rapidly built Hunter's confidence in Ellie's readiness to be open with her. In every way.

AS PROMISED, ELLIE returned early the next morning. She and Hunter saw each other briefly — long enough for Ellie to give her a nutritious breakfast. She also spent time with Dani, held the baby for a long moment, and thought about what Hunter had asked her about children. Baby Ezra was adorable but as selfish as it sounded, Ellie was ready to live her life for *her*. She didn't think that made her a bad mother. She loved Jessie with all her heart and had given her everything. Because of that, Jessie was well on her way to starting her future. Wasn't it time for Ellie do the same?

She stood outside Blaise's hospital room and leaned against the wall. Whoever said change was hard was severely understating.

Either that or they didn't make so many *major* changes within such a brief period of time. Problem was, life doesn't stop just because you want to take a breath. Ellie pushed away from the wall. She had a daughter to raise, pies to make, a diner to run, a grand opening to cater. She could breathe when she taught yoga. Well, she could if she stopped missing the damned classes.

"*Bitch.*"

Ellie stopped in her tracks. "Good morning to you, too, Iris."

"You stole her from me."

She tried *really* hard not to roll her eyes. "I'm not going to do this with you, Iris. Hunter was never yours and we're not in high school."

Iris got in Ellie's face. "I'm sure you remember how much she was mine in the on-call room."

"I remember she dropped you, literally, when I walked in." Ellie closed her eyes for a brief moment and took a breath. "That was rude. I'm sorry."

"Save it. Go ahead and gloat, but I'll get her back."

"How low must your self-esteem be that you would waste time on someone who doesn't want to be with you? I'm not done," Ellie said, stalling Iris's retort. "What happened in that room was not the beginning of a relationship. If you doubt that, think of all the times you two have interacted. Has she *ever* expressed interest in you?"

"Obviously," Iris smirked snidely.

"Other than that day when she was upset and confused?" Iris didn't have an answer. "Move on, Iris. I'm not saying this just because I'm seeing Hunter now. I'm saying this because by giving up on someone that doesn't want you, you can finally find someone who does."

"Screw you! You can't just barge in on people's lives and expect to get away with it." Nurse Ruderton stormed away, leaving Ellie to shake her head in disbelief.

"Don't mind her."

Ellie turned at the sound of Mo's voice.

"She's pissed about Hunter, but she'll get over it."

"Hmm." Honestly, Ellie couldn't care less if Iris got over it. She simply didn't have the time or inclination to worry about the idiocies of the young nurse. "How are you, Mo?"

"Fine." Mo shuffled her feet nervously. She screwed up with Hunter. Royally. Which had pissed Patty off even more. It seemed Mo was screwing up all the time these days. "This thing between you and Hunter? What is it?"

Ellie raised a brow. "Private."

Mo frowned. "Whatever your plan is, don't drag it out."

"My plan?" Ellie shook her head. "My 'plan' is to go about my business and take this thing with Hunter one day at a time. Now, if you'll excuse me." This was probably why Ellie didn't have an overabundance of friends. Too many personalities could sometimes clash. And Ellie could definitely see her clashing at times with Mo.

"I'm jealous," Mo called out to Ellie's retreating back.

I'm never going to get out of here, Ellie thought with a silent sigh and turned back around. "Jealous?"

"I've been trying to figure out what my deal has been since you and Hunt met." Mo blew out a breath. "It's not like I don't like you."

"Thanks, I think," Ellie muttered.

"I think you're good for Hunter, but I miss that feeling you get at the beginning. I think that's what has me being so stupid." Mo scrubbed her face, dragging her hands through her short hair which caused it to spike up. "And, I don't know why I'm telling you this shit."

Ellie couldn't help but feel sorry for the woman. Truth be told, Mo looked a bit rough. She had dark circles under dull eyes. Quite a departure from when they first met at the diner.

"Have you talked to Hunter about this?" Ellie certainly didn't want to step on any toes. But when Mo shook her head, Ellie couldn't find a way out of this without hearing Mo out. "How long have you and Patty been together?"

"Almost thirteen years." She ushered Ellie to a more out of the way spot for more privacy. When she saw Ellie talking to Iris, it wasn't her intention to eavesdrop or even talk to Ellie. But her feet – and apparently, her mouth – had other plans. "It's not the sex, that's still great. I mean, maybe we could spice it up a bit, but I think that's kinda normal for such a long relationship."

Ellie winced. *Too much information.* She wondered if anyone else thought it was ironic that *anyone* would come to her to talk about relationships. The one woman who had never been in a relationship in her life. But, one thing she did know was how to observe and listen. If what she had learned through years of being around diverse types of people could help others, she would use it.

"There was this couple that came into the diner every day at the same time," Ellie began. "They would sit in the same booth and order the same thing. The only thing that was different each day was the conversation. They made a pact that they would tell each other at least *one* thing they've never told before. It could have been a dream they'd never talked about, a feeling they had, a childhood memory. It didn't matter what it was, as long as it was something new. Something they once thought was too insignificant to speak aloud."

Ellie eyed Mo to see if she was paying attention. The stout woman was thoroughly captivated. "The wife told me once that the reason her husband asked her to do this was because their relationship had grown stagnant. What they both found out was that even after forty-two years of marriage, there was still more to learn about each other."

"Whoa. Forty-two years." Mo shook her head in wonder. "Are they still coming in? They gotta still be together, right?"

Ellie smiled sadly. "The wife died a little over a year ago. Big Al still comes in at the same time every day. But he can't sit in their spot and he rarely talks anymore. I think he's still in mourning. Either that or he hasn't met anyone as worthy as his wife to talk to."

"Shit. That's sad as hell." Mo cleared her throat and sniffed.

"Yes, it is." Ellie hesitated, then decided. "Mo, by no means am I an expert at relationships. But, would you like my advice?" Mo nodded eagerly and Ellie took a pen from Mo's shirt pocket. She then took Mo's hand and wrote a number on her palm. "Call this number and order a bouquet of Patty's favorite flowers. On the card, ask her out on a date."

"But, we're married, we don't go out on dates . . . Oh. Gotcha."

"When she says yes, make it good, Mo. It's not about sex, it's about getting to know each other again."

Mo nodded, squinting at the number on her palm. Did she even know what her wife's favorite flowers were? "I know she thinks I'm cheating on her," Mo said suddenly. "I would never . . ."

"Mo, stop." Ellie patted Mo's shoulder and squeezed it. "Whatever you're about to say is going to come from your heart. The only one who deserves that right now is Patty."

Mo stared at Ellie. "I can see why Hunter is so interested in you." She sighed. "I'm sorry for what I said to her about you."

Ellie lifted a brow. "I don't even want to know. I'd rather keep this clean slate and move on from here. Agreed?"

"Yeah," Mo grinned. "Hey, um, could Patty and I use the diner as 'our place'?"

Ellie smiled brightly. "I'll make sure I have enough chocolate pie."

Chapter Twenty-Two

If Ellie believed in things like the universe being against her, the next couple of weeks would have been hard evidence. When she was stuck at the diner, Hunter would spend as much time as she could there. And if Hunter was at the hospital, Ellie would try to find the time to bring her something other than hospital cafeteria food to eat. It had become a bit of a routine in their busy lives.

When they did have free time — at the *same* time — others needed their attention. With Dani's release from the hospital was getting close, both Hunter and Ellie were helping to get things set up at Claire's place to make it more accessible. Then there was the science fair that Jessie and Piper had worked so hard for. Ellie finally got to see what had been taking up so much of her daughter's time. She couldn't have been more proud and surprised. Perhaps if she had known Jessie was interested in being a doctor, she wouldn't have been so taken aback. But Ellie now knew more than she ever thought she would about how stem cells may be used to bioengineer a vital organ. The fact that Jessie *personally* invited Hunter was just icing on the cake.

Of course, the grand opening of Sumptor Gallery, LA loomed largely. Ellie shouldn't have been nervous about the menu. Food was what she did best. But for some reason, Eve Sumptor made her feel a bit inferior. So, she worked and reworked the menu until it drove her — and those around her — crazy. The only thing that saved Ellie from being lynched was the fact that everyone got to eat the rejects.

With the birth of Ezra, even girls' night was postponed for 'no more than one week'. Blaise's instructions. Ellie was pretty sure it was because Blaise would go insane if she missed more than one week of pure gossip, food, pampering, and more food. Ellie had hoped that with the cancellation of the tradition, she and Hunter would have some time alone. Unfortunately, Hunter was called in to the hospital for most of the night.

Tonight, though. Tonight, they would finally have some alone time. Jessie was going to the movies with Piper. If they stopped for food — which they usually did — that would give Hunter and Ellie at least four hours alone. Blaise was in motherly bliss with Ezra and promised not to call unless it was an extreme emergency. And it was Hunter's day off and she was on her way over right now.

Ellie was cooking a romantic dinner at her apartment, not the diner. They would be absolutely alone for the first time since their first date. Obviously, she couldn't predict where the night would take them, or if she was even ready to be intimate with Hunter. But she promised herself that she would allow the night to develop organically. That's why she rented a few different genres of movies that could work with any mood that was happening at the moment.

The doorbell rang, causing Ellie to realize just how nervous she really was. While she was alone and cooking, she could forget what the night might bring. Yet, now that Hunter was here, there was no denying the effect the prospect had on her body.

Ellie took a deep breath. "Okay. Just relax and let things flow naturally," she told herself as she walked to the door. She opened it and her heart skipped a beat. Hunter – all five foot eleven of her – was clad in espresso cargo pants, a crisp white tank top, and flip-flops. The woman definitely had a style that Ellie found extremely sexy. "Hi."

"Hey," Hunter grinned. "You, uh, said to dress comfortably. I hope this is okay." She discreetly — she hoped — took in Ellie's black lounge pants and a pale pink t-shirt. She tried not to stare too much at the hint of Ellie's bra and the soft swell of her breasts, but they were like a damn magnet. *Beautiful.*

"Perfect." Ellie took a step back. "Come on in. In fact, you can leave your shoes right here by the door. Tonight is all about comfort. That's why I chose to make cheeseburgers and fries and picked out a few different movies. Sound good?"

Hunter slipped her shoes off. "Sounds relaxing and great. Oh! Um, I got this for you." She held out a teddy bear garbed in dark blue surgical scrubs and stethoscope. She shrugged shyly. "I didn't want to overdo it with flowers."

Ellie chuckled. "It's adorable, thank you."

She followed Ellie to the kitchen, smiling when Ellie hugged the teddy bear to her chest. "I thought that maybe it could remind you of me when I'm not around," she said, hoping she wasn't moving too fast. They had known each other for a little over a month now and had spent most of their free time together. But technically this was only their second date. Did she know she wanted to move forward with Ellie? Hell, yes. She just didn't want to push too hard.

"I don't need any help with that," Ellie answered coyly. "But, I love it."

Hunter didn't even try to fight the toothy grin. *She loves it!* "Good. So, burgers. Does that mean I get some of that homemade mayo?"

"I made a spicy aioli for tonight. Do you like spicy foods?"

"The spicier the better." It wasn't her intent to make that sound so sexual. But she took the cute little smile that Ellie gave her as a good sign that she wasn't offended.

HUNTER PLOPPED ONTO the sofa and rubbed her belly. "That was awesome. But I'm pretty sure I passed my limit of food to stomach ratio."

"Food to stomach ratio?" Ellie laughed. She sifted through the movies she had rented. Dinner had consisted of light conversation and fun memories. There was an underlying tension there that she always felt when she was around Hunter, but she wasn't sure if she should accentuate that with a romantic movie.

"Mmhmm. My stomach has had to expand to accommodate the amount of food I've just ingested and I don't know if it has enough room." Hunter lifted her shirt and pooched her tummy out. "See this? Your delicious food has exceeded my stomach ratio."

Ellie's grip on the movies tightened until she heard a small crack. Even with Hunter's stomach jutted out, Ellie could see the definition of her toned physique. Her fingers itched to find out if Hunter's skin was a soft as it looked.

"El?"

Ellie cleared her throat and tore her gaze away from Hunter's exposed skin. She refused to let Hunter's sly grin get to her. She was caught. She knew it, Hunter knew it. No sense in denying it. "So, no popcorn with the movie?"

"Uh, popcorn is a must." She let the hem of her shirt fall back down. Oh yeah, she saw Ellie staring. And her body responded in the most luscious way. It was a pretty great first step and she would keep taking her cues from Ellie as the night progressed.

"You can fit popcorn in there?" Ellie lifted her chin in the direction of Hunter's stomach.

"It's just a bunch of air. But, more importantly, I think there's a rule written somewhere that when a movie is playing, popcorn must be consumed."

Ellie's lips twitched in amusement. "Well, we wouldn't want to break the rules, would we?"

"Nope. I hear the punishment is horrible." She leaned up and looked both ways before lowering her voice. *"They make you watch* all *of Adam Sandler's movies back to back."*

Ellie laughed out loud. "That *is* horrible! I'll make some popcorn. Want to pick the movie?"

"Left hand."

"Huh?"

"Whatever movie is in your left hand, that's the one we'll watch. Don't look at it!" she practically shouted before Ellie could see which movie she had in that particular hand. "Let's be surprised."

"You're a goof," Ellie shook her head and smiled. It was something she really liked about Hunter. The woman was a successful doctor but never took life too seriously. At least not when she was with Ellie. Nevertheless, Ellie did as Hunter asked and put the chosen movie in without looking at it. "Is tea okay, or would you like wine?"

Hunter pondered her options. Truth be told, she wasn't much of a drinker anymore, but she didn't want to hold Ellie back. "I'll have whatever you're having," she said finally, giving the decision to Ellie.

It didn't go unnoticed. Ellie began to recognize how Hunter would defer to Ellie when there was a mention of alcohol. "You know, alcohol is never my first choice. What do you say we stick to tea?"

Hunter flashed her a grateful smile. "Sounds like a plan."

A few minutes later, Ellie came back with a bowl of popcorn – flavored with Ellie's own blend of seasoning, of course – and two tall glasses of iced tea on a tray.

"Need any help?"

Ellie gave Hunter a look. "This is my area of expertise, Dr. Vale. You don't see me walking into your OR asking if *you* need help, do you?"

Hunter laughed. "Didn't mean to offend you, Miss Montgomery." She sat back and purposefully put her arm across the back of the couch. As Ellie was busy preparing their snacks, Hunter fretted with where to position herself. Should she tuck herself into the corner and leave the rest of the couch to Ellie? Should she be more welcoming, yet unobtrusive? Or should she be a bit assertive and see if Ellie accepted the offer?

After much back and forth, Hunter went with the latter. She

JOURDYN KELLY

watched as Ellie glanced at her, then at the rest of the couch, and back again. A slight, precious blush colored Ellie's cheeks before she laughed softly.

"It's crazy how much you make me feel like a teenager," she said as she sat close to Hunter, tucking her shoulder under her Hunter's waiting arm. She shivered when Hunter's fingertips grazed her upper arm with soft strokes.

The fact that Ellie chose to sit so intimately close to her gave Hunter a boost of confidence. "Is that the only way I make you feel?" she breathed close to Ellie's ear.

Ellie's eyes fluttered closed. "No. You definitely make me feel like a woman." She tilted her head back and captured Hunter's lips with hers.

It was a tentative brushing of their lips at the beginning. Their first *real* kiss. Hell, it was Ellie's first real kiss with a woman. Her heart was practically pounding out of her chest. *So soft.* When Hunter shifted, deepening the kiss, Ellie moaned softly. Her body felt as though it was burning from the inside out. The sensation was both pleasurable and painful. And incredibly exciting.

So good. The kiss surprised Hunter initially, but the feel and taste of Ellie quickly turned that surprise into arousal. Hunter had to force herself to stay in control and that wasn't easy. She had never kissed anyone like she was kissing Ellie. She had never wanted anyone like she wanted Ellie. And her body had never, *ever* even come close to being this aroused before.

Ellie touched Hunter's face with one hand and buried her other hand in Hunter's silky tresses. It was all the encouragement Hunter needed. Her tongue glided over Ellie's bottom lip and she was immediately granted entrance. The moment their tongues met, both women would swear they felt a shock of electricity. Ellie's hand tightened into a fist in Hunter's hair and she pulled her closer. Hunter slipped her arm around Ellie's waist and moved in until she was practically on top of the smaller woman.

"I love this couch," Hunter mumbled through the kiss and felt Ellie smile.

Somehow, through the haze of their lust, they heard the distinct jingle of keys in the lock. Hunter pushed herself away from Ellie so fast she ended up sliding off the couch. Her ass hit the floor with a thud causing Ellie to snicker.

"Are you okay?"

"Mmhmm. Yep." Hunter cleared her throat and sat there as though that was exactly where she meant to be.

Jessie walked in before Ellie could make any other comment. She looked up at her daughter. "Hey, sweetie. You're home early." *Way too early*, she thought with a bit of disappointment.

"Hey, guys." She plopped herself into one of the plush chairs that flanked the couch. "Yeah, Piper got sick so we left the movie early." She leaned over and grabbed a handful of popcorn. "Mmm, spicy. Hunter? Why are you sitting on the floor?"

"Um," Hunter gestured towards the TV which was clearly off. "We were about to watch a movie."

Jessie waited for a beat, but Hunter offered nothing more. "Wouldn't the couch be more comfortable?"

It was extremely *comfortable just a minute ago.* Of course, she couldn't say that and now she was at a loss at how to explain.

"Wait." Jessie looked at Hunter's expression which, if she had to guess, exhibited unease. Then she looked at her mother, whose face held a bit of a glow. *Crap.* "I interrupted something, didn't I?"

"No!" Ellie and Hunter exclaimed simultaneously.

Jessie smirked. "Right. Hunter's on the floor, mom looks a little heated," she laughed when Ellie hid her face behind her hands. "And, the TV is off, but you were 'watching a movie'."

"Technically, I said we were *about* to watch a movie," Hunter muttered.

"I'm sorry, guys. I didn't mean to mess anything up. Want me to go back out?"

"You didn't 'mess' anything up, Jessie," Hunter said sincerely. "Why don't you watch the movie with us?"

"I don't want to intrude."

"You're not," Ellie chimed in and smiled at her daughter.

Jessie narrowed her eyes. She *knew* she had disrupted their night, but they sounded pretty genuine about her watching a movie with them. Maybe this would be a clever way to see how Hunter treated her mom. A little covert spying wouldn't be terrible, would it?

"What movie?"

"We, uh, don't know." Hunter shrugged and Ellie laughed. "I told El not to look."

El. She had only heard Blaise call her mom by the nickname. Not sure how that made her feel, Jessie shook it off and popped up to look at the movie sleeve. And snorted.

"Deadpool?"

Hunter leaned her head back on the couch and eyed Ellie who lifted a shoulder.

"I heard it was funny."

"It's terrible, mom," Jessie laughed. "But, hey, if you want to see full frontal male parts . . ."

"What are our other choices?" Hunter interrupted.

THE TRIO FINALLY agreed on a light-hearted comedy. Hunter took up her original spot on the couch and was thrilled when Ellie did the same. They laughed, shared popcorn, paused the movie for more popcorn, and simply enjoyed their time together.

Jessie did take a few surreptitious glances at the couple — it still felt weird to think of her mother as part of a couple. What she found was Hunter was the perfect, um, gentlewoman. No underhanded groping, no sleazy kissy moves. Hunter never once made Jessie feel like a third-wheel or that she was cramping her style. In fact, it was the exact opposite. When Ellie got up to make more snacks, Hunter engaged Jessie in a resourceful conversation about her science project. The verdict was; she liked Hunter.

"Well!" Jessie proclaimed loudly once the movie was over, causing the two women to jump slightly. It had taken them more than three hours to watch a ninety-minute movie, but now Jessie was beginning to feel as though she was overstaying her welcome. Her mom and Hunter deserved to have more alone time. "That was fun, but I'm exhausted and I have school tomorrow."

Subtle, oh daughter of mine.

"I should get going, too," Hunter said reluctantly. The thought of going back to her empty house — as beautiful as it was — held little appeal after the night she just had.

"You don't have to go," Jessie said a little too eagerly.

"I . . ." Hunter swiveled her head from Jessie to Ellie – who looked as confused as Hunter felt. "Unfortunately, I have to work in the morning."

"Oh. Hey, do you think I could come and do rounds with you one day?"

"Jessie, I don't think that's allowed," Ellie warned softly.

"Actually," Hunter hoped she wasn't overstepping her bounds. When they had gone to Jessie's science fair together, Hunter got the feeling Ellie was blindsided by Jessie's career choice. "We have a program that offers high school students an opportunity to get clinical exposure." She turned her attention to Jessie. "If you're serious about this, and your mom approves, I'd be honored to have you shadow me on rounds."

Jessie's eyes sparkled with excitement when she turned them to Ellie. "Mom?"

Ellie exhaled. *My kid wants to be a doctor. I should be happy about that. So, be happy. Besides, that'll mean she'll get to know Hunter better.* "Sure."

Jessie jumped up and ran to her mom, throwing herself into her arms. Not easy since Ellie was still seated. "Thank you, thank you, thank you!"

"Don't thank me, thank Hunter."

Jessie lifted her head from her mom's shoulder. "Thank you, Hunter. It means a lot."

"My pleasure," Hunter grinned. At that moment, she became aware of how much she enjoyed watching mother and daughter interact with each other. *I could really get used to nights like this.*

"'Kay, well, I'm out. Can you text mom whenever you think is a good time for me to come to the hospital?"

"Will do. It'll be on the weekend. You good with that?"

"Yep!" Jessie kissed her mom on the cheek. "Goodnight!" The teen disappeared down the hall within seconds.

"It's going to take her forever to calm down and get to sleep now," Ellie laughed.

"I probably should have talked to you before telling her about the program."

Ellie shook her head. "Knowing my daughter, she probably had that information before she asked you."

"Tenacious."

"Mmhmm." Ellie glanced the direction her daughter went. "I just don't know why she didn't tell me she wanted to be a doctor. She tells me everything."

"I had a hard time telling my mom I wanted to be a doctor," Hunter revealed. "In my case, it meant telling her I wanted to move across the country to go to school in Boston."

Ellie sat up quickly. "Oh, God. Is that? Is she? . . ." She looked towards her daughter's bedroom again. A bedroom that could be empty soon with her daughter thousands of miles away. What if that was the reason Jessie had been so hesitant to talk about college recently?

Good going, Hunter. "I'm sorry, Ellie. I didn't mean to upset you."

Hunter's words invaded Ellie's inner trepidation. "No, I . . . I." She waved her hand, dismissing the apology. "Don't mind me, I'm having a small 'overreacting-mother' moment."

Hunter covered Ellie's hand with hers. "I've never really thought about it from the mother's point-of-view."

"Well, you should call your mother and apologize," Ellie teased, squeezing Hunter's hand.

"I'll get right on that," Hunter chuckled. "But, if Jessie feels anything like I felt back then, she's suffering, too."

"I'll try to keep that in mind," Ellie said genuinely.

"Good. I should probably get going." She stood and pulled Ellie up and into her arms for a heartfelt hug. She kissed her on the top of her head, nuzzling for a moment. "Thank you for tonight." She pulled back a little. "I didn't think we could top our first date. Now I'm not sure we're going to top this one."

Ellie grinned. "I'm sure we'll figure something out." She ran her hands up Hunter's arms and wrapped them around her neck. "About earlier."

"Regrets?" *Please say no.*

"Of course, not." She hesitated. "Hunter, I'm not sure how far things would have gone even if we weren't interrupted." To Ellie's surprise, Hunter smiled.

"As much as I want to make love to you, Ellie, tonight wouldn't have been the night." She recognized the conflicted emotions that flickered in Ellie's eyes. "Jessie was a little early, but we knew she'd be back before our night was over." She tucked Ellie's hair behind her ear and traced a finger down her cheek. "This is brand new to both of us and I don't want to be rushed when I'm with you. I don't want to have to carve out an hour here and there. I want to take my time, explore every inch of you. And, if I'm lucky, we won't have to say goodnight. Instead, we'll say good morning and do it all over again."

Oh, my. Ellie swallowed audibly. She wondered if Hunter could hear her heart beating. It was a surprise it wasn't beating out of her chest. "You," she cleared her suddenly dry throat and tried again. "You certainly know all the right things to say."

Hunter chuckled softly. "I told you, I'm following my heart when it comes to you."

Ellie tugged Hunter's head down and kissed her soundly. She was seriously going to need a *very* long run after tonight. She felt Hunter pull back slowly. The doctor glanced towards the hallway that Jessie disappeared in.

"Does Jessie being here make you uncomfortable?" Ellie asked gently.

"No," Hunter shook her head. "It's just that I don't want to make *her* uncomfortable. I can't imagine how challenging this has all been for her. For both of you. I don't want to make it any more difficult."

Ellie laughed softly and placed a hand over Hunter's heart.

"This is leading you well. Stick with it," she said and kissed her again. Ellie moaned softly and gave Hunter a slight push towards the door. "You should go before I don't let you."

"Not much of an incentive to leave, Miss Montgomery," Hunter smiled. "But, I'll go. See you tomorrow morning at the diner?"

Ellie ran through her schedule in her head. *Run (must), go to the diner to start the pies of the day, yoga, Sumptor Gallery menu sampling.* She was tired just thinking about her day tomorrow. "I have a class to teach in the morning. But if you don't have to go in too early, I'm sure I'll have some time to see you and make sure you have a proper meal."

"You know I don't only visit so you can feed me, right?"

"I know. It's an added bonus knowing that you get at least one nutritious meal," Ellie grinned.

"That it is," Hunter laughed as she slipped her shoes on. "Are you going to watch me walk down the hall again? Because I don't think I can do a jump in these things," she said indicating her flip-flops.

"Yes. You'll just have to do your best." Ellie lifted onto her tip-toes and gave Hunter a quick, yet toe-curling, kiss. "Goodnight, Hunter. Text me when you get home?"

The doctor smiled, giving Ellie another hug. "First thing after the door closes behind me. Goodnight, El. Thank you for everything." She made her way down the hall knowing full well Ellie was watching her. Hunter quickly kicked her shoes to the side and leaped in the air to click her heels together. With a cheeky grin, she put her shoes back on and disappeared around the corner.

Ellie was still laughing when she closed the door. She adored how much of a goof Hunter was. The doctor was also an unbelievable kisser. Not that Ellie had much experience to compare with. Kissing Jessie's father was messy at best. With Hunter, there weren't just tingles. There were bells and whistles, racing hearts and breathlessness, need and want. She touched her fingertips to her lips. Desire.

"You really like her, don't you?"

A muffled oath escaped from Ellie through her fingers. "Holy crap, kid! Don't think you're getting the inheritance if you intentionally kill me. I thought you were sleeping. And, yes, I do."

"Inheritance? Nice!" Jessie giggled. "Sorry for scaring you. I like her, too, by the way. I didn't want to, but I do."

"Why didn't you want to?"

Jessie shrugged. "Because I'm a selfish teenager."

Ellie snorted with laughter. "At least you're honest."

"So? If you two like each other so much, why didn't she stay over?"

This time Ellie choked. "Um, I have to clean up and you need to go to bed. You have school in the morning."

"How about I help you clean up and you can give me an answer," Jessie negotiated.

Ellie's eyebrows shot up. "Maybe I *should* call Hunter back. You must be sick if you're offering to help clean."

"Ha. Ha." Jessie rolled her eyes but peeked over at the kitchen and living room. "It's only a few things."

"Exactly. Nothing I can't take care of myself. Now, go to bed," Ellie shooed her daughter away.

"You're not going to tell me, are you?"

"Sweetie, there's nothing to tell. We're just not there, yet."

Jessie stood her ground, putting her hands on her hips. At that moment, she looked very much like her mother. "You've been seeing each other for a couple of weeks now. Known each other for longer. Isn't that, like, a lifetime in lesbian relationships?"

Ellie bit her lip to keep from laughing. "You're terrible. I blame Blaise. Besides, Hunter and I have only been on two official dates."

"Official, schmofficial. Dating isn't like it used to be when you were young."

"You're really pushing it, kid."

"I'm just sayin' that there's no date count these days, mom. You just do it when it feels right. Not that I know!" she said quickly when she saw her mom begin to frown. "I'm just going by what I've seen. People don't really date anymore. They hang out. You and Hunter have totally been doing that."

Dating advice from my teenage daughter. No, wait, sex *advice from my teenage daughter. What has my life come to?* "I — I got nothing. I have no idea how to respond to what you've just said to me. Your mother. So, what I'm going to do is say I love you and goodnight."

Ellie kissed her daughter on her cheek and walked away. Towards her bedroom. Without cleaning.

"*I broke my mom,*" Jessie whispered staring after Ellie. "*Time to bring in the big guns.*"

MEANWHILE, HUNTER WAS still smiling as she let herself in her house. As promised, she sent Ellie a text saying she made it home safe. She laughed out loud at the responding text.

Good. Dr. Bearington and I are happy about that. Now, get some rest. Doctor's orders.

Attached to the text was a selfie of Ellie giving 'Dr. Bearington' a kiss on the cheek.

"Lucky bear," Hunter sighed. "She's so beautiful." She sent a cheeky selfie of her saluting back, chuckling as she did. The snicker died in her throat when a manila envelope caught her eye. "Goddammit!"

Hunter snatched up the offending mail, knowing precisely what it was. It wasn't the first. She opened it and took out a photo of a different kind. One that certainly wasn't as pleasing as the one she just got from Ellie. It was of Hunter and another one of Susan's victims. Even though they, too, used Hunter, she couldn't help but feel responsible for their possible exposure.

A note floated out and Hunter caught it in mid-air. *Get rid of the whore or she gets the next one. I expect to see you here next weekend to make it up to me. Susan*

Hunter's fists bunched, ready to shred the envelope and its

contents to pieces. The thought of two people stopped her. The first was Dr. Woodrow.

'If you're not going to take this to the police, Hunter, I advise you to at least keep anything she gives you to use as evidence. I hope this doesn't escalate, but if it does, I want you to be ready.'

The second was Ellie. She didn't want to keep anything from her. Of course, she didn't exactly want to show this shit to Ellie, either. But when the time was right, she would. There was no way she was going to let Susan have the upper hand. Not anymore. *Ellie knows about my past. I won't lose her because of this. Susan can't hurt me. She can't hurt Ellie.* Hunter kept those thoughts in her head as she threw the envelope in a drawer with the others.

She hated that her wonderful night was now contaminated by Susan's attempt at manipulation. To make herself feel better and get nasty thoughts out of her head, she pulled up Ellie's picture again. With that photo, all thoughts of Susan disappeared.

Chapter Twenty-Three

Ellie placed the laptop on the counter in front of her and checked her watch. Since she got up earlier to run on days she taught yoga, she and Rosa made an agreement that Ellie would come in to start the days' pies before heading off to her class. Rosa appreciated the extra sleep and Ellie appreciated the "me" time.

As of now, Ellie had a little more than an hour to get things going before Rosa waltzed in. Luckily, most of the prep was done the night before and that gave her the opportunity to do some . . . research while she was alone. She felt a bit odd sitting in the kitchen of her diner doing anything other than cooking. Especially doing something like this. But times were changing. And she certainly couldn't do things like this at home with Jessie around.

With shaky resolve, Ellie typed in a web address she had googled and hesitantly pressed enter. She was immediately met with images that caused her to question what she was doing. But Ellie Montgomery was not one to back down from tricky situations. So, she found what she was looking for and . . .

"Hello?"

Ellie snapped the computer shut with embarrassment. "What? Nothing! What?" Wide eyes took in a frazzled Blaise standing in her kitchen, bouncing baby Ezra in her arms. "What are you doing here? I didn't think you knew this time of the day existed."

Blaise narrowed her eyes. "What are you doing?"

"I asked you first."

"Ezra obviously does not have the affinity for sleep that I have. He usually calms down when we go for a drive. Today it was apparently my turn to take that drive, though Greyson's punishment for not at least offering to go is no sex for a month."

Ellie rolled her eyes. "That's how much longer you have before you *can* have sex, weirdo."

"Yeah, well, other things could have happened before then. But since he refused to do this for me so I could sleep, that's out, too. Your turn. What were you doing when I walked in?"

"Nothing."

"You were looking up recipes, weren't you?"

Ellie gasped, completely offended. "I was not! How dare you even suggest that!"

"I don't know, El," Blaise smirked. "You looked quite 'caught' when I walked in. So, you're either looking up recipes or porn." Blaise watched, fascinated, as a blush crept up Ellie's neck. "Oh my God! Porn?" Ellie lowered her eyes. "Wow, you'd rather I know you're looking up porn than recipes?"

"I do *not* look up recipes." Ellie scooted back from the counter. "Now, give me my godson."

Blaise gratefully handed over the baby who was currently blowing bubbles with his spit and making cooing noises. She loved him dearly, but a sleep deprived Blaise was not someone *anyone* wanted to deal with. Even a newborn.

"So? Getting ideas for sex with the good doctor?"

Ellie covered Ezra's ear with her free hand. "This is not appropriate talk in front of the kid."

Blaise laughed. "He doesn't understand what we're saying, stop avoiding the question." Ellie walked away, telling Ezra how odd his mother was. "El, I understand you're probably hesitant. This is all uncharted territory for you. Literally," Blaise chuckled at her own joke. "But, how long do you think someone like Hunter will wait to be asked to stay?"

Ellie turned around and frowned at her best friend. "You've been talking to my daughter, haven't you?" Blaise shrugged in lieu of answering. "First, Hunter isn't in any kind of hurry. Second, I'm not hesitant, but I'm also not trying to rush into things. I've been waiting for this, for something I never thought would happen, for a very long time. That doesn't mean I'm just going to jump in for the sake of jumping in."

"I get that. So does Jessie. I think we're afraid you'll talk yourself out of a good thing because of fear. You and Hunter have known each other for over a month now."

"*Known*," Ellie interrupted. "Not dated. And, yes, I have been informed by my daughter that *dating* is obsolete now, but it's not for me. Or Hunter. Besides, I'm not afraid, really. I may not be experienced, but that doesn't mean I'm naïve." She hoped she sounded more convincing than she felt.

Blaise nodded in understanding. Ellie may be innocent, so to speak, but Blaise had never known the woman to have an ounce of naiveté in her body. "Answer me one thing. *Honestly.* Jessie's afraid you're not taking the next step because of her. Is there any truth to that?"

Ellie opened her mouth to answer, then shut it again. "I don't want to say yes, but I don't know." Ezra started to fuss a bit and Ellie bounced him calm again. "It's weird. She's going to know what's going on behind the closed door of my bedroom."

"That's the life of a parent, sweetie. Jessie is an intelligent young woman. You two have been extremely close her whole life. El, she practically *told* you that you should be having sex right now without blinking an eye. Yes, she told me what she said," Blaise confirmed. "She doesn't want to be the one that holds you back. Don't *make* her be."

Blaise reached for Ezra who began to cry. She hoped that her words were getting through to Ellie. When Jessie had called her the night before, she had sounded miserable, thinking she was holding her mother back. Blaise knew the one thing Ellie would never want was to let *anything* change her relationship with her daughter.

"I need to feed this big boy, but how about this. Let's get together later tonight. An impromptu girls' night. It'll give me a good way to punish Greyson more and we can invite Hunter's friends to see what more we can learn about the tall beauty."

Ellie raised a brow. "Tall beauty?" Blaise shrugged with a wink. "Who did you want to invite?"

"Well, we kinda know Rebecca already and you've told me a little about Patty. I'd like to get to know them a little better. Maybe I can talk Greyson and Cade into inviting Hunter and the other significant others over for a game of poker."

"Cass and Mo," Ellie supplied absently. The thought of Hunter and Cade in the same room for an extended period of time made her eyeballs itch. "Do you really think it's a good idea to have Hunter and Cade spending time together?"

"Actually, I think it's a great idea. He needs to get it through his thick head that you're with Hunter and it will never be him. Greyson will keep him in line."

"Tonight?"

"Yep."

"It's the middle of the week."

"That's what's so great about being adults. We can do these things in the middle of the week and get away with it." Blaise widened her eyes comically at Ellie who stuck her tongue out at her. "I'm aware that people have jobs – wait, what does Rebecca do?"

Ellie frowned as she thought about it. "I have no idea. Strange. Patty and Mo are nurses. Cass is an artist." She lifted a shoulder. "Maybe we'll find out tonight if Rebecca can make it."

"Okay, now that we have a plan to solve that riddle, back to the original thought. Since I'm aware people have jobs and school in the morning, we'll just hang for a few hours, gossip, get to know each other, and stuff."

"It's the 'stuff' that worries me."

"Trust me," Blaise grinned. "We'll have fun."

"If we do this, I hope everyone comes away from it well on the road to being friends," Ellie said. "Hunter wanted to invite everyone to a barbecue at her house sometime soon. I don't want to ruin that for her."

"Ooo, fun. Don't worry. This will simply be a prelude."

"HEY, CAN WE talk?"

Hunter looked up from tying her shoe and saw a nervous Mo rocking back and forth on the balls of her feet. Her hands were stuffed deep into her pockets. It was something Mo had been doing since she was in elementary school and got in trouble.

"I'm late for rounds," Hunter responded, standing to put on her white lab coat. She hadn't spoken to Mo since that day her so-called best friend went nuts. It was childish, but she didn't want to hear Mo's idiotic ideas about what Hunter should be doing.

Mo stood her ground in front of the door. "Come on, Hunt. We've been friends way too long to keep avoiding each other like this."

Hunter stared at Mo for a long, uncomfortable minute. "Did you cheat on Patty?"

Her first impulse was to get angry, but Mo knew she had made this mess. Now she had to clean it up the way she did with her wife. "No. I would *never* do that to Patty. I love her."

"She know that?" Much to Hunter's surprise, Mo smiled.

"Yeah. We had a long heart to heart. Ellie was right about that."

Hunter's head snapped up. "Ellie?"

"We, uh, ran into each other a couple of weeks ago when her friend had her baby."

"You didn't tell her what you said, did you?"

"No, not really. I thought maybe you had, so I tried to apologize. She stopped me. Said she didn't want to know. That she wanted to stick with the clean slate and move on from there."

Hunter grinned. That definitely sounded like something Ellie would say.

"Look, Hunt, I'm sorry for the things I said. Ellie? She's good for you. You deserve that."

"Hmm, so I shouldn't be out there screwing every chick that looks at me twice?" Hunter asked acerbically.

Mo flinched. "I had that comin'. And, I *know* that's not who you are or what you want. I let my own issues cloud my good sense."

Hunter snorted. "Since when have you had good sense?"

"Hey! I'm friends with you and I married Patty. I'd call that some good sense."

"These 'issues'? How much do I have to worry about them? You know I love you, Mo. We've been friends since you were actually taller than me. But, you fuck things up with Patty by disrespecting her, I won't be on your side. Got me?"

"I do and I understand. I don't think *I'd* be on my side either. We're working on my stuff. Both of us. I have Ellie to thank for that, too. She told me this story about an older couple who used to come to her diner every day and talk." Mo shook her head with sadness. "Sucks that the wife passed away."

"It was true," Hunter said with a soft, sad smile.

"Huh?"

"Big Al, right?"

"Yeah! She told you about him?" Hunter nodded. "Sad story, man. But she also gave me some great advice. Now I'm buying Patty flowers, asking her out on real dates, and knocking on my *own* door to pick her up. We go to Ellie's and talk. Patty and I have been together for years, but I'm learning new things about the woman I love that makes me love her even more."

Hearing those words coming from Mo made Hunter feel a whole hell of a lot better. Mo's opinions about what she should do with Ellie — and others — was forgivable. But cheating on Patty? That was one thing Hunter didn't think she could forgive.

"You free tonight?"

Mo, surprised by the unexpected question, quickly thought what her night looked like. This morning Patty had mentioned something in passing about last minute plans with friends. Of course, Mo had been busy trying to get some morning nookie, so she wasn't really paying attention to words that weren't 'yes', 'more', or 'right there'.

"Uh, I think so? As long as I come home to Patty, I'm gold. Since I'll be with you, I don't think she'll have a problem with me going out."

Hunter's eyebrows furrowed. She took out her phone and looked at the text from Ellie again. "Didn't Patty tell you that El invited her and Rebecca to dinner at her place tonight?"

Mo snapped her fingers. "*That's* what she said! Right, right. Then, yeah, I'm free," Mo grinned. "What you got planned?"

Hunter shook her head at Mo's quirkiness. "Believe it or not, we've been invited to play poker with Greyson, Blaise's husband. And his friend, Cade."

Mo snickered at the scowl that graced Hunter's angular face. "This Cade guy got a thing for Ellie?"

"Yep."

"Hunt, all you gotta do is strut in there with your head held high and a big ass smile on your face. You got the girl. He never had a chance."

Hunter laughed. "It's good to have you back, Mo."

ELLIE WALKED INTO Sumptor Gallery, LA bearing a tray of intensely aromatic food. Even she, the 'chef', was having trouble keeping her stomach from growling. *Should have sampled more of the samples.*

"Whatever that divine scent is, I want it. All of it."

Ellie turned at Eve's sultry voice, fighting off a shiver from the sheer sexuality that seemed to exude from the woman. How did she make such innocent words sound so suggestive?

"This is your lucky day." Ellie raised the tray, causing another waft of spices to float through the air. "These are samples of what I want to put on the menu for the opening." Eve gestured where she should put the covered platter and Ellie gingerly set it down. This place was filled with priceless art and she didn't want to have to ask Blaise for a loan to pay for any accidents. She lifted the lid. "Now, I know you wanted simple – which these are – but I also thought more elegant would be perfect for the night. The top row is what you've already approved. I would like you to choose two or three others from the rest."

"Oh, God. You want me to choose?" Eve leaned over and took a deep breath in. "That seems impossible. But, let me go get Lainey. She's good at this stuff. Besides, she'd punish me if she was left out of this," Eve grinned with a wink and set off to find her partner.

Ellie replaced the cover to keep the food warm for her friends, then decided to take a look around as she waited. There was a particular piece that caught Ellie's eye when she walked in. The colors were chaotic. There didn't seem to be any distinct purpose other than . . .

"Interesting piece, yes?"

Ellie tilted her head to look at the piece from a different angle. "Confusing." She turned to the unfamiliar voice and came face to face with a stunning woman. She was tall with long, golden-brown hair that fell past her shoulders and shimmered in the sunlight. She had flawless skin, high cheekbones, a regal nose, and full lips that held the hint of a smile. Her eyes, framed by long lashes, were a fascinating shade of green.

"Most of the paintings from this artist are confusing. I can't imagine what it's like being in his head," the woman laughed lightly. She had a heavy accent that piqued Ellie's curiosity.

"I'm pretty sure we're seeing exactly what it's like in there," Ellie chuckled, gesturing to the work.

"True enough." The woman held her hand out in greeting. "I'm Kiara Adler."

"Ellie Montgomery." Ellie shook the taller woman's hand,

noting how they seemed delicate considering their size. "Do you work here?"

"Oh! No, no. Although I love art, I know absolutely nothing about it."

"Are you here on holiday, then? Your accent." Ellie continued when the woman looked at her questioningly. "German?"

"More of a working holiday and yes. Good ear," Kiara smiled. "I am from Berlin. Have you been?"

Ellie shook her head. "It's one of the places on my bucket list, but I have yet to make it there."

"Ah, if you decide to go, be sure to let me know. I'd love to show you around."

Ellie smiled politely. Surely the woman wasn't flirting with her. Right?

"Stop flirting, Kiara. You're not getting any of that food." Eve bumped shoulders with the woman who rolled her eyes. "Kiara is here to provide the attire for the opening, Ellie."

"Oh, you're a designer?" Ellie asked.

Kiara smiled. "No, I merely work with the designers."

"She's being modest," Lainey chimed in, giving Ellie a welcoming hug. "Kiara is a supermodel turned fashion mogul. As artists do with Eve, designers flock to have Kiara represent their work in her stores."

"Don't you have food to stuff in your mouth?" Kiara teased grouchily and turned to Ellie. "Don't listen to them. I'm just here to get measurements and find a talented designer to do everyone justice."

Eve groaned playfully. "Okay, now that we've established that Kiara is successful, yet humble, can we get on with the tasting?"

Ellie laughed as Lainey smacked Eve on the arm — something Ellie was sure *only* Lainey could get away with — and Kiara flipped her off. "Yes, let's. I have a diner to run, you know."

It took another thirty minutes for Eve to decide — with little help from Lainey as she told Eve to choose all of them. That boosted Ellie's confidence and she was sure no matter what they selected, it would be a hit at the opening. But, eventually, the menu was narrowed down and finalized, which was one less thing for Ellie to worry about.

"Ellie?"

Ellie paused in gathering the remnants of the samples (which wasn't much) and turned to Kiara. She could certainly see why the woman had been a supermodel. "Yes?"

"Would you happen to be free later? We could get your measurements taken care of and then perhaps you would permit me to take you to dinner?"

"Oh! Um." *Well, shit.* She felt a pang of guilt in her belly that confused her. It wasn't like she was flirting back. *I should tell her I have a girlfriend. Is that what Hunter is?* "Actually, I have plans tonight." Disappointment flashed in Kiara's eyes. *She's probably not used to being turned down,* Ellie thought, then almost laughed out loud at the absurdity of her musings. The invitation was most likely nothing more than an innocent suggestion. Kiara was probably not even gay. "Are you on a schedule?"

"We do need your measurements soon as time is running short. We could get that done promptly." Kiara took a card out of her purse. "Or, if you have someone you regularly go to, just have them email me with the information. You can also email or call me with your preferences if that's easier for you."

Ellie looked at her watch. She had three hours before everyone was expected at her apartment. Thankfully, she had everything she needed to make dinner, but still, she had to actually *make* the dinner. However, if she took a bit of time now to get this done, it would be one more thing checked off her list.

"I really do have plans tonight, Kiara, so I hope you don't think I'm being ungrateful for what you're doing. But, I can spare a few minutes before I have to get back to the diner."

"If you're sure, my assistant has sequestered one of the offices to work out of." Kiara gestured towards the back of the gallery, signaling for Ellie to precede her. "I apologize for my presumptuousness before. I didn't mean to assume you were gay and would be interested in a date with me. I hope I didn't offend you."

Oh, God. She was *asking me out.* "Oh, um, no. I mean yes, I am, but you didn't offend me. It's just," Ellie hesitated, not sure how to continue without sounding even more foolish.

"You're taken," Kiara guessed.

"I — It's complicated." Ellie winced. "I know that's vague, I'm sorry. But . . ."

Kiara stopped and placed a hand on Ellie's elbow. "You don't owe me any explanations, Ellie. If your situation changes, I wrote my private number on the back of that card. Even if it uncomplicates and you're still not in the position to go out with me, I would like to think we could be friends."

"Berlin is quite a long distance, Kiara," Ellie smiled. She didn't want to feel bad for turning the model down. But, as beautiful as Kiara was, Ellie had no interest in dating her.

Kiara chuckled. "Friendship only requires communication and in this day in age, that's easy. If there is a chance for more, I've lived long enough to understand the importance of being able to go where life takes you at any given moment."

"Just like that?"

"Just like that. Now, let's get you measured and on your way. You have plans," Kiara winked.

Chapter Twenty-Four

"Are you sure you're okay with this?" Ellie smoothed the front of Hunter's already smooth shirt.

"Are you sure I can't stay here with you?" Hunter grinned. Ellie's hands on her were causing all kinds of chaos with her hormones. She didn't mind one bit.

"Rules."

"Rules, shmules." Hunter bent her head and kissed Ellie gently. Part of her still couldn't believe she got to do this. Part of her wanted to do so much more.

"Mmm, nice." Ellie smiled against Hunter's lips. "But, seriously." She pushed Hunter back a bit. "Are you going to be good spending time with Cade?"

"I'm good, El. I'm the one kissing you, not him."

"Try not to antagonize him, please. He's a good friend and was very helpful when Blaise needed him."

Hunter traced a finger down Ellie's cheek. "I promise. I want this to go as well as you do. I'll be on my best behavior. And I'll make sure Mo doesn't muck anything up."

"Hey! I heard that!" Mo shouted from across the room. She and

Cass were currently saying their goodbyes to their women — like Hunter — as Jessie, Blaise, and Piper looked on with humor.

This was a side of her mom Jessie had never seen before. She was happy Ellie was happy, even if it was still a little weird to witness. It made her feel a bit bipolar, being delighted that her mother found someone to be with and apprehensive at the same time. Not that she thought Hunter was bad for her mom. She simply wanted to be sure that when she went off to college — hopefully to the school she wanted to go to — her mom would be in a healthy, supportive relationship. In Jessie's mind, Hunter had to prove herself. And not only with this kissy-face stuff (however cute it was).

"Okay, okay! It's not like they're going off to war. All this smooching is seriously cutting into my eating time." She side-eyed a smirking Blaise. "At least you had the decency to do it in Greyson's car."

Blaise's smirk fell as the others in the room laughed.

"I can assure you, there was nothing decent going on in that car," Ellie joked.

"When did this become a dig on Blaise bit?" Blaise grumbled. She wasn't offended, really, but talking about what happened in Greyson's car was making her rethink her husband's punishment. One month is *way* too long to be celibate.

"As fun as all of this is, I'm getting hangry," Jessie called out over the fits of laughter.

"And, that's our cue to go!" Hunter shivered.

"Coward," Ellie teased.

"You bet. Teenagers can be scary!" Hunter tossed a wink Jessie's way. "Come on, you yahoos. Let's let these beautiful ladies' get on with their night. We have money to take from some military dudes."

"Remember your promise," Ellie cautioned with a grin.

"Of course, baby."

It was unclear which of the two women was more surprised by the endearing term. In an effort to cover her embarrassment, Hunter gave Ellie a quick kiss and walked out.

Ellie stood there shell-shocked as Rebecca ushered Mo and Cass out. She wasn't a stranger to being called cutesy nicknames. Blaise did it all the time. But hearing them from Blaise *never* affected her like this.

"*Feels good, doesn't it?*" Blaise whispered close to her best friend's ear.

"*Feels amazing.*"

"WHY DID I call her that? It's too soon. It's too soon, right?" A very fidgety Hunter asked her snickering friends. "It just came out. Do you think I screwed things up? She looked kinda freaked. Did she seem freaked to you?"

"Hunter, calm down!" Cass laughed and pulled her friend to a stop. "You didn't do anything wrong. There's no timetable with this stuff. Hell, look at me and Rebecca. She was doing things to me I never thought I'd allow before I even knew her name."

"Yo, TMI, Cass," Mo mumbled. "But, she's right. You gotta just go for it. Isn't that the point of this stuff?"

"I don't know."

"We do." Mo and Cass said simultaneously. "First," Cass continued. "You can't walk into that poker game all frazzled and shit. Second, you can't let Ellie think you feel like you're making a mistake with her."

"I don't think that!" Hunter said urgently. "I just don't want to fuck it up by going too fast for her."

"Dude, you're acting like she's some kinda virgin or something," Mo scoffed in jest. Her smile faded completely at the look on Hunter's face. "Bullshit! That woman is no virgin! She has a kid! I don't know what kind of game she's playing with you . . ."

"Mo, stop," Cass chided quietly. She could see Hunter getting upset and wanted to diffuse the situation quickly. "Hunter?"

"Not my story to tell," Hunter muttered.

Cass held a hand up to stop Mo's retort. "Okay, that's fair. Just know that if you need to talk, we're here, Hunter. You know it goes no further. Not even to Rebecca if that's what you want."

Mo lost the attitude as fast as it came on. "Not Patty either. Sorry about that."

Hunter sighed heavily and sat down on the parking stop. "I know you're looking out for me, Mo. But Ellie isn't playing me. You don't know what she's been through. I can't tell you much without her permission, but suffice it to say, I'm her first 'real thing', ya know? Kind of like she's mine. Do you see now why I'm a little on edge about screwing things up?"

"Man." Cass plopped down beside Hunter. "That's heavy. Honestly, though, maybe this is for the best. She's not jaded by bad relationships." She shrugged. "You know that I'm the first real, *healthy* relationship Rebecca has had. I admit that it can be stressful sometimes wondering if I'm doing everything right. Becca gets upset with me for feeling that way, though. She says it's not my job to make everything perfect. It's my job to be me and to treat her with love and respect, not kid gloves. If you want to call Ellie cute little pet names, do it. Seems to me, she would tell you if she didn't like it."

"Agreed," Mo said wholeheartedly. "I don't believe that woman would have a problem telling you what's on her mind. Patty is the same way. I mean, she wants the romance, flowers, and shit, but what she really wants is for me to *want* to give her that." Mo frowned. "Did that make sense?"

Hunter and Cass both chuckled.

"Yeah," Hunter tapped Mo on the leg with her foot. "Don't do it because you think that's what she wants, do it because it's how you want to treat her."

"That's what I said. More or less."

"I think the moral of our convoluted story is," Cass threw in, "be yourself. That includes calling her 'baby' if that's what you're feeling. You wouldn't want her to hold back, would you?"

"No, of course not. But I also don't want to scare her off."

Cass nodded. "You know, the first time Rebecca spent the night with me, I woke up that next morning in absolute heaven. The most beautiful woman I'd ever seen was naked and wrapped around me. I also felt this terrible sense of fear." Hunter and Mo stared at Cass in confusion. Neither could understand fearing waking up to a beautiful woman. Knowing that she could trust the two women, Cass explained. "I hadn't seen Rebecca in two months. She had run away thinking it was what was best for me. Before then, I had been with her a total of two times. Missing her was like missing the air that I breathe. The fear came from worrying she would run again and I would never experience that form of heaven again or breathe again. So, I did what any insane person would do. I asked her to move in with me."

"Whoa." Mo knelt down next to her friends. "She didn't get up and run?"

"Nah, thank God. But what it did was open up the lines of communication. She learned about my fears and I learned she was serious about giving us a chance." Cass bumped Hunter's shoulder. "See? It could be a good thing being ready and willing to take leaps instead of baby steps."

Hunter's response was interrupted by the trill of her phone. She dug it out of her back pocket and winced when she saw Ellie's name. "It's El." She took a deep breath. "Hello?"

"Are you all right?"

"Huh?" Ellie's question was filled with concern, causing Hunter alarm.

"Are you all right? Are you safe?"

"I'm fine, El. What's going on?"

"Greyson called Blaise. He said you hadn't shown up yet. You should have been there by now. I was afraid something had happened to you."

Hunter felt terrible. She stood, ready to sprint back up the apartment and grovel if it would make Ellie feel better. "I'm sorry. We're still down in the parking lot. We, uh, stopped to talk." She heard Ellie release what sounded like a relieved breath. "We didn't mean to worry you, El."

"No, it's . . . is everything okay?"

Hunter hesitated.

"Hunter? Are you stressing over what you said before you left?"

"Kinda."

"Oh, honey." Hunter's heart soared at the endearment. Not to mention the emotion she heard behind it. "Do you want to know how I really felt when you called me baby?" she heard Ellie ask.

"Y-yes?"

Ellie laughed softly. "It made me feel whole. It made me feel like *me*. Years ago, when I chose the path I've been on, I thought I'd never hear someone like you say something like that to me. My parents broke me and I was terrified that I would always be a coward. Then you walked into my life. Hearing that from you made me feel that in the end, I won."

Hunter wiped a tear from her cheek. "Baby, it's not the end. This is only the beginning. And, what you did for yourself and Jessie? That was anything *but* cowardice."

"Let's agree to disagree on that. You have a poker game to get to. If you win, I expect a nice dinner."

"If? *If?* You doubt my skills?"

"Oh, I don't doubt your skills at all. In fact, I've been thinking about them a lot lately."

Holy shit! Did someone just turn up the heat? She cleared her throat and wondered which one of her friends would administer CPR if she had a heart attack. *Please don't let it be Mo.* "Yeah?"

"Mmhmm. See you later, Hunter."

"Yo, Hunt! You good?"

Hunter stared at her phone for a second, then a wide, toothy grin formed. "Oh yeah. I'm fantastic. Let's go win some money!"

"ARE THEY ALIVE?" Patty asked from her perch at the bar.

Ellie smiled. "Yes. They're still down in the parking lot. Apparently, they had to stop to talk."

"Hunter was over-analyzing what she said before she left, wasn't she?" Rebecca asked with a shake of her head. She was standing close enough to see the shimmer of *something* in Ellie's eyes. This was something she was going to have to nip in the bud if she wanted to become friends with the woman her best friend was falling for.

Ellie hated the twinge of jealousy she felt at Rebecca's familiarity with Hunter. She knew it was foolish. If she believed both Hunter and Rebecca — and she did — she knew nothing had ever happened between the two. So, why the jealousy? It was something Ellie would have to figure out if she wanted a friendship with one of Hunter's best friends.

"Yes. But, I think I talked her down from the ledge. For now," Ellie grinned. "Let's eat."

"I heard that!" Patty clapped her hands and rubbed them together. "I've been smelling whatever delicious scents are going on in here since I walked in. If you had made me wait much longer, child, I would have given your daughter a run for her money in the 'hangry' department."

"I don't know, Patty, Jessie can get pretty cranky. Even Blaise without red velvet hasn't touched that level of crankiness, yet."

"Getting crankier by the second!" Jessie called out in jest as she stuffed her mouth with one of the pepperoni cheese sticks her mom selfishly kept her from eating earlier.

"I call that being a teenager!" Blaise called back.

"So, what's your excuse?" Piper asked her mom quietly, blushing a bit when everyone laughed.

"You come from my vagina. You're supposed to be on my side," Blaise grumbled, then winked at her shy daughter who blushed even more.

"Stop embarrassing your daughter by talking about your vagina and help bring food to the table," Ellie chided. She laughed when Blaise pouted. "Doesn't work now that you're not pregnant anymore."

315

"I'm still making my list," Blaise muttered and took a platter of stromboli that was making her mouth water. It never ceased to amaze her how Ellie could cook just about anything. Italian, Greek, American. It didn't matter where it originated, Ellie was able to put her own spin on it and make it even better.

"Hunter is going to have to seriously up her workout regimen," Rebecca commented when Blaise set the platter in front of her. "And, I'm going to have to take more yoga classes! This looks absolutely delectable, Ellie."

Ellie graciously accepted the kudos, telling everyone to dig in. As she had hoped, the Italian cuisine was a hit with adults and teenagers alike. *So far, so good,* she thought as the conversation remained playful and light.

Jessie watched and listened to the banter and benevolent chatter. She found that liked Hunter's friends and thought they'd make great additions to girls' night. Especially if her mother kept cooking like this to impress them. Her only issue was that *no one* was talking about the important things. Things she thought her mom needed to hear. It was time for her to initiate things. Hence, her slight kick to Blaise's shin.

Blaise frowned at Jessie who widened her eyes and inclined her head. When Blaise shook her head in confusion, Jessie repeated the motion.

"What is going on over there?" Ellie asked suspiciously.

"I have no clue," Blaise answered, rubbing her shin.

Jessie rolled her eyes. "Fine. I guess I have to do all the dirty work. Ladies," she addressed everyone at the table except her mom and Piper. "How long did you wait to become intimate with your partners?"

"Jessica Anne!"

Blaise, Rebecca, and Patty stared at Jessie with a mixture of shock and hilarity. And perhaps a bit of trepidation. Ellie's face reddened with chagrin. Jessie was never particularly blunt, but she also never shy. Something Ellie was regretful about right at this moment.

"What? Come on, mom. It's not like I'm asking for details." She sighed. "All I'm asking is how long they waited. Aren't you a little curious yourself about the dating rituals of older people?"

Piper laughed softly. "You should have stopped while you were ahead."

Jessie lowered her head, but couldn't suppress the smile at the indignant look on Blaise's face.

Rebecca looked at Ellie with interest. "I take it from the line of questioning that you and Hunter haven't, um . . ."

"No." Ellie gave Jessie the motherly version of the evil eye. She wasn't happy that she felt she now had to explain herself to Hunter's friends.

"Well, that's not uncommon," Patty comforted. "Many couples take their time. There's no schedule. At least not for us old folks," she teased, winking at Jessie. "How long did you wait with others?"

Ellie's eyebrows rose. "Hunter didn't tell you?" Both Rebecca and Patty remained silently baffled and Ellie felt a sense of pleasure knowing Hunter had been loyal to her. She had expected that at the very least Rebecca would know. However, now Ellie had to figure out how to explain this to the women without having to go into *everything*. "She's my first," she said softly.

"You've never been with a woman?" Rebecca reiterated a bit harshly. "I thought you were a lesbian. Is this a game to you? Is Hunter some sort of experiment for you?"

"Hey! My mom isn't like that!" Jessie defended vehemently.

"It's okay, Jessie. Rebecca is only protecting Hunter," Ellie soothed even though calm was not what she was feeling. But she tried to put herself in Rebecca's shoes and knew she would be the same way if things were turned around. Green eyes locked with gray. "I am a lesbian and Hunter is *not* an experiment for me. There were circumstances in my life that have prevented me from . . ." Ellie's voice trailed off.

"Mom denied herself to protect me," Jessie declared defiantly. She heard Ellie say her name quietly, but she wasn't finished. "Her parents forced her to be someone she's not by threatening to take me away from her. She's not playing Hunter. But, you better believe that Hunter is *very* lucky that my mom chose to be with her." Ellie reached across Blaise to squeeze Jessie's hand. No words were needed. Just that one simple gesture told Jessie everything she needed to know.

"I'm sorry, Ellie. I had no idea." Rebecca made a mental note to scold Hunter for not at least giving her a heads up about Ellie's situation. The tiniest morsel of information would have been better than a huge helping of "foot-in-mouth" she just had. And Hunter's "CliffsNotes" version didn't count.

Ellie waved away the apology. "I'm not going to fault you for looking after your best friend." She couldn't deny that Rebecca's genuine contrition made her feel marginally better. Besides, she had to be happy that Hunter had good friends to safeguard her heart.

"Great. Now that we have that cleared up, back to my question." Jessie held up a hand to cut off her mom's objection. It was most likely the last time she'd have use of said hand, but she had to believe it was for a noble cause. "We're all friends here, right? And, I know you all probably think I'm too young for this kind of talk, but I'm not because I'm not asking for details. Let's start with Blaise. How long did you and Greyson wait?"

Blaise stuffed her mouth with cheesy greatness and shrugged. She was actually *willing* Ezra to wake up needing to be fed. Anything to get her out of this conversation.

"That is the longest you've ever had food in your mouth, mum," Piper laughed. "Surely it wasn't that bad."

Blaise swallowed and narrowed her eyes at her daughter. "Allowance? Gone." She then took another huge bite of food.

Ellie chuckled. "A couple of dates, wasn't it? Though I may be stretching that a little."

"What happened to loyalty between best friends?" Blaise mumbled with her mouth full.

"Apparently, my daughter is trying to educate me on the ins and outs of 'old people dating'. That means you're obligated to answer." Ellie shrugged. "I'm simply helping you out."

Blaise tapped her temple. "List. And, *technically*, we had three and a half dates before we . . . got intimate."

Patty laughed until Jessie turned the attention on her. "And, you and Mo, Miss Patty?"

"Oh! Child, you are precocious, aren't you?"

"Ha! Precocious. That's the subtle way of saying you have a brass set of . . ."

"Blaise!" Ellie stuffed a garlic knot in Blaise's mouth.

Jessie shook her head. "Rules," she mildly reminded Patty who had yet to answer.

Patty shook her head. "Mo and I were a bit different. It took me a while to come to terms with what I was feeling for Mo because she was a little wild for me. But that nut pursued me for months before I gave in to a date. Took a couple more months of dates after that before we, ahem, became intimate."

Jessie nodded. She had only met Mo for a brief time and could tell that the couple was very different. But she thought they complemented each other pretty well. She looked to Rebecca. *This* was the one she was really interested in. Rebecca exuded sensuality and Cass was just plain hot. "Rebecca?"

"Um."

Ellie could have sworn Rebecca turned at least fifty shades of pink. *She's embarrassed.* If she hadn't seen it with her own eyes, Ellie wouldn't have believed it. Rebecca had always seemed so poised and . . . in control.

"You don't have to answer," Ellie told her.

"Hello? You said I was *obligated!*" Blaise groused playfully. She had seen Rebecca's discomfort, as well, and felt for her.

"Rebecca is our guest and new to this girls' night. She can take some time to get used to us. Mostly you and Jessie."

"No, Blaise is right," Rebecca said bravely. "Rules are rules. Cassidy and I, well, we met at a club. We weren't exactly dating when we . . . got together."

"Okay!" Ellie picked up her plate and handed it to Piper. "Why don't you girls start cleaning up."

"Yes, and then perhaps you can check on your brother," Blaise suggested. She wanted to hear this story and she didn't think Ellie would allow Rebecca to tell it if the girls were in the room.

"Why am I being punished? I didn't start this thing." Piper gave her mom a sly smile. "Come on, Jess. We're being banished to the 'kids table' so they can have grown-up talk."

"I see she's starting to take after you more and more," Ellie laughed.

Blaise smiled proudly. Piper was still incredibly shy, but Blaise could see her blossoming increasingly each day. And if Piper really was taking after her, Blaise would consider that a blessing after missing so much of her life.

Jessie grumbled and Piper snickered as they collected the dishes. Ellie was pretty sure she heard her daughter complaining about never hearing the good stuff. She wasn't sure *she* was ready to hear what Rebecca had to say. Something about the woman made Ellie feel strangely unsophisticated.

"Are you sure you want to talk about this?" Ellie asked when the girls were in the kitchen making all sorts of noises. *Please don't let them break anything or scratch my pans.*

Rebecca took a deep breath. "What is the protocol about things said here?" she asked.

"Stays here if that's what you want," Ellie guaranteed.

Rebecca nodded. "I want to preface this by saying I'm not ashamed of anything concerning me and Cassidy. But I'm also a very private person and the business I'm in necessitates confidentiality."

"Hold on." Patty sat up in her chair and stared at Rebecca. "You know, I've known you for a few years now and I have *no* idea what you do for a living. Does that finally change tonight?"

Ellie glanced at Blaise knowing they were both thinking about their earlier conversation.

"I don't want you to think I don't trust you, Patty." Rebecca brought her gaze to her hostess for the evening. "And, I don't want you to think of me any differently."

"The thing about Ellie," Blaise interjected before Ellie could answer. "She's the least judgmental person I know. Me, on the other hand, I'll judge you all day long." She winked and stuck her tongue out at Rebecca who chortled. "Do you need some more wine to loosen your tongue up?"

Rebecca grinned wickedly. "Do you ask all the lesbians that?"

Ellie snorted and gave Rebecca a high-five. Patty covered her full mouth and hoped not to choke as she laughed. Even the teenagers — who weren't supposed to be listening — giggled uproariously.

Blaise blushed uncharacteristically. To cover, she glared at the girls and pointed towards the guest bedroom where Ezra was sleeping. "Go!"

"Sorry," Rebecca chuckled. "I couldn't resist."

"She'll get over it." Ellie bumped her best friend on the shoulder.

"As long as lesbian humor is not just for lesbians, I'm good," Blaise quipped.

"Do your worst," Rebecca allowed freely.

Blaise saluted cheekily. "Okay, enough stalling. What kind of club were you at when you met Cass?"

Rebecca pursed her lips and considered her options. Full truth? Or as little as she can possibly get away with? Eager eyes stared at her. "A sex club," she said finally.

"Shut up!" Patty sat back in her chair with an audible thump. "How did I not know this!"

"A sex club?" *Now we're talking!* Blaise barely resisted rubbing her hands together with excitement. This was the most she had talked about sex with other women. Ellie never could. Of course, Blaise *now* understood why, but perhaps that would change now that El had a potential lover. "What kind of sex club are we talking about here? Swingers? Singles? Fetish?"

Ellie stared at Blaise suspiciously. "How exactly do you know about sex clubs?"

"I — it's common knowledge that they exist!"

Rebecca laughed at the banter between the two friends. *Okay, here goes nothing. I suppose I'll know if these friendships were meant to be.* "BDSM," she said simply. Patty remained quiet and Rebecca wasn't sure what to make of that. Blaise's eyes got enormously wide. But, it was Ellie's reaction that intrigued Rebecca the most. The young chef looked . . . pensive. Whether there were other emotions hiding behind those green eyes, Rebecca didn't know.

"Whoa." Blaise managed to pick her jaw up off the table long enough to peek over at her best friend. "BDSM," she began to explain, "is . . ."

"I know what it is." Ellie's eyes never left Rebecca.

Though Blaise was a bit surprised by Ellie's statement, she let it go. Whatever was going on between Ellie and Rebecca, though? *That* she would find the underlying cause of when they were alone. "So, Cass is your, um?"

Rebecca tilted her head and waited. She had to admit that watching Blaise squirm was pretty fun. When the New Zealander started looking to the others for help, Rebecca decided to put her out of her misery. "Cassidy is my girlfriend."

"Well, sure. But, if you met at the club, that means she's also your — what do they call them? — Dominant, right?"

"Other way around."

The three women stared at Ellie who spoke quietly.

"Ellie's right," Rebecca confirmed. "I am Cassidy's Mistress."

"The business you're in," Ellie repeated Rebecca's earlier words. "You own the club."

Ellie's emotionless demeanor was starting to worry Rebecca. She wished that she could read the woman's mind. *What a trip that would be.* "Yes. And, Hunter was right. You are kind of scary with how observant you are," she smiled.

"Somehow, I don't see Cass submitting to anyone," Patty broke the momentary silence and shook her head. "I still can't believe I don't know any of this. Does Hunter know?"

Rebecca swept a lock of hair out of her face. Her answer was *not* going to win her any points with Hunter's girlfriend. "Yes. It's, to some extent, how we met."

Ellie's hackles went up and she narrowed her eyes. "She's been to the club? *Your* club?"

Well, at least she's no longer emotionless, Rebecca thought with an internal wince. "No, Hunter's never been there. I just meant that she knows about my lifestyle. I ended up in the hospital because of it," she finished quietly.

"I'm sorry." Ellie looked appropriately chastised.

It was Rebecca's turn to wave away Ellie's apology. Another tilt of the head. "Do you think they're having discussions like this at the poker game?"

Chapter Twenty-Five

"How about a little seven-card stud? Or is that offensive to you ladies?" Cade blew a puff of cigar smoke out the side of his mouth. Greyson had told him to behave and he swore he would. Then again, that was before he saw Hunter's smug face walking into the room. Okay, so he wasn't taking losing the girl as well as he thought he was. Any man who had seen Ellie's ass in jeans would understand.

"Cade," Greyson warned.

Except for Greyson, apparently, Cade thought irritably.

"Little must be the operative word if you're this moody," Hunter deadpanned. "I'm pretty sure we can handle anything you throw out there."

When Cade began to snarl, Greyson knew it was time to put a stop to this madness. Otherwise, Blaise was going to make him wait even longer to get some!

"Oh, for fuck's sake! We're adults here, let's start to act like it, shall we?"

"Says the man who has everything he wants," Cade mumbled.

"Ellie's gay, brother. Let it go." Greyson saw Cade eye Hunter as though it was her fault. "You do know she was born that way, right?

Hunter didn't steal her from you. She didn't turn Ellie. You *never* had a chance. That's life."

"Who the hell's side are you on, Grey?"

"The side that finishes this bullshit and gets on with the damn game!" *Shit! I need this damn month to be over with. Maybe I could talk Blaise into a . . .*

"Blow that smoke somewhere else, man." Cass waved her hand in front of her, staving off another round of Cade's cigar smoke. "Rebecca is never going to let me get near her smelling like an ashtray."

Hunter flexed her neck, savoring the feel of the popping loosening up the tension she held there. *For Ellie.* "This is ridiculous. We are intelligent, successful human beings. We should be capable of having a pleasant evening without all of this unnecessary drama. Greyson, you're married to Blaise — Ellie's best friend — and, Cade you're Greyson's best friend. *Obviously,* we're going to be seeing a lot of each other since I'm with Ellie now. I don't have to be friends with you, but I'm not about to cause any undue stress for Ellie by fighting with you. She's going through enough with coming out, don't you think?"

Cade didn't want to agree, but Hunter made a valid point. Ellie had been scared of what would happen when/if she was *truly* herself. She had told Cade as much. He told her never to compromise. If she had chosen him in order to be deemed what society thought was 'normal', that's exactly what she would have been doing. The Marine — hell, the *man* — in him needed to check his ego. He stood and held his hand out to Hunter.

"You're right. I apologize for my behavior." He grinned when Hunter stood as well and accepted his handshake. Cade lost the grin and pulled her a fraction closer. "You hurt her, this truce will be null and void. Get me?"

"If I hurt her, *brother*, I'll deliver myself to you," Hunter said seriously.

The grin returned with a slight nod. As much as he hated to admit it, he felt Hunter could be good for Ellie. She *seemed* legit. He wasn't allowed to do any background checks, but that, too, would be invalid if things took a bad turn. "Do me a solid, yeah? Don't tell Ellie about this? She'll kick my ass for sure."

"Scared of her?" Hunter looked amused. The tension from before began to roll off of her in waves.

"Fuck, yeah!" He clapped Hunter on the shoulder. "You are, too, if you're smart."

Mo threw her hands up. "Finally! Are we done with all this emo chick stuff? Can we get on with this game now? Jesus! I need to win my money back. Courting my wife is expensive!"

"Hear, hear!" Greyson raised his glass of whiskey to Mo before slamming it back.

"What the fuck, Grey? You're married to an heiress. Nothing is expensive to you," Cade laughed gruffly and dealt the cards.

Cass and Mo turned their heads to stare at Hunter, who shrugged. *An heiress? Thank goodness Blaise is straight!* She slid two bucks to the center of the table. "Why are we playing this penny-ante stuff, Mr. Heiress?"

Greyson scratched his beard and peered at the growing pile of money in front of him. "It would be a bit of an overkill if I took *more* money from you to line my already stuffed pockets, wouldn't it?" he grinned.

"MAY I HELP?"

Ellie paused with dish in hand and closed her eyes briefly. She felt awful for feeling any kind of jealousy towards Rebecca. The poor woman had been through so much and Hunter helped her. Unfortunately, she didn't know how to stop it. This wasn't something she had a lot of experience with.

"No, please. You're a guest. You should be having fun with the others."

"Ellie?" Rebecca waited until Ellie turned towards her. "You know there's no reason to be jealous of me, right?"

Ellie sighed. "Logically, I know that. It's just that," she faltered, not sure she wanted to say what she was feeling. "On paper, you and Hunter are perfect for each other."

Rebecca's eyebrows shot up. Personally, she thought it was a brave, honest, and quite vulnerable thing for Ellie to say. She's *perfect for Hunter.* "I could see how you'd think that, but I don't agree." She rested her hip on the counter and explained. "When Hunter came into my life, I was broken. Literally and figuratively. She saved me by becoming not only my doctor but a cherished friend. Ellie, I wasn't in a mindset to see anyone in a romantic way and, as gorgeous as Hunter is, I've never felt that way for her."

"But you two have this deep connection."

"As do you and Blaise. Which Hunter has noticed, by the way."

Ellie chuckled at that thought. "The difference is Blaise isn't an experienced lesbian." She cringed. "That sounded better in my head. I didn't mean that the way it came out."

Rebecca smiled. "I know what you meant. I assume that's what your biggest issue is. Your lack of experience?"

Ellie lifted a shoulder and returned to the task of washing dishes. "How do we know we're compatible? How do I know what I like? What *she* likes?"

"When I met Cassidy," Rebecca began after a moment of silence, "I had no clue how to have a healthy relationship. That, along with my reservations about our age difference, had me running away from the woman that *is* perfect for me." She pushed away from the counter. "Turns out, despite being younger, Cassidy was the wiser one. She told me that no matter how many relationships we've had — and she's had a few — they're all different. 'There's no magic recipe. We work at it and we find our own way.'" Rebecca smiled softly when she recalled Cassidy's words.

"Wow."

"Yeah. Ellie, in my opinion, you and Hunter have the potential to be perfect for each other. Enjoy finding each other. I promise you, the journey is spectacularly fun," Rebecca grinned wickedly.

Ellie glanced into the living room where the others were. Blaise looked back at her questioningly. It was strange to be talking to someone else about the most intimate things in her life. She would talk to Blaise later, but for now, Rebecca was the one with the answers she needed.

"Your lifestyle? Is it just something you know you like?"

Rebecca shook her head. "No. I was introduced to it by my ex, though in a different role. Cassidy wasn't a fan of the lifestyle until she met me." She batted Ellie's shoulder with the back of her hand. "Like I said, the journey is fun. And, if you both decide that bondage and flogging are something you want to explore, I have a special room at the club just for you," she winked.

Ellie took a second to think about that. How would it be to give up control like that? Would Hunter enjoy finally being the one in charge? She gasped at how quickly she defined their roles. Her body was *definitely* reacting to the thought of submitting to Hunter and she cleared her throat in hopes it would help clear her mind of those images.

"I'll, um, keep that in mind. You mentioned your and Cass's age difference a couple of times. You can't be that much older than her."

"Hey, mom! Hunter is texting you saying they're here and on their way up. *Baby*." Jessie waved her mother's phone in the air with laughter.

"Looks like we'll have to save that conversation at another time." Rebecca held Ellie's gaze. "Any question, anytime. There's not much that shocks me and I know how to be discreet."

"Thank you. About earlier."

Rebecca held up a hand. "We both made mistakes. How about we call it even and move on?"

"Deal."

"SO, HOW DID everything go?" Hunter caught the look that passed between Ellie and Rebecca. She pulled Ellie a bit closer, hoping the look meant a budding friendship was in the works.

"Good. And, with you and Cade?"

Hunter flashed back to the poker game. Yeah, it didn't start so great, but by the end, she and Cade had come to an almost friendly cease-fire. "Absolutely," she smiled and glanced around. With the teens and BFFs all around, Hunter couldn't help but feel a bit on display. "Can we maybe talk in private for a moment?"

"Yes, of course." Ellie guided Hunter to her bedroom. "Are you okay? Did something happen at the game?"

Hunter turned to Ellie. "No, no. Everything was good. I even won some money. Enough to take you out on the town for . . . hotdogs."

Ellie laughed. "I can do hot dogs. What did you, mmph!"

For the second time since they met, Hunter surprised Ellie with a kiss. Only this time she embraced it. Fingers were buried into hair and dug into hips. Moans blended as tongues melded together. The heat that Ellie felt deep inside singed her soul. Regardless of how things progressed between them, Ellie would remember this one moment for the rest of her life. The heated kiss came to its natural end when both women needed to breathe.

"*Whoa.*"

Ellie swayed a little and Hunter tightened her hold. "Mmm. I've been thinking about doing that all night. I just didn't want an audience when doing it." She touched her forehead to Ellie's. "Is it wrong for me to wish we were alone?"

"If it is, we're both very, *very* wrong." She took Hunter's face in her hands. "*Kiss me again.*"

Hunter complied, this time taking it slow. She kissed Ellie in a way she had always dreamed of kissing someone she . . . loved. *Love.* Such a huge word with even more intense consequences that Hunter wasn't sure either of them was ready for. Yet. But, she knew her heart was speeding towards that magnificent awareness and there was nothing she could do about it. Except embrace it.

"As much as I want to stay here doing this," Hunter panted softly, "I should get everyone home safely."

"Are you always this responsible?"

The tall doctor chuckled. "Not even close." She delicately extracted herself from Ellie's arms and immediately felt the loss. "See you in the morning?"

"Mmhmm. Are we still on for next weekend?" The time had finally come for the Sumptor Gallery, LA opening. With the menu done and her dress fitting out of the way, all Ellie had to worry about now was showing up at a publicized event with Hunter. It was a big step for the normally very private diner owner.

"Wouldn't miss it for the world, baby." Hunter winked cheekily, but the truth was, she couldn't wait to see Ellie all dolled up for the opening. She already had her outfit for the night and with Ellie by her side, it was going to be awesome!

Ellie smiled and took Hunter's hand, holding it as they left the room and walked to the front door. Naturally, she felt all eyes on them and squeezed the hand in hers. If her face looked as flushed as Hunter's, Ellie knew what the others were thinking. But, these people were friends and family. If she couldn't be herself in front of them without being embarrassed, she'd never make it next weekend. "Be careful," she said when they got to the door.

"Always. And, I'll text you when I get home," she promised with her lopsided grin.

"Thank you." Ellie pulled Hunter down for another quick kiss and then said her goodnights to the others. There may have been awkward moments at the beginning of the night, but Ellie — with blessings from Jessie, Blaise, and Piper — ended up inviting Rebecca and Patty to be girls' night regulars.

Blaise sidled up to Ellie with Ezra in her arms. She leaned close to Ellie's ear as they watched the women leave. "That woman is *so* ready for you," she murmured, laughing because Hunter kept turning back to look at Ellie.

"Let's hope I'm ready for myself," Ellie replied faintly.

"MOM! I — WHOA!" Jessie, who had come barreling into Ellie's bedroom, froze in her tracks.

Ellie turned, nervously smoothing her hands down her dress. "Is it too much? Not enough?" She checked herself in the mirror again. Turning every angle. She had given Kiara carte blanche when it came to the dress and now Ellie wondered if she had made the right decision. Okay, she had to admit the black, off-one-shoulder dress was beautiful. Its column silhouette ended in a sweeping train and the sweetheart neckline boasted shimmering crystals that cascaded down the length of the gown. All of that was perfect. It was the open back and the side split up to . . . there that caused Ellie's trepidation.

"Mom, you look amazing!" Jessie circled Ellie. "I'm totally stealing that dress." She fluffed Ellie's hair lightly. Her mom's hair fell in a beautiful, wavy, honey-colored waterfall down her bare back. A crown braid completed the elegant look. "I'm so glad you chose to keep your hair down. It looks *so* good!"

Ellie hugged her daughter. "Thank you, sweetie. That makes me feel good. But, you're not getting this dress."

"Ha! That's what you think. I know where you keep your clothes! Speaking of which." She gave Ellie a sly grin. "I took the liberty of packing you an overnight bag. It's in the sick limo Mrs. Sumptor-Riley sent over."

Ellie blinked at Jessie. "An overnight bag. Jessie, I . . ."

"It's just in case, mom. I'm not saying you have to use it. But, you know, if you want to, I'm totally fine with that."

"Is this as awkward for you as it is for me?" Ellie joked. "You're my daughter and you're packing me an overnight bag to go and stay with my, um, girlfriend."

Jessie shrugged. "It's a little awkward. But, if I had let Blaise pack it, you would only have a toothbrush."

Ellie let out a hoot full of mirth. "Oh my God, you're so right. So, I guess I should thank you." She pushed a stray strand of hair out of Jessie's eyes. "Are you going to be okay tonight?"

"Yes, mother."

"Ugh, don't call me that," Ellie laughed. "Reminds me of *my* mother."

Jessie snickered. "Well, you know you're *nothing* like her. Anyway, I'll be fine. I'm going over to Piper's to help her babysit Ezra. Then, I'll probably, um, stay there. So, you know, if you're more comfortable coming back here with Hunter . . ."

"Okay! Getting even more awkward!"

"Just giving you options," Jessie winked. "But, on a serious note, can you do me a favor?"

"If I can," Ellie answered carefully. She knew her daughter well enough to be cautious. Jessie had been around Blaise enough to make bizarre demands.

"Don't call her sweetie, please?" Jessie lifted a shoulder self-consciously. "That's always been mine. And, I know you call Blaise that sometimes, but that's different."

The request was easy enough to adhere to. And if it made Jessie feel better, Ellie was more than happy to do it. "You got it. *Sweetie*," she smiled.

Jessie rolled her eyes but chuckled. "Good. So, what *are* you going to call her? Boo? Bae?" She laughed harder when Ellie pushed her and walked away. As her mom slipped on a pair of stilettos that Jessie was in awe of, she continued. "Bugaboo."

"We're still on B's?" Ellie asked dryly.

"Cuddle-bunny? *Dah-ling?*" She pronounced the word with an overly-dramatic accent. "Ooo, I got it! Punkin-pie!"

Ellie snorted with laughter. "You are a nut!"

"Gotta choose one," Jessie ordered. "I gave you some good choices! Which one?"

Jessie was interrupted by the ding of the doorbell.

"Aww, saved by the bell." She stuck her tongue out at her daughter. "Excuse me."

HUNTER FIDGETED AS she waited for Ellie to answer the door. She was nervous again and wondered if that feeling would ever go away. Or if she wanted it to. Pulling the lapels of her black blazer closer together, she mulled over what had possessed her to forego a shirt. It wasn't that she didn't look good. Hell, even at the age of forty-one, the surgeon still knew how to bring out the sexy. She just hoped the form-fitting slacks, heels, and 'sneak peek' of what's under her jacket pleased Ellie. Perhaps Hunter could distract Ellie with the *over*-abundance of flowers she had brought and her outfit wouldn't even be noticed. She laughed quietly at her nervousness. It felt as though there was so much riding on tonight. This was their first outing as a couple where friends and acquaintances would be in attendance as well. If that wasn't enough pressure, the press that would be there certainly filled the void.

She was lost in thought of how Ellie would handle the imminent attention when the door opened. All coherent thoughts drained from her brain and her blood took a bullet train to regions further south when she saw the vision before her.

"Breathe, Hunter."

Somehow, beyond the haze of lust and awe, Jessie's command seeped through Hunter's paralyzed mind and she drew in a ragged breath. "You," she cleared her parched throat and tried again. "You look . . . exquisite."

Exquisite. Leave it to Hunter to deliver a compliment Ellie wasn't expecting. "Thank you," she smiled coyly. "Please, come in."

Hunter, still dazed, pushed the flowers at Ellie. "These are for you." *Great, Hunter. You sound like an idiot.*

"Thank you. Again," Ellie laughed softly. "They're . . ." It was Ellie's turn to be rendered speechless when the removal of the flowers revealed all that was Dr. Hunter Vale. Oh, what an unveiling it was. Ellie couldn't have torn her eyes away from Hunter's exposed cleavage even if she wanted to. Which, coincidentally, she didn't. "Beautiful."

Jessie observed the exchange – or lack thereof – with amusement. Even her friends from high school weren't this bumbling when going out on a date. She had to admit, though, her mom and Hunter looked amazing together. "Okay, okay. Enough ogling each other. You can do that later. Right now, I want to take a pic." That got a groan from her mother and a "deer-in-headlights" look from Hunter.

"We're not going to the prom," Ellie argued.

"Yeah, but you never went to yours," Jessie reminded her as she brought out her phone. "Come on, you two, get close. You know you want to."

"You're pushing it, kid," Ellie warned.

"Can't say she's wrong," Hunter murmured close to Ellie's ear as she pulled the smaller woman into her arms.

"Told ya. Now smile!" Jessie centered the two in the frame and paused. There was a light in her mother's eyes that Jessie had never seen before. And the way Hunter looked at her, the adoration was almost palpable. Jessie wasn't sure if she believed in true love or souls belonging together. Sure, she had seen the chemistry between Blaise and Greyson. She thought maybe they were just an anomaly. But seeing her mom with Hunter gave her an all new perspective. Perhaps it really *did* exist. She snapped a few photos, getting away with more than she thought she would before Ellie declared she'd had enough.

"You're going to make us late, paparazzi girl. When did you become so trigger-happy with that thing?"

"When my mom started dating." Jessie stuck out her tongue. "Tell me you're not going to do the same thing for prom or graduation," she challenged.

Well, shit. She got me there. "Fine. Now come over here and give me a hug so we can go."

Jessie obeyed, even giving Hunter a quick side hug. "Have fun. And, be good!"

"Bye!" Ellie practically dragged Hunter to the door. There was no telling what Jessie would say, but Ellie was sure it would be exceptionally embarrassing.

The teen giggled at her mom's discomfort. She rarely had the chance to tease Ellie, so she was going to take advantage of this situation as much as she could. She swiped through the photos she just took until she came across the perfect one. It captured the moment her mom looked up at Hunter and their eyes met. *Now, that is chemistry.* "Totally Instagramming this," Jessie murmured as she thought about what hashtags to use.

"HAVE I SAID how amazing you look?" Hunter fought to keep her hands to herself. Not an easy thing to do when Ellie's tanned, toned thigh peeked out at her, begging to be touched. Okay, so Hunter was the one begging. Semantics.

"I believe the word was exquisite, which I liked very much." Ellie took Hunter's hand and squeezed it. "Have I told you that I'm having a really tough time keeping my eyes off your cleavage?"

Hunter let out a bark of surprised laughter. "My plan has worked!" She put her arm around Ellie and pulled her closer.

"This isn't helping." The move opened Hunter's blazer, even more, giving Ellie a view of . . . more. She was pretty sure tape was involved in keeping Hunter decent, otherwise, Ellie would be getting her first up-close glimpse of a different side of Hunter. She was ready for that. Right?

"It's helping me." She nibbled Ellie's earlobe, toying with the diamond stud that rested there with her tongue. It was a bold move, but with Ellie's declaration, Hunter was feeling rather fearless.

"Hunter." Ellie shivered.

"Am I going too fast?" There was that damned insecurity. Hunter was determined to get over that with Ellie. Soon.

Another shiver after another nibble from Hunter. "Yes. I mean no." She laughed softly. "I can't think when you're doing that." Ellie turned her head and pressed her lips to Hunter's, kissing her gently. "We're almost there and I don't want to start something we can't finish."

"Do you want to? Finish, I mean?"

"Definitely." She watched the grin spread on Hunter's face and a kaleidoscope of butterflies took up residence in her stomach. Oh, yeah. Ellie was ready. Nervous, but *so* ready.

Chapter Twenty-Six

They walked into the gallery arm in arm. It was a huge step for Ellie and she thought she was handling it pretty well. So what if she was practically squeezing the life out of Hunter's arm. She was still holding on to it.

Hunter leaned in close. *"You good with this?"*

"Mmhmm."

"I could . . ."

"Stay right here," Ellie finished for her. "I'm fine, Hunter. Just getting my bearings."

Hunter smiled at her companion. "Let's look around before we go find Cass." The suggestion was made to hopefully put Ellie at ease, but Hunter was kind of interested to see how the gallery turned out even though she didn't know much about art. What she did know was Cass was super excited to have her work shown in a Sumptor Gallery and she wanted to support that.

"Do you like art?" Ellie asked as they strolled together casually, taking in all the different mediums.

"What answer would impress you the most?"

Ellie chuckled and looked up at Hunter. "The truth will always impress me the most, Hunter. No matter what it is."

Hunter grinned. "I know jack about it. I like Cass's stuff, but other things confuse me. How do people get so gaga over splatters of paint on a canvas?"

"So, you're not a Pollock fan." Ellie laughed as Hunter shrugged humbly. "Art is very subjective. What one finds inspiring, others find odd and vice versa. I don't think there's a right or wrong answer."

"Hmm. I guess you're right." Hunter lifted her shoulder again. "I always thought it was because I have more of a scientific or analytical mind. I'm not artistic at all."

Ellie studied one of the black and white photos on display. The artist certainly knew how to bring out the emotions with this simple, yet powerful photo of a young, obviously malnourished, child. She squinted at the name of the artist. *Eve Sumptor.* "I think we're all artists in some aspect," she said at length. "You as a surgeon, me with food. We just use different media and techniques. Have you always wanted to be a doctor?"

Hunter thought about Ellie's comment before answering her question. She supposed it could be true. Ellie was certainly gifted at what she did. And Hunter had a healthy enough ego to know she was an exceptional surgeon. "Yeah, I think so," she answered finally. "My mom used to tell me that if any of my stuffed animals ever got a 'booboo' I'd ask her where her sewing kit was so I could fix them up."

Ellie imagined a young Hunter concentrating on doing surgery on her stuffed friends and smiled softly. *I bet she was cute.*

"What about you? Have you always wanted to cook?"

"Not really." She pulled Hunter towards another aisle, this one featuring the 'splattered' look Hunter wasn't a fan of. "My mother hated cooking, but according to my father it was her job."

"Chauvinist?"

"To say the least. He's very old school." Ellie shook her head. "Anyway, when I got older, my mother decided it was time for me to pull my weight around the house. I was resentful at first because I was in track and having to be home to make dinner every night was cutting into my running time. But, it turns out that I was naturally very good at it. If I hadn't enjoyed it so much, I would have been pissed off that it soon became my job to cook almost every meal. Ruined my Olympic chances, though," she joked.

Hunter stopped abruptly. "You wanted to be in the Olympics?"

"It was a child's dream." Ellie tugged Hunter in motion again. "One that was born out of the want to get out of the house as soon as I could. I loved my parents and I thought they loved me, but living there was stifling. Anyway, it was all moot once I got pregnant."

"If you could go back and do things differently, would you work for the Olympics?"

This time Ellie stopped in front of Hunter and gazed up at her. "Knowing now how my life turns out, I wouldn't change anything."

Hunter's response was interrupted by a feminine voice with a thick accent. Her eyes widened with shock when she saw who the voice belonged to. Then narrowed at the woman's over-friendliness with Ellie.

"You are a vision!" Kiara kissed Ellie on each cheek. "I knew that dress . . . no, that *you* were made for that gown. *Sehr Schön!*"

Ellie bowed her head. "*Dankeschön.* Don't be impressed," she said when Kiara's eyebrows lifted. "It's the only word I really know and you can thank Wayne Newton for that."

Kiara chuckled. "I'll be sure to do that if I ever meet him." She glanced at Ellie's companion. "My apologies for interrupting the two of you."

Damn. I should have introduced them right away. "Kiara, this is Hunter, my . . ."

"Friend," Hunter supplied dully. It hurt that Ellie hesitated. Hell, it hurt that Ellie didn't think to introduce Hunter to her *friend*. Maybe she didn't know the woman as well as she thought.

"Date," Ellie corrected immediately. "Hunter is my girlfriend."

"Ah, so you're the lucky woman." In Kiara's line of business, being able to read people was important. Her take on Hunter? She was not happy. Kiara could deal with jealousy. That was easy. But underneath that, Kiara saw a sadness in Hunter. This relationship was important to both women. Far be it for Kiara to get in the middle of that. "Again, I apologize for interrupting. I saw you and just wanted to tell you how beautiful you look. Both of you are stunning. Now, I must mingle." Kiara graced them both with a genuine smile and left them alone.

Hunter grabbed two flutes of champagne from a passing server and handed one to Ellie. "Wanna tell me how you know Kiara Adler and why she's so familiar with you?"

"Want to tell me why that sounded like an accusation rather than a question?"

"*Guilty conscience?*" Hunter muttered.

Annoyed, Ellie turned on her. "I have nothing to be guilty about," she whispered hotly. "What about you? How did you know her last name? Is there something I should know?"

"I'm a lesbian," Hunter said stonily. "Kiara Adler was one of the first out and proud lesbian supermodels. She came out when she was sixteen and never looked back. It gave those of us around the same age as her someone to admire. She was on every lesbian's wall back in the day. Mo probably still has hers."

Ellie stared at Hunter as though she grew two heads. Growing up denying who you were could put you so far out of touch with what's out there. "To answer your questions, Kiara is a friend of Eve's. She also works with designers." Ellie indicated her dress. "We met a few days ago when she was collecting measurements."

"*She* took your measurements?" Hunter scoffed. "Of course, she did." *Oh, my God, shut up, Hunter! You're fucking up so badly right now.*

"No, her assistant did. Where is this coming from?" She pulled Hunter to a semi-secluded corner. "I get that we're both pretty new to this, but I thought we were moving forward. *If* I were interested in Kiara, I would have said yes when she asked me out."

Hunter's heart sank. She couldn't compete with someone like Kiara Adler. Regardless of Hunter's success, her track record with women was subpar at best. How could she expect Ellie to *settle* with her? The woman just came out. She should be out there doing exactly what Mo said Hunter should do. Right?

"Maybe you should say yes." *God, that hurt.*

"Excuse me?"

Hunter shrugged. "You should say yes. Experience what it's like to be a lesbian. You have a supermodel asking you out. That's not an everyday occurrence." She looked around, willing herself not to cry. When she spotted Cass, she took the cowardly way out. "I should, uh, go see Cass and congratulate her."

"Hunter!" Ellie watched in bewilderment as the surgeon walked away. *What the hell?* How did the night go from flirtatious seduction to Hunter walking away from her and telling her to go out with someone else?

Rebecca sidled up to Ellie, touching her lightly on the shoulder. "You look stunning." She lost her smile when she saw the look on Ellie's face. "And, a bit stunned."

"Hmm? Oh, thank you. You, too."

Ellie's distraction was not lost on Rebecca. In fact, she hadn't even looked in Rebecca's direction. So, she followed Ellie's line of sight until she was looking at Hunter.

"What's up with tall, dark, and goofy?"

"Why don't you go and ask her? She's your friend." Ellie slammed her eyes shut. This wasn't Rebecca's fault and taking it out on her would only complicate things even more. "Sorry. I'm sorry." Finally, she turned her attention to the other woman. She really did look beautiful, too, in her pale pink, knee length dress. "The whole point of a relationship is to be honest, right?"

"That's one of the main objectives, yes." Rebecca decided not to take offense to Ellie's snarky comment. Obviously, something was going on between the new couple and she'd rather focus on fixing that than the petty stuff. "Do you want to talk about it?"

Ellie relayed the condensed version of what just went down with Hunter. As she was saying it, she tried to see Hunter's side of things. While she could *somewhat* understand, that didn't make what Hunter was doing right.

"Kiara Adler asked you out?" Rebecca asked after she picked her jaw up off the ground.

Ellie rolled her eyes. "You know her, too?"

"Every lesbian does. She was our . . ."

"Role model."

Rebecca shook her head. "Fantasy."

"ARE YOU CRAZY?" Cass stared at Hunter.

"She has options," Hunter grumbled moodily. "Maybe she should take them."

"Options," Mo scoffed. "You practically just handed Ellie over to a . . ."

"I know! Fuck!" Hunter downed the rest of her champagne and switched the empty flute out for a full one. "It's the right thing to do."

"Bullshit." Cass wanted to slap Hunter upside the head. Rebecca had tried this shit with Cass when they first met and it pissed her off. Having the choice to be with someone you feel strongly for taken away from you sucked royally. "You don't get to decide what Ellie wants."

"Cass is right, Hunt. You're making a big mistake."

"This from the person who basically told me to slut it up and not be tied down by one woman."

"That was my mistake," Mo acknowledged. "And, I apologized for it. You really want to screw up this thing you have with Ellie?"

"No, I don't. But I also don't want to hold her back." Hunter hung her head. The night had started out so promising. She could only imagine how it would have ended. Why couldn't she have just let this thing with Kiara go? It wasn't even that big of a deal, according to her friends who were having no trouble telling her how stupid she was being. She couldn't disagree. She had let her insecurities take over and now she may have ruined what could have been an amazing relationship.

"CAN YOU UNDERSTAND her fear?" Rebecca asked. By this time, Blaise had made her way over to join the conversation.

Ellie thought of the women Hunter had been with. All married. All cheating on their spouse. She hoped that Hunter didn't believe that was the way relationships were destined to be, but there was no telling the extent of the damage that Susan did. "Yes," Ellie sighed. "However, that doesn't mean she gets to make this decision for me." She looked at her best friend. "You know how I feel. We've had this discussion."

"I know." Blaise, dressed impeccably in slate blue, silhouette gown, rubbed Ellie's arm with affection. Actually, she hadn't fully understood the intensity of Ellie's reaction to Hunter. What was it about the woman that touched Ellie so deeply? She glanced over at the surgeon who was watching Ellie and receiving what Blaise hoped was an earful from her friends. Then she glanced over at Kiara. If Ellie wasn't attracted to *that* woman, Blaise knew what she felt for Hunter was real and powerful. Obviously, it wasn't just about beauty. There was something more profound that made Ellie gravitate to Hunter. "Maybe if you went out on a date with Kiara Hunter would be forced to get her head out of her ass."

Ellie shook her head. "No playing games, Blaise. I don't want to use Kiara like that or manipulate Hunter's feelings. But I also don't want to be in a relationship that dictates who I can and can't talk to. I think I've had enough of that in my life."

Blaise and Rebecca both agreed with Ellie. There was going to be a huge learning curve with these two. Of course, Rebecca loved and respected Hunter, but she couldn't help being delighted that someone as strong and independent as Ellie was in Hunter's life. This was exactly the type of woman Hunter needed.

"Ladies," Kiara greeted. "May I steal Ellie for a moment?"

They both looked to Ellie, who nodded, and each wandered off hoping that by the end of the night this whole situation would be resolved.

"I noticed there seems to be a discord between you and your girlfriend. I'm sorry if I am the cause." Sincere verdant eyes captured Ellie's. "I'm not a manipulative person, Ellie. So, if I did anything to make Hunter believe there was something between us, it was purely unintentional."

Ellie smiled kindly. "It's just a misunderstanding. This is not on you, Kiara."

"In any case, if you would like me to talk to her, I'd be happy to tell her how you rejected me."

Ellie chuckled. "I already told her. Full disclosure and all that. Relationships are not easy."

"Believe me, I know."

"Somehow I find that hard to believe. I mean, you *are* the subject of many lesbian fantasies."

Kiara laughed gleefully. "Ironic, isn't it? That in reality, I can't find a woman to spend my life with? I suppose fantasies are much easier to navigate than real life."

EACH TIME ELLIE laughed with Kiara it was like a knife to the heart. Hunter had just made up her mind to beg the diner owner for forgiveness when she saw them together.

"I'm going to go." She finished the glass of champagne she held — her fourth — and handed the empty flute to an always present server. "Sorry, Cass. Congratulations. You deserve all of this. I don't want to screw it up even more than I have already."

"Don't do this, Hunt." Cass looked to Rebecca who took her hand. "You're compounding the situation by avoiding her. This could all be worked out if you just talk to her."

"She seems to be doing just fine."

"And, you've had too much to drink," Rebecca chastised. "You're acting like a moron, I hope you know that. But, if you insist on leaving — even though it's a big night for Cass — you better tell Ellie. Don't just walk out on her."

"And, before you ask," Patty, who had been thoroughly filled in on the situation, began. "We're all on Ellie's side here. We love you dearly, child, but you're wrong about this."

"Thanks for the support," Hunter grumped.

"Right back at ya," Cass retorted. "Get your shit sorted, Hunter. I wanted you here to celebrate with me and you pull this." Cass sighed resignedly when Rebecca squeezed her hand. "I expect you to buy a painting or two to make this up to me." She gave Hunter a hug. *"Don't leave without saying goodbye to her. You'll regret it."*

Hunter apologized again and heeded the warning. Maybe she was wrong about this. In fact, that possibility was close to one hundred percent. But, while she loved her friends, she needed to talk to Dr. Woodrow. She *must* be a head-case to be sabotaging something as good as this.

Slowly, she made her way to where Ellie was standing with the supermodel. It hadn't occurred to her until right at that moment that Ellie never once came after her. Unsure how to feel about that, she approached the woman she longed to be with cautiously. "El?"

Ellie turned. She wanted to stay mad at Hunter, but her glassy-eyed appearance told her how much this was affecting the doctor. Still, she needed Hunter to realize this wasn't how things should be dealt with.

"I'll leave you two." Kiara tried to extract herself from the situation when Hunter stopped her.

"No, it's okay." She looked at Ellie. "I — I'm not feeling well, so I'm going to take off." It wasn't exactly a lie. She actually felt sick to her stomach for being such an idiot. Without taking her attention off Ellie, Hunter vaguely registered Kiara slipping away, leaving them alone.

"I'll go with you." Ellie glanced around, ready to make excuses for her early departure.

Hunter shook her head weakly. "Stay. Have fun. You worked

hard on the food." Food that her stupidity wouldn't let her enjoy now. "I'll, uh, call you." She turned away on heavy feet.

"Hunter?" The tall woman stopped but didn't look back. "Figure this out. I want to be with you, but I won't keep running after you. I have too much self-respect to do that." Ellie saw Hunter barely nod and heard a nearly inaudible apology. That, at least, gave Ellie hope that maybe they could work things out once Hunter got it out of her head that she was unworthy. Until that happened, Ellie could do nothing but watch Hunter disappear out of the gallery.

"Girl troubles?"

Ellie glanced over, ready to give the intruder a piece of her mind when she saw Lainey's kind eyes.

"You could say that. I'm sorry. I know this is a big night for you and Eve."

Lainey waved off the apology. "Please. We're no strangers to opening night drama. The night we re-opened the gallery in New York, my husband and I had a huge fight and he walked out on me." She hesitated for a moment, then continued. "That was also the night that Eve and I first made love."

Ellie choked on the sip of champagne she just took. She would have never guessed that Lainey would be so open with that information. Especially being married.

"Eve told me you knew about us." Lainey patted Ellie's back gently. "The reason I'm telling you this is because I see something between you and Hunter that reminds me of us. A belonging. A fear. A need. A want."

"Why aren't you together?" Ellie asked gently.

Lainey smiled sadly. "It's complicated. Besides, this is about you and Hunter. Don't let fear stand in your way. Hers or yours. All of the best things in life are worth fighting for, Ellie. Don't live with regret." Lainey's eyes traveled to Eve. No matter how big the crowd, she could always find her. And Eve would always be gazing back. "There's nothing standing in your way but you. Nothing holding you back. Seize the opportunity to be happy."

With those words, Lainey left Ellie, being drawn towards Eve by some invisible force. The only thing amiss was that Adam was standing next to Eve and Lainey ended up in the arms of her husband, Jack. It made her sad and determined at the same time. She would fight for Hunter, but she couldn't keep doing it alone. Hunter needed to fight, too. She caught Blaise's eye and her best friend nodded towards the door. The others, who Ellie was quickly beginning to think of as her 'crew', all motioned her to go. Even Cass — on her big night — was encouraging her to leave. *I owe you big time!* Ellie mouthed as she placed her hand over her heart and rushed out.

ELLIE HAD THE limo driver drop her off at her apartment first. It was impossible to determine how the night would go, so a change of clothes and her own vehicle could be advantageous. After a quick call to Rebecca for an address, Ellie followed the GPS to what she hoped was a happy future with Hunter.

"You've arrived at your destination."

Ellie raised an eyebrow at the contemporary one-story home. The clean lines of the stucco and stone were beautifully adorned by a massive frosted glass entrance.

"Nice." The way Hunter had described the place, Ellie had imagined something a little more . . . humble. Or, perhaps it was just Hunter that was being humble. Hunter's truck sat in the driveway alongside a metallic brown Mercedes. Either Hunter had a second vehicle or she had company. Ellie tamped down the stab of jealousy. Surely, Hunter wouldn't be so stupid as to recreate the little fiasco in the on-call room. With shaking hands, she pressed the doorbell.

The door swung open and Hunter's red-rimmed eyes widened. "Ellie!" She grabbed the stunned blonde and hugged her fiercely. "You're here!"

"Hunter." Ellie tried pulling away, but Hunter held on tighter. She was trembling and that spooked Ellie.

"She said you left with Kiara Adler. She said you were holding hands. But you're here. You're not with her."

Ellie pushed Hunter back gently so she could see her face. "Honey, I don't understand. Who are you talking about?"

"Susan. She said . . ."

"She's *here*?"

Hunter nodded. "I don't know where she came from. She just showed up. I . . ."

Ellie's blood boiled and she didn't wait to hear any more. She stormed past Hunter. Even though she had never set foot in Hunter's house, fury must have guided her straight to where the repulsive woman stood.

"Finally, darling. I was about to get started myself."

So, this was Susan. Nothing particularly good stood out about the older woman. She was – in Ellie's biased opinion - average at best. Average height. Average weight. Just . . . average. Her black hair — obviously colored to cover the gray — was cut in an obnoxious bob that did nothing to soften her sharp features. If Ellie hadn't already hated the woman, that damn haircut would do the job. "Get out." She watched Susan pause in whatever the hell she was doing and look at her. Dark, soulless eyes matched the smile Ellie received and it made her boiling blood run cold.

"And, who might you be?"

"You know damn well who I am." Ellie stood toe to toe with the bitch. It was a term she rarely used, but this woman fit the bill like no other. "But, just so we're clear. I'm the woman who's going to make sure you never hurt Hunter again."

Susan's laugh was pure evil. "Ah, yes. You must be the diner whore." She looked Ellie up and down. Something akin to appreciation shone in dull eyes before she laughed again. "As you can see, Hunter and I weren't expecting company."

Ellie eyed the bag of sex paraphernalia. She somehow resisted the urge to clock Susan. But, oh, it would be so satisfying to feel the crack of the woman's long nose under her knuckles. She picked up the bag and thrust it – hard – into Susan's chest. "Get out."

"Hunter . . ."

"Do not talk to her." Ellie knew Hunter had followed her in, but the surgeon had yet to say a word. It worried her. "You've done enough damage."

"Do you have any idea who I am, little girl? Are you sure you want to get involved?"

Ellie laughed mirthlessly. "Little girl? Don't you wish. I know who you are. You're a perverted, pathetic pedophile who preys on innocent young girls, manipulating them until you break them." She stepped closer even though it made her sick. "I *am* involved now. And I'll be damned if I let you get near Hunter again." She felt a glimmer of satisfaction when Susan's face turned red.

"I would be careful if I were you. You're playing with the adults now. I have friends . . ."

"Ha! You have no friends, *Susan*. You have puppets you are blackmailing. Oh, yeah. Hunter told me everything," she said when those soulless eyes widened. "What happens when you lose your leverage, hmm? Who will stand with you then? Because let me tell you something, *I* have friends. Friends who love me and have my back no matter what." She lowered her voice. "Friends who will do *anything* to keep those I care about safe."

Ellie could swear the woman actually snarled. Wild eyes looked to Hunter, then back at Ellie.

"I know things, too, *Ellie*. It must be hard being a single mother. How is that daughter of yours? Jessie, is it?"

Before Ellie even had a chance to register what Susan had said, Hunter was there. Her large hand wrapped around Susan's throat and she pushed her back until she was pressed up against extensive sliding glass doors.

"No." Hunter's voice was deep. Threatening. "If you go near Jessie, I will kill you. No more, Susan. I will never allow you to hurt Jessie the way you did me."

Stunned, Ellie went to Hunter, gingerly laying a hand on her arm. The woman who had sworn to help people was currently squeezing the life out of someone right in front of her. Susan's eyes bugged out as she clawed at Hunter's arm, unable to break free. "Hunter, you have to let go."

"I won't let her hurt Jessie."

"I know, honey. Look at me." Ellie waited until Hunter's eyes met hers. "You have to let go now. You're killing her. And, as much as I would love a world without Susan, I don't want to lose you. We've just started. Please."

Hunter released her grip, albeit reluctantly. She didn't want to admit how satisfying it felt to be hurting Susan for once. She stepped back, flexing her hand to keep it from returning to Susan's throat. "I believe Ellie told you to get out. I would do that if I were you."

Susan grasped at her neck and coughed. "You've made a big mistake," she rasped. "You'll regret this." She aggressively pushed past the couple who stood arm in arm.

"Don't forget your little bag of tricks," Ellie called after her.

Susan stopped and pivoted on her heel. "Just remember that every time you're with Hunter, it was me who taught her everything she knows."

Ellie allowed her hand to drift over Hunter's stomach, right below her breasts. She felt the taller woman shudder and hoped she hadn't just made a huge blunder after everything Hunter had just been through. "Just know that when Hunter is with me, she forgets all about you because she *finally* knows what it's like to make love to a woman." Of course, she knew she and Hunter had yet to become intimate, but Susan didn't need to know that.

Susan let out a cry of fury, slinging the bag at the couple. The floor was littered with sex toys. It would've been funny had the situation not been so terribly awful.

"I'm so sorry, Ellie." Hunter stopped her groveling apology when Ellie placed a finger over her lips.

"Make sure she's gone first?" She watched as Hunter did as she was asked, noting the sheer exhaustion in Hunter's gait. How long had Susan been here? What had she said that had left Hunter utterly defeated. The woman who had let Ellie in was not the confident, successful surgeon Ellie knew. Nor was she the goofy, sweet woman she had come to care about. It was almost as if Hunter had reverted back to that vulnerable, confused child that Susan had exploited all those years ago.

"She's gone," Hunter said listlessly. "I understand if you want to leave, too."

"Is the door locked?"

Hunter frowned. "Yes, but . . ."

"Come on. Let's get you ready for bed so you can rest." She held her hand out to Hunter, who remained hesitant. "I'll stay with you if you want."

Hunter took Ellie's hand. "Please?" She started them towards her bedroom, then stopped. "This isn't how this night was supposed to go. I wanted . . ."

"I know. Me, too. Right now, you need to rest. Do you want me to call someone else to come over? Rebecca? Mo?"

Hunter shook her head. "I only want you. You stood up for me when I couldn't do it myself. Thank you."

"And, you stood up for Jessie." Ellie knew deep down that Hunter could get past this. She had proven there were fight and protection in her still. If Hunter needed someone in her corner fighting with her, Ellie was ready to tag in any time. What better way is there to thank someone that threatened another's life for the sake of her daughter? She got on her tiptoes and kissed Hunter softly on the cheek. "*Thank you.*"

Chapter Twenty-Seven

Ellie turned down the bed as she waited for Hunter to come out of the bathroom. If the night had turned out differently, she would feel much more nervous than she did right now. At the moment, all she could think about is comforting Hunter.

"Hey," Hunter said shyly, still standing at the bathroom door. She had changed into a pair of plaid boxers and a black t-shirt that read **Surgeons do it with precision**.

Ellie read the shirt and smiled. "Come here." She nudged Hunter onto the bed. "In you go."

"You're a good mother."

"I don't want to be your mother, honey," Ellie chuckled.

"Me either," Hunter mumbled sleepily. "Will you sleep with me." Tired eyes opened wide. "I mean just sleep!"

Ellie brushed the hair from Hunter's forehead. "I know what you meant. And, yes, of course."

Hunter relaxed against Ellie's soft touch. She couldn't believe she had this beautiful woman in her bedroom, ready to get in bed with her, and she was too exhausted to do anything about it. *She probably wouldn't want to after what she saw earlier*, Hunter thought miserably.

"I'm, uh, sure I have something you can sleep in." She started to get up, but Ellie stopped her.

"It's fine, honey. I can sleep in this."

"Jeans aren't very comfortable." *No matter how amazing you look in them.*

"They come off. Unless you're uncomfortable with that," Ellie continued when Hunter's eyes widened once again.

"No! I, uh, no, please. I want you to be comfortable." She took Ellie's hand in hers and rubbed her thumb across her knuckles. "I didn't want to be too presumptuous, but I bought an extra toothbrush for you."

"That was sweet, thank you," Ellie smiled. "Why don't you get settled in. I'll be out in a bit."

"'Kay." Hunter smiled when Ellie kissed her on the forehead. "Thank you for being here."

"Anytime."

ELLIE CREPT OUT of the bathroom as quietly as she could. She was grateful for the floor to ceiling windows that illuminated the room in a magnificent amount of moonlight. It certainly saved her from stumbling around in the dark. Once she made it to the opposite side of the bed, her nerves hit her. Here she was, about to get partially naked and get into bed with another woman. A woman she was passionately attracted to.

"Come on, Ellie," she whispered to herself. *"You're an adult. Act like one."* With a quick, deep breath Ellie shimmied out of her jeans and slid into bed next to Hunter. The heat radiating off the sleeping woman warmed her instantly, soothing her jitters. When Hunter languidly wrapped her arms around Ellie, she sunk into the embrace as though she was always meant to be there. She

lifted her head, giving Hunter a feather of a kiss on her neck. *"Goodnight."*

"Ellie?"

She had thought Hunter was asleep and her name was called so quietly, she almost missed it. "Hmm?"

"Don't want you to go out with Kiara Adler."

Ellie chuckled softly at the way Hunter always had to use Kiara's full name. She patted Hunter's stomach. "Okay. I won't."

Silence. Then a soft, "El?"

"Yes?"

"Want to be exclusive. Just you and me," Hunter mumbled drowsily.

Ellie smiled against Hunter's shoulder. "Okay, honey. Sleep now. We can talk about this in the morning."

There was another long moment of silence and Hunter's breathing had evened out. Ellie barely refrained from yelping when she heard Hunter's voice again.

"Baby?"

Ellie traced patterns on Hunter's tummy in hopes it would help the woman finally get some rest. "Yes, honey?"

"Think I'm falling in love with you."

Ellie froze. Should she respond? Was Hunter even lucid enough to know what she was saying? A soft snore from Hunter did nothing to help answer any questions. In fact, she had more. The most important one being; Did she feel the same way? Yes, she felt something deep for Hunter, but was that love? *God, I wish I could run right now. I need to think.* But Hunter needed her even more. So, Ellie tried turning her brain off and snuggled in closer.

AN HOUR PASSED without a wink of sleep for Ellie. Turning

her brain off was proving to be impossible. As pleased as she was that Hunter trusted her enough to sleep peacefully — snoring softly — beside her, she just couldn't relax enough to doze off herself. And as much as she wanted to stay right where she was, she needed to move. Carefully, she disentangled herself from Hunter and left the warmth of the bed. She kicked her jeans out of the way as she strode to the sliding glass door that led out to an impressive balcony. Hunter was definitely going to have to give her a tour of this place she thought as she stepped out into the cool breeze of the night.

The sound of the ocean embraced her as she leaned on the railing, taking it all in. It was beautiful. The silvery moon reflected off the shimmering water and waves crashed against the shore. Ellie longed to feel the sand beneath her feet and the spray of the surf as she ran. For now, she would be content just standing out here listening to the melodic sounds of the sea.

Hunter watched silently as Ellie leaned over the railing. The shorter woman's eyes were riveted on the beach and Hunter couldn't help but wonder what was going on in that beautiful head. Her own eyes wandered down the length of Ellie's body that was covered only in the oversized, white, button-up shirt she had been wearing when she showed up at Hunter's house. It left Ellie's toned legs prominently on display and Hunter marveled at the muscles that jutted out in her calves as Ellie stood on her tiptoes. *I wonder how they would feel wrapped around me.* Her stomach flipped at the thought.

"Couldn't sleep?" she called out softly.

Ellie gasped, tightening her hold on the railing. She hadn't realized how far she had been leaning over. "You scared me."

"Sorry," Hunter apologized tenderly. "Would it help if I asked you not to jump?"

Ellie smiled over her shoulder. "No jumping. I was restless and the ocean seemed to call out to me. I can see why you come out here after a distressing day." She glanced over at Hunter who now stood by her. "I didn't mean to wake you."

"You didn't. Just missed you," Hunter confessed demurely. "What's on your mind?"

"Running," Ellie answered honestly.

Hunter's heart dropped. "I understand. I don't blame you for wanting to get away from me after what you saw tonight."

"No, honey." She took Hunter's hand and pulled her closer. "Running. Down there," Ellie pointed towards the beach.

"You still run?"

"Mmhmm."

"Wow. I guess we still have a lot to learn about each other, huh? Unfortunately, as you saw earlier, it's not all going to be pretty." Hunter felt Ellie tug her until she was standing behind the shorter woman. When Ellie leaned back into her, Hunter wrapped her arms around her waist, grateful that Ellie was still here. Her heart had shattered a little when she woke up to an empty bed. It was only when she saw Ellie standing out here on the terrace that she began to breathe again.

"I'm old enough to realize that life is not a fairy-tale, Hunter. Though, Susan does make one hell of a villain."

"Cruella suddenly flashed through my head," Hunter laughed.

"Yes, I can see poor puppies suffering around that woman," Ellie snickered. "My point is, I don't expect you to be perfect. Lord knows I'm not. And, this process of getting to know each other? I hope that lasts for a long, long time. We have thirty plus years of life before meeting each other. We may never know everything about one another."

"But we can try, right?" Hunter tightened her hold. "Like Big Al and his wife?"

"Absolutely." Ellie leaned her head back and kissed Hunter briefly on the lips. She couldn't quite gauge how the taller woman was feeling now. That brief time of sleep seemed to have helped a great deal, but Ellie was still wary of coming on too strong.

Little did she know Hunter was trying to figure out the best approach to letting Ellie in on just how much she wanted her. Would Ellie still be interested after the stunt Susan pulled? Perhaps she should just leave well enough alone and bask in the glory of merely holding Ellie in her arms like this?

They stood in comfortable silence, both lost in their thoughts. Neither could deny the way it felt to be this close to each other.

Alone. With the entire night ahead of them and no other distractions. The possibilities were endless. *Or,* Hunter thought sourly, *the possibility will end when I tell Ellie everything she needs to know.*

"El?"

"Yeah?"

"There's something I need to tell you."

Ellie detected the fear in Hunter's voice and it wasn't at all what she expected to hear. She had hoped they were both on the same wavelength.

"Does it involve being with someone else?"

"No!"

"Is it something that will ruin this moment?"

"Probably."

"Will it still be there tomorrow?"

Hunter frowned. "Yeah, but . . . ."

"Hunter? There's nothing you could say to me that would change the way I feel about you. However, it could change the way I feel right at this moment. And, that's something I don't want."

"What do you want?" Hunter managed to grind out as Ellie's hands reached back and found their way into Hunter's hair.

"To know if this beach is private."

"In the middle of the night, it certainly is." Hunter kissed Ellie's neck, groaning softly when Ellie tilted her head to give her better access. There was something unmistakably seductive about standing behind Ellie, her breasts pressed up against Ellie's back, breathing in that sweet scent that was distinctly Ellie.

Hunter's kisses left trails of fire on Ellie's neck. Even in her wildest fantasies — which had only started very recently — she didn't imagine this intensity of pleasure. Without changing their positions, Ellie turned her head and kissed Hunter passionately.

"Are you okay with this?" Ellie asked through the haze of desire. She needed to make sure Hunter was in the right frame of mind to be doing this and wasn't feeling pressured.

"You're kidding me, right?" Hunter panted. "I've been wanting this from the moment I saw you."

Ellie laid her head back on Hunter's shoulder. "I just want to make sure after everything that happened tonight . . ."

"El," Hunter interrupted gently. "When I'm with you, nothing else exists. There is no past. Just right here, right now." She brushed Ellie's hair off her neck and kissed the soft skin she exposed. "Are you scared?"

Ellie moaned when she felt Hunter's tongue graze her pulse point. "I don't think scared is the word I'd use," she managed.

"What word would you use?"

She thought about how best to answer. There was absolutely no fear in being with Hunter. And, if she were honest, there was no anxiety about knowing what to do. All you could do was what came naturally. So, what did she feel? Ellie lowered her arms, placing her hands on the outside of Hunter's thighs. She was effectively giving Hunter all of the power. "*Awakened.*"

Hunter growled in Ellie's ear. She had never known what it was like to feel control in this situation. The fact that Ellie gave it to her so freely meant the world to Hunter. With hands that were trembling from the flood of emotion coursing through her, she began unbuttoning Ellie's shirt.

Ellie shivered when the cool air hit her overheated skin. Her knees buckled slightly when Hunter's fingertips began at her cleavage and feathered down to her bellybutton. Her head fell back and her eyes slammed shut when Hunter skimmed her fingers underneath the lace of her panties. "*Hunter.*"

Fingernails dug into Hunter's thighs, heightening her lust. Her experiences never involved touching without some kind of protection. But that wasn't how she wanted things with Ellie. No barriers. "*I need you to know that I'm clean, Ellie,*" she whispered. "*I never would have started anything with you if I wasn't.*"

"*I trust you.*"

"*Let me feel you?*"

"*Yes.*"

Hunter closed her eyes and lowered her hand until she felt the silky folds of Ellie's aroused sex. It wasn't clear who moaned louder when she dipped her middle finger into the eager pool and touched the slippery bundle of nerves that awaited her. It didn't matter. All that mattered at this moment was the feel of Ellie. It was awe-inspiring and she needed more.

One of Ellie's hands left Hunter's thigh and dug itself into Hunter's dark tresses, dragging her down to until their lips met in a fiery kiss. The passion that burned between them threatened to consume Ellie. No matter how ready she thought she was, how does one possibly prepare for the emotions that fought to burst free from every pore of her being? Her hips undulated of their own volition. She needed more.

"Don't stop," she pleaded when Hunter began to withdraw her hand.

Hunter gripped Ellie's hips, shifting her until they were facing each other. "I'm not even close to stopping, baby." She started backing up, pulling Ellie along with her. "I don't want to share you. Not even with the moonlight."

As they made it to the foot of the bed, green stared into blue, never losing the connection. Ellie lifted Hunter's t-shirt with the taller woman bending down a bit, allowing Ellie to pull it over her head. The remainder of clothes were slowly peeled away until they stood there, souls bared. No barriers. Hunter watched in wonder while Ellie closed her eyes and lightly trailed her hands down Hunter's chest and stomach. The woman had yet to fully touch her and Hunter was ready to explode.

Without a word, she nudged Ellie onto the bed. She wanted Ellie more than she could ever vocalize, so she let her actions speak for her. Taking it slow and deliberate, needing to be present for each touch, each kiss, each emotion. She let all of that affection shine through clearly, holding Ellie's gaze as she lowered her body until they were unified.

Both women gasped at the contact, neither prepared for the overwhelming rush of feeling flesh on flesh. Ellie's arms immediately engulfed Hunter in a strong hug. She couldn't stop the flood of tears if she tried, so she let them come in a quiet sob.

Pure instinct told Hunter that Ellie's soft weeping was not out of sadness or regret, but joy. And she was profoundly honored that Ellie chose to share this incredible experience with her.

"I'm sorry. This isn't very sexy." Ellie gave Hunter a watery smile.

"You sharing your soul with me is the sexiest thing I've ever witnessed," Hunter professed warmly. "Don't ever apologize for that."

She was acutely aware that merely being on top of Ellie, her thigh nestled between Ellie's legs, could bring her to climax. It was unequivocally different than what she was accustomed to. Normally, at this point, she was losing focus. Anything to get her mind out of the situation she had so often found herself in. She wouldn't be losing focus tonight. She couldn't bear that.

"There's so much I want to explore with you." Hunter caressed Ellie's face reverently.

Ellie smiled shyly. "There's one thing in particular that I would love to experience with you right now."

"Anything, baby."

"I've never . . ." Being this open, especially about sexual matters, wasn't easy for Ellie. She found herself blushing slightly, which was silly. She was naked for crying out loud. Things couldn't get any more personal than this. After a deep breath, she tried again. "I've never had an orgasm," she practically whispered.

Hunter was surprised. "Never?" Ellie shook her head. "Not even, um, self-induced?" She knew Ellie had never been with anyone except Jessie's father. But she imagined — quite a bit during the last couple of weeks — that some "self-love" would have been involved during all those years of celibacy. Hell, that was the only way Hunter was able to do it — again, quite a bit during the last couple of weeks.

"Kind of goes with the whole 'not wanting to know what I'm missing' idea I had."

Hunter shook her head in awe, tears threatening. "You're gifting me with so much."

"I'd say we're gifting each other. Hunter, you changed my life when you walked in my diner. Was I waiting for you? I don't know the answer to that. But, I do know there's no one I'd rather be with. No one I could even *imagine* being with. It's you."

"*El.*" The best response Hunter could give Ellie was to give her *everything* she longed for. Everything she waited for. And Hunter would do everything in her power to be the woman Ellie deserved. She kissed Ellie deeply, shifting enough to dip her hand between them.

Hunter slid her tongue seductively against Ellie's. She used the same rhythm as she circled her coated fingers over Ellie's swollen nub. She felt Ellie jump at the contact and she would have pulled away if her girlfriend hadn't spread her legs even further. With unhurried movements Hunter moved her fingers down, positioning them at Ellie's opening. She broke the kiss long enough to silently ask for permission to go inside.

Ellie nodded. It amazed her how much Hunter made her feel like a virgin. In some ways, she was, which made this moment even more special for them both. She gasped as she felt Hunter fill her. The thrill of Hunter being inside her caused her sex to clench around Hunter's fingers. The added friction felt incredible and Ellie's body moved, matching Hunter's rhythm.

"Hunter!"

"It's okay, baby. I got you." Her stomach pitched and her dripping center trembled with desire when Ellie's thigh made direct contact. "Let go for me. Give yourself to me. Please?" Hunter kissed Ellie again, wanting to capture every moan, every cry, every murmur of joy and savor it all.

When the palm of Hunter's hand grazed the area that ached most, Ellie couldn't have stopped the delicious pleasure of the looming orgasm if she wanted to. For once in her life, Ellie didn't want to hold back *anything*. Not from Hunter and not from herself. She gave in to Hunter's quiet demand. The intensity of what was happening inside of her caught Ellie off-guard and, without a mind of what she was doing, she bit down. The emotional cry of ecstasy came from deep down in Ellie's soul.

Hunter couldn't say if it was the bite Ellie gave her, Ellie's nails scraping down her back, or the incredible sound that came from somewhere deep inside Ellie. Whatever it was, the climax that ripped through Hunter nearly caused her to pass out. In fact, she wasn't absolutely positive that she *didn't* lose consciousness for a heartbeat. Luckily, she had the presence of mind to keep her hand exactly where it was and was rewarded with the feel of Ellie pulsing around her fingers.

"*Oh my God*," Ellie panted. For a moment, she was sure she had gone blind. Then she opened her eyes. "Oh my God!" she exclaimed again for a completely different reason. A drop of blood trickled down Hunter's chin. Ellie reached up and wiped it gently with the pad of her thumb. "I'm so sorry."

Hunter grinned. "Don't be. It was, um, hot."

"Hot?" Ellie watched with rapt interest as Hunter's tongue snaked out to lick the blood, then captured Ellie's thumb between her teeth. Hunter sucked it in her mouth for a moment before letting it go again.

"Oh, yeah. What I *really* want to know is if you'll do it every time I make you come."

Ellie's stomach fluttered at Hunter's words. If her body hadn't already been stimulated, those words and the lust in Hunter's eyes certainly would have done it. "We're not done yet are we."

Even though it wasn't a question, Hunter answered. "Not even close."

Ellie smiled at Hunter's roguish expression. And she was so, *so* glad they weren't done. "I want to touch you." She was surprised there was no hesitancy in her voice. Then again, after what she just experienced, she was definitely ready for more.

Hunter's grin waned. "You do?"

"Of course."

"But, I . . . why?"

"Why?" Ellie frowned in confusion. Then she remembered exactly why Hunter was flustered. "Honey, we're in a relationship, right?" Hunter nodded. "Now, I'm no expert, but I'm pretty sure give and take are part of what makes a good relationship. I just took from you. Now I want to give back," she smiled, knowing she was making light of a situation that broke her heart. It was a decision she hoped would allow Hunter to avoid traveling down the path of the past.

Hunter's responding smile was tremulous. "I — I don't know if I can."

"Can you tell me why? Do you not want me to touch you?"

"I do!" Hunter briefly closed her eyes, trying to make sense of her jumbled thoughts. "I do want you to. I — I'm afraid."

"Do you think I'll hurt you?"

Hunter shook her head. "I know you never would. I just . . ." She growled in frustration. "With the, um, others I would lose my concentration, trying to think of something else. Medical procedures, working out, a book I was reading. Anything to keep my mind off of where I was and what I was doing."

"Okay," Ellie said carefully. "That's understandable. Do you think you would do that with me?"

"I don't want to. But I've never had experience with things being the, uh, other way around." She kissed Ellie, lingering for a moment. "If I can't focus with you, it would kill me."

"Did you have any problems earlier?"

"No," Hunter answered emphatically. "It was easy to stay focused when I was trying to please you."

"Succeeding," Ellie corrected with a wink. She took a breath, trying to think of a solution that would help Hunter relax. With a slow smile, she shifted them until they were side by side. "Okay. You said you wanted to explore, right? So, we find a way to keep you right here with me."

"I'll do anything and everything you want."

Ellie chuckled. "You might live to regret those words."

"Never," Hunter said seriously. "I want it all with you."

To Ellie's ears, those words carried the promise of so much more than what they were currently talking about. Remarkably, it didn't scare her. Ellie gently pushed Hunter to her back. Without pause, she straddled Hunter's stomach. "I'm giving it all to you."

It was the first thorough inspection Hunter got of Ellie's body. She had been so determined to see to Ellie's comfort, and ultimately her pleasure, that she didn't think about ogling her. Oh boy, was she gawking now. Pert, full breasts beckoned Hunter with their taut, rose-colored nipples. Her hands lifted, cupping both breasts. *Perfect*, she thought as they fit as though they were molded especially for her hands. She let the weight of Ellie's breast anchor her there as she allowed her eyes to travel the length of the woman who sat astride her.

Though Hunter could see the definition of muscles in Ellie's stomach, she still carried the soft curves that screamed femininity. Her slim waist flared slightly at her hips and those thighs. Good Lord, those thighs. Strong and so incredibly beautiful. The sight of them on either side of her did things to Hunter that she had never experienced before. *This* was what it was like to *want*. To *need*. To be aroused to the point that it almost became painful.

The press of the apex of those thighs touching her body was beyond description. Ellie's smooth, velvety core branded Hunter with its hot, slick arousal. Hunter dropped her hands to Ellie's hips, gripping them tight. She tugged, then pushed, coating herself with Ellie's wetness.

Ellie gasped. "This was supposed to be for you."

"Believe me, baby, it is." Hunter repeated the gesture until Ellie rolled her hips and took over.

Her view of Hunter's flawless, rounded breasts was going to make it hard for Ellie to control herself. Gravity caused them to fall ever-so-slightly to the sides when Hunter was on her back and sway gently as Ellie moved on top of her. It was mesmerizing. Ellie grasped them both, squeezing gently and raking her thumbnails over the hard, darkened tips. She smiled when Hunter's hips bucked in response.

"Touch me, look at me, do whatever you want," Ellie breathed. "But don't leave me." Keeping her cadence, she reached behind her with one hand until she found Hunter's wet center and continued to stimulate Hunter's rigid peak with the other. She moaned along with the doctor as she touched Hunter for the first time. "*You feel so good.*"

Hunter's eyes rolled back into her head. It wasn't just being touched for the first time by someone else. It was being touched by Ellie that made her body sing. "*El,*" she ground out through gritted teeth. Bending her knees slightly, she opened herself completely to the woman who was quickly stealing her heart. And breath, she thought as she gasped when Ellie tweaked the center of her pleasure.

The bedroom became a wondrous litany of sounds from the symphony of their lovemaking. Low moans, pleasured sighs, body writhing against body, and the increasing of heartbeats and breaths surrounded Hunter bringing her closer to the edge. She was ready to go over. And she wanted to take Ellie along with her into that blissful space between reality and fantasy. It was the only way she knew how to describe this euphoric moment.

Hunter's felt her body begin to shudder and she knew she was close. She surged up, wrapping her arms around Ellie to keep her moving. Keep her close. Keep her. *"Ellie."* It was a breath, a sigh, a promise, a dream, a future all wrapped up in one word. One name. And when Ellie's teeth clamped down on her shoulder, Hunter came hard with a sharp cry of pure ecstasy.

Ellie followed close behind as Hunter's body erupted beneath her. It was an incredible sight to see a woman like Hunter become vulnerable and powerful at virtually the same moment. To see her allow herself to abandon her fears and give in to her desires while demanding the same in return.

Hunter fell back onto the bed, never relinquishing her hold on Ellie. "That was . . ." she shook her head slightly with a small laugh. "I don't think the word that could possibly describe how that felt has been invented yet."

Ellie chuckled lightly. "Would you like to make one up?"

Hunter thought about it for a second before giving Ellie a definitive 'nope'. "I love the idea that only I can know what it's like being with you." She bucked her hips and wiggled her eyebrows as Ellie laughed harder.

"We're not done yet, are we." Ellie had seen this same look in Hunter's eyes the last time she made the same statement. She had to admit, she could *really* get used to seeing that look very often.

Hunter rolled them over until she hovered over the smaller woman. She gave Ellie a lopsided grin. "Nope."

Chapter Twenty-Eight

Hunter woke gradually with a smile on her face. She wouldn't be surprised if the smile was permanent. Images of the night before flooded Hunter's thoughts and her arm involuntarily tightened around the woman currently using her shoulder as a pillow. There was no doubt that waking up with Ellie's leg thrown over her thighs and her hand resting over Hunter's heart was — how did Cass describe that moment with Rebecca? — heaven.

"Your heart is beating so fast," Ellie murmured sleepily, rubbing the spot in a soothing manner.

"Because I'm with you," Hunter responded truthfully.

Ellie gave Hunter's shoulder a sweet kiss and looked up. "Is this okay? Me being here with you like this?" It was something she had wondered about. Surely Hunter wasn't used to waking up with someone still in her bed. Hopefully, the galloping of the heart beneath her hand didn't convey fear.

"This is more than okay, baby." Hunter peered down at her girlfriend — God, she loved that — and smiled. "I woke up a few minutes ago and do you know what I've been thinking about?" Ellie shook her head. "I've been thinking about what it was like to kiss you, how it felt to touch you, how you tasted."

Oh yeah, *that* happened during their 'exploration' last night. Just as Hunter suspected, Ellie tasted a sweet as she looked and Hunter couldn't get enough. Judging by Ellie's reaction, Hunter's performance left her just as insatiable.

"Is your heart racing?" Hunter asked with a knowing grin.

"Yes," Ellie exhaled.

"Now you know why mine is doing the same. It's not because this feels wrong. It's because it feels so right."

Ellie groaned and rolled on top of Hunter. "If you keep saying things like that we're never going to leave this room again."

"I fail to see how that is a terrible thing." Hunter grinned when Ellie bent to take a nipple in her mouth. "Nothing terrible at all." She gasped at the feel of Ellie's hand between her legs. Oh, she was primed and ready to make more amazing memories with Ellie.

THE SMELL OF bacon — being slightly burnt — drifted past Ellie's nostrils. She stretched languidly, prying open an eyeball to catch a glimpse of the clock on Hunter's nightstand. Both eyes popped open when she noticed the framed photo that also sat there. It was the one she had texted of her and the teddy bear Hunter had given her.

"Sweet," Ellie smiled. "How did I miss that last night?" she wondered aloud. "Oh, yeah. I had other things to focus on." She chuckled at herself, then sniffed the air again. Slightly burning was rapidly becoming — well, less than slightly. "Whoops! Better get up now."

After a quick freshening up, Ellie made her way towards the scents of breakfast. The view of the ocean from the incredible wall of windows pulled Ellie off course until she heard a crash and an expletive from the kitchen. She pivoted back to her original path and padded off in the direction of the chaos with a chuckle. When the kitchen came into view, Ellie's jaw dropped.

The kitchen was modern and sleek with crisp, white cabinets surrounding dark granite countertops. The enormous island boasting darker, gray cabinets was illuminated by a beautiful modern chandelier. There was so much to look at in the large space, but Ellie's eyes were drawn to the range Hunter was currently standing — and cussing — at. The stainless steel, six-burner range was simply elegant and it took Ellie's breath away.

Hunter heard what sounded like a whimper and looked over to see Ellie standing there staring. Okay, so she was having a bit of an issue with breakfast, but it wasn't that bad. Plus, she was a little disappointed that her surprise of making Ellie food for once was foiled. Oh well, she could fix this.

"Hey, baby. I . . ."

Ellie held up a finger. "Shh!" She ran that finger longingly over the stove, trying not to cringe at the mess Hunter was making.

Once Hunter figured out that Ellie was gawking at her kitchen, she laughed. "Does it pass the test?"

Ellie tossed a look at Hunter who was back in her boxers and t-shirt. "Your mom did a wonderful job."

"Hey! I . . ." Hunter looked around for something she could claim. She pointed at the stove. "I picked this!"

Ellie laughed softly. "You did an excellent job, honey." She wound her arms around Hunter's neck, pulling her down for a kiss.

"I was going to surprise you with breakfast in bed," Hunter said against Ellie's lips. "You like eggs and bacon, right? Oh, and I have some bread toasting."

"I do and thank you." Ellie nonchalantly reached over and turned off the burners and manually popped the toast. "Sorry I ruined your plans. I don't think I've ever slept in this late."

"You thought I was going to burn the place down, didn't you?" Hunter teased with another quick kiss.

"Of course not." Ellie feigned innocence. "It smells good."

"You're a terrible liar," Hunter laughed. "It may not — okay, it's definitely not going to be as good as what you make, but I tried."

"Don't do that, honey. I adore you for doing this. And I'm sure it'll be great if not just for the fact that you did it for me."

Hunter's heart rate doubled at Ellie's words. So, she didn't exactly say love, she said adore, but it was close, right? It had Hunter thinking this was the perfect time for the conversation she knew they needed to have.

"Do you want to talk about it?"

Ellie's question startled Hunter. Was she thinking about the same thing? Why did it always seem like Ellie was reading her mind?

"Talk about what?" Hunter asked carefully.

"What happened last night with Susan. Why she was here, what she said."

No, that was definitely not what Hunter wanted to talk about. *Ever.* "Would it be okay if I said no?" She turned to face Ellie. "I mean, I want to talk to you about it, but not now. Not after the night we just shared together. I think we have much more pleasant things to talk about, don't you?"

Ellie smiled brilliantly. "Of course." She cupped Hunter's cheek. "Just know that I'm here, honey."

The affection she saw shining in Ellie's eyes thrilled Hunter. She knew then that last night was not a fleeting moment for Ellie, but as real and beautiful as it was for her. And that brought her back to the things she said.

"Um, why don't you go sit down," she gestured to the island. "I'll make you a plate. Do you want coffee?"

Hunter's nervous demeanor baffled Ellie. Did she say something wrong? Or was Hunter really that anxious about her food? While that didn't bode well for Ellie's taste buds, no matter what the food tasted like, she was grateful that Hunter cared enough to even attempt cooking for her. *'Think I'm falling in love with you.'* Oh, boy.

"I can get the coffee if you just steer me towards the cups." She giggled — ugh, she was too old to giggle! — when Hunter took her literally and "steered" her by the hips towards the coffee pot.

"Creamer is in the fridge and sugar is in the cabinet."

"Aye, aye, Cap'n." Ellie saluted with a wink.

"So, how long do I have you for this morning?" Hunter called over her shoulder.

"I don't have anywhere to be." She had already decided to take the day off from the diner. Something that confused and pleased Rosa at the same time. If Ellie didn't know better, she would think Rosa wouldn't mind taking on even more responsibility. However, Rosa didn't have the recipes for Ellie's pies, so that circumvented any little mini takeover Rosa may have had in mind. Ellie laughed silently at the thought, knowing Rosa was one of the most trustworthy people she knew.

Hunter glanced back with raised eyebrows. "Does that mean I get to keep you forever?"

Ellie chuckled nervously. "Well, I do have a daughter to get back to eventually. Wouldn't want her to think I've abandoned her to have hot sex for the rest of my life."

"Hot sex?" Hunter tossed her a roguish grin.

"You don't agree?"

"Oh, yeah, baby. I definitely do." She came up to Ellie, hugging her from behind. "Want to see if we can really heat up this kitchen?"

"Tempting. *Very* tempting." Ellie couldn't help pushing her backside into Hunter. "But, I'm hungry."

"Tease." Hunter nibbled Ellie's ear causing her to shiver.

"Who's the one teasing? Food, baby. Then we can play some more."

It was the first-time Ellie had called her baby and it revved up her already feverish body. "Promise?"

In lieu of an answer, Ellie kissed Hunter lustfully. "Food," she mumbled through the kiss.

Hunter laughed and smacked Ellie's ass.

"YOU HATE IT."

"I do not! Stop saying that." Ellie chuckled at Hunter's shenanigans. She could understand people being afraid to cook for her. Jessie and Blaise always complained, but Ellie had a sneaky suspicion they did that just so Ellie would cook. "It's good, honey. I promise."

"Hmm." Hunter narrowed her eyes playfully at Ellie. "I guess you're telling the truth since your eye isn't twitching like it does when you're lying."

"My eye does not twitch, you goof!"

"Does so." The spirited banter between them warmed Hunter's heart. This was what her mom imagined for her when she designed this kitchen. Someone wonderful to share wonderful times with. Though, she probably never would have guessed that Hunter would be the one cooking. At least this once. "I meant it," she said, suddenly serious.

Ellie chewed her food and glanced up at Hunter. "That my eye twitches when I lie?"

With a small smile, Hunter shook her head. "I wasn't sleep talking, El. I knew what I was saying. And, I don't expect you to say anything . . ." her voice trailed off when Ellie took her trembling hand.

"Do you know what I was thinking about out on the balcony last night?"

"About running?"

"Well, yes. Running helps me think. But, other than that, I was examining my feelings for you." She pushed her mostly empty plate to the side and held out her other hand, smiling when Hunter took it. "I have no reference for this stuff, Hunter. Whether things are too fast or too slow. Yet, I *do* know that when I'm with you, I'm happy. When we're apart, I'm constantly thinking of you, missing you. And, when you made love to me for the first time last night, I felt whole." She paused, searching for the right words. "I've never felt incomplete, honey. I have a great life, a great daughter, great friends. Then you came in and gave me something I didn't know I was missing. Is that love? Can it happen that fast?"

374

Ellie shrugged. "Maybe it is and maybe it can. Who's to say any different?"

Unchecked tears rolled down Hunter's cheeks. "Everyone keeps telling me there's no timetable," she sniffled. "I want to believe that. And, I want to give you the time to figure it all out. It's a little scary, though."

"Why?" Ellie reached over and wiped a tear from Hunter's cheek with her thumb.

"What if . . ."

"Stop," Ellie ordered gently. "What-ifs never work in life. That's one thing I have learned. Could you imagine all of the things we would miss because we're scared of the what-ifs? What if I hadn't taken the chance to tell my daughter who I really am so I could be with you?"

The woman had a point. Even "what-if'ing" the negatives in life wasn't worth it because everything brought Hunter here to this point in time with this beautiful woman.

"Okay. No what-ifs," Hunter agreed. "One day at a time?"

"Sounds like a plan." She pulled Hunter off her stool to stand between her legs. "I don't want you to be afraid to say things to me. I may balk at times. I think we both will while we navigate this new path. But it's better to know how each other feels rather than speculate, right?"

Hunter dipped her head and kissed Ellie. "Right." She deepened the kiss, tracing Ellie's lips with her tongue. Just as things were getting *real* good, a cell phone started vibrating on the counter. Hunter groaned.

"Not mine," Ellie mumbled.

"I'm sorry, baby, I have to get that. It's the hospital." Hunter adored the beautiful smile Ellie always seemed to offer her so freely. It made her feel special, especially when coupled with the sparkle in Ellie's eyes. Hunter cleared her throat, hoping to clear her mind of all the sexy thoughts she was having before answering the phone. "Dr. Vale," she said in her most professional voice. Not an easy feat when Ellie was looking at her *that* way.

Ellie didn't want to intrude on Hunter's phone call, so she

busied herself collecting the dishes and trying not to drool all over the large, apron sink with its pulldown faucet. As someone who spent most of her time in the kitchen, Ellie put a lot of thought and money into her kitchens at home and at the diner. But even she had a bit of envy at all of the high-end materials and components Hunter had here. "*I could do so much in this kitchen,*" she whispered to herself. What surprised her more than the thought of a future in this kitchen, was all of the *non*-cooking things that ran through her mind.

"I understand that, but I'm not on call." Hunter turned to Ellie, wondering about the blush she found on the woman's face. *What are you thinking, El?* "Where is Dr. Mackenzie? I see." She sighed heavily and gave Ellie an apologetic look. "Yeah. I'll be there as soon as I can."

"Duty calls?"

"I'm so sorry, El. They need an attending there and apparently, I'm the only one available at the moment." She blew out a frustrated breath. "I shouldn't have answered the damn phone."

"Honey, it's fine."

"But, I wanted to spend the day with you." Okay, that was perilously close to whining.

"I know, me too." Ellie clucked her tongue. "This is what Jessie would call 'having to adult'."

"When did 'adult' become a verb," Hunter laughed.

"Don't ask me. Sometimes I wonder if my daughter and I are speaking the same language. I am lucky, though, that she doesn't do that very often." She tugged on Hunter's t-shirt. "Why don't you go take a shower and get ready. I'll clean up in here."

"Or, you could take a shower with me." Hunter wiggled her eyebrows suggestively.

"I'd love to."

Those wiggling eyebrows shot up. "You would?"

"Yes," Ellie chuckled. The two sides of Hunter – one so seductive and the other so innocent – fascinated Ellie. She found she loved both of them equally. "But, we both know that you need to be quick and that wouldn't happen if I were with you."

"Oh, I can be quick."

Ellie shook her head, laughing at the speed at which Hunter could change directions. "I can't. Not with you. Now, go."

"Okay, okay," Hunter reluctantly conceded. "But, you don't have to clean up. I can . . ." She looked at the mess she made and dreaded coming home to an empty house with this waiting for her instead of Ellie.

"You cooked, I'll clean." Ellie patted Hunter's chest. "Remember that," she winked.

Hunter moaned playfully. "I'm going to be doing a lot of cleaning, aren't I?" *Please.*

"Oh yeah."

HUNTER HELD ELLIE'S shoes out to her. "Hey, I got a little sidetracked, but I meant to ask you if Jessie was, um, fine with you staying here last night."

"Yes," Ellie smiled. "In fact, she packed me an overnight bag."

Hunter coughed. "Wow. Progressive. I can't even think of my parents doing . . ." Hunter shivered with a barely audible 'yuck'.

"Same here," Ellie snickered. "However, as weird as it is for me, I'm glad she's attempting to make this change in our lives painless. It can't be easy for her."

Hunter pulled the front door closed behind them, locking it. "She's a great kid, El. You must be proud of her."

"I am. I —"

"Shit!"

Startled by Hunter's unexpected outburst, Ellie glanced in the direction Hunter was looking in. She spied a manila envelope on the windshield of her Jeep. Frowning, she rushed to keep up with Hunter's accelerated pace. She plucked the envelope from Hunter's hand, despite her protests.

"El."

Ellie ignored the unspoken plea and opened it. Shock. That would probably be the first word that came to her mind when she saw the picture. Then perhaps anger.

Judging by Hunter's reaction, the "gift" didn't seem like much of a surprise to the doctor. "Does this have anything to do with what you wanted to tell me last night?"

Hunter nodded sadly. She hadn't seen the photo, yet, but she imagined it was like the rest of them. God, she didn't want Ellie to see her like that with other women. Yes, she would have told her about the photos, but that didn't mean she had to look at them.

Questions rolled around in Ellie's head. How many had Hunter gotten? Were any of them like this one? Were the photos the only threat she was receiving or was there something else? None of the questions she particularly wanted answers to. Yet. Instead of asking, she handed over the envelope. If Hunter had told her about this last night, Ellie didn't know if she could have understood how violated Hunter must have felt. Now, she knew.

Hunter wished she could rewind the morning. She would have ignored that phone call and she and Ellie would be snuggled together in bed. Unfortunately, she had to now deal with the woman she was falling in love with seeing her at her worst. *Fuck*, she thought. *Rewind back to when I had my hands around Susan's throat. Let me finish the job!* Though she didn't want to, Hunter took out the photo. "Oh, God!"

"I have to admit, we do look pretty sexy," Ellie dead-panned. Somehow Susan had gotten a photo of the soon-to-be lovers when they were out on the balcony. Ellie's shirt barely covered her breasts, and Hunter's hand was buried in the modest bit of fabric that shielded Ellie from being completely embarrassed.

The guilt that coursed through Hunter's veins burned. She *knew* she was damaged goods and that Susan was a psycho. Yet, she still pursued Ellie, bringing her into this mess. If she had just stayed away . . .

"No, Hunter." Ellie stepped close to her lover, taking her face in her hands. "You are not going to shut down on me. What you're thinking right now, is *exactly* what that bitch wants. We'll get through this. Together."

She should have been freaked out by Ellie's dead-on observation. For some reason, it calmed her instead. "You're not mad?"

"Of course I am." In truth, Ellie had never been more pissed. But she would be damned if she let that vile woman ruin what she had shared with Hunter last night. The bitch has caused Hunter enough suffering. "At Susan, not you. This is not your fault."

"But." Hunter prudently stopped at Ellie's raised eyebrow. "Can I at least say I'm sorry?"

"No. You have nothing to be sorry about." Ellie held her hand out for the package.

Hunter hesitated. "What are you going to do with them?"

"*We're* going to go to the police."

"El, no. Please? She'll tell my parents!"

While Ellie felt sorry for Hunter, they couldn't let Susan get away with this. "Honey, this has to stop. Things are going to start escalating when she figures out the photos and idle threats aren't working to get you back. Who knows what she's capable of? After this, I know no one is off limits, and I won't jeopardize my daughter's safety. Not even for you."

The doctor understood completely and nodded. It was bad enough that Ellie now had to deal with this. The last thing she wanted to do is drag Jessie into it. "Is there a way for us to wait, just for a little while, until I tell my folks? A week or two, tops," she pleaded.

After an uneasy moment of silent thought, Ellie responded. "I'll agree to delay going to the authorities *if* we allow Cade and Greyson to investigate this woman." She saw the resignation in Hunter's eyes and it made her heart ache. It wasn't as though she was keen on having Cade – or Greyson – seeing these photos, but she would do whatever she had to do to keep her daughter safe. "I'm sorry, honey. I don't like it, either. But, they care about me and Jessie and will do everything they can to protect us. That includes protecting you."

She caressed Hunter's cheek. "You need to tell your parents before she does."

"I know." She shuffled her feet nervously. "Will you be there with me when I do?" It may have been childish to ask, but having Ellie near her made Hunter feel stronger. If she could find someone like Ellie to care about her, she couldn't be all bad. Right?

"If that's what you want, yes."

Hunter inhaled deeply, letting it out slowly. "Okay. I'll call them and see about making arrangements." It wasn't exactly how she wanted to introduce Ellie to her parents, but at this point, she'll take what she can get. She's damn lucky Ellie hasn't told her to go to hell. God, she wanted to touch Ellie but didn't know if it would be welcome right now. "I, uh, hate leaving you like this, but I guess I should be getting to the hospital. Are you going to be all right?"

"I will be if you are. Will you talk to your therapist, honey? Tell her what happened last night. All of it. And this," she lifted the envelope. When Hunter agreed without hesitation or shame, Ellie stood on her tiptoes and kissed her. She poured everything into that kiss, making sure Hunter knew nothing had changed between them. "I'll miss you," she said softly.

Hunter hugged Ellie to her tightly. The relief and gratitude that flooded her heart caused her knees to buckle. *Thank you.* The words stuck in her throat, a lump threatening to become a sob. She hoped Ellie felt them in her hug. "When can I see you again?"

Ellie indeed felt the emotion in Hunter as though it was her own. She wished they could go back to earlier when everything was lighthearted and flirty. *We'll get it all back tonight, baby. I promise.* "Stop by the diner when you're free. Or, if you're going to be late, come by the apartment."

"You're sure?" She still couldn't quite fathom how the woman hadn't run fast and far from her. It wasn't like Hunter to look a gift horse in the mouth, but she needed one more reassurance before she could hold on to the hope.

Ellie kissed her again. "Don't forget your overnight bag."

Chapter Twenty-Nine

Ellie's vehicle idled as she sat in the alley behind her diner. The emotions inside her were running rampant and she needed a moment. Her first instinct had been to run, but at this point, she didn't think that even that would work. Last night was one of the most incredible nights of her life. To have it marred by Susan, *twice*, hurt. And, knowing Hunter still felt responsible — and possibly unworthy — made Ellie angry.

She slid the photo out of its packet once again. It, like the night, gave her so many different emotions. Their private moment turned out to not be so private. Her *first* time being touched like that was caught on film. How could anyone conceivably wrap their brain around that and find one solid response? Ellie huffed out a breath, stuffed the photo back, and slipped the envelope under her seat. She would tell Blaise about it, but she would like to avoid anyone else seeing it if possible.

She got out and instead of going to her diner, she headed two doors down. Using the key she rarely got to use, Ellie let herself in the back door of Knight in Bloom. She stood there for a moment and watched Blaise at her desk. Fourteen years. That's how long they had been best friends and Ellie was about to do something she had never done before.

"I'm a biter."

"YO, HUNT!" MO moseyed into the hospital cafeteria, flipped a chair around and straddled it. "Thought you had the day off?"

"Yeah, me too." Hunter took another bite of her bland turkey sandwich. She could be eating something good right now. She grinned as she let her mind linger on that thought, then sighed. Instead of that pleasantry, she was stuck here because Mack was M.I.A.

Mo lifted her chin at the doctor. "Ellie beat you up for all that drama shit you put her through last night?"

Hunter stopped chewing. "Huh?" Drama? How did Mo know about . . . oh, right. The gallery opening. Kiara Adler. *Shit, I owe Cass a huge apology.*

When Mo tapped her own lip, Hunter remembered the bite. Her lip was a little swollen and busted and she could understand how Mo would think the worst. She smirked.

"Nah. Ellie's a biter."

"JESUS!" BLAISE LAID a hand over her rapidly beating heart. "You scared the bitch out of me."

"I don't think that's possible." Ellie laughed at her best friend.

"Ha ha. Why are you coming in the back? And, what did you say?"

Ellie plopped herself down in the chair in front of Blaise's desk, wincing. She never considered how sore she would be after . . .

"Ellie?"

"Hmm? Oh. I came in back here because I wanted this conversation to be private." She noticed Blaise scoot up in her chair and lean on her desk with interest shining in her eyes. *Weirdo.* "And, I said 'I'm a . . . biter'."

"What does that mean? Did you and Hunter work things out last night?"

You could say that. Ellie sighed. "It means that when I, um," she waved her hands in the air. "When I . . ."

Blaise caught a clue about what Ellie was having such a tough time saying. She had known the woman long enough to know her quirks. "Orgasm? Climax? Arrive? Cream? Come?"

"Okay! Stop!" Ellie covered her heated face. "Yes, all right? When I do all of the above, I bite!"

"SHE BITES?"

Hunter had a second of indecision. Maybe Ellie didn't want her telling anyone about this. But Mo was her best friend. Surely Ellie would talk to Blaise, wouldn't she? Hunter leaned closer.

"Yes. But if you tell *anyone* this, I swear I will pummel you. Got me? Not even Patty."

Mo raised two fingers. "Scouts honor."

"You were never a scout, boy or girl. And, it's three fingers, you boob."

"Whatever. You got the gist. Now stop trying to distract me with boob and go on."

Hunter rolled her eyes. Maybe she should have chosen Rebecca or Cass to confess this to. At least they would be more mature about it. Or they'd think she and Ellie were into more kinky stuff. *Are we?*

"Hunt? You can't just leave me hanging!"

Hunter sighed and scooted her chair closer to Mo. Hospitals were notorious for gossip and Ellie didn't need more shit to deal with after what happened this morning. She lowered her voice. "When I make El, you know, she bites."

"Holy shit! You hit," Mo stopped abruptly. Hunter's look and thinking of Patty's disapproval had her rethinking her words. "I mean, finally!" She had a plethora of questions, but the first and foremost was:

"HOW MANY BITES are we talking?"

By this time, Blaise had left her seat and took up residence right next to Ellie.

"Is that important?" It was a serious question from Ellie. Again, she had no reference for things like this. Was biting weird? Unheard of? Normal? How many orgasms are normal the first time you have sex. And, yeah, she knew it wasn't technically the first time, but . . . it really *was* the first time.

"Not really. But it is to me because I'm nosy and we've never had a talk like this before," Blaise grinned. "Here, I'll start. My first time, I had zero orgasms. But, I was also fifteen and so was my partner. We had no clue what we were doing. Now, my first time with Greyson? Off the charts. That man *knows* what he's doing." She sat back with a satisfied grin. "Your turn."

Between Jessie packing her an overnight bag to Blaise giving her details about orgasms, Ellie's head was about to explode from all the bizarreness.

"Um, off the charts."

"Wow," Blaise smirked. "Good for you. Did you return the favors?"

"Blaise."

"Come on, sweetie. We have years of you clamming up every time we begin to have a conversation like this to make up for. You know you have nothing to be embarrassed about, right? There's no need to be shy around me."

"That's easier said than done. I've done a one-eighty in my life and my head is spinning."

"I know. But it's me, El. If you can't talk to your best friend about all of this, who can you talk to?" Blaise winked playfully, hoping to lighten Ellie's mood.

Ellie chuckled. "Yes, I returned the favors."

"SOUNDS LIKE IT was everything you've ever wanted." Mo stole a chip from Hunter's plate. A small part of her may have still been a little jealous, but since she had started following Ellie's advice things with Patty have been really good.

"It is. Mo, I think she's the one." Hunter made a conscious decision not to tell Mo anything about Susan. That was one subject that had been a thorn in their friendship. Mo never understood the hold Susan had on Hunter. And Hunter never explained how or when things actually began. Whenever she thought she would confess everything to Mo or even Rebecca, she couldn't do it. She was too afraid of what they would think of her.

In fact, no one knew the full extent of what Susan had done to her. Except for Ellie and Dr. Woodrow. The fact that Hunter had the courage to tell Ellie everything proved to Hunter that Ellie was different from anyone else. Woodrow was a great therapist and it seemed as though she cared. But it wasn't the same as having someone you *want* to talk to as opposed to having someone you pay to listen. Be that as it may, as promised, she made a call to her shrink and scheduled a time for them to talk. She wondered if Ellie would consider speaking with Dr. Woodrow as well.

"I'm happy for you, Hunt," Mo said, unknowingly interrupting Hunter's thoughts. She stole a glance over Hunter's shoulder and noticed a certain infatuated nurse staring at her tall friend. She couldn't tell if Iris could hear them, but she definitely didn't look happy. *Talk about dodging a bullet,* Mo thought with a grimace. Something was seriously unstable about that woman. At one time, Mo might have pushed Hunter towards a fling with the redhead. Okay, she *may* have suggested something similar. Whatever. Now she knew better. "You deserve to have a happy relationship."

"SOUNDS LIKE EVERYTHING is going great. We should all be so lucky to find that our first time out." Blaise smiled, reaching over to squeeze Ellie's leg. She was thrilled to see Ellie so happy. And if she *was* lucky enough to find someone without having to go through the drama of failed relationships, Blaise would be eternally grateful. Ellie had suffered enough having to hide who she really is.

"Hmm." Ellie gave Blaise a small smile. She hadn't yet told her about Susan. It wasn't a conversation that just came up during coffee. Or in Blaise's case, red velvet.

Ellie's lack of enthusiasm provoked a frown from Blaise. "It's not great?"

"No! I mean, yes. Things between me and Hunter are incredible. She's charming, beautiful, attentive, erotic, and a lot of other amazing adjectives. I *am* lucky to have found her."

"But?"

"What is it that song said? Every rose has its thorn?" Ellie sighed. "Not everyone is happy to see us together. Hunter is being blackmailed."

Blaise sat up a little too quickly and it caused her head to spin a little. Either that or what Ellie just told her was making her head spin. "What? By who? An ex?"

"Not exactly. I mean they . . ." Ellie paused. What Susan did to Hunter did not constitute a relationship. In Ellie's mind, it wasn't even sex. It was abuse. To explain the blackmail to Blaise, she'd have to explain Hunter's past. That's exactly what she did as delicately as she could while trying her best to keep Hunter's integrity intact.

"My God." Blaise slumped back, stunned. "And, this Susan bitch? That's who's blackmailing Hunter?"

She could always rely on Blaise to understand how malicious a woman could be when they wanted something they couldn't have. Especially having dealt with Pricilla. Susan, though, was on a whole other level. "Yes. She manipulated Hunter when she was a child. She's doing everything she can to keep her hooks in."

"El, sweetie, are you sure you want to get involved in this?" Blaise knew as she was saying it that it was a stupid question. That was made even more clear by the annoyance she saw written all over Ellie's face.

"I'm already involved, Blaise. Whether I stopped seeing Hunter or not — which I don't want to do — I'm already on Susan's radar. She was at Hunter's last night when I showed up."

"Oh, shit. What the hell was she doing there?"

"Hunter and I haven't had time to talk about it in depth, but my guess is she's stalking Hunter. She was at the opening last night and followed Hunter home when she left. When I got there, Hunter was agitated because Susan was lying to her about me." Ellie shifted in her seat. Remembering that particular part of the night was unpleasant. "You should have seen her, Blaise. She was so vulnerable. So scared."

"I can't even imagine." Blaise shook her head. "When I think of something like that happening to Piper or Jessie," Blaise shuddered. "I don't think I would let that woman live."

Ellie recalled Hunter's reaction when Susan mentioned Jessie.

"Hunter almost didn't." When Blaise cast her a look, she explained what had happened. "I didn't think she was going to let her go."

"I can't believe that damn woman had the audacity to even utter Jessie's name. Maybe you should have let Hunter do it." Blaise wasn't normally a violent person. Except when it came to the people she loved. Then all bets were off.

"I had the same thought this morning when I got Susan's little gift," Ellie confessed.

"Do I want to know what this 'gift' is, or should I just go kick her ass now?"

Ellie actually contemplated having Blaise confront Susan. When the woman was mad . . . well, the name Blaise suited her very well.

Blaise ran out of patience with Ellie's hesitation. "El? What are we really talking about here with the blackmailing?"

"Photos."

Blaise raised an eyebrow. "Of?"

"Hunter." She knew very well that wasn't going to satisfy the inquisitive best friend. Ellie took a deep breath. "Hunter in compromising situations."

"Sex." Ellie nodded. "That means she's willing to expose the other women as well? Her so-called friends?"

"She doesn't have friends, Blaise. She has lackeys. And, I don't feel one ounce of empathy for them. They knew exactly what they were doing to Hunter. To their husbands." Unable to keep sitting, Ellie got up to pace.

"Can this hurt Hunter?" Blaise watched Ellie pace. She had never seen her friend this worked up before. Hunter had better be worth it.

"She says it can't. At least not with her job. She was mostly afraid of her parents finding out, but I think I've talked her into telling them herself. It can only help having more people in her corner and eliminating one of Susan's threats."

"But, you're still worried about something." This was more than just photos of Hunter and other women.

"I'm worried about things escalating. These photos are trite and simple. I suspect Susan thought they were enough to control Hunter. She didn't count on me being in the picture." *Literally.*

"Okay. How powerful is she?"

"I don't know. She has politicians in her back pocket, but from what I've heard from Hunter they're small time." Ellie blew out a breath and ran a hand through her hair. She knew she was avoiding telling Blaise about the more personal photos, but she was doing her best with all of this.

"Has Hunter gone the police?"

"No. She's afraid of what Susan would do for retaliation, I think." Ellie sat down again and held Blaise's stare. "Honestly, Blaise, I'm reluctant to trust the cops in this situation. I'm just not sure how deep Susan's pockets go. That's why I need Greyson and Cade's help. And, I need them to be discreet."

Blaise nodded. "I'll call Greyson. Give me all the information you know about this woman and they'll get started."

Ellie reached over and plucked a piece of paper and a pen off of Blaise's desk. She would talk to Hunter later tonight to get more if Drake & Associates needed it.

"I feel like there's something else, El. Something you're reluctant to say and I don't like that. It makes me itch."

Ellie laughed softly. "I should have known that I couldn't keep anything from you. But, this has to stay between us unless it can somehow help Hunter."

There wasn't much that Blaise kept from her husband, but if Ellie was asking for confidentiality she had no qualms. "Deal."

"The photo I got this morning was of me and Hunter."

It was said so matter-of-factly that it took Blaise a moment to catch on to the actual meaning. She sprang up from her chair, furious. "That bitch! Oh, no. She is not getting away with this shit."

"Blaise."

"That was a special moment for you. *And* for Hunter. How dare she intrude? Oh, I'm going to . . ."

"Blaise!" Ellie got up and hugged Blaise tightly. "Thank you. For caring, for having my back, for not blaming Hunter." She pulled back. "I need you to keep doing that. And, I need you to tell the guys that if they try to put the blame on Hunter even *once* I will be a very unhappy person."

Blaise widened her eyes. "Cade would hate that. And, I think both of them are a little scared of you." She rubbed Ellie's shoulders. "I could never blame Hunter, sweetie. None of this is her fault. I'll make sure the boys know that very clearly."

I wish I could make Hunter know that. "I have one more favor to ask," Ellie said softly.

"Name it."

"I want Cade to have someone shadowing Jessie."

Alarmed, Blaise tightened her grip on Ellie's arm. "Do you think she's in danger?"

"No, but I want to make sure she stays that way." Ellie sighed deeply. "I don't want her to know, Blaise. She's doing so well, handling everything with me like a champ. She has enough on her plate with college applications, school, and everything else. She doesn't deserve to feel anything but safe, happy, and, you know, like a regular teenager."

"We're going to find out everything we can about this woman and bring her down before she can do anyone any more harm," Blaise vowed.

Ellie smiled. "I believe you." Her phone buzzed in her back pocket and she brought it out hoping it was Hunter. Disappointed, she held up the cell. "It's Rosa. Hello?" Ellie frowned. "Rosa, slow down, I can't understand you." She glanced at Blaise. "They're there now? Okay, okay. I'll be right there."

"What's going on?" Blaise was up, cracking her knuckles, ready for combat by the time Ellie hung up.

"I think Susan is flexing her muscles. There's a health inspector at the diner."

Blaise barked out bitter laughter. "Wrong move. Your diner is so clean I could eat red velvet off the floor! They'll be hard pressed to find a speck of dirt anywhere in there."

"Not if they're being paid off." Ellie held up her hands, stopping

Blaise from following her. "Call Greyson. Find me something on her, Blaise. I'll take care of this."

BLAISE PACED UNTIL she couldn't stand it anymore. After doing her due diligence and calling her husband to get the ball rolling on Susan, she needed to be at the diner backing Ellie up.

"Mer, I'll be back," she called as she plowed out the front door and smack into Eve and Lainey. "Excuse me."

"Blaise? Is everything all right?"

Blaise peered at Eve thoughtfully. If *anyone* had friends in high places — even higher than her — it was this woman. "There's an insane person mad at Ellie for dating Hunter. Apparently, she's somewhat 'connected' and has sicced a health inspector on the diner as we speak. I'm sorry, I have to go."

Lainey watched Blaise speed down the sidewalk to Ellie's Diner. "Eve?"

Eve brought her gaze to Lainey's. "I'll take care of it."

"MR. WILLMAR, SOMEONE from your department was here last month and the diner score near perfect." Ellie was furious. She stood her ground, arms crossed with a stern look on her face. It always worked with Jessie, though she was pretty sure it wasn't as intimidating in this situation.

"Nevertheless, Miss Montgomery, I'm here to do another inspection." The robust man peered at her over his glasses. He was sweating as though he was in the hot seat. Tug after tug at his necktie told Ellie that he was either extremely out of shape or guilty of something. Perhaps it was both. "If you refuse, I will shut you down. Is that what you want?"

Ellie raised an eyebrow and spread her hands in front of her. "Knock yourself out."

Rosa let out a string of what Ellie was sure were curse words in Spanish as she stormed off. *Yep. That one I know.* As ridiculous as she knew this inspection was, Ellie kept her eyes focused on the man rounding her kitchen. She didn't trust him not to do something he could knock her for. She watched helplessly as he made check marks, scribbled notes, and more marks. Throw in a few grunts here and there and Ellie was ready to pull her hair out.

This was so much different than the last person that came to inspect the diner. He was such a pleasant man in his late fifties with a smile at every turn. His personality and willingness to go over every single detail with Ellie had impressed her. The only impression this ass was making was a bad one. Especially when he tapped his pen on his clipboard with a smirk.

"My findings are that this place not up to code."

"You can't be serious! You barely look around, ask no questions, do nothing in your 'inspection' except make little marks on your list." Ellie moved towards the stove, the walk-in freezer, the prep area — all exceptionally clean per usual — and gestured wildly. "Clean, clean, clean! Everything is clean. I want to see the report."

"It is not my duty to show you anything. It's my duty to keep these patrons safe." The man started for the door leading out into the seating area.

Ellie rushed to keep up with him. "This isn't legal. If I'm in violation of some code, I have the right to know what it is and have the opportunity to fix it before the inspection is over."

"The inspection *is* over. This place is being shut down for health code violations," he called out loudly.

Ellie looked frantically at Blaise who materialized beside her once she came out of the kitchen. She then turned her gaze to her patrons who sat there as stunned as she was.

"Get up, people! Clear out!"

"Wait!" Ellie purposefully stood in front of the inspector. "Please. I'm not in violation of any codes. This is all some huge misunderstanding." She turned back to the man. "Mr. Willmar, you can't do this."

He tapped his identification smugly. "This says I can."

"I say you can't," a deep, somewhat familiar voice sounded from the door. "What on earth are you doing here, George?"

Mr. Willmar's already flushed face became even redder if that was possible. "My job."

Ellie finally took a good look at the man behind the voice. It was the pleasant gentleman from the previous inspection. *Oh, thank God.* "Mr. Salgado, I don't understand what's going on here. Your department . . ."

"My department," he interrupted gently, "has nothing to do with this, Miss Montgomery." He motioned for Ellie to give him a moment and grabbed Willmar's arm. Whatever was being said right outside the door of the diner was undoubtedly heated. She wouldn't have thought a man as congenial as Mr. Salgado could get that angry.

"You in trouble, girl?"

Ellie looked up at Big Al and shook her head. "Like I said, *old man*, just a misunderstanding." She gave him her best smile – as tremulous as it was — and bumped Big Al's hip. "You'll still have your gross drink every day."

Big Al nodded once and gave her what she took as a grin (whether it was one or not). "Thought so." With that, he left Ellie and Blaise alone.

"Wow. That was almost an entire conversation *and* a smile." Blaise would have hugged the cantankerous old fella if she thought she could get away with it. She was sure he knew exactly what he was doing by allowing Ellie a moment of mirth in this terrible situation.

"Miss Montgomery?" Mr. Salgado joined them with an apologetic expression. "Is there somewhere we can speak in private?"

"Yes, of course. But, first, can you tell my customers something so they can finish their meals in peace?"

"Oh, right! Ladies and gentlemen, I sincerely apologize for the interruption. This was nothing but a terrible misunderstanding. Ellie's Diner is *not* in violation of any codes whatsoever. In fact, this diner is one of the highest rated establishments in our city. I implore you to forgive the Health Department's mistake today and keep frequenting this fine restaurant."

Ellie raised her eyebrows. "Huh. That ought to do it. But, just in case." She addressed her customers. "Everyone gets a slice of pie on the house for the inconvenience." She chuckled lightly at the raucous round of applause. "Please, get back to your meals. Mr. Salgado, if you'll follow me." She gestured for Blaise — who had kept surprisingly quiet — to follow them.

She settled in behind her desk and waited as Mr. Salgado sat in one of her visitor's chairs and Blaise made herself comfortable on the small couch.

"I can't tell you how sorry I am that this happened, Miss Montgomery."

"Call me Ellie, please. Why was he here?"

Mr. Salgado rubbed his hands over his face. "I don't know, yet, but I will. George is on leave." He hesitated as though he was contemplating how much to say. "He's being investigated."

"Investigated for what?"

"Taking bribes."

"Shocking," Blaise piped up sarcastically, causing Mr. Salgado to visibly wince.

"My diner is clean, Mr. Salgado. If this damages my reputation . . ."

"Juan, I insist. And, I assure you, we will get to the bottom of this, Ellie." He stood. "Your establishment speaks for itself. However, if necessary, my department can and will speak with local media in order to clear up any misgivings."

"I appreciate that." Ellie shook Juan's extended hand in a show of gratitude and grace. "One question. If he was on leave, how did you know he was here?"

Juan smiled. "You and the department have a mutual friend it seems. Give Mrs. Riley my best, will you? Good day, Ellie." he showed himself out and Ellie fell back into her chair, blowing out a whoosh of breath.

"Did you call Eve?" Ellie didn't even bother opening her eyes. A killer of a headache was forming and she longed for fresh air and the burn of her lungs working hard. There was something else she longed for even more than running which surprised her. *Hunter.*

"I ran into her and Lainey on my way here. I made an executive decision to tell them a *very* condensed version of what was going on down here."

"Thank you."

Blaise was worried. She wouldn't say Ellie looked defeated, but she certainly looked exhausted. It shouldn't have been this way for her. Both Ellie and Hunter should be celebrating what they had shared the night before. Not dealing with some deranged sicko.

"Do you want to talk about what's going on in your head?"

"Besides the drum line?" Ellie rocked her office chair gently, using the motion to help calm her. "Everything that she's doing – the photos, bribing someone to shut me down – it's mediocre child's play at best."

"So, maybe she's not as powerful as she thinks she is."

"And, that's what scares me. She's delusional. She was expecting to be able to control Hunter with all of this. But she didn't count on Hunter standing up to her. And, she didn't count on me being in the picture. Literally."

"Do you think she'll do something out of desperation?"

Ellie shrugged. "Maybe she overplayed her hand with today's failure and she'll leave us alone." Of course, she didn't believe that. Neither did Blaise, judging by her skepticism. She waved off the strange feeling in her tummy, chalking it up to side-effects of her headache. "Whatever she comes up with, Hunter and I will face it together."

Along with the rest of your family, Blaise added silently. If she had to pay Greyson in sexual favors to speed up their investigation . . . well, she would shoulder that burden. What were best friends for? "Are you going to tell her about this?"

Ellie opened her eyes and sighed. "I have to. This thing between us, I don't want to mess anything up by keeping things from her."

"You love her, don't you?"

For a divine moment, Ellie's headache weakened and she smiled.

Chapter Thirty

The rest of the week following Susan's attempt to shut Ellie's Diner down was notably quiet. Hunter wasn't sure whether she should be nervous about that or grateful. Naturally, when Ellie told her everything that happened, Hunter felt that familiar stab of guilt. Ellie never let that last for long and Hunter was finally beginning to believe that she was not the one to blame. Her anger towards Susan, however, was something she was going to have to control a little better. The only thing that kept Hunter from going after the despicable woman was the stiff consequence of possibly losing Ellie.

Because of that, Hunter scheduled as many sessions as Dr. Woodrow could fit in. Even Ellie had agreed to sit in on a couple, which Hunter appreciated immensely. It had been very enlightening seeing how Ellie's brain worked. And she realized during those sessions that her girlfriend minced no words. She could trust Ellie to be upfront with her and that eased Hunter's mind and heart into opening further.

What pleased Hunter the most was Ellie's willingness to let her stay over at her place. She had thought with Jessie being there that it would be Hunter's place or none and that their time together would be limited. But Ellie had said that she wanted Jessie to get used to seeing them together. Hunter suspected that it was to give Hunter and Jessie a chance to bond as well. Strangely, that was going exceptionally well. This coming weekend the three of them were going to spend some family time at the beach house, much to Jessie's — and Hunter's — excitement. Until then, Hunter kept an overnight bag in her truck and had used it every day since her and Ellie's first night together. It was amazing!

"Dr. Vale to the nurse's station."

"Aww, come on!" Hunter had managed to talk Mack into letting her go a couple of hours early tonight and she wanted to surprise Ellie. Being called to the nurse's station was *not* on her agenda. She made her way there, irritably. If this altered her plans she was going to be one unhappy surgeon. When she rounded the corner, she stopped dead in her tracks. This was definitely going to alter her plans. "Mom? Dad?"

"ENJOY YOUR MEAL." Ellie gave her customer a pleasant smile. The diner, thankfully, did not lose any patrons after everything that happened. Ellie liked to think that her customers knew her well enough to know she would never jeopardize their health or her diner's standing in the community. She may live and do business in Los Angeles, but she had a small-town mentality when it came to how she treated those who ate at her restaurant.

The bell signaled a new arrival and, per usual, Ellie looked up with a smile. The courtesy smile turned happily surprised when Hunter walked in. Then Hunter ushered in two people behind her and Ellie faltered. *Oh boy.*

Hunter practically pushed her parents into a booth close to the door and rushed up to the counter towards her somewhat dazed girlfriend.

"Hey, baby."

"Hi, honey. This is a surprise." She peered over Hunter's shoulder briefly. "I thought you were working until six tonight."

"I was, but I talked Mack into giving me a few of the hours back that I've given. I wanted to surprise you."

"Well, you have certainly accomplished that."

Hunter glanced back at her parents who were watching them. "Um, my folks are here," she said unnecessarily. Ellie may not have met them, yet, but there was no mistaking they were related to Hunter.

"You don't say," Ellie smirked. "Did you know they were coming?"

"Nope." Hunter shuffled her feet nervously. Introducing Ellie to her folks was not what made her edgy. It was the fact that they were here and now she had to come clean about Susan and the others. "Apparently, they couldn't wait to hear what I had to tell them. So, they made a special trip."

Ellie and Hunter had agreed to wait until after the coming weekend to drive up to her parents' place. Not only did it give them an opportunity to spend a bit of uninterrupted time with Jessie first, it gave Hunter a little extra time to get mentally prepared for "the talk". Well, Ellie hoped Hunter was ready now. At first glance, Hunter's father looked rather reasonable. Her mother, however, reminded Ellie of a mama bear. Mess with her baby and they won't be able to identify the body. That didn't bode well for Susan. Which caused Ellie to smile wickedly.

"We're being rude, honey. Introduce me before your mom thinks I'm not good enough for her daughter."

Hunter chuckled. "No chance of that. Just bring her a piece of pie." She placed her hand at small of Ellie's back, using the contact to calm her nerves. "This isn't exactly how I envisioned this," she murmured.

"It'll all be okay." *I hope.* They were about to find out.

"Ahem, Mom? Dad? I'd like you to meet Ellie."

Alton immediately stood, hand held out amicably. "It's a pleasure to meet you."

Now I know where Hunter gets her charm. Ellie smiled warmly. "The pleasure is all mine, Mr. Vale."

"Ah ah." Cece scooted out of the booth and stood in front of Ellie. "No one that makes Hunter smile the way she does when she says your name or," she continued through Hunter's whine. "Or talks about you as though you were the only woman in the world calls us Mr. or Mrs. You call us Cece and Alton." She hugged a speechless Ellie. *"Until it's time to call us mom and dad,"* she whispered.

Oh boy. "Hunter wasn't kidding about all of the stories she's told me about you." Ellie winked at Cece. "I have to respect a mother who isn't afraid to speak her mind."

"Or embarrass her kid," Hunter mumbled.

"Don't be dramatic, honey." Ellie patted Hunter's arm. "It's a mother's job to embarrass her kid every once in a while."

Oh, I like her. Cece watched the exchange with interest. When Hunter had told her that Ellie had a kid, she had been surprised. Unfortunately, Hunter didn't offer any further explanation. No matter. She would just have to get her information straight from the source.

"Hunter tells me you have a child of your own?"

Ellie had never had the opportunity to "meet the parents" before, but she knew what she would do when Jessie brought home someone she was serious about. With that in mind, she couldn't begrudge the inquisition. "Why don't we all have a seat. Will you be eating?"

"A slice of that heavenly pie sounds wonderful. Baker's choice." Cece slid into the booth next to an amused Alton. A less amused Hunter sat opposite of them.

"Done," Ellie said easily. "Let me get that and a pot of coffee and I'll join you. Then you can grill me as much as you like."

Cece laughed as Ellie walked away. "She's perfect, Hunter."

"I think so." Hunter gave her mom a toothy grin. Even being embarrassed couldn't put a damper on how happy it made her that her mom approved of her girlfriend. It was silly. Here she was, an adult, and seeking her parents' endorsement.

"Are there any subjects we should avoid?" Alton asked carefully.

All he knew was the woman had a kid. He would hate to seem inconsiderate by asking about the father.

"Nah, I don't think Ellie would want you to sidestep anything with her. She's pretty private, but she's also very candid with those she deems important."

"You sound quite enamored with her."

"What your father is trying to ask is; is this thing with Ellie why you needed to talk to us?" Cece tapped her blue painted fingernails on the table. She had been waiting for years for Hunter to find someone special. And, while this may have happened a little fast, she was happy. Of course, Alton would scold her for being hypocritical since the two of them were engaged mere months after meeting.

Hunter blushed a little but was completely honest. "Ma, believe me, when I ask Ellie to marry me — and, I will when I think she's ready — I'll be shouting it from the rooftops." She spotted Ellie coming back with a tray full. Her first instinct was to get up and help but knew better. She snorted softly when she thought of Ellie sashaying into her OR and handing her surgical tools.

Ellie eyed Hunter suspiciously and was rewarded with a cute wink. "Today's pie of the day is lemon-cream cheese. I chose that for you, Cece. Alton, Hunter tells me you enjoy gardening and grow your own berries and produce." Alton nodded, a spark of eagerness in his eyes. "I thought you might enjoy double berry vanilla cream."

"Oh, yeah!" Alton rubbed his hands together in anticipation. "Now if I could just keep my wife's hands off my pie." He scooted the pie piled high with beautiful berries closer to him, using his arms to protect it.

Ellie laughed at his antics and Cece's response which was to pluck a berry right out from under his nose.

"What do I get?" Hunter sat up tall in her seat trying to get a glimpse.

"You get to try a new recipe I've been working on. Banana and peanut butter."

"Ha!" Hunter stuck her tongue out at her parents as though she won the grand prize. In her mind, she did. Knowing Ellie most likely wasn't ready for public displays of affection in her diner, Hunter refrained from kissing her when she sat next to her. *"Thank you, baby,"* she said for Ellie's ears only. The sweet, shy smile she got from Ellie made her heart soar.

Cece watched them interact with each other. All any mother wanted was what was best for their kids. It was quite possible that all of Cece's hopes for Hunter rested within this one woman. "So, tell me about your . . . daughter, is it?"

"Yeah," Hunter answered first with a proud smile. "She's awesome."

Ellie grinned and leaned closer to Hunter. "Jessie. She's sixteen going on forty."

"Sixteen?" Astonished, Cece glanced at her own daughter. She really needed to have a conversation with Hunter on how much information to supply her with. "You certainly don't look old enough."

"Ma," Hunter warned.

"No, it's fine." Ellie patted Hunter's thigh under the table. "I had Jessie when I was young. Too young. I was a teenager and going through life-altering changes. I made a mistake, had sex with a boy for the wrong reasons, and became pregnant. That's the shortened version."

Cece nodded. She approved of Ellie's no-nonsense attitude. The one thing she *didn't* want was someone who was going to be fake with her just to win points. Fortunately, her gut told her that there wasn't a fake bone in Ellie's body. "Perhaps one day we'll have an opportunity to have a more in-depth conversation."

"I would love that."

"And, your parents? Are they still with us?" Alton asked, then stuffed his mouth with a glorious bite of pie. He was so devoted to savoring this bite that he missed Hunter burying her face in her hands.

Ellie squeezed Hunter's thigh. "They are, but we don't speak very often." She knew what the next question would inevitably be, so she continued. "They do not approve of who I am, so it's best for me to keep my distance."

Cece gripped her coffee cup tightly. This was one subject that irked her. Former friends of her often asked how she could stand having a gay daughter. To her, who Hunter loved didn't change who she was or the remarkable woman she had become. "It's such a shame when parents can't support their children."

Hunter stared at her mom. "I don't think I've ever seen you rein in your temper like that."

"Keep it up, kid of mine. I'm not above turning you over my knee right here in this diner."

"She's not kidding," Alton mumbled with a mouthful.

"While I would pay to see that," Ellie teased. "My customers may find it a bit odd."

"Can we change the subject, please?" Hunter couldn't believe her mom just threatened to spank her in front of Ellie.

"We can talk about what brought us here." Cece wondered how terrible it would be to get a second piece of pie. Or maybe a sampler. To take home, of course. At least half of it. Thinking about the pie didn't prevent Cece from catching the look that passed between Hunter and Ellie. There was unmistakable fear in Hunter's eyes which put Cece on alert.

"I think," Ellie began, still watching Hunter. Seeing that Hunter was more than willing to let Ellie do the talking, she turned to Cece and continued. "That conversation would be better somewhere more private."

She's protecting Hunter. Cece couldn't have been more satisfied with the woman that her daughter chose. Anyone who would choose to challenge a mother was worth it.

"Yeah, um, maybe I could order some take-out and we can, uh, talk over dinner? And, I would like for Ellie to be there if you don't mind."

It was unusual for Cece or Alton to see Hunter being anything but confident and they exchanged a look of their own. If she's this nervous, whatever she had to say couldn't be good.

"Yes, okay, dear. If that's what you two think is best."

"I just have to finish up here," Ellie told Hunter. "I can be there in a couple of hours. Is that okay? Only don't order anything, I'll cook."

"Yeah, baby. But, I don't want you to have to . . ."

"Honey, let me do this for you. Besides, it'll give me a chance to use that amazing kitchen," she grinned.

"Oh! You've seen the kitchen?" Cece was excited. This thing with Ellie must be very serious. Hunter was never the type to invite people over. Except for Mo. That girl nearly drove Cece crazy.

"Yep!" Hunter beamed. "*I* made *her* breakfast." She heard a little squeak come from Ellie and she realized what she had just revealed. To her parents. "Um . . . what I mean is . . ."

Laughter rumbled from Alton, but he wisely kept eating. Cece tried her hardest to look stern, but couldn't keep the façade up because the look on both women's faces was priceless.

"Hunter, you're over forty. I think it's safe to say I know you two are . . ."

"Ma!"

"Stop torturing our daughter, Ce." Alton winked at Hunter and Ellie. "Ellie, if your cooking is a good as this pie, I for one would be extremely appreciative if you cooked tonight."

"Will you be bringing Jessie?" Cece had long ago given up having grandchildren. Hunter had made it perfectly clear that she was not interested in having kids. Knowing that Ellie had a child and Hunter was perfectly fine with that made her relationship with Ellie even more special, Cece thought.

"Oh, I . . ." This probably wasn't a conversation to have with Jessie around. Especially if they spoke about what was going on now.

"Bring her, baby. She can hang out by the pool while we talk. Do you mind? I'd like for my folks to meet her."

"Sure, honey. I'll talk to her and see if she has any plans tonight. On that note, I should get back to work." She offered Cece and Alton a dazzling smile. "It was wonderful meeting you both. I look forward to seeing you later." Ellie wished she had the courage to kiss Hunter right then. However, being in her diner with so many people surrounding them . . . well, she wasn't that fearless. Yet.

Instead, she took Hunter's hand and squeezed it. "See you soon, honey."

AS IT TURNED out, Jessie was thrilled to be invited over to Hunter's for dinner. The pool was a great incentive, but her real motivation came from the thought of meeting Hunter's parents. They sounded like great people from what her mom told her. How could they not be? At least they supported Hunter, unlike her mom's parents. It was going to be interesting to see what real grandparents were like. Of course, she didn't tell her mom this. Maybe one day, but for now she wanted them both to enjoy this night.

"So, what are you making for dinner?" Jessie looked out the window as she spoke. The setting sun made the ocean look as though it was on fire. She always loved this time of day. Especially when she got to spend it with her mom.

"Pork cutlet parmigiana." Ellie glanced over at her daughter. She looked so peaceful and happy. She would do anything for Jessie to stay that way. Hopefully, by getting everything out in the open with Hunter's parents, Hunter would be more inclined to hit back hard when it came to Susan.

"Yummy. Can you put extra parmesan on mine?"

"Your love for cheese is bordering on weird, kid."

"There's nothing weird about loving cheese, mom. It's the food of life." She made a face at Ellie, then turned her attention back to her surroundings. When her mom pulled into the driveway of one of the coolest houses she'd ever seen, her jaw dropped. "Holy crap! This is Hunter's house?"

"Mmhmm. And, please don't say crap in front of her parents. At least not in the first fifteen minutes."

Jessie rolled her eyes. "Don't worry. I'll be the smart, well-behaved kid you raised all by yourself."

Ellie laughed. "You're a brat. Just try not to embarrass me."

"Do I get extra cheese?"

Ellie raised her brow. "Are you negotiating good behavior payment with me? Because if it's cheese you want, I'll take it out of your allowance."

"Gah, why you gotta be so harsh? Okay, how about this. Triple the cheese, raise my allowance five bucks more a week, and I'm an angel." She circled the space above her head like a halo.

"I don't think you get how negotiating works, sweetie. Here's the deal." Ellie parked her Jeep behind Hunter's truck and cut the engine. She turned to her daughter. "You be on your best behavior and I won't tell embarrassing stories about you. I'll make sure you get double the parmesan, but your allowance remains the same."

"You drive a hard bargain, woman." Jessie held out her hand. "Deal."

Ellie snickered and shook her daughter's hand. "Sometimes I wonder about you."

"You only have yourself to blame!" Jessie called out as she hopped out of the Jeep.

ELLIE STOOD UNDER the hot spray of the shower and reflected on everything that had happened tonight. Despite Hunter's reservations, the night actually turned out better than expected. At least the beginning did. The Vales took to Jessie immediately and doted on her as if she were their granddaughter. As for Jessie, she was relaxed, talkative, and open. Something Ellie had never seen with her own parents. That fact alone caused such resentment for her mother and father. Ellie couldn't help but wonder what Jessie's life would have been like if she had grown up with grandparents like Cece and Alton.

Then the time came for the unpleasantness of Hunter telling

her parents about Susan. Oh, how Ellie was glad Jessie was out in the pool enjoying herself. Inside Hunter's beautiful home there was a stream of ugly curses, whisper-yelling (for Jessie's benefit), and complete outrage. If Susan had shown up at that moment, it most likely would have been the last thing she ever did. It was the only time Ellie would ever wish to see Susan.

It literally took a group effort to keep Cece from storming out to find the woman who hurt her daughter and . . . well, there were some extremely colorful suggestions of what to do with her coming from Cece. Some of those were directed at the three of them for having the gall to stop her.

One beautiful thing did happen that brought tears to Ellie's eyes. Both Alton and Cece bent over backward to make sure Hunter knew they in no way blamed her. That they loved her unconditionally and would stand by her no matter what happened. That *was the true love of a parent*, Ellie thought whimsically. In return, Hunter made it clear, especially to her mother, that they had no fault in what happened to her.

Ellie stepped out of the shower and wrapped a towel around her body. A body that constantly hummed for Hunter's attention. Unfortunately, she took the unselfish route and came home so Hunter and her parents could spend some quality time together. After a week of devoting most of their free time together, it felt a little off getting ready for bed with Hunter waiting for her. She laughed quietly at the absurdity of that. She'd been 'alone' all her life when it came to the bedroom. But now she couldn't deny how much she missed the companionship of her girlfriend. *And more,* she thought with a groan.

The buzzing of her phone on her nightstand caught Ellie's attention. *Only one person that could be,* she thought and rushed to answer it, chuckling when it turned out to be a facetime call. She touched the button to connect and Hunter's gorgeous face filled her screen.

"Hi." She climbed up on her bed, propping herself up on her pillows.

Hunter's eyes widened and she craned her neck in a failed

attempt to see more than Ellie was showing. "Did you just get out of the shower?"

"Yes. Good timing."

"Good? Baby, that is perfect timing. But you need to work on your angling of the phone. And lose the towel."

"Did you call to see my breasts or to talk to me, honey?"

"I can't do both?" Hunter grinned that oh-so-charming lopsided grin and Ellie laughed.

"How is everything there?"

Hunter gave Ellie a playful, resigned sigh and leaned back on her own bed, mirroring Ellie's position. "Better. I think mom is winding down. At last count, I think we were at number 573."

"573?"

"Unusual ways to kill Susan."

Ellie's laughter was swift and she slapped a hand over her mouth. "I shouldn't laugh about that. But, have I told you how much I adore your mother?"

Hunter chuckled at her girlfriend. "She adores you, too. And, Jessie. They've always wanted grandkids." She closed her eyes and pressed her lips together when she realized what her words indicated.

"Jessie's always wanted fun grandparents. I think both parties were happy with the results of their meeting tonight."

Incredible blue eyes popped open. Had Ellie just presented her with the gift of a long future or was she just trying to make Hunter feel better? "Yeah?"

Ellie smiled softly. "Yeah. How is Alton?" He had been quiet throughout Hunter's tale. If Ellie were a good judge of body language, and she was, he was silently seething. Only the clenching of his fists gave away what he might be feeling inside.

"Stoic," Hunter answered, never questioning the change in subject. Most of their conversations were like a branched tree. No matter what direction they veered off in, eventually they go back to the root of things. "That kinda worries me. Though for every 573 ways mom came up with, pop always made the same joke. At least I think it was a joke." She lowered her voice to mock her dad. "'Just leave me enough to fertilize my garden'."

Ellie gave a full out belly laugh. "Oh, God. It is so wrong to be laughing about that. I'm going to hell." She snorted. "Eh, according to my parents I was headed there anyway."

Hunter didn't like thinking about everything Ellie's parents put her through. She had watched the interactions between her girlfriend and her parents. Though Ellie's demeanor remained casual and pleasant, Hunter caught those brief moments of melancholy. Ellie missed so much love growing up that it broke Hunter's heart. She knew with Jessie and Blaise that void had been lessened. Her hope was that *she* could close it for good.

"I miss you. I know that's probably silly to you."

Ellie smiled softly. "I miss you, too." They sat in silence for a moment and Ellie studied Hunter's face. It was scrubbed clean of enhancements and her hair was pulled back in a loose ponytail. "You're so beautiful."

Hunter crinkled her nose. She had a healthy enough ego to accept the compliment, even looking as she did now. But what caused her heart to race was the frank desire in Ellie's eyes. "I'm constantly thinking the same about you. God, baby, I wish you were here."

"So do I, honey."

"Will you still come over this weekend? I have an extra room for Jess. And I, uh, hope you'll be staying in my room with me."

"How long are your parents staying?"

Hunter sighed. "I don't know. That's why I'm prepared to beg you. I'm almost afraid my mom isn't going to want to leave now."

"I don't blame her. You're being threatened and you're her baby." She laughed when Hunter grunted and mumbled something about not being a baby. "No matter how old you are, you will always be her baby."

"I want to be *your* baby."

Ellie grinned. "You are. Only in a very different way."

Hunter threw her head back. "Ah! This is torture! I want to be able to touch you." Her body responded powerfully when Ellie's eyes fluttered closed. "Be my hands, baby."

Green eyes sprang open. "What?"

"Be my hands," Hunter repeated huskily. "And I'll be yours."

"Honey, I – I've never . . ."

"I know," Hunter said softly. "I would like to be your first."

Ellie raised a brow. "You were. And, my second, third, fourth, fifth, and so on."

Hunter inhaled sharply through her nose. She vividly remembered each and every one of those times. *"Drop the towel and let me see you. Let me touch you, baby."*

After another quite vigorous first — and Ellie agreeing to stay with Hunter as planned — the lovers fell asleep still connected to each other via the wonders of technology.

Chapter Thirty-One

After the weekend she just had, Hunter Vale was flying high. She had never been happier and she was making no secret about it. There was an extra pep in her step, she was smiling more, and she even started greeting almost everyone that she passed. And why the hell shouldn't she? Life was marvelous.

During their preliminary search, Cade and Greyson came up with nothing solid to take down Susan. And, while she remained quiet for the time being, both Hunter and Ellie agreed that Drake & Associates should dig deeper. It was unlike Susan to just give up. When she came after Ellie or Hunter again, they wanted to be ready to fire back.

"Hey, Hunter." Hunter rolled her eyes as Iris slinked up beside her and touched her arm.

Hunter pulled away. She felt way too good to let someone like Iris ruin it. "Iris."

The short nurse had to trot to keep up with Hunter. "I was thinking that maybe we could get a drink after shift."

"Not interested." Hunter whistled a cheery tune and kept walking.

"Okay, we don't have to drink. We could always just go back to the on-call room."

Hunter stopped suddenly and waited for Iris to figure out she was no longer next to her. When the redhead finally turned back, she was greeted with a scowl.

"Don't ever mention that again. What happened that day was a huge mistake never to be repeated." She lowered her voice dangerously. "Get it through your head that I'm not interested. I will never be interested. I'm in love with Ellie and I'm sure as hell not going to jeopardize that with anyone, especially you. Leave me alone, Iris. Go chase one of your other targets. I'm off the market. For good."

Fate stepped in at that moment as Hunter was paged just as Iris was about to respond. It was a bittersweet reprieve considering she was being called into surgery a mere hour before her shift ended. Still, she smiled when she thumbed the key in her pocket. *"I want you to know that you can come over anytime, honey. No matter how late."* There would always be a light at the end of her tunnel. Ellie.

JESSIE YAWNED AND stuffed the application back in her folder. It was the last college application she had to fill out. And the hardest. She dreaded the moment she would have to tell her mom she had changed her mind about what school to go to. Never wanting to leave her mother alone, Jessie had always talked about going to school here in L.A. But now that her mom had found . . .

HUNTER OPENED THE door as quietly as she could. It was extremely late and she was exhausted both mentally and physically. The surgery she had been called into turned out to be a terrible, impossible case. But, Hunter being Hunter, she refused to give up until she ran out of options. At the end of the night, her patient had run out of time. Although she knew she was fighting a lost cause, the loss hit her hard.

"Hey."

"Shit!" Hunter stood motionless, the door still open behind her, staring at Jessie. "Sorry, I didn't mean to say that. You just scared me."

Jessie giggled. "I've heard worse from Blaise. Are you coming in?"

"Um, where is your mom?"

Jessie checked her watch. It was well past midnight and her mom had been awake since five that morning. "It's late, doc. Mom's sleeping."

"Oh. Maybe I should . . ."

"Come in? It is what mom gave you the key for. You've been coming over every night, what's different about now?"

Hunter sighed and shut the door. "It's never just been you and me, I guess. What are you doing awake? It's late."

"Eating and filling stuff out." She stuffed a grape in her mouth. "Is there always going to be an awkwardness between us?"

Hunter kicked her shoes off and made her way to the kitchen island. "Nah. I think I'm getting a little better." She winked and stole a grape. "College apps?" she asked, nodding at the papers on the countertop.

"Yep."

"Any top prospects?"

"Yeah."

"You don't sound very sure about that." Hunter was proud of herself. She was having a full conversation with Ellie's daughter without stumbling over every other word. Yep. Progress.

"I'm sure about where I want to go. I'm just not sure how to tell mom."

"Ah. Out of state?"

"Across the dang country," Jessie grunted on her way to the refrigerator. She grabbed the leftover apple pie, two bottles of water, and two forks on her way back. Handing Hunter a fork, she planted herself on a barstool next to the surgeon. "I don't know why, but mom's apple pie is extra good when it's cold."

Hunter took a healthy bite and hummed in delight. "Your mom's pie is great no matter how it's eaten."

Jessie stopped chewing and gave Hunter a stony stare. "Is that a euphemism?"

If Hunter ever wondered if choking on apple pie was better or worse than choking on coffee, she now knew. "No! I — I didn't! I meant . . ."

Jessie burst out laughing. "Oh my God, you're so easy! Blaise and I are going to have so much fun with you!" She wiped tears of laughter from her eyes. "I'm so glad mom found you."

"Because I'm easy to tease?" Hunter coughed and wiped tears of almost dying from her eyes.

Jessie bumped Hunter's shoulder. "No, because you make her happy." She waited a beat. "*And* because you're easy to tease."

Hunter chuckled. "You're a brat."

"Yeah, I know. Mom tells me that almost every day." Jessie sighed and set her fork down. "How did you do it?"

Hunter took a pull from her bottle of water. "Do what?"

"Leave your parents. Every time I think about moving away from mom, it's like I get the hives. But, I *really* want to go to Harvard."

Dark, arched eyebrows raised. "Harvard?"

Jessie reached over and grabbed the application, handing it to Hunter. "Medical school. I haven't told mom about this, yet. I don't know how. So, how did you do it?"

Oh, man. Ellie is not going to be pleased with this. But Hunter thought she knew her lover well enough to know she wouldn't want Jessie giving up anything she wanted. "It's never easy, leaving your home, Jess. However, if this is something you feel you need to do, you have to go for it. Your mom will support you, I think you know that."

"Ugh! I'm sure I could be just as happy going to UCLA or Berkeley. Somewhere close."

Hunter swiveled her chair until she was facing the teen. "What's honestly holding you back?"

Jessie propped her elbows on the counter and rested her head on her palm. "Fear?"

"Are you asking me or telling me?"

"Telling. I mean, I know mom is going to be okay without me. She has you now. How do *I* survive without her?"

"You want to be a doctor, kiddo. You're going to be too busy trying to survive that. Are you going to miss your mom? Of course. Is she going to miss you? More than you know. But, she would never want you to give up on your dreams." Hunter laid a hand on Jessie's shoulder. "If it means anything when I saw you presenting at the science fair, I saw someone with extraordinary talent and a great mind for medicine. Don't let fear hold you back from changing the world."

Jessie beamed. "Thank you, Hunter. That means a lot coming from you."

She squeezed Jessie's shoulder. "Talk to your mom. Let her help you through all of this. It'll make you both feel better. And, if Harvard is what you really want, I'd be happy to write you a recommendation letter."

"Oh my God! That would be so great, thank you so much!" Jessie hopped off her stool and gave Hunter an impromptu hug. Amazingly, neither of them felt awkward at that moment.

COMPLETELY DRAINED, HUNTER nearly groaned out loud when she finally laid down in bed. Her talk with Jessie had allowed her to focus on something other than her dreadful night at the hospital. But it was being next to Ellie that soothed her soul as nothing else could. When her girlfriend automatically rolled over to cuddle with her, Hunter wasted no time wrapping her arms around Ellie, reveling in the comforting warmth.

"*You're home.*"

That one small declaration caused tears to form in her eyes from the sheer accuracy. Regardless of where they were, when Ellie was in her arms, Hunter was home. "*Yeah, baby. I'm home.*"

Sleepy eyes opened and peered up at Hunter in the darkened room. "Are you okay?" She wasn't sure what it was that had alerted her to Hunter's mood, but she learned long ago not to question a gut feeling.

"Yeah, I'm just tired. I didn't mean to wake you, baby. Go back to sleep."

Ellie had seen *tired* on Hunter after long shifts at the hospital. This? This was something more. Because of that, she stubbornly pressed on. "Talk to me, honey."

Hunter took a deep breath, letting it out with a whoosh. "I don't know how much more I can take, El."

"You lost someone." Even though it wasn't a question, Hunter nodded. "Talk to Mack, honey. Get out of trauma before it tears you apart."

"But, it's who I am." It was a weak argument since Hunter wasn't convinced that was true anymore.

"It's what you do," Ellie corrected gently. "And, yeah, trauma may have been something you needed years ago. But, you're different now. I think it's safe for you to try something new."

"Still be a surgeon?"

"If that's what you want."

"And, if I want to quit altogether and become a beach bum?"

"As long as you shower off all the sand before you get into bed with me, go for it."

"*Go for it.*" Isn't that what she had just told Jessie? Must be sound advice if Ellie's giving it as well.

"Whatever it is you want to do," Ellie continued, "I support you, Hunter."

Hunter kissed Ellie's forehead. "Thank you. I'll talk to Mack tomorrow." She rolled over until her body was deliciously on top of Ellie's. "Whatever I want?"

A soft, beautiful laugh filled the room. "I thought you were tired."

"I must have gotten my second wind."

"Oh, well in that case." Ellie flipped their positions easier than Hunter would like to admit. "*I'm hungry*," she whispered against Hunter's ear and took the long journey down Hunter's body.

Hunter forgot all about being tired. In fact, when her body arched off the bed at the touch of Ellie's tongue, there was only one thought that looped in her brain.

Home.

"MORNIN', MOM."

Ellie looked up from cooking breakfast to see her daughter fully dressed and ready to go.

"Good morning, sweets. You're up early. Want some breakfast?"

Jessie reached over the counter and grabbed her mom's glass of orange juice. "No time." She took a gulp that drained half the glass. "I'm picking up Piper this morning, remember?"

"Oh, that's right." Ellie watched as her daughter guzzled the rest of her juice. She grabbed a protein bar from her ever-present stash and tossed it to Jessie. "You're welcome for the juice, now eat that and you should be good until lunch."

"Yes, mommy." Jessie snickered when her mom gave her "the look".

"By the way, Hunter is here." Even though Hunter's presence

had become a constant, Ellie always wanted to make sure Jessie wasn't surprised by the company.

Jessie gave her mom a devilish grin. "I heard."

Ellie's eyes grew wide and she felt a warmth that had nothing to do with standing near the stove. "I —"

Jessie roared with laughter. "I'm kidding! I was awake when she came in."

"You!" Ellie had half a mind to throw the wooden spoon she was holding at her jokester kid. "I will get you back for that."

"Sure, sure. Hunter is just as easy to tease as you are." Jessie knew she was about to get scolded for her antics, so she rushed on. "Hey, is she okay?"

Ellie narrowed her eyes. "You know I know you're changing the subject, right?"

"I know that you know that I know, etcetera," Jessie joked. "But seriously, mom. She seemed kinda down when she came in last night."

"She's fine, sweetie. She's just getting a little burnt out with trauma."

"I can understand that. Trauma must be pretty difficult sometimes. Why doesn't she go into something else?"

"She is."

Both Ellie and Jessie jumped at the sound of Hunter's voice and she chuckled. She wondered if the two of them knew just how alike they were.

"Morning, kiddo." She got a fist bump from the teen who mumbled something about a bell. "Morning, baby." Hunter accepted a sweet kiss from her girlfriend.

"So, I take it you don't recommend going into trauma?" Jessie asked as she gathered up her stuff for school.

Hunter glanced at Ellie who was listening carefully. "It takes a certain personality to work in trauma. It's not for everyone, that's for sure. And, it's not for me anymore."

"That was a great non-answer," Jessie laughed. "But, I'll let you off the hook, cuz I gotta go. Maybe we can talk more about it later?"

"Um." Hunter looked at Ellie again who nodded. "Yeah, I'd like that."

"Cool. Oh, and, mom?"

"Hmm?" Ellie finished making a plate for Hunter and looked up at her daughter.

"I would like to talk to you later, as well. I could, uh, use your help on some stuff."

Ellie wasn't pleased about having to wait to find out what this was all about, but she would never deny a request like that. "Sure."

"'Kay. Love you!"

"I love you, too." Ellie immediately turned to her lover as soon as the door shut behind Jessie. "Do you know what all of that was about?"

Hunter stuffed her face with food in lieu of answering. Yeah, she was a coward and Ellie knew it. She felt herself being pushed onto a barstool and automatically spread her legs so Ellie could stand in between them.

"Fine. You want me to wait, give me something else to occupy my mind."

Hunter swallowed audibly, then leered at Ellie who was wearing nothing more than a t-shirt and shorts. God, she loved Ellie's legs. "I can do that." She brought Ellie's lips to hers and kissed her deeply. When their tongues met, images from the night before flooded Hunter's brain and she moaned into Ellie's mouth. There was a good chance that she was going to be late for work and Hunter was absolutely content with that.

"Mom!"

Ellie pushed away from Hunter, tugging her shirt down in hopes of keeping some of her dignity in front of her daughter. Both had been captivated with each other and the kiss — not to mention what their hands were doing — that they never even heard the door open. She expected perhaps shock, maybe a little disgust, when she faced Jessie. What she didn't expect was the frantic, almost scared look she received.

"Jessie? What's wrong?" She rushed to her daughter, examining her for any possible injuries. Her first thought went to Susan and she vowed that if that immoral woman did *anything* to hurt her daughter there would be hell to pay.

Jessie swatted at Ellie's hands. "There's nothing wrong with me. It's this!" She shoved her phone in Ellie's face.

She had to step back a bit to focus on the photo Jessie was showing her. "Is that my Jeep?!"

Hunter — who stood poised to battle anything or anyone that was causing Jessie anxiety — pulled the phone to her. Ellie's Jeep Wrangler was destroyed. Tires were slashed, the windows were busted out, and vulgar messages were spray-painted everywhere. *'Whore', 'Bitch', 'Cunt', 'Psycho girlfriend stealer'.* Rage coursed through every vein in her body, propelling her to the door. "I'm going to kill her."

Ellie snapped out of her shocked daze just in time to catch Hunter's arm. "Honey, stop."

"No, El! I won't let her get away with this!"

Ellie took a deep breath. The last thing any of them needed was to start fighting with each other. Besides, something about this just didn't feel right to her. Perhaps her gut instinct was wrong, but Ellie's first thought had not been Susan. Witnessing Hunter's current state, Ellie made a conscious decision to keep those thoughts to herself.

"I understand how you feel, but you can't just go after her. We will report this to the police and let them handle it."

"Can someone please tell me what's going on!" Jessie demanded impatiently. "Who are you talking about?"

"Susan," Hunter and Ellie answered simultaneously.

Jessie frowned. "Wait, the wacko that hurt Hunter? She did this?"

"Yes," Hunter grumbled.

"We don't know," Ellie countered sharply.

"El." Hunter had seen that look before from her own mother. It worked just as effectively as Hunter immediately shut her mouth. Even the smirk Jessie gave her didn't faze her as much as *that* look.

Ellie turned to her daughter. "You need to go pick up Piper and go to school."

"I'm not . . ." This time Hunter smirked when Jessie's mouth snapped shut at her mother's look. "Why does that work?"

"Because it's scary as hell?" Hunter suggested carefully.

Ellie put her hands on her hips. "Because you both know I'm right. Jessie, sweetie, there's nothing you can do here. Go to school, have a good day, and don't let this ruin any of your plans. It's not worth it."

Jessie sighed. "Okay, but you're going to call the cops, right?"

"Yes."

"And, you'll text or call me if anything else happens?"

"Or, I'll wait until you get home to tell you. Seriously, sweetie, nothing is that important that we need to interrupt our day."

Jessie eyed Hunter, who shrugged. "Fine. Good luck, doc." She pivoted towards the door, but stopped and turned back. "I love you." She gave her mom a hug. "When you find whoever did this, maybe you should give them 'the look'."

Ellie laughed, which lifted her spirits a little. She would continue to pretend to be unbothered by this for the sake of the ones she cared about. "I love you, too, brat. Now, go."

Once they were alone, Ellie took Hunter in her arms. "I know this is hurting you, honey. But the best thing we can do is report it to the police. If it turns out Susan did do this, having the report can only help us."

"I don't understand how you can doubt it's her." She squeezed Ellie to her, doing what she found herself doing quite a bit. Finding comfort. It almost made her feel guilty. This happened to Ellie, and Hunter should be comforting her. "But, we'll do this your way. May I make one request?"

"Of course."

"I want to pay for the repairs and you to drive my truck while your Jeep is in the shop."

"Honey, the insurance will cover it." Hunter looked so defeated it broke Ellie's heart. "But, I will need your truck today. I need to go to the farmer's market and get some produce for the diner. It's shopping day," she grinned.

"I'm kinda surprised you don't grow your own," Hunter teased.

Ellie tapped Hunter on the nose. "Cute. But, the only thing green on me is my eyes. I can't even keep plastic plants alive, much to Blaise's horror."

"It's nice to know you have flaws." Hunter winked at her, then sighed. "I'm sorry about all of this."

"Nope. Still not going to do this, baby." She caressed Hunter's face. "Like I told Jessie, it isn't worth it. We do what we have to do, then go on with our lives. They're not allowed to win."

"They?"

"Anyone who has a problem with us being together and being happy." Ellie kissed Hunter sweetly. "I'm going to call the police. Why don't you get ready for work?"

"Yes, ma'am." Hunter patted Ellie on the ass. "Thank you."

"For letting you smack my ass?"

"Well, yes. Always for that. But, also for being so strong." Hunter knew this had to bother Ellie more than she was letting on. Flowers and a special dinner were definitely in order. Maybe they'll even have a glass of wine. After that, Hunter was determined to take Ellie's mind off of everything except what her body was feeling.

ELLIE PULLED UP to the curb of the hospital to drop Hunter off a bit later than they anticipated. The entire process of reporting the vandalism, getting the Jeep to the shop, and, of course, calming Blaise down for not calling her right away, took forever and a day.

"Sorry, honey."

"Not a problem. The attending still owes me a few hours. Besides, I have a meeting with Mack." Hunter had already called Dr. Mackenzie requesting he set some time aside for her. She had a feeling he already knew what was coming, but to make it official would be one less burden on her shoulders.

"Good luck." Ellie leaned over and kissed Hunter. It had meant to be just a quick goodbye kiss, but one of them deepened it to quite a bit more. Since she wasn't sure which one of them it was, she gave credit to both.

Hunter pulled away slightly and tucked Ellie's hair behind her ear. "I don't want to leave you."

Ellie smiled. "As much as I would love to spend the day with you, I have shopping to do. And you need to go save lives. Then I'll come pick you up, we'll eat, talk, go to bed, make love, and start all over again. Everything will be fine, love."

"Sounds like heaven." She cleared her throat. "Love?" Hunter grinned. That was a new one and one she wholeheartedly approved of.

"Jessie tells me I need more pet name options. Love sounds so British."

"I like it."

God, how Ellie loved that big, toothy grin. It made Hunter look so carefree and happy. "I'll keep it on the list. Now, kiss me again before you go."

"My pleasure." She started to lean in, then stopped. "Should I be calling you something else?"

Sweet laughter filled the cab of Hunter's truck. "I like when you call me baby. And, you also have El. Don't change anything."

"Gotcha."

They kissed, lingering for more minutes than Hunter had. When they finally came up for air, something in Ellie's peripheral caught her attention.

"I think we have an audience."

Without making it obvious by turning her head, Hunter looked out of the side of her eye. Iris. She shook her head. "Hundreds of sick people needing attention in that hospital and she's out here gawking."

"You're out here kissing me," Ellie reminded her with a chuckle.

"Whose side are you on? Mouth to mouth. Totally a doctor thing to do."

"You better not be doing this with any of your patients!"

"Nobody but you, baby. Nobody but you." To prove her point and give Iris something to pout about, she gave her girlfriend another intense kiss. This time it took a lot more effort to pull away. "Be careful?"

"Always. I'll be here about six to pick you up."

"Good deal. If I happen to get called into surgery, I'll do my best to let you know. Wouldn't want you sitting here at the hospital all night waiting for me."

"Thank you. But, just so you know, I would wait."

"I love you, Ellie."

"I love you, too, Hunter."

She watched as Hunter hopped out of the truck and jogged inside the hospital. Iris was still staring through the windshield, an uneaten sandwich barely grasped in her limp hand. *Yeah, I know it was you,* Ellie mused with a touch of anger. She had no evidence other than her gut, but what happened to her Jeep had Iris written all over it. Literally. Hopefully, the cops that were investigating would find something conclusive. Until then, "the look" would have to be enough.

Chapter Thirty-Two

"Thank you for this, Mack."

Mack looked over at Hunter as they walked down the corridor. "I actually surprised it took you this long, Hunter. My offer to put in a word for you for chief of surgery is still open. You know old man Floyd is retiring."

Hunter laughed sharply. "I'm trying to lessen my stress, Mack, not add to it."

"Do me a favor and think about it. You'd make a fine leader, Hunter."

Maybe after another month or so with my therapist. Or a little more time with Ellie. "I'll think about it. For now, all I'm going to think about is using some of the vacation time I've accrued." She smiled as she thought about talking Ellie into going on vacation somewhere secluded. Or maybe taking Jessie with them to Europe. That could be educational, right?

"I hear that." Mack clapped Hunter on the shoulder. "Recommendation letter is already written. I'll hold on to it for as long as the position hasn't been filled." Mack's phone sounded. "Ah. Duty calls."

Hunter snickered as he jogged off. As she agreed, she would

think about the chief position. It wasn't the first time she was offered such a promotion, but she had been focused on surgery alone. She had never wanted to deal with all of the other aspects of the job and still wasn't sure she wanted to. *I'll talk to Ellie and see what she has to say.*

"Well, hello, stranger."

Hunter leaned on the nurse's station. "Hey, Patty. Mo." She nodded at her best friend, who seemed a little perturbed.

"Oh, you remember my name?"

Okay, maybe a little more than a little. Yeah, she had been a little preoccupied with Ellie and Jessie, but surely her friends understood that. Rebecca gave the impression that she got it when they spoke on the phone a few days ago.

"Come on, Mo. Don't be that way. You know, I didn't see you for like three months when you and Patty started dating."

"She just misses you, child. We all do." Patty rubbed her wife's arm. Mo wasn't always good at showing much emotion besides anger. And, Patty knew she wasn't angry with Hunter, just a bit left out.

"I know, I'm sorry. You remember what it's like, though. I want to spend every moment with Ellie. It's hard being away from her." She looked at Mo. "I've waited so long for this, Mo. I'm doing my best."

Mo sighed heavily. "Yeah, I know."

"Hey, my parents should be coming back from Santa Monica in a couple of days. They're going to stop back by here before heading home. Why don't we all get together and have a barbecue at my place? Me, Ellie, Jessie, my folks, you and Patty, Rebecca and Cass, Blaise and Greyson." She hesitated. "And Cade if he wants. We'll go all out."

"Will you have beer?" Mo asked, suddenly interested.

Hunter laughed. "Yeah, just for you."

Patty shook her head, ready to respond when the alert came in. "Incoming!"

"Damn. I'll get this one since I'm down here. If I get caught up in surgery, can you call Ellie and let her know?"

"I will. Go!"

Hunter ran towards the ambulance bay, pulling on a pair of blue medical gloves. "What do we have?"

The paramedics raced in with the gurney. "Female, early thirties, motor vehicle collision, multiple lacerations," the female paramedic spouted out in rapid succession. "Head trauma, hasn't regained consciousness. Left side of the body looks pretty bad . . ."

Preferring to make her own assessment on the extent of the damage, Hunter listened with half an ear and went into trauma mode. Though the ER docs usually handled this part, it wasn't out of the ordinary for Hunter to take charge if she was near when the bus came in. "Neck?" she asked as she caught up to the gurney.

Years of working in trauma could never prepare Hunter's heart for what she saw lying on that gurney. Nothing she had ever witnessed or had to do before could have possibly destroyed her more than this.

"Ellie?" Hunter's brain completely stalled. She had been in countless stressful situations. Never once did she falter. Never once did she lose her ability to think, to act, to do *something*. Seeing Ellie lying motionless, blood caking her honey hair, contusions across her beautiful face; the one time she needed every ounce of her training and calm, Hunter just couldn't comprehend what was happening.

"Doctor?" The paramedics were waiting to turn over the patient and get their gurney back. They had no idea of the unimaginable turmoil they were witnessing.

Sounds became muted to Hunter's ears. Her tunnel vision was focused on the love of her life. They were together just this morning, laughing, talking, kissing. Ellie wasn't due at the hospital to pick her up for another few hours. She wasn't supposed to be here now. Not now. Not like this.

"No. No, no, no, no. This isn't happening." Hunter bent over Ellie, gently touching her face. "Ellie? Baby? Wake up. Please?"

"Dr. Vale?" Mack walked in on a scene he would not soon forget. The usually unflappable Hunter Vale was trembling, crying, and begging. "Hunter, we need to treat the patient."

"She's not a patient! She's Ellie!" Hunter yelled, keeping her arms protectively around her lover.

Patty heard Hunter's cry from across the room, her hand flying to her mouth. "Oh, sweet Jesus! Mo!"

"Shit!" Mo ran to Hunter, grabbing Hunter just as her knees gave out. "Hunter, you gotta let Dr. Mackenzie help her."

"It's Ellie."

The fear and utter anguish in Hunter's voice was gut wrenching.

"I know, Hunt. That's why Mack needs to get in here. She needs help." Mo looked up at Mack.

"Hunter?" Mack called out gently. He knew all about Ellie, the woman who stole Hunter's heart. He often joked with Hunter that it must take an awfully strong woman to put up with the indomitable surgeon. Mack hoped to hell that was true. "I have her. I won't leave her side, I promise."

Patty laid a hand on Hunter's arm. Precious moments were ticking by. Moments that could determine life or death for Ellie. If Hunter had been in her right mind, she would have realized that. "Time is of the essence, Hunter. Let Mack take care of our girl."

Hunter nodded and stepped back. "I need to stay with her."

"You can't, Hunter, I'm sorry." Mack motioned to the nurses and doctors that were standing by watching the entire tragedy unfold. They immediately started working on Ellie. Mack passed by Hunter, pausing just long enough to lay a gentle hand on her shoulder. "Trust me to take care of her. I'll get word to you as soon as I can."

They rolled Ellie away from her and Hunter collapsed. With tears in her eyes, Patty knelt beside her and took Hunter in her arms as sobs wracked her body.

Mo used the back of her hand to wipe the tears from her eyes. The damn things flowed even harder when she took just a second to stop and think about what was going on. She sniffled, bending down to rub Hunter's back.

"Come on, Hunt. Let's get you somewhere more private." She touched Patty's cheek briefly before helping her lift a bone-weary Hunter.

Hunter allowed herself to be ushered to wherever they wanted to take her. She didn't care. The only thing she cared about was

Ellie fighting for her life and there was nothing she could do to help. She stopped suddenly. "Jessie!"

Patty tightened her grip on Hunter's arm, automatically reaching out for Mo's hand. "Oh, Hunter, please tell me she wasn't with Ellie."

"No, she's at school." *Thank God.* "I – I have to tell her about . . ."

"I can call her," Mo offered.

Hunter shook her head emphatically. "I don't want her driving her while she's upset. If something happened to her." She couldn't finish the thought. "I'll take care of it. I just need to splash some water on my face."

Patty swiped her I.D. card to enter the on-call room and kindly guided Hunter through. "Take your time. Mo is going to the OR to see if she can find anything out."

Mo nodded. "I'll come back as soon as I can." After a brief hesitation, she quickly hugged Hunter and ran out before she became a blubbering mess.

"I'll leave you alone for a minute," Patty said. "I'll be right outside the door."

"I don't need a babysitter," Hunter groused.

"No, you need a friend. Sorry, sugar, but you're not going through this alone. We all love Ellie and we'll all be here for her, Jessie, *and* you." Without waiting for a response, Patty began to close the door.

"Patty?" She waited until Patty poked her head around the door. "Thank you."

Hunter sank into a nearby chair and buried her face in her hands. The tears seemed endless, but she couldn't allow herself to just sit here and break down. She needed to be strong for Ellie and Jessie. She had no clue how she was going to do that when it felt as though her heart was shattered and each piece was cutting her from the inside out. But she would find a way. With a deep, cleansing breath, she tried to steel herself for the phone call she needed to make. Her hands shook uncontrollably as she dialed.

After two rings, the line was answered and Hunter had a moment of doubt that she would be able to get the words out.

"*Greyson Steele.*"

"Greyson?" She cleared her parched throat, wishing she had taken more time to gather herself and think about what to say.

"*Hey, Hunter. What's up? If you're calling for an update, we don't have one, yet. But, I think we're getting close.*"

"What? Oh, um, no. I . . ." Another deep breath. "I need you to do something for me."

"*Okay? What is it?*"

She had a fleeting thought of what a great guy Greyson was. Loyal and doting both as a father and a husband. Blaise was lucky to have him. *Oh, shit! Blaise.*

"I need you to pick Jessie up from school," her voice cracked and she cleared it again. "I need you to bring her and Blaise to the hospital."

"*What happened?*"

Hunter heard Greyson go from relaxed to alert and vaguely recognized that she was on speaker phone when she heard rustling on the other end as though Greyson was getting ready to hang up and leave right then.

"It's – it's Ellie. She's been in an accident."

"*Fuck! How bad?*"

"Just get them here, Greyson. Soon."

"*Oh, God. Okay, I'm leaving now. We'll be there ASAP.*"

He didn't even bother saying goodbye and Hunter didn't need it. The phone clattered on the floor as it slipped from Hunter's hand. She was never one to pray, but she would do *anything* if it meant Ellie would be okay.

NOTHING WAS HELPING calm Hunter as she waited for Jessie. She paced until Patty forced her to sit. When she sat, her legs bounced with nervous energy. Tears kept up a steady flow and the chairs around her were littered with tissues. Thankfully Patty had chosen a private waiting room.

"Where is Mo? Why haven't we heard anything, yet?" Hunter got up again, ready to tear some heads off if that's what it took to get information on Ellie's condition.

"Sit. You know Mo will be here as soon as she knows anything." Patty's heart was aching for Hunter. She had made the calls she thought Hunter needed her to make and now all they could do was wait. In her years working at the hospital she had learned that waiting was one of the hardest parts for family. The not knowing was agonizing and Patty was quite surprised she was able to keep Hunter from fighting her way into the operating room.

"Yeah," Hunter sighed wearily. "I can't stand this, Patty."

The older woman brushed crumpled tissues to the side and sat next to Hunter. "I know, child. We just have to believe."

"Hunter?"

Hunter's head snapped up at Jessie's broken voice and she shot out of her seat. She took Ellie's distraught daughter into her arms with a crushing hug, finding solace in Jessie's returned hug.

Jessie eventually pulled back but kept a connection with Hunter. Her eyes were red and puffy from crying and still, she looked so much like her mother that it hurt Hunter's heart.

"Where is she?"

"In surgery."

Jessie squeezed Hunter's arms, unwittingly digging her nails in painfully. "Why aren't you with her! You need to be with her!"

Taken aback by Jessie's outburst, Hunter stuttered. "They – they won't let me. I . . ."

"You are the only one I trust, Hunter. You need to tell her I'm here. That I need her!"

There was a desperation in Jessie's voice that Hunter could understand deep down in her soul.

"Please. She needs to know I'm here, Hunter. That I can't lose her."

"Okay, okay." Hunter brought Jessie to her again, hugging her tight. "I'll go."

Patty quietly snuck out of the room to give them and herself some privacy. She had never been blessed with children herself, but still had that maternal instinct. Seeing Jessie and Hunter hurting so much made her heart heavy. If she were going to be of any help throughout this tragedy, she was going to need to pull herself together.

"What happened?"

It was the first Blaise had spoken since they arrived. Hunter could see the toll this was taking on Ellie's best friend who was just as red and splotchy as the rest of them. Greyson had one arm protectively around Blaise and the other around Piper, who held Ezra. Hunter noticed Blaise leaning heavily on him as though she couldn't stand by herself.

"I don't know." She continued to give Jessie all the comfort she could possibly give, continuing her answer to Blaise. "Th – they just said MVC."

"Motor vehicle collision," Greyson translated softly to his wife.

Hunter nodded. "I haven't learned anything else, yet. I kinda lost it when I saw . . ."

Blaise closed her eyes and a tear rolled down her cheek. Hunter reached over and squeezed Blaise's arm briefly, then took Jessie's face in her hands.

"I'm going to go see what I can find out. I'll stay with her for as long as they'll allow me to."

"You'll tell her what I said?" Jessie's voice trembled, sounding so young and vulnerable.

"I promise." She kissed Jessie on the forehead and entrusted her to Blaise once again as she went to deliver on her promise.

"Grey?" Cade called out quietly.

Greyson knew better than to try to talk to Cade privately. Blaise needed to know why her best friend was laying in the hospital, fighting for her life right now. He wouldn't deny her that.

"What did you find out?" he asked, instinctively tightening his grip on Blaise.

Cade glanced at Jessie. But the teen, no matter how distraught she was, wasn't going anywhere. That much he knew for certain. *She got that look from her mom.*

"It wasn't an accident."

HUNTER STOOD IN the scrubbing area of the OR, staring through the window. From here, it looked like any other surgery on any other patient. But her heart knew the truth and it made it difficult for her to go in. She had meticulously scrubbed her hands until they felt raw, but she couldn't feel any pain other than the one in her chest. With almost robotic movements and the help of her circulator, she continued the routine she had done innumerable times. She only "came to" when she was standing near the table, close enough to see the woman she loved so much looking incredibly pale and fragile.

"Dr. Vale, you can't be in here." Between the surgical mask and scrub cap, only Mack's eyes were visible. They were intense and focused, but they were also not happy with the intrusion.

"I just needed to be with her, Mack. Please? I promise I won't get in the way." When he didn't respond immediately, she went all in. "Her daughter needs me to be here."

Mack sighed. "Fine. But don't interfere."

"Thank you." Those two simple words were so heartfelt, the sentiment filled the room.

"I was going to come tell you what was going on," Mo muttered from behind her mask. "I just couldn't leave her."

Hunter knew better than to hug Mo in this sterile environment, so she nodded, ignoring the tears that fell from both of them.

Unfortunately, due to the various colleagues — all great doctors and nurses that Hunter approved of — trying to save Ellie's life, Hunter wasn't able to get as close as she would've liked. Nonetheless, she had important messages for Ellie and she couldn't care less who was listening.

"Hey, baby," she called out softly. "Jessie's here." Hunter paused, listening carefully to the machine announcing Ellie's heartbeat. She took solace in the fact that it was steady. "She wanted me to tell you she loves and needs you. We both do, baby. Can you hear me? I'm begging you, El. Please don't leave us."

"WHAT THE HELL do you mean it wasn't an accident?" Blaise demanded. Her arm protectively surrounded Jessie who was staring in disbelief.

Piper stood by silently, listening intently, rocking Ezra gently. She couldn't help but feel grateful that her own mother was standing here, healthy. At the same time, Ellie had become like a second mother to her and she could hardly believe this was happening. She was definitely no longer the sheltered little girl in New Zealand.

Cade had tried to shrug off his anger before he came in here to announce the news. Problem was, someone deliberately hurt someone he cared about. A great woman who was as sweet as the pies she made. That pissed him off.

"I don't have much intel, just what I could get from the uniform that followed the paramedics here. The initial report is, Ellie was run off the road. I'm going out to the scene to see what else I can find out."

"I'll go with you." Greyson eyed his wife who nodded. His first priority was always his family and Ellie was part of that family. If someone purposefully did this to her, he and Cade would find out who and why. And they would pay.

"Wait, wait." Jessie rubbed her temples. She felt as though she had been crying for days and it had only been an hour since she found out about her mom's accident. "Does this have anything to do with what happened to mom's Jeep this morning?"

All three adults focused on Jessie, but Blaise spoke up first. "What happened?"

Jessie took out her phone and showed them the photo she took this morning.

Blaise grabbed the phone, zooming in on the damage. "Why didn't she tell me about this?"

"I'm sure she was going to, but you know mom. She didn't want to make a big deal out of it and calling you would have done exactly that for her."

Blaise couldn't argue with Jessie's logic. It wasn't that Ellie thought Blaise was quick to anger — which she readily admitted she was — but telling her would have made it all real. Sometimes Ellie just needed the time to process things on her own first.

"Did Ellie call the police to report it?" Cade asked, taking the phone from Blaise. He texted the photo to himself and his tech genius, Jules, at Drake & Associates with the instructions to gain access to any and all security camera footage around Ellie's building. This could be the break they needed to nail Susan if Jules came up empty on her more in-depth search into Susan's deepest, darkest hiding places.

"Yeah. Was this Susan?" Again, all eyes went to Jessie and she shrugged. "Yes, I know about her. And, if she's the one that did all of this, I want her punished. That bitch should already be in jail for what she did to Hunter. If she did this to mom . . ." Jessie began to cry again and gratefully burrowed into the hug that Blaise gave her.

"We'll investigate the vandalism independently from the police," Cade assured both Jessie and Blaise. "If Susan is involved, we'll find out."

Blaise shook her head distractedly. She didn't even chastise Jessie for saying "bitch". *We'll just leave that little part out when we tell Ellie this story.* She refused to believe she wouldn't get the chance. "It's too childish."

"What, doll?"

"Ellie's Jeep. That just doesn't feel like Susan to me."

"I think mom had doubts it was Susan, too," Jessie announced.

Greyson was inclined to agree. "What was Ellie driving, Jessie? Did she get a rental?"

"No, she was driving Hunter's truck."

Greyson caught his wife's eye and saw the doubt. Was it too much of a coincidence that Ellie ended up in the hospital the one day she was driving Hunter's vehicle?

"Grey, let's go, brother. I want to get to the scene before they fuck it up." Cade grimaced. "Sorry, ladies."

Blaise shook her head. "Go." She gave Greyson a kiss. No words were needed, no promises were given or received. She knew her husband and Cade would do whatever it took to find out what happened to Ellie.

"Are we going to tell Hunter about this?" Jessie asked Blaise.

"Yes." Jessie and Blaise turned to Piper who answered. "I think we all know what it feels like to be lied to. Even when the person was doing it for what they felt were the right reasons." She looked pointedly at Jessie. They had had a few conversations about Jessie feeling slightly betrayed by her mom keeping such an important thing as being gay from her even though she understood. Wouldn't Hunter feel the same way?

"But you didn't see her, Piper. When Hunter thought Susan had vandalized mom's Jeep, she was ready to race out the door and kill her. She *literally* said, 'I'm going to kill her'."

Ezra was becoming cranky and Piper handed him over to Blaise who seemed quite satisfied with letting Piper handle this conversation. Piper was convinced it was because she had no qualms if something did happen to Susan. Hunter would certainly be justified. "That's understandable, don't you think? Do you think your mum would want you keeping things from Hunter?"

Jessie sighed deeply. "No. She wanted their relationship to be open and honest."

"There's your answer." Piper gave Jessie a small smile, then frowned as a thought came to her. She turned to her mum. "What if it wasn't Ellie?"

"What do you mean?"

"I mean, she was driving Hunter's truck. What if Ellie wasn't the one they were trying to . . . hurt?"

"*Shit!*" Blaise hitched Ezra up, holding him with one arm as she brought her phone out to call Greyson.

HUNTER SCRUBBED HER face wearily. She had been in this position many times. It had always been her least favorite part of the job. Having to face the family, no matter the news, was too emotional. If they weren't crying because of loss, they were crying because they believed Hunter had performed a miracle. She wasn't able to do that tonight. Hell, she wasn't even allowed to try. And that killed her inside.

She pushed through the door, zeroing in on the one person she needed to talk to the most. She walked straight to Jessie, who was sitting between Blaise and Rebecca and knelt down in front of her.

"Is she?" Jessie's lip trembled and she blindly reached out for Hunter.

Hunter took Jessie's hand in hers and kept a firm hold. "She made it through the surgery."

Murmurs and thanks to God were heard around the room, but Hunter kept her attention on Jessie. *She knows there's more.*

"Tell me," Jessie said softly. "And, don't speak to me as a doctor, Hunter. Tell me as though you're speaking of the woman you love."

Hunter briefly closed her eyes, trying to keep the tears under control. When her eyes opened, Jessie was staring back intently. "She's in a coma." She caught the teenager who simply melted off the chair in despair. Hunter sat on the floor with Jessie cradled in her arms, rocking her gently. "I know it's very hard for both of us to accept, sweetheart, but doctor to future doctor, it's what's best for Ellie right now."

She glanced up at Blaise who was huddled together with her kids, quietly sobbing. The rest needed to be told, but she was finding it difficult to find the words. This *wasn't* like any other time she'd done this. This was personal.

"She had a significant blow to the head and the left side of her body is . . . broken." She silently berated herself for her choice of words. But, not having the luxury of hiding behind the fancy medical terms and calmness of being a surgeon, she found herself floundering to find the right approach.

"Broken?"

Jessie's voice sounded so small, all Hunter wanted to do was protect her from everything bad in the world. Regrettably, she couldn't protect her from this.

"The impact," Hunter's voice quivered with raw emotion. "Broke her arm, hip, and leg. They did their best to repair most of the damage, but now it's a waiting game."

"To see if she walks again?" Hunter nodded at the teen, who began to cry again. "She's left-handed. Will she be able to use her hand again?"

"I think so." Truth was, she had no idea what the real extent of the injuries was. Ellie would need to wake up before they could make that determination "Listen, Jess, it's going to be a long, very tough road for your mom. But, I'm here with you both, okay?"

Jessie, unable to express how safe that made her feel, merely nodded. "Can I see her?"

"Of course. They should have her settled now." Again, she brought her eyes to Blaise. "I'm going to let Jessie sit with Ellie by herself for a few minutes. Then, I'll have you brought back. Is that okay?"

"Yes, by all means. Let Jessie be with Ellie for as long as she needs to. I'm not going anywhere."

Hunter glanced around. "Greyson?"

"He and Cade are looking into things." Blaise shook her head.

"We'll talk about all of that later. Right now, Jessie needs to be with her mum."

"Yeah, okay." The surgeon got to her feet and pulled Jessie up, keeping an arm around her. She reached out to both Rebecca and Cass, who had been quietly listening. Rebecca had tears in her eyes and she held onto Cass's hand as though it was her life-line. "Thank you both for being here."

"Nowhere else we'd be," Cass answered knowing her girlfriend was too emotional to speak. "G'wan. We'll stay here with Blaise and Piper. Patty and Mo went to get coffee for everyone, so don't worry about us. Just take care of our girls, yeah?"

Hunter gave Cass a small, grateful smile, then guided Jessie out of the room. It was going to be a long, emotional walk down that corridor. Nothing like the last time the two of them were here together when Jessie had shadowed Hunter during one of her rounds. The experienced doctor had been impressed with Jessie's willingness to listen and her capacity to learn. Jessie's compassion and empathy may not be favorable for trauma, but Hunter was willing to bet they would make Jessie an excellent doctor one day. Between the both of them, Ellie could have no better team in her corner.

Chapter Thirty-Three

As Jessie slept fitfully on the small couch in Ellie's room, Hunter kept vigil in the chair next to the bed. She had yet to give up Ellie's hand, hoping that the constant connection would help Ellie find her way back to them. She spoke in muted tones to her girlfriend, words of love, of encouragement. Pleas tumbled out every now and then and Hunter would temper them with soft kisses to the small hand she held in hers.

A parade of visitors had already come through with Rebecca, Cass, Patty, and Mo promising to return soon. Hunter appreciated their understanding of the need to be alone for a bit, just Hunter, Ellie, and Jessie. Even Blaise took off with Piper and Ezra, but only long enough to bring back food. And it was only with promise after promise to wake her if there was *any* change did Jessie agree to rest for a little while. That left Hunter somewhat alone with Ellie for the first time since she was brought in.

"I love you, baby. If I could trade places with you, I'd do it in a second. Jessie needs you. I'm doing the best I can, but she needs her mom." A tear ran down Hunter's cheek when she recalled the moment Jessie walked in and saw Ellie laying in the hospital bed. Tubes and bandages replaced Ellie's vibrant smile and enthusiasm. Jessie's wavering

utterance of *"Mommy"* shattered what was left of Hunter's battered heart.

A quiet knock brought Hunter out of her reverie. She looked up to see *her* mom standing at the door. It was at that moment when she understood the sentiment behind Jessie's youthful plea.

"Mom." Her voice hitched. Any other time, Hunter would be up and in her mother's comforting arms in a flash. Now, she was reluctant to leave Ellie's side or relinquish her hold on her.

"Oh, Hunter." Cece bustled over to her daughter, hugging her as close as she could with the chair between them and Hunter not letting go of Ellie. "Patty called us and told us what happened. We got here as soon as we could." She looked over at Ellie and gasped softly. "How is she?"

Hunter shook her head. "As well as expected. The next twenty-four hours are crucial."

Cece squeezed Hunter's shoulder. "I'm asking *you* how she is, not Dr. Vale."

Hunter lowered her head. "I don't know, ma. She needs this rest, but it's killing me to see her like this."

"I know, honey. But, we have to believe she'll wake up soon. How's Jessie?"

Hunter gestured over at the couch just as Jessie whimpered. "Could you go to her?"

Cece patted Hunter's shoulder and did as she was asked. With a gentle shake, she woke Jessie up.

The teen was momentarily confused seeing Cece sitting there beside her. When she saw her mom and remembered everything she slumped into Cece's waiting arms.

Jessie peered over at Hunter. "No change?"

Hunter shook her head. "Not yet, sweetheart."

"You should really be sleeping somewhere more comfortable," Cece suggested to Jessie, who immediately shook her head.

"I don't want to leave my mom."

Hunter looked over at them. "I'll stay, Jess. You need to eat and get some real sleep."

Jessie sighed. She knew that Hunter was just looking out for her, but there was no way she could stay away. What if something happened while she was gone? She shuddered at that thought and pushed it aside. *Positive thoughts.*

"How about a compromise?" Jessie held up a hand when Hunter looked as though she would argue before even hearing the compromise. "I can't stay away, Hunter. I think you know that better than anyone. But, grandma Cece . . ." she glanced over at Hunter's mom who looked a little shell-shocked. "Is that okay?"

With tears in her eyes, Cece squeezed Jessie closer. "Yes, of course, sweet girl."

Jessie smiled her first genuine smile since hearing about her mom's accident. "Grandma Cece can drive me home where I can shower and change. I'll also pack a few things for mom. I'm almost positive she's complaining about that itchy hospital gown somewhere in there."

Hunter let out a little chuckle. She could definitely see that. Ellie was all about comfort. Hospital gowns were certainly not that.

"Blaise should be back soon with food," Jessie continued. "So, we'll be quick. But I'm staying here with you and mom."

Hunter knew better than to argue. Thing was, she didn't want to. If being here with Ellie helped Jessie, and potentially helped Ellie, Hunter was all for it. She knew she would have to do a bit of begging to clear this with the hospital, but she would do whatever she had to do.

"Deal." Hunter's gaze bore into her mom's. "Be careful, please?"

"We will. I'll take your father with us. He wanted to come in here, but I think he needs a little more time to prepare himself."

"I know he hates hospitals." Hunter tried being understanding, but it hurt that her dad couldn't get past his distaste for hospitals to see Ellie.

"It's not that, Hunter." Cece stood and walked to Ellie's bed, placing a hand on the uninjured, blanket covered foot. "He thinks of Ellie as a daughter and seeing one of your children like this is never easy. He'll be in when we get back."

Hunter wiped a tear from her cheek. "Thanks, ma."

TWENTY-FOUR HOURS turned in to forty-eight. There was no change in Ellie's condition or Hunter's vigil at her bedside. The will to stay positive and believe that this was what Ellie needed was waning quickly. She just wanted Ellie to wake up and tell her everything would be okay. Instead, Hunter would continue to whisper optimistic words in Ellie's ear and try to sound sincere. When she wasn't reassuring Ellie in hushed tones, she was reading or singing to her. She had no clue if Ellie could hear her, but she kept up the routine nonetheless.

The staff – at Patty's request – had brought in an extra bed for Jessie to sleep in. Though the teen would only utilize it when she was so exhausted she couldn't keep her eyes open anymore. Even then it felt as though she never fully rested. Jessie knew she probably wouldn't sleep well again until she had her mom back.

Hunter had refused a bed for herself, opting to stay in the chair close to Ellie's side. The only time she gave up her position was to let Jessie take her place. Still, she never went far and she rarely took her hand off of Ellie. She practically willed all of her strength into the woman she loved. The only way Hunter would survive was believing Ellie would, too.

She jumped slightly at the touch on her shoulder. Wearily, she looked up at Jessie who stared back with concern.

"You need a break from being in here."

"I'm not leaving."

"Hunter, you're not sleeping or eating. Do you know how mad mom is going to be about that?" Jessie placed her hands on her hips, a replica of her mom. "We need you. *I* need you. You said you were going to help me, but you won't be able to do that for much longer if you keep this up." Truth was, Hunter looked like shit and needed a shower in the worst way, though Jessie would never say that out loud.

Hunter took a deep breath in, holding it for a moment before blowing it out. Okay, so she could use a toothbrush. And perhaps a shower. Maybe a nap. But all of that sounded so trivial to her when Ellie was still in a coma fighting for her life.

"I'll compromise with you," Hunter said, echoing Jessie's earlier remarks. "I'll go to the on-call room to take a shower and brush my teeth. That's as far away from this room as I go, no exceptions. When I'm done, I'll come back in here and lay down for a spell. I'll even do my best to eat, but no promises. That's the best I got, kiddo."

Jessie considered it, then nodded. "Deal. But you'll do more than try to eat. Don't make me write a list of the things you're not doing to keep yourself healthy and show mom when she wakes up." Her voice cracked, but she refused to back down. She remembered when Blaise had brought food from Ellie's, Hunter couldn't bring herself to eat it. Jessie wondered if it was because she wasn't hungry or because it reminded her of what was missing in their lives at the moment.

Hunter nodded, unaware of where Jessie's inner thoughts had gone. She just hoped the food didn't come from Ellie's. It may have been foolish, but for some reason it made Hunter feel she was being disloyal if she ate it.

She stood and took Jessie's hand in hers and placed it over Ellie's. It physically hurt Hunter to leave that room, but she did it for Jessie. If she was going to stay strong for the teen, she was going to have to do better. She slipped past Blaise who was coming in and walked away.

"How did you get her to leave?"

Jessie held on tightly to her mom's hand and looked up at Blaise. "I threatened to tell on her when mom wakes up." With her free hand, Jessie pushed Ellie's hair away from her face. The bruising was darkening and looked so painful. "She will, won't she?"

God, I hope so. "Yes, sweetie." Blaise set down the enormous bag of food she had brought in. "After the stressful month or so that she's had, I'm sure she's just using this as an excuse to rest."

Jessie gave her a tremulous smile. "Yeah." She sighed. "We need to tell Hunter what really happened."

"I know." Blaise walked over to Ellie and bent down to give her a little kiss on the cheek. *"Wake up, sweets. We miss you."* She pulled a chair over and sat next to Jessie. "I'm afraid she's going to go a little crazy and go after Susan. Not that I'm against that, but I would like for Greyson and Cade to be absolutely sure Susan was involved before Hunter tears her apart."

"I guess you're right. I just hope she understands why we waited."

"Hunter is smart, sweetie. And, right now, she's focused on Ellie waking up."

Jessie nodded, rubbing her thumb across Ellie's motionless hand. "There's something else I need to do and I don't want to. I'm scared."

Blaise turned her chair towards Jessie, laying a hand on her knee. "Scared of what, Jessie? You know we're here for you and you never have to do anything alone."

Jessie sighed dramatically. "I have to call grandmother and grandfather. It sucks. They don't deserve to be here, but she *is* their daughter." Frightened eyes caught Blaise's. "What if they take me away from her? If they come here and see Hunter, I mean, they're going to know. Hunter can't hide how she feels. What if they try to take mom or make me live with them? You *know* that's what they're going to do. That's just how they are."

"There's nothing they *can* do, sweetie. They can't take you or your mom anywhere."

"But they're her parents."

"And I'm your mom's power of attorney and your legal guardian while Ellie is . . ."

"Resting?"

"Right. So, while I agree with you, they don't deserve to be here, it's only right to call them. Would you like me to do it?"

Jessie shook her head sadly. "I should be the one." She laid her head on Ellie's bed, placing her mom's hand on her cheek. She would call her grandparents. Later.

HUNTER SANK ONTO the bed in the on-call room and let the tears flow. She had held them in as much as she could for Jessie's sake. Now that she was alone, the strength she tried so hard to hold onto in that room, evaporated. She would allow herself a couple of minutes. No more.

"Hunter?"

The surgeon swiped angrily at her tears and stood up abruptly. "Don't do this. Not now, Iris."

"I – I just wanted to say how sorry I am about your, um, girlfriend."

Hunter looked at the nurse. Something was different. There was genuine sorrow in her eyes and more. Regret? Guilt?

"She knew," Hunter said suddenly, startling Iris. "Ellie knew it was you who did that to her jeep." Iris lowered her eyes. "She didn't tell me, but now I know."

"I never meant . . ."

"Never meant what?" Hunter shouted. "For this to happen? For the woman I love to be in a coma? For her to be fighting for a life that may include paralysis? *Fuck you, Iris!*" She approached the young nurse until she was cowering in the corner of the room. "Don't ever come near me again. Don't speak of me, don't look at me. If you see me, turn around and walk the other way. Do you understand?" She leaned in threateningly. "God help you if Ellie doesn't wake up. You may not have caused the accident, but in my eyes, you're just as responsible."

"I'm sorry," Iris sobbed. "I'm so sorry!" She squeezed by Hunter and ran out the door. Even bumping into Patty and Mo didn't slow down her retreat.

"Did she try something with you?" Mo asked incredulously. "That woman is sick if she thinks . . ."

"She didn't try anything," Hunter interrupted, scrubbing her face dejectedly. "I'll tell you about it later. Right now, I have to take a shower and get back to Ellie."

ELLIE ROLLED OVER and snuggled up close to Hunter. She hummed softly when Hunter's arms tightened around her.

"*I miss you, baby.*"

Ellie raised her head and kissed Hunter tenderly. "*I'm right here, honey.*"

The tender kiss was deepened and Hunter's heart began to pound. Feeling Ellie's lips on hers was comparable to finding an oasis in a parched desert.

"*I love you.*"

Ellie smiled against Hunter's lips. "*I love you, too.*" She stopped suddenly and looked into Hunter's eyes. "*Hunter, you need to wake up.*"

"*Don't want to. Want to stay here with you.*"

"*You can't, honey. Wake up, Hunter.*"

Ellie began to move away from her and Hunter reached out for her in panic.

"Ellie!"

Jessie rushed to Hunter's side. "Hey, hey." Jessie soothed. "You were dreaming, Hunter. You fell asleep. Whatever it was, it was only a dream."

Hunter searched Jessie's face for any sign that something had happened. When she found no answers, she darted off the bed and was at Ellie's side in two strides. The surgeon in her listened carefully to the machines that Ellie was hooked up to. She checked and rechecked Ellie's vitals. Once she was satisfied, she leaned down and kissed Ellie delicately on lips that were slightly chapped.

"*I'll have to bring you some Chapstick, baby. Gotta keep those beautiful lips healthy.*"

"Get away from my daughter!"

Hunter barely flinched at the angry, male voice. Her nerves were beyond frayed, but the hell if she was going to leave Ellie's side. She merely glanced up to see a distinguished, yet very outraged couple, standing at the entrance to Ellie's room. He was a tall, slender man with thinning silver hair. She couldn't tell if it was his weathered face or the deep frown that made him look old and mean. Perhaps it was both. Ellie's mother had a more youthful look to her, but there wasn't an ounce of kindness in her dark eyes. Her brown hair was coiffed in a way that reminded Hunter of women from those old fifties television shows. Even the outfit that the woman was wearing could have come straight out of some sexist black and white film.

"Grandfather!" Confused, Jessie jumped up, almost at attention. That's how her grandfather always made her feel. As though she was a soldier being scrutinized for any imperfection possible. She hadn't had the chance to call her grandparents and hoped to have more time to prepare for their visit. Seeing them here now was a bit of a shock. Yet, even though her grandfather scared her, Jessie stood her ground next to Hunter. She couldn't allow him to dictate her mom's life any more. Especially since Ellie couldn't fight for herself right now. "How did you know mom was here?"

John Montgomery glared at his only granddaughter. "I had to hear it from the authorities, young lady. I can see your mother hasn't taught you good manners."

Jessie bristled with anger. "Don't talk about my mom! It's no wonder I didn't call you right away. God, I *knew* you'd barge in here and do exactly what you're doing!"

John stepped towards Jessie, fury written all over his face, stopping only when Hunter positioned herself between the two.

"You should have been disciplined more."

"Like you disciplined mom? By hitting her?"

"Jess," Hunter warned gently. She never imagined she would meet Ellie's parents, especially like this. As first impressions went, Hunter didn't think things were going very well on either side. She was caught practically kissing Ellie and, even though Ellie's mother had yet to say a word, Hunter concluded they were just extremely unpleasant people.

"I don't know who the hell you are," John barked at Hunter. "But I want you out of my daughter's room. My family is none of your concern."

Jessie glanced at Grace Montgomery, her grandmother, who stood behind her husband, a look of disgust on her pinched face. How these two managed to have such a beautiful, sweet daughter like her mother, Jessie would never understand.

"This is *Dr.* Hunter Vale," Jessie announced with pride. "She is a prominent surgeon at this hospital and mom's girlfriend. Hunter has *every* right to be here."

Hunter was both impressed and flustered by Jessie's frankness with her grandparents.

John's nose flared with rage. "Grace, get security," he ordered. "And, I want to talk to hospital administration. This," he gestured angrily toward Hunter, "deviant should not be allowed anywhere near this room. I want her banned immediately."

"You can't do that!" This time Jessie stood in front of Hunter with a defiant stance.

"I can do as I please, young lady. And since you seem to have lost your sense of respect, you will be coming home with us. Consultation within the church is in order for you. I will not allow you to be corrupted by this . . . this nonsense!"

Jessie laughed mirthlessly. She knew exactly what 'consultation within the church' meant for her mom. She'd risk going to hell before she did that or left this room. God, she hoped Blaise meant what she said. "I'm staying here with my mom."

"Your mother will be going to a private institute."

"The hell she will." Hunter had held her tongue for as long as she could. She had no idea how she would stop him, but she sure as hell would fight. "I won't allow you to take her."

John scoffed. "You have no authority over any of this."

"But, I do."

Everyone turned towards the door where Blaise stood with her arms crossed. She had heard part of the exchange from down the hall and wasn't surprised one bit that Ellie's parents were already causing a scene. Dramatics were one thing they did very well.

"Hello, Mr. Montgomery. I would say it's nice to see you again, but under the circumstances." She let the statement hang unfinished in the air. Both of them knew there was no love lost between them. Blaise was too independent and John Montgomery was too misogynistic to ever become friendly.

"Ms. Knight, this doesn't concern you."

"It's Mrs. Steele now. And, since I'm Ellie's power of attorney it most certainly does concern me. Also, let me be very clear about this, I am Jessie's legal guardian until Ellie wakes up. Neither of them are going anywhere."

John's face reddened. Clearly, he was a man who was used to getting his way. Having women challenge him must have been extremely frustrating. Hunter loved it.

"I will not stand for this." He turned towards where his wife had been standing, grumbling when he didn't find her there. "My lawyers will straighten this out."

Blaise couldn't help but chuckle. "Sorry, Mr. Montgomery. There's no 'straightening' anything out anymore when it comes to Ellie. She's found her happiness. And she was of sound body and mind when she put me in charge. But, you can try fighting it if it makes you feel better."

Grace entered the room at that moment and Hunter wondered if she would choke herself if she clutched her necklace any tighter.

The older woman took her place by her husband and sneered at Blaise. "She has never been of sound mind. Her *choices*," she croaked the word out as if it burned. "clearly show she has a mental . . ."

"Stop! You miserable, homophobic, bit-" Hunter covered Jessie's mouth and Blaise held her back from doing something she would regret. Jessie wrenched herself away from the two and glowered at everyone. "I want them out of here. This isn't good for mom."

"She's right." Hunter turned on her doctor mode. "Ellie doesn't need this stress while she's trying to recover from this trauma."

"I couldn't agree more," Mack said from the doorway. Security flanked him, but he wasn't going to utilize them unless he absolutely had to. "I think you all need to take a break."

"Mack," Hunter began.

"I have to examine Ellie anyway, Hunter. I'm not asking you to leave the hospital, but go down to the cafeteria or take a walk around the campus. All of you." He walked to Ellie, stethoscope in hand. "If you keep this up, I will have to insist on no visitors."

The prospect of not being able to be with Ellie shook Hunter to her core. "Please don't do that, Mack."

"Then act like the adults you are. I understand this is a trying time, but the fighting is not helpful to anyone." He turned to who he assumed was Ellie's parents who made complaints. "I don't care who thinks they have authority right now, Ellie cannot be moved at this time. You're her parents, yes?" John gave him a curt nod. "I will not ask you to leave unless you continue to cause a commotion. Ellie is my patient," Mack said over John's protestations. "You can protest as much as you want, but her health and recovery are the only things I care about. I would think you'd feel the same way."

With that scathing remark, he dismissed the lot of them from Ellie's room. Ellie's parents marched off in one direction and Hunter, Jessie, and Blaise stood there for a moment, not sure what to do with themselves.

"Coffee?" Blaise suggested.

"Did you bring any of your whiskey?" Hunter sighed.

Blaise laughed as Jessie muttered 'gross'. "No, but the coffee here isn't worthy of it. Come on. This will give us a chance to talk."

"About?" Hunter was too mentally exhausted to hold much of a conversation.

Blaise glanced at Jessie. Though Greyson had told her they hadn't found any evidence tying Susan to the crash, she knew they couldn't keep this from Hunter anymore. Cade had kept the authorities at bay for as long as he could, allowing Hunter to be with Ellie and not deal with everything else. But he could only stall them for so long. "Important things."

Chapter Thirty-Four

"Hunter! Hunter, slow down!" Blaise and Jessie both had to jog to keep up with the long-legged surgeon. They barely avoided hitting her and each other when Hunter stopped abruptly.

"How — why," Hunter grunted with frustration. She turned to start walking again, but stopped just as suddenly. "How could you not tell me *right away* that someone tried to . . . that this wasn't an accident!"

Hearing that someone purposefully ran Ellie off the road filled Hunter with a myriad of emotions. Rage, fear, guilt, anguish. At the moment, she couldn't distinguish one from the other, except anger.

Blaise walked straight up to Hunter and grabbed her shoulders. She stared directly into the doctor's betrayed eyes. "Because you are *exactly* where you're supposed to be. I know who you're thinking did this and I have to tell you, Ellie does *not* need you going off all half-cocked and getting yourself in trouble. If this was Susan, I promise you, Greyson and Cade will find out."

Hunter exhaled heavily, the weight of the guilt bearing down on her. "This is all my fault. If I had just . . ."

"Stop it, Hunter. What do you think mom would say if she heard you?" Jessie interrupted.

"She'd probably kick my ass," Hunter admitted with a rueful smile. "I can't help it, Jess."

Jessie shook her head. "You aren't to blame. You know what she'll say. 'This is the fault of the person who did the deed.' That's it. End of story."

"Yeah, I know." Hunter patted Blaise's hand that was still holding on to her. "You can let go now. I'm not going to run off and kill Susan."

"Well, normally I would encourage you," Blaise smirked. "But, I really do think Ellie needs you here. We all do."

Hunter nodded. They made their way back to Ellie's room, disheartened to see the Montgomerys there alone. Hunter was sure she was overstepping some imaginary line, but she didn't trust the pair. For all she knew, they could have been plotting on how to smuggle Ellie out of there. She snorted softly at the thought. Even if they did take her somewhere, Hunter would scour the earth to find her.

"I've informed the hospital that visitors are to be family only," John Montgomery announced as soon as Hunter and Jessie took their respective spots next to Ellie.

"Did they tell you to go to hell?" Hunter muttered, deliberately leaning down to kiss Ellie softly on the forehead. *"They can't make me leave, baby. I'll tie myself to your bed if I have to."* She heard a slight blip in the machine that was monitoring Ellie's heartrate. To Hunter, that was as good as a smile at this point. She continually wondered if Ellie could hear her. Or if she could feel her there? That one blip gave her more hope than she had had the past forty-eight hours.

"The decision is not yours, Mr. Montgomery," Blaise interjected before more fighting could ensue. "I appreciate that Ellie is your daughter, but all decisions go through me. And, since I would be excluded from this room if you had your way, that's certainly not going to happen. Ellie has all that she needs and wants right here."

Grace huffed as John fumed. "What *my* daughter needs is to be away from this . . ." he gestured towards Hunter, "filth."

Blaise advanced on him, her fiery nature coming to the surface. "Hunter is one of the best people you will ever have the privilege of knowing. More importantly, she treats Ellie with love and respect. You should be proud of that and take notes." Blaise took her "Ellie" stance, hands on hips, and looked squarely at John. "If you don't like seeing them together, you can be the ones to leave. Otherwise, let's focus our attention on what's really important here. Ellie's recovery."

"Grace, we're leaving." He took Grace roughly by the arm and marched towards the door. He turned back, a sour look on his face when he witnessed Hunter holding Ellie's hand. "This happened because she defied . . ."

"Don't even go there, gramps," Jessie interjected and rolled her eyes. She had a momentary fear that her mom would sit right up in bed and reprimand her for disrespecting her grandfather. Then, she sighed. If that happened, Jessie would do it over and over again. "This has nothing to do with your religious beliefs."

"Gramps" left without another word, dragging his wife with him. Both Hunter and Blaise stared at Jessie.

"Do you feel better?" Hunter asked her.

"I do. You have no idea how annoying it is to have to say 'grandfather' when addressing him."

"It's not the best idea to antagonize him, sweetie," Blaise scolded gently.

"I know. But," Jessie lowered her voice. *"I don't believe this was punishment for who mom is like he does. And, I didn't want her to hear that."*

"Can't argue with that logic." Hunter winked at Jessie causing Blaise to tsk.

"Ellie is going to have her hands full with the two of you."

"IT'S BEEN FOUR days, Hunter." Jessie gently brushed her

mom's hair the best she could. She let Hunter, Mo, and Patty take care of the things that required more experience than she had, but the little things like brushing her mom's hair, Jessie insisted on doing them. She wanted to be as involved in her mom's recovery as she could.

"I know, kiddo." Hunter knew very well. Every hour, every minute, every second since Ellie was brought in was burned into Hunter's brain. "But, her vitals are strong. That's a very good sign."

"Do you think she's in so much pain that she doesn't want to wake up?"

Hunter winced at the sadness in Jessie's voice. "No, sweetheart. The meds we have her on should be making her comfortable."

"Could the meds be keeping her from waking up?"

Hunter reached across Ellie to take Jessie's hand. "Jess, she's going to wake up. I'm sure she misses you and is trying her hardest to come back to us. Just keep talking to her so she knows we're here, okay?"

Jessie nodded and squeezed Hunter's hand in appreciation. Even though she knew Hunter was exhausted, mentally and physically, the surgeon was always reassuring her. Never tiring of the questions, never snapping at her. But supportive and loving. There were no words that Jessie could ever say that would express her gratitude.

Thirty minutes later, Jessie was still sitting in the chair, asleep, with her head laying on Ellie's bed. It didn't seem like a very comfortable position to Hunter, but she couldn't blame the teen for wanting to stay close to her mom.

Hunter leaned close to Ellie's ear. *"Come on, baby. Jessie needs you. I need you. I miss you so damn much."*

"Hunter?"

For a split-second Hunter's heartrate spiked thinking Ellie had called out to her. She stared intently, disappointed when there was no change. *I must be hearing things.* She jumped when she felt a hand on her shoulder.

"Easy there, Hunt. It's just us."

Tired eyes focused on Cass, Rebecca, Patty, and Mo. "Hey,

sorry. I just . . ."

"It's okay," Rebecca interrupted gently. "You really need some sleep, honey."

Hunter frowned sadly. "Ellie called me that."

"And, she will again." Rebecca kissed Hunter on the cheek before moving to Ellie and doing the same. "*Wake up, sweet one. You're sorely missed.*"

"We brought you some clothes, Hunt," Mo announced. "You have to be tired of wearing scrubs."

Hunter looked down at the blue scrubs she had donned after her last shower. It didn't really matter to her what she wore, but she thanked Mo nonetheless.

"Your fan club is starting to arrive, baby," she said mildly to Ellie, hoping she could hear. Everyday around this time, people who loved Ellie flooded the room with gifts or flowers or food. Rosa would bring pies and cards signed by patrons from the diner. Cade would bring fresh orchids from Blaise's shop to keep the room beautiful. Greyson, Blaise, and Piper always had food or drinks for everyone who visited. Hunter's own parents brought magazines or books for Hunter to read to Ellie. Even Eve and Lainey stopped by offering anything and everything Jessie, Ellie, or Hunter needed.

Truth was, as much as she appreciated the love everyone was showing Ellie, all Hunter needed was Ellie herself. At least Ellie's parents had stayed away since their last visit didn't go quite how they expected it to. Plotting on how to get their way, she was sure.

"Dinner has arrived!" Blaise announced as she came into the room followed by Greyson (holding Ezra), Piper, Cece, Alton, and Cade. "Your mom was sweet enough to cook for everyone, Hunter."

"I will find any excuse to use that kitchen of yours." Cece and Blaise had agreed to try to stay positive for Hunter's and Jessie's benefit even though it wasn't easy. That was especially true for Blaise as Cece knew she was hurting just as much as the others. But they did their best to keep Hunter and Jessie optimistic.

Hunter, however, knew exactly what they were doing and she silently thanked them. Of course, they were currently breaking so many rules having everyone in the room at one time, but somehow it made Hunter feel better when they were all there. Maybe it was the extra energy. Or, maybe it helped her to think Ellie knew how much she was loved.

"Thanks, ma." She leaned into the kiss on the forehead Cece gave her.

"How's our girl?" Alton asked from the foot of the bed. He laid his hand gently on Ellie's foot just to let her know he was there.

"No change."

"Jessie is going to regret that position when she wakes up." He smiled sadly as the teen mumbled in her sleep as though she knew she was being talked about. Frankly, he didn't know how she could sleep with all these people surrounding her. But the poor girl must be as mentally exhausted as his daughter is.

"Yeah, but I just didn't have the heart to wake . . ." Ellie's hand, which rarely ever left Hunter's, twitched.

"Hunter?" Blaise's attention was focused on Hunter who was watching Ellie intently.

"Shh! Do it again, baby." She stood up and leaned close to Ellie, their hands still linked. "Ellie? Can you hear me? Move your hand again, baby."

"She moved her hand?" Blaise moved closer, nudging Jessie awake as she did.

"Wha?" Jessie looked around in a state of confusion. So many people! And they were all looking at . . . suddenly alert, Jessie shot up out of her chair, ignoring the pain in her neck. "Is she awake?"

"She moved her hand," Hunter answered, her eyes never leaving Ellie. "El? Can you open your eyes?" She gasped when she felt the twitch again. Blindly, she reached over with her free hand and grabbed Jessie's, placing it on Ellie's wrist. "That's it, baby. Come back to us. I know you can do it!"

"I don't . . . oh my God! She moved! Blaise, she moved!"

Tears formed in Blaise's eyes as she watched with new found hope. *Please let her be okay,* she prayed silently.

Ellie's eyes felt as heavy as anvils. She could faintly hear the muffled voices surrounding her, but she couldn't open her mouth to respond. With extreme effort, she tried flexing her hand again. The muffled voices got excited and Ellie realized she was doing something they liked. Now if she could just talk. Her lips felt so dry and her mouth felt like a desert. *Try harder! You have to know if Jessie is okay!*

"*Jessie,*" Ellie managed. Her voice sounded odd to her ears and it hurt like hell to talk. She just hoped someone else heard it as well.

"I'm here, mommy!"

Jessie came into view. Her hair was a bit mussed and her eyes were red from crying, but to Ellie seeing her daughter was perfection.

"*Hunter?*"

"Right here, baby. We all are."

There were the blue eyes Ellie loved so much. She tried to raise her hand, wanting to touch both Jessie and Hunter to make sure they were real. When her left hand didn't move, she tried the other. It felt heavy and moving in any way created an agonizing pain throughout her entire body.

"*Hurt.*"

Unchecked tears — some from joy, some from the heartache of knowing Ellie was in pain — rolled down Hunter's cheeks. "I know, baby." She glanced up at Patty. "Can you get Mack in here, please?"

"Of course!" Patty bustled out of the room, a small feeling of relief flowing through her. *One hurdle down.*

Ellie's eyes felt heavy. The effort it took to keep them open was draining what little energy she had.

"Mommy, please don't leave me again." Jessie framed Ellie's face with her hands. "Stay with me."

"*Still here, sweetie.*" She lost her battle with staying awake, however.

"She's just sleeping, sweetheart," Hunter reassured Jessie. "The pain is taking a lot out of her."

"Can I get through, please?" Mack pushed his way through the crowd of people surrounding Ellie's bed. "You know this is against the rules, Dr. Vale."

Hunter gave him a trembling, watery smile. "Don't tell my boss. She woke up, Mack. She was coherent. Knew Jessie, knew me."

Mack nodded with approval. He had spoken briefly to Hunter about the possibility of brain damage. Against his better judgment, the decision was made not to tell Jessie of the chances Ellie wouldn't know her when she woke up. He was happy it seemed as though the head injury didn't cause as much damage as it could have. "I need to check her vitals and I need everyone cleared out of here while I do."

They had learned during the run-in with Ellie's parents not to argue with Mack. Fact was, he had been incredibly patient and lenient with them. The least they could do was comply with his rare demands. They filed out one by one, with Hunter and Jessie being the last ones to leave.

"Can't you stay in there with her?" Jessie asked Hunter as she leaned into her. "You're a doctor."

"I trust Mack, Jess."

"So do I, but I trust you more."

Hunter hugged Jessie to her. "I wouldn't leave Ellie unless I knew she was in great hands. Having Mack as her doctor allows me to be out here with you."

"I'm glad you're here."

Blaise heard the mumbled words come from Jessie and caught Hunter's bashful eyes. *Me, too*, she mouthed with a smile.

THE NEXT FEW weeks seemed to crawl and move at lightning speed at the same time. Ellie was finally able to stay awake for more than a few minutes at a time. The fact that she was alert and showed no signs of permanent damage to her memory or motor skills was remarkable. However, Ellie was devastated to learn that she could not feel her legs. That, along with the fact that her left arm was useless, caused Ellie to retreat into herself.

Hunter did her best to cheer Ellie up, but she knew it would take time to come to terms with the changes. Despite Ellie's low spirits, Hunter was determined to do everything it took to help her recover. Which brought them to the conversation — not argument — they were having now.

"I don't want to be a burden."

"Ellie, baby, you could *never* be a burden." Hunter sat on the edge of the bed and lifted Ellie's hand to kiss it. They were having a rare private moment and Hunter was taking advantage of it. "You know I love you, right?"

"Yes. Tell me the truth, Hunter. Would you have asked me to move in with you this early in our relationship if this hadn't happened to me?"

"El, I would have asked you to move in with me after our first date if I thought you would have said yes." When Ellie rolled her eyes, Hunter caught her chin with her free hand. "You know I'm telling the truth, baby. I never wanted to be away from you. I still don't."

"I'm not," Ellie paused, wondering how to explain how she felt. "You deserve more . . ."

"Please don't say that. We can get through this, baby. I want to help you. *And* Jessie. I don't care if you both move in with me or if I move in with you, I just want to be with you."

"Because you feel responsible?" It hadn't escaped Ellie's attention that Hunter fawned over her out of some sense of guilt. The surgeon never was good at hiding that particular emotion.

"Because I love you," Hunter corrected with gentle force, though she couldn't deny culpability for the 'accident'. When the detectives came to speak to her and Ellie about what happened, she felt as if she were being interrogated. Were they having problems? Did they know of anyone who would want to hurt Ellie? Why was Ellie driving Hunter's truck? Was that normal?

They were honest about everything. About Susan and about the vandalism the morning of the accident. Ellie held Hunter's hand the entire time, never once giving the impression that she blamed her. Unfortunately for Hunter, the detectives weren't quite as magnanimous. She was almost expecting them to arrest her right there.

"So, did you ask her?" Jessie waltzed in, oblivious to the tension in the room, and plopped herself in "her" chair. She took a sip from her Frappuccino, looking from one to the other as she waited for an answer.

"Yeah, I asked."

"Cool. I can pack some of the important stuff that we'll need right away. Blaise offered to hire someone to come in and pack the rest."

Ellie raised her brow which cause a sharp pain behind her eye. "Do I have a choice here?"

"Of course, you do, baby."

"Wait, you didn't say yes?"

"We hadn't gotten that far, yet, kiddo."

"What the heck have you been doing? Making out?"

Both women blushed furiously. Truth of the matter was, Hunter had been apprehensive about initiating more physical affection than a kiss on the forehead or cheek. Not only was she unsure it would be reciprocated, she didn't want to hurt Ellie in any way.

As for Ellie, she didn't feel beautiful, whole, or desirable. Therefore, she became reserved, not blaming Hunter for not wanting her like this.

"Jessie," Ellie said in her most motherly voice, betrayed only by the lowering of her eyes.

"Sorry." Jessie tossed Hunter a questioning look and received a sad shrug in return. Something was different about her mom. While she could understand some mood change due to the situation, this was drastic for Ellie. Insecurity and irritability weren't normal traits for the woman Jessie strived to be like. "But, I don't understand what the issue is. Grandpa Alton, Greyson, and Cade have already rigged up Hunter's place to make it easy for you."

Ellie slanted her eyes to Hunter who failed to tell her that little tidbit. But she addressed what caught her attention the most.

"Grandpa Alton?" They told her she had been out for four days. Why did she feel like she missed an entire year?

"Yeah, um, is that okay with you?"

"Y-yes, of course. I just didn't realize." She stopped and blew out a breath. "Fine. We'll move in with Hunter. At least until . . ."

"No, baby. No until." Hunter scooted off the bed and kneeled down so Ellie could look into her eyes. "I'm not asking you to move in until you're recovered. I want you and Jessie to live with me, but I'm not going to force you into it. If this isn't something you want, I'll respect that."

Ellie slipped her hand out of Hunter's and brushed the doctor's cheek with her fingertips. "I want to."

Hunter grinned broadly. "Yeah?"

"Yeah. But," Ellie said and saw Hunter's grin falter. "If I'm going to be living with a brilliant doctor, I should be able to get out of here soon, right?"

Though she was against Ellie leaving too early, Hunter nodded. "I'll go find Mack." She took a chance and kissed Ellie sweetly on the lips. Her heart relaxed for the first time what seemed like years when Ellie kissed her back. She patted Jessie's shoulder amiably on the way out.

"You two seem to be getting along well," Ellie voiced softly.

Jessie shrugged. "We bonded while sitting here next to you. What's going on? Have your feelings changed for Hunter?"

"Of course, not!" Ellie responded immediately.

"Then why the reluctance to let her help?"

Ellie sighed. How did she explain something she didn't fully understand herself? She loved Hunter. Nothing about that had changed. There was just something in her own mind that held her back. It frustrated the hell out of her that she didn't know what it was. If she could figure it out, she could fix it. Instead of saying all of that to her daughter, she went with an answer that was just as true. "Because I don't want to be a burden for her, Jessie."

Jessie set her cup to the side and scooted closer to her mom's bed. "Mom, you don't understand how Hunter was when you were, um, not waking up. She hardly left your side. I had to threaten to tell you how she wasn't eating or taking care of herself to get her out of this room for ten minutes." She made a mental note to apologize to Hunter for "tattling", but her mom needed to hear this. "She held your hand or made me promise to hold your hand if I forced her to sleep for a minute. And that was *before* she found out someone ran you off the road! So, if you're thinking she's doing this because she feels guilty, she's not. That woman loves you, mom."

Ellie felt hot tears run down her cheeks. She had been questioning how Hunter could love her like this and it shamed her. She was letting her own insecurities overwhelm her. The doctors told her it was normal for her to feel confusion, and even depression, after waking up. To Ellie, there was nothing normal about the past couple of months. Her life, once again, had changed in the blink of an eye. She was going to have to learn how to deal with that or risk losing someone she loves so dearly.

Chapter Thirty-Five

Hunter closed the door to the study behind her and let out a breath. They had been home for almost two weeks now and she was trying so hard not to get discouraged by Ellie's mood swings. Lately, they swung in the direction of bad. The only solace she had was that it wasn't just her that Ellie was abrupt with, though that really didn't make her feel any better. Jessie was getting less and less tolerant of her mother's outbursts. Even Blaise was limiting her time with her best friend.

Mood swings weren't enough to change how Hunter felt about Ellie. In fact, she felt as though she could see through the hostile façade to the remorseful woman beneath, and it made her love Ellie even more. Maybe she was crazy, but she would continue to love Ellie even if the woman kicked her out of her own house. Which was entirely possible in Ellie's current state.

"Knock, knock." Blaise had taken to letting herself in these days, which was fine with Hunter. Ellie wasn't seeing many people and the people she didn't mind around her were the people Hunter trusted the most. To save herself from having to answer the door each time someone wanted to visit, she gave them all carte blanche to come and go as they please.

"In the kitchen!" Hunter called out as she continued to load the dishwasher. Mack had granted her as much time off as she needed to get Ellie acclimated. It was taking a little more time than she anticipated, but she couldn't complain. Despite the occasional blow-ups, she loved being near Ellie.

"Hey." Blaise held up her hand, already knowing what Hunter's question would be. It had become something of a routine. "Greyson and Cade haven't found anything linking Susan to the crash, yet. She's obviously good at covering her tracks. But they're not giving up. One new development, Jules thinks she may be on to something. I don't know what because I don't understand half of the things she says, but you'll be one of the first to know what, if anything, she uncovers."

"I'm that predictable, huh?" Hunter grinned sheepishly.

Blaise chuckled. "No, I just know that you're as desperate as the rest of us to find out what happened. How is she today?"

Hunter shook her head. "She's quick to temper."

"Tell me, as a doctor, is such a drastic change normal?"

"She's had a severe head trauma. She's also dealing with being in a wheelchair and the frustration of not being able to use her dominant hand. As a doctor, I would say her personality adjustment is within the realm of typical."

Blaise blinked at Hunter. "Wow. That was, um . . . informative."

"You asked," Hunter mumbled grumpily.

"That I did. Where is Jessie?"

"She said she had to go out for a little bit. It's hard for her to see her mom like this. I don't think Ellie has ever been this short with her before."

"She hasn't." Blaise was trying hard to be empathetic to Ellie's changing behavior. She wasn't as good as Hunter at "turning the other cheek". The good doctor deserved a medal. "Even when Ellie didn't agree with something Jessie did, she tried talking things out before getting anywhere close to punishment. This must be hard for her."

"It's hard for Ellie."

"Hunter, I'm not knocking her. She's my best friend and I love her dearly. I understand how difficult this is . . ."

"Do you?"

Blaise turned to see Ellie glaring at her. She had lost weight and there were dark circles under her eyes. No matter how much they tried to get her to eat and sleep, she made excuses. 'I'm not hungry. I can't get comfortable.' Once they threatened to hook her up to an I.V. if she didn't get something nutritional in her body.

"El, sweetie."

Ellie looked pointedly at Blaise's perfectly working legs. "Are you in a wheelchair? Do you get migraines more often than not? Do you have to ask someone to help you when you have to use the bathroom? Have you had to stop doing *everything* you love doing? I see you walking around. Coming and going as you please. So, tell me, do you *really* understand how difficult this is?"

"She may not, but I do."

Ellie looked over her shoulder — as best she could and cringed internally. "Dani."

"Yep." Dani maneuvered her wheelchair towards the opposite side of the house. Jessie had begged her to come over and talk to her mom. After hearing how Ellie was reacting to her situation, she was happy to do so, but not with an audience. She wouldn't do that to Ellie. Not after everything Ellie had done for her. "You coming? That thing is electric, right? Ain't no one has to get you to follow me but you."

With that, Dani disappeared down the hall. She didn't care where the hell she landed, just as long as Ellie followed.

Ellie looked at her daughter, who had come in with Dani, but said nothing. The only sound was the whirr of Ellie's wheelchair as she took off after Dani.

"WHERE ARE YOUR legs?"

Dani chuckled. "You and Claire are probably the only ones who could ask me that and not get punched. To answer your question, they're being adjusted. They were pinching."

"So, you didn't just take them off to prove something to me?" Ellie asked suspiciously.

"Cynical Ellie is new. Can't say I approve."

"That's not fair," Ellie said quietly.

Dani rolled closer. "You know what's not fair? Your daughter wondering if she's going to get her old mom back. Or, Hunter wondering every day if you blame her. Or, Blaise willing to spend every dime she has to make sure her BFF gets better."

Ellie lowered her eyes in shame and was full on crying now. Not because Dani held nothing back, but because she wasn't wrong. She could no longer pretend she couldn't hear Jessie cry. She couldn't pretend she didn't see the pain in Hunter's eyes or the frustration in Blaise's.

"Jessie told you all of this?"

"She thought I could help. I get it, Ellie. Better than anyone else, I get the anger. It was *you* who taught me that it solved nothing." Though physical contact with anyone but Claire made her a little uncomfortable, Dani took Ellie's good hand. "I don't know if I have the right words like you did. And, Lord knows I can't bake worth a damn, so I don't have pie to bribe you to open up."

Ellie sniffled and laughed softly. "I did *not* bribe you with pie."

"Spiked pie."

"Is that what you tell people?"

Dani grinned. "Think I'm gonna say that you just walked in and I spilled my guts?"

"You're still as ornery as ever," Ellie smiled.

Dani looked down at her non-existent legs. "Well, there's less of me so it cycles faster."

The older woman shook her head. "It's not them," she said finally. She slipped her hand out of Dani's and touched her fingertips to her temple. "There's something in here nagging at me and I can't . . . I can't figure it out. It feels like something important, but it eludes me no matter how hard I try to grab ahold of it."

"Have you told Hunter this?"

"I don't know what to say! They come to me in an instant, like the flash of a bulb and then it's gone. I don't even know if they're memories or dreams. Or nothing at all and it's just driving me insane." She backed away and steered herself to the large, picturesque window at the far side of the room. It was both a blessing and a curse staying here in the beach house with Hunter. A blessing because, well, Hunter. A curse because every day she could look out and see the beach, see the expanse of sand, and ache to have her feet pounding through the surf.

"Whenever I had a problem, something in my mind that I couldn't solve, I would run. Every rhythmic beat of my feet on the ground calmed me. If I couldn't run, I would cook. I can't do either now and so it builds up inside and I end up taking it out on those I love the most."

Dani rolled up next to Ellie. "So, get back out there. You still have your legs."

Ellie narrowed her eyes at Dani. She couldn't tell if she was joking or serious, but the small hold she had on her temper was quickly slipping.

"My legs are useless."

"I heard the doctors told you there was a possibility you would never use your legs again."

"Exactly. And, prosthetics won't work for me."

Dani hoped to hell she wasn't making things worse. She didn't have any experience with this shit. But she owed Ellie to give it her best. Perhaps doing it the "Dani" way will be just as effective as the "Ellie" way. Different, but effective.

"I never took you for the self-pitying type. Or the type that gave up. You never let me do that."

"This is different, Dani."

"Yeah, it is. Because what *I* got out of all of that hubbub the docs told you was there's a possibility you *will* use your legs again.

But you've got it in your head that it's over. You're letting it beat you."

Ellie raised a brow. "When did you get so smart?"

"The day some stranger walked into my hospital room and offered me pie and a shoulder to cry on." Dani backed away and headed for the door. "Talk to Hunter. Maybe she can help you figure out what's driving you crazy."

"Dani?" Ellie called out. "Thank you."

Dani shook her head. "You never have to thank me. We're not even close to even. Because of you, I'm starting a job next month, I'm living with my soulmate, and I'm happier than I've ever been. I'll never be able to repay you for that."

"You know I love you, right?" Ellie declared softly. "You're part of my family now."

"And, you're the mom I wish I had," Dani confessed just as quietly. "I'm sorry I didn't visit you in the hospital. I just couldn't . . ."

"You're here now. That means the world to me."

Dani nodded. "Uh, love you, too," she said quickly and rushed out.

ELLIE STAYED IN the study, contemplating Dani's words long after the teen left. Hunter, Jessie, and Blaise had left her alone. Whether that was because they were scared she would be angry with them or they just thought she needed time, she didn't know. But she appreciated the gesture nonetheless.

She heard a faint noise outside the door and it triggered one of her "flashes". This one was pleasant and Ellie found herself smiling for reasons she didn't understand.

"Hunter?"

Hunter winced. "Sorry, El. I didn't realize I was humming that loud."

Wow. How terrible have I been? "Honey, would you mind coming in here for a minute?"

Hunter's heart jumped. It felt like forever since she heard that beautiful word come out of Ellie's mouth. "Of course not." Hunter walked in immediately and crouched next to Ellie. She had learned early on not to ask if she needed anything. Not being able to take care of basic needs by herself, cook, or work was difficult enough for Ellie. She didn't want people constantly offering to do things for her that she so desperately wanted to do for herself.

"Did Dani leave?"

"Yeah. She visited for a bit, then Blaise offered to take her home."

Blaise left without saying goodbye to her. Jessie hasn't come to see her for hours. Hunter was apologetic about humming because she thought it would bother her. "I haven't been handling this very well, have I?"

"Baby, there's no right or wrong way to deal with everything you've been through the past few months."

"How I've been treating Jessie, you, Blaise," Ellie scoffed. "And, *everyone* else is wrong. I should have tried talking to you instead of getting angry. Why could I do that with Dani and not you?"

"Because Dani understands."

"But I love you."

Hunter smiled. "I love you, too." She held Ellie's hand. "I'm a doctor. If you want to know what your body is going through physically, I can tell you that. I can tell you anything you want to know about anatomy or surgery. But I've never been through what you're going through. Jessie bringing Dani here was a genius move on her part. I wish I had thought about it. I wanted to be the one to fix everything for you. I'm sorry for being selfish."

"I'm the one who needs to apologize, honey. Not you." Ellie squeezed Hunter's hand. It was going to take hours to atone for the way she had been acting. "May I ask you something?"

"Anything."

"The song you were humming. Do I know it?"

Hunter's eyes widened slightly. "Um, I made it up. But I used to sing it to you when you were . . ."

The pain she saw in Hunter trying to say the word "coma" made Ellie ache. "Is it possible? For coma patients to hear what's going on around them, I mean?"

Hunter nodded. "I think so. I mean, I know a lot of scientists are skeptical because they can't see it for themselves, but there are too many stories out there to disprove it. Do you think you heard me?"

"When I heard you just now, it was familiar. It made me happy." Ellie took a breath. "Everything is so jumbled in my head. It's confusing and frustrating. It's one of the reasons I've been lashing out." She reached up and cupped Hunter's cheek with her palm. "That's not an excuse, honey."

Hunter leaned into Ellie's touch. "There's no need for excuses, baby."

"I know it hurts you. And, I've heard Jessie crying. It kills me. Yet, I couldn't control it."

"What hurts is knowing *you're* hurting. Jessie cries because she misses the closeness you two had and doesn't know how to get that back. I tell her that all we need to do is love you and be patient. Baby, it has only been a few weeks. As amazing as I think you are, adjusting to something like this takes a while."

Ellie sniffed when Hunter brushed her tear away with the pad of her thumb. "Am I going to walk again, Hunter?"

"Yes."

"You seem so sure."

"Because I believe in you. And, when you're ready, I'll be right here. Always."

"Until I run you off with my bitchiness."

Hunter laughed. "Not possible." She took Ellie's hand again, kissing her palm before lowering it. "When they rolled you into my ER, I felt my heart stop. I knew before that I loved you, but when I saw you, when I thought . . . my heart is yours, Ellie. The *only* way you could get rid of me is if you told me you didn't love me and didn't want to be with me anymore."

The vision of Hunter blurred behind Ellie's watery eyes. "I don't think that could ever happen."

God, I was hoping you'd say that. "Marry me, Ellie."

Okay, she knew she was still suffering some from a head trauma, but . . . "What?"

"Will you marry me?"

"After how I've been and how I am," Ellie thumped their linked hands on her dead leg. "You can seriously ask me that?"

Hunter tilted her head and smiled. "You may not think you're perfect, but you're perfect for me."

For me, not to me, Ellie thought with amazement. That one tiny difference touched Ellie deeply. She had always felt pressure to be perfect because of how she grew up, but that's not what Hunter wanted. Hunter wanted *her,* imperfections and all.

"There are so many people who wait and wait and wait for the perfect moment to propose, you know?" Hunter continued when Ellie remained quiet. She hoped she could convince the woman she loved that her timing was actually quite impeccable. "It has to be romantic or extreme. But, if I'm pledging my love and the rest of my life to you when things *aren't* perfect, that has to tell you how serious I am. Life isn't perfect, baby. Neither are we. But, in sickness and in health, through good times and bad, I'm here. Forever." Hunter dropped to one knee and fished a beautiful, antique ring from her pocket.

Already crying, Ellie snorted. "You just happened to be carrying that in your pocket?"

Hunter reached over to the small table next to Ellie and plucked tissues for both of them out of the box. "It was my Gram's. Ma gave it to me the day I brought you home. She told me to keep it with me because I'll know when the time is right. Moms. If I tell her she was right she'll never let me forget it," Hunter rolled her eyes playfully. "What do you say, baby? Will you make me the happiest woman alive?"

"I say you're crazy."

If she hadn't seen the twinkle in Ellie's eye, the one that had been missing for far too long, she would have been more nervous. "Crazy about you."

Hunter grinned that silly, lopsided grin and Ellie's heart melted. With her good hand, she pulled Hunter to her and kissed her hard. "Yes!" she exclaimed against Hunter's lips.

"Yes?"

"Yes!"

That silly, lopsided grin turned into a full blown toothy smile. "Thank you." And, because she had missed it so incredibly much, she kissed Ellie again. She moaned softly when Ellie deepened the kiss. They hadn't kissed like this since the morning of Ellie's accident, which Hunter had understood completely. Even now, she let Ellie take the lead and, oh boy, she would follow her anywhere.

"Never thought I'd say this, but I missed seeing you two like this."

Ellie slowly pulled away from Hunter and smiled at Jessie. "I don't miss being interrupted."

"Yeah, well, you do this in an unlocked room, it's always going to be a possibility." Jessie stuck her tongue out playfully at her mom. This is the happiest she'd seen her in weeks and she felt a weight lift off her shoulders.

She hurried over to her mom when she held her hand out for her. Tears flowed as Ellie whispered apologies in her ear and held her tight. Dani had refused to go into everything she and Ellie talked about, but she did tell Jessie that she believed Ellie was ready to open up. Hope was high that this was the beginning of that.

"So? Is there a reason for this make-out sesh?"

"She said yes!" Hunter announced proudly.

"Shut up!" A broad smile formed on Jessie's face and she wiggled her butt in a little happy dance without removing herself from her mom's embrace. "I'm so excited!"

"You knew?" Ellie asked, looking between the two. It made her happier than she ever imagined knowing their bond had become so strong. There would never be a question that Hunter would be there when Jessie needed her.

"Yep. Hunter asked me for my blessing."

If Ellie hadn't loved Hunter with all her heart before, hearing that would have done the trick. Her daughter meant the world to her and knowing that Hunter went to her first, basically asking for Ellie's hand in marriage, moved her deeply.

"I love you both so much." Ellie's voice hitched. "I'm so sorry . . ."

"Nope! None of that," Hunter decided energetically. "This is a time for happiness and celebration."

Hunter pulled the ring out of the box and Ellie noticed it was attached to a necklace.

"I wanted to give you the option to wear this around your neck until your hand heals."

"That's perfect." Ellie leaned up as best she could, closing her eyes when Hunter clasped the chain under her hair and feathered her fingertips across her neck when she was done.

"It looks beautiful. It'll look even better on your finger," Jessie said softly.

"Jess?" Hunter pivoted her body slightly to face the teen. "I never had the desire to be a parent. Getting to know you and the fantastic person you are, has changed my mind. I may not be related to you by blood, but that doesn't make you any less my family. If you'll have me." Hunter lifted the bottom of the box and produced another chain. The pendant that dangled from it looked similar to the diamond in Ellie's ring, only smaller.

Mother and daughter cried. Jessie threw herself in Hunter's arms, giving her a sound hug. It was because of this woman that Jessie was able to keep her sanity when her mom was in a coma. Even more so when Jessie was afraid she wouldn't get the mom she grew up with back.

"I would be honored to call you family." She was pretty sure she was ugly crying all over Hunter's shirt.

"*Thank you,*" Ellie mouthed when Hunter looked at her over Jessie's shoulder.

She shook her head with a smile. "*I love you.*"

"Gramps is going to *love* this!" Jessie exclaimed, unaware of the silent exchange going on around her. She lifted her hair so Hunter could put the necklace on her.

"Gramps?" Ellie asked. She watched as Jessie and Hunter exchanged a look. "What else did I miss?"

"Grandfather," Jessie explained.

Ellie frowned. "You're going to have to tell me a little more."

Jessie drug a chair over and sat down. "They came to visit when you were in the hospital. Gramps being gramps decided he wanted to take over. Said he was going to take you to a private facility and I needed to go to counseling. At the church."

Ellie furrowed her brows. "Blaise stopped him."

Hunter eyed Ellie. There was something about the way she said the words. A statement, not a question, that made Hunter think it was more of memory than an inquiry.

"Heck yeah, she did. Like a boss."

"They know about me," Hunter added.

Furrowed eyebrows raised. "Oh. That must have been fun. Is that why they haven't been back to visit? Did they even call to find out where I was now?"

"I think grandfather is just mad that he couldn't do anything he came to the hospital to do, mom. I'm kinda glad they're not bothering you. Does it really upset you?"

Distracted, Ellie looked up at her daughter. "Hmm? Oh, um, no. It's what I expect from them, I guess."

"They're fools, baby. But, if you want, I can contact them and invite . . ."

"No!" Ellie grimaced. "Sorry, I didn't mean to yell. Don't call them. It's not worth it, honey." Her head was beginning to hurt. "I think I'm going to take a nap."

Hunter was immediately alert. "Are you okay?"

"Yeah, I'm just a little tired." Ellie smiled wanly. Though it was quickly concealed, she noticed Jessie's disappointment. "But, hey, why don't you two go and get things for a barbecue?"

"Huh?"

The expressions on both of their faces caused Ellie to laugh. "Ow, don't make me laugh until after my nap. Barbecue.

Hamburgers? Steaks? Am I making any sense here?" They simultaneously shook their heads and Ellie laughed again. She held up the ring dangling from the chain around her neck. "We have something to celebrate, remember? Invite everyone over — if they can still tolerate me and will allow me to apologize — and let's celebrate."

"Baby, there's nothing for you to apologize for."

"Your parents are still in town, we have plenty of room here and they chose to stay at a hotel, Hunter."

Hunter chuckled at Ellie's stubbornness. "Babe, they wanted you to get acclimated to being here without extra people around. They love you."

"Hmm." She was skeptical, but then Ellie couldn't blame anyone if they were miffed at her. "Well, I hope you're right because I can't make any pies to win them over again."

"You can't make them yet," Jessie corrected. "And, it was never your pies, mom, it's just you. Which reminds me, Rosa wanted me to let you know that she wasn't serious when she said she wanted to take over so hurry up and come back." She laughed when her mom smiled. "And, Big Al grunted something about his drink. But, he also said he misses you. Weirded me out hearing him say an entire, nice sentence. Oh, and all of our regulars are asking about you and sending their well wishes."

And, now Ellie was crying again. "Thank you, sweetie." She brought her gaze to Hunter. This was the part she hated the most. However, today felt different. She didn't feel like an invalid in Hunter's eyes. She felt like the woman she knew Hunter cherished. "Care to help me to the bedroom and into bed?"

Hunter flashed a roguish grin. "Don't have to ask me twice, baby." She hopped up and guided Ellie out of the room.

"Ugh. Did I say I missed you guys being like this?" She smiled behind their backs. "Don't take too long or I'm going to the store by myself and taking your credit card, Hunter!" she called out, rolling her eyes when Hunter laughed heartily. "*Welcome back, mommy.*"

Chapter Thirty-Six

"Cade?"

The ex-Marine was dressed casually in cargo shorts and a tight t-shirt. He had always had an air of indifference about him, but Ellie could invariably detect that military stiffness. *Always ready to pounce*, she thought humorously.

"Hey, sugar. Great party. Have I said congratulations, yet?" He bent down and kissed her lightly on the cheek. When he had heard the news of her and Hunter's engagement, he could admit to being a bit jealous. But the profound change in Ellie's demeanor from when he saw her last couldn't be ignored. He knew her injuries had taken a toll on her. Hell, he'd been injured a time or two in combat. A bad attitude after trauma like this was assumed and Cade never took it personally.

"Thank you and yes." Ellie glanced over her shoulder and spied Hunter laughing joyously with her friends. Everyone was thrilled about the news and greeted Ellie with open arms and words of love and encouragement. If she hadn't still been in the wheelchair, she would have thought things had gone back to how they were before the car accident. But she *was* in a wheelchair and she needed answers. "Do you have a minute?"

"For you? As many as you want."

"You know that flirting with me doesn't work, right?"

Cade shifted on his feet. Ellie had never been afraid to call him out. It was one of the things he liked the most about her.

"Can't blame a man for trying. What's up?"

"I wanted to talk about the investigation."

Cade motioned for her to follow him. Since everyone was outside by the pool, they made their way into the living room where it was quiet and private.

"Nice set up you have here," he said, looking around the extensive area. He grinned at her raised eyebrow. "Okay, no stalling. What do you want to know?"

"Everything."

Cade took a deep breath. There was *one* thing he hadn't disclosed to anyone. "All right, listen." He sat on the edge of the couch. "There really isn't more to go on right now that connects Susan to your accident. We're looking into her 'friends' to see if she had help. We're also looking into her husband's businesses. Some companies create 'shell' companies to cheat the government. If he has one, she could have used it. This is all assuming she paid someone to run you off the road. The other scenario, which will be even harder to prove, is she blackmailed someone into doing the deed."

Ellie nodded, but couldn't shake the feeling that something else was up. "There's more you want to say."

"When are you going to come work for me? I could use your brain."

"Well, at the moment, it's the only thing that's working. And I'm not even sure how well. So?"

Cade sighed. "Thing is, I shouldn't be telling you this, but Jules did find something. Not related to the accident," he said quickly when anticipation flashed across Ellie's features. "With the blackmail situation Hunter is in."

Ellie shifted in her chair, just as hopeful. Although it had been put on the backburner after what happened with Ellie, Susan's little photo scheme was never far from Ellie's mind. They haven't received anything as of late, but that would make sense if Susan was responsible for the accident. "What did you find?"

"Something that could possibly put Susan away for a long time." He stalled any other questions from Ellie. "Look, I can only say so much because the information was obtained, uh, illegally. Without a warrant, we won't be able to use what Jules found. I have a buddy at the DOJ who I'm hoping can help us out. That's all I got for you, Ellie. And, if you can keep it to yourself, or at least just between you and Hunter until things get ironed out, I'd appreciate it."

"As long as I can tell Hunter, I'm good with that." She paused, questioning her sanity one last time. "You're doing so much for me and I appreciate it more than I can tell you."

He shrugged sheepishly. It still amazed him how he reacted to this woman. Even knowing she would never be his, one simple thank you and he was mush. *Some tough Marine*, he thought, laughing at himself. "It's my job, Ellie."

"It's above and beyond and you know it, Cade. And, regrettably, I have to ask you for another favor."

"Anything, sugar."

"THINK THIS IS a last ditch effort to get her not to marry you?" Mo took a swig of her beer, eyeing Cade and Ellie suspiciously from outside.

Hunter laughed as she flipped burgers on the grill. "Nah, I think he gets it that he's not her type." Her answer was flippant, but she couldn't help but wonder what was going on in there. "Probably just interrogating him about the investigation."

"She seems to be feeling better," Rebecca chimed in cautiously. Of course, she couldn't blame Ellie for being angry about her situation. She just hated how it affected Hunter and made her feel even more guilty.

Hunter glanced over at Rebecca, who leaned on Cass and sipped water out of a bottle. She often wondered how different Rebecca was in *Mistress* mode.

"She is. Dani came to visit her earlier today. I think it helped her a lot."

"Full circle," Cass mumbled. When everyone looked at her she shrugged and explained. "Ellie was the one to bring Dani out of her funk. Makes sense that when Ellie's going through something similar, Dani would be the one who could help her."

"Yeah, wish I would have thought about it weeks ago. Ellie's moods weren't just hard on others, they were hard on her." Hunter absently flipped the burgers again.

"Give me that." Cass took the spatula from Hunter. "You can't keep messing with the meat like that."

"Spoken like a true lesbian," Mo snorted and received a flip of another kind from Cass.

Rebecca rubbed Cass's arm and whispered something in her ear that made the tall woman grin and blush. "I'm just glad Dani was able to help. It's going to be a tough road for Ellie. I hope she's ready to let us in."

Hunter thought of the way Ellie hugged each of their friends when they arrived. It was heartfelt and apologetic. The hug with Blaise lasted for a good long while and Hunter was sure she was going to have to use a sandblaster to separate them. No complaints, though, because the two best friends uncomfortable with each other was just wrong. The world didn't make sense when Ellie and Blaise fought.

"I think she is," Hunter confirmed. "She's opened up more to me, which is awesome. Get this, I think she heard me talking to her when she was, you know." It was ridiculous that a *doctor* couldn't say the word coma. But when Hunter thought about Ellie like that, it made her ache inside.

Mo choked a bit on the gulp of beer she just took. "No shit! That's real?"

Hunter wiped spit beer off her arm. "It would seem so. She remembered a song I was singing to her and a few other things.

Though I think that's one of the things that has been making her a little crazy. Her words!" she said hurriedly. From her peripheral vision, she saw movement from inside the house. Cade had stood up and was now pacing anxiously. "Excuse me."

"YOU'RE SERIOUS?"

Ellie watched Cade go back and forth, anger and frustration apparent in every step. "Unfortunately, I think I am."

"Think?"

"It's hard to explain, Cade. And, you can't tell *anyone* I asked you to do this. Not even Greyson."

"Hunter?"

"Let me deal with Hunter. For now, this stays between us. *If* you find something, we'll bring everyone else in and handle it accordingly."

Cade scratched his head, shaking it slightly. "It's up to you how to handle this, Ellie. But if you ask me, I think you should tell Hunter. You shouldn't have to deal with this by yourself."

"I don't even know if what I'm asking of you will amount to anything, Cade. Why concern anyone else until we actually know something?"

Cade sighed. "And, what about the vandalism? I hear you know who did it. Want to share?"

Ellie shook her head. "I'm not worried about that and you shouldn't be either. I need you to focus on what I've just told you without letting anyone know. Can you do that?"

"You know I'll do anything for you, sugar. Just think about what I said, yeah?"

"And, what's that?" Hunter asked from the door.

Shit. "Cade said Jules found something," Ellie said quickly, shooting an apologetic look to Cade.

"Uh, yeah. But, like I was telling Ellie, I can't say much about it."

Hunter hurried to Ellie's side and crouched down beside her. "About the accident?"

"No, the blackmail," Ellie answered.

Hunter waved her hand dismissively. "That's not important."

"Yes, it is," Ellie argued.

"El."

"Hunter." She took Hunter's hand in hers. "They haven't found anything to connect Susan to what happened to me, yet. Cade says that what they've found could put her away for a long time. Honey, I don't care why she goes away, I just want her gone."

Hunter conceded. "Fine, baby. But you'll still investigate the accident, right?" she asked Cade. The look that Ellie and Cade exchanged made her edgy.

"Yes, ma'am. I'm almost as eager to find out who did this as you are." There was an awkward silence with Ellie and Hunter staring each other down before Cade cleared his throat uncomfortably. "I'm, uh, out of beer. I'll . . ." He made a hasty retreat after realizing no one was paying attention to him any longer.

"Are you going to tell me what you were really talking about in here?" Hunter asked quietly.

"Surely you're not jealous." She knew avoiding the situation wasn't going to help. But how was she supposed to explain the inexplicable to Hunter and keep her from going all vigilante?

"El, I'm not jealous. I'm concerned."

"Honey, I know. But, can you trust me?"

"I *do* trust you, baby. It's not about that." Hunter leaned in a kissed Ellie on the cheek. "It's about being able to share your burdens. We're getting married. That means your worries are mine and vice versa."

Ellie touched Hunter's face gently. "Okay. I'll try to explain to you, but later. And, you have to stay calm and let me handle it the way I need to."

Hunter kissed Ellie's palm. "Deal. What do you say we go back out there and gloat about getting to spend the rest of our lives together?"

Ellie chuckled. "Sounds like a plan."

Jessie stood at the entrance to the living room silently watching her mom and Hunter together. The air around them seemed lighter somehow. That palpable love and chemistry Jessie had missed so much was back. Hunter was displaying that by lovingly massaging Ellie's legs with lotion. With a deep breath, Jessie plastered a smile on her face and walked in.

"Hey, mom, could you look at these and make sure everything is good?" She plopped on the couch as close to Ellie as she could get and handed her two packets.

"What are they?"

"Applications for Berkeley and UCLA."

Hunter stopped her massage and looked up at Jessie. Of course, she knew better than to interfere, so she continued her task while keeping an ear open.

"I thought you decided on Harvard." Ellie refused to take the applications from Jessie. She saw the look her daughter gave Hunter. "Don't blame her. She didn't tell me, but you should have."

Jessie slumped back, dumbfounded. "How did you know about Harvard?"

"I'm a mom."

Hunter looked up in time to see Jessie eyeing her and shrugged. "I'm still trying to figure out how my mom knew things before I told her. I got nothing."

"Jessie, I saw the application in your room when I was putting your clothes away a few weeks ago. I was waiting for you to come to me."

"I was going to! I promise. Mom, I was going to talk to you about it the night of your, um, accident."

Ellie reached for Jessie's hand. "Okay. So, talk to me about it now."

Jessie sniffled. She still got upset when she thought about that day. Could still feel that excruciating pain when Blaise showed up at her school and told her that her mom was in the hospital. She could still remember feeling almost numb until she got to the hospital and saw the agony on Hunter's face. It was at that moment when she felt an emptiness she didn't ever think would be filled again.

The day she knew her mom would be okay was the day she made the decision to give up Harvard. She could study to be a doctor right here in LA. Her mom needed her more than Jessie needed to go to some school across the country. If she were being honest with herself, Jessie needed her mom more than anything else.

"I'm not going to Harvard, mom. Berkeley is a good school. I could even try for Stanford. No offense to Hunter, but there are some schools on par with Harvard, really good schools right here at home."

Ellie had started shaking her head the second 'I'm not going' popped out of Jessie's mouth. "You're not staying here just because I'm handicapped."

"You're not handicapped, you're stubborn."

"Jess," Hunter warned.

"No, it's okay. Let her say what she needs to say. I owe her that."

"I don't mean to be mean, mommy. I feel like you've given up. That light and drive is no longer there. Like, you're just going to take what the doctors say about how you may never use your legs again and not fight to prove them wrong. That's not my mom."

Ellie held up her hand when Hunter opened her mouth to say something. "You're right. I've let the anger and self-pity get to me. Even you can't argue with that, honey." She looked at her daughter and grinned. "The way I've treated the both of you and everyone else wasn't fair and I don't know if I can apologize enough." She rolled her eyes a bit when they argued that she was entitled to be in a bad mood. "No one is entitled to be a bitch to those she loves the most. And, I can't promise I won't be that way again. But, I'm *can* promise you that once my bones heal and I'm cleared to start physical therapy, no more bullshit. I'll give it my all to walk again."

"There's my mom," Jessie smiled. "And, I'm going to be here to help you."

"That gives us a little more than a year." Ellie brought her attention to Hunter, who was listening intently to the conversation. "Is that enough time?"

Hunter blinked as her mind caught up with being asked a question. "Um, yeah. You should get the cast off of your arm in a few weeks. A little longer for your hip and then we'll get a better look at the spine. Physical therapy can conceivably start in a few months. Perhaps as little as six if you put your mind to it."

Ellie smiled at her fiancée. "You're so sexy when you speak doctor," she teased, chuckling softly when Hunter blushed and Jessie made gagging noises.

"Wait," Jessie frowned. "What do you mean a little more than a year?"

"I mean, I will promise this to you *if* you promise to send in the Harvard application."

"That's blackmail!"

"No, that's making sure you don't pass up the opportunity of a lifetime," Ellie countered calmly.

"Look, mom, there's not even a guarantee I'll get in. Plus, Berkeley is cheaper, has a higher acceptance rate, and is close to home. All pros, no cons."

"The con is it's not your first choice, sweetie. Blaise is helping with your tuition, so take advantage. You're brilliant, you have an alumnus to write a recommendation letter, and did I mention you're brilliant? If they don't accept you, they're idiots. And, just because you'll be on the other side of the country . . ." Ellie paused. That really *was* a con for her, but she couldn't be selfish. No matter how much she was going to miss her daughter. "Doesn't mean we won't see each other. You'll come home as often as you can. And when you start to get so busy you can't find the time to visit your old moms, we'll come to you and embarrass the hell out of you."

'Moms'! She thinks of me as a parent to Jessie! Hunter grinned at Ellie and hid her excitement by continuing her massage. She knew Ellie couldn't feel it — yet — but it made Hunter feel a little more helpful.

Jessie pursed her lips. "You're really not going to let this go, are you?"

"Nope."

"I thought you wanted me to stay close."

"I did. When I thought that's what you wanted, too." She reached over and tugged Jessie's hair. "Don't give up on your dreams because of this, sweetie. What kind of mother would I be if I let you do that?"

"One that loves her daughter and wants her close by?"

Ellie laughed. "I love you so much that I'm willing to let you go, daughter of mine."

Jessie smiled. "Fine. I will send in the application. But, I reserve the right to make my final choice if Berkeley and Harvard accepts me depending on where you are in your recovery." She held her hand out to her mom. "Deal?"

"I don't know if I should scold myself or Blaise for your impeccable negotiating skills." Despite her reluctance to agree to such terms, Ellie shook her daughter's outstretched hand. "Deal. Now go get that application."

Jessie popped up from the couch. "Hunter, you're my witness. You know, just in case she tries to worm her way out of this deal and tries to ship me off to no man's land."

"Boston is hardly no man's . . ." Ellie flinched. "Ouch, honey, that hurts."

Hunter's hands froze and Jessie slowly turned back from the doorway.

"Mom?" Jessie rushed back over.

"You felt that, baby?" Reluctant to hurt Ellie again, Hunter gently prodded the spot she had been rubbing.

"There. My thigh, I can feel that." She winced again when Hunter touched a certain spot. "Is that normal?"

"The scar tissue could be clearing up and the swelling could be going down," Hunter answered distractedly. She was still poking at the spot with clinical interest until Ellie grabbed her hand and stopped her.

"Honey, I love you. But if you keep poking me like that, I'm going to thump you on the forehead."

Hunter grinned sheepishly. "Sorry, baby. I'm just excited that you can feel this." She stood up abruptly. "We need to get to the hospital. I want Mack to run some tests."

Ellie rolled her eyes at Jessie who giggled as Hunter paced and mumbled unintelligible things. "Hunter?"

"Hmm?"

"It's late, love. I'm sure this can wait until tomorrow."

"But . . ."

"No buts. The party wore me out and I would like to just spend some quiet time with my two favorite people." She glanced at Jessie. "Don't tell Blaise I said that."

Jessie crossed her heart with her finger. "I kinda agree with mom, Doc. She needs to rest, especially if they're going to be putting her through a lot of tests."

Hunter weighed the options. It most likely would be a long, exhausting night of tests. She would have to page Mack to come in and he'd probably be pissed at her. More importantly, Ellie would probably be pissed if Hunter went against her wishes.

"Yeah, okay." She kneeled in front of Ellie again. "But we go in the morning, right? First thing?"

"I promise." Ellie pulled Hunter to her and kissed her before whispering in her ear. "*Maybe later you can explore some more and see where else I have sensation.*"

For the first time in weeks Hunter felt the stirrings of arousal. It wasn't that she didn't find Ellie beautiful and desirable still. Seeing Ellie in such pain — mentally and physically — didn't exactly translate into sexual feelings. But now, with Ellie's warm breath brushing against her ear, saying these things in that way? Oh, yeah. *She* was the one feeling something now.

"Ahem. In case anyone is listening, I'm going to go get that application now." No response. "And, I've decided on orthopedics."

Still nothing. "Unless I meet a nice woman and we decide to get married and have kids."

"Pick a good donor, sweetie. Maybe a doctor?"

Hunter snickered against Ellie's lips as Jessie groaned something about her mom being a meanie. "You shouldn't tease her like that."

"How will she know I love her if I don't tease her?" Ellie asked innocently. It felt good to feel good again. To feel positive and unburdened. She still had a long way to go, but at least she was finally feeling like she was back on the right track.

Hunter looked over her shoulder to make sure they were alone. "Do you think she was kidding about finding a woman?"

Ellie smiled. "I think our daughter thought she could shock us. But, if she wanted to leave her options open, I'm good with that."

TEST RESULTS WERE encouraging and Ellie continued to regain feeling in her legs. Each day was both a blessing and a curse. She had no doubts now that she would walk again. That was her determination speaking when she had good days. On her bad days, when she could feel nothing but the pain, she almost wished she could go back to the days she couldn't feel anything. *Almost.*

And, while she was cranky during those times, she tried her hardest not to revert back to her bitchy ways. Dani became her go to person when she was having a challenging time with that and their relationship continued to flourish. Dani had even begun to call Ellie mom.

Hunter went back to work — after much protesting and compromising. She agreed to go back part-time if and only if someone else was with Ellie when she was gone. At first, Ellie had been pissed that Hunter was treating her with kid gloves. Then she remembered that she couldn't even go to the bathroom by herself. So, she conceded and spent more time with their friends and her future in-laws. Surprisingly, Ellie actually found it much easier to stay upbeat when she let herself be surrounded by love. They were all optimistic about Ellie's recovery and she allowed their positivity to wash over her whenever she was feeling particularly low.

When she was feeling up to it, she would spend some time at her diner. It was astonishing how her patrons flocked to her with well wishes. If she was ever curious about the affect she had on the people that came into Ellie's Diner, her answer came the first time she rolled through the door. Even her employees cried when they saw her, telling her they hoped she would return soon. As great a job as Rosa was doing, Ellie longed to come back and bake again.

ELLIE TILTED HER head up to bask in the sun and breathed in the salty air. She was having a rare moment to herself out on the deck and the peace and quiet was incredible. She loved Hunter and Jessie. She loved Blaise and everyone else. But she also loved her alone time and without being able to get out and run, she took it where she could get it now. Of course, it wouldn't last long, but she was learning to appreciate that people cared for her.

"Ahem, hey, sugar."

Ellie opened her eyes to see Cade, Blaise, Greyson, and Hunter — who was not amused by Cade's nickname — watching her.

"Five minutes. I think that's a new record," Ellie deadpanned.

Hunter pushed past the others and made her way to Ellie. "Sorry, baby. I know you could use more 'me time', but Cade said he had something he needed to tell us." She kissed Ellie on the forehead. "I didn't realize he meant the gang, too."

"I should have asked before I brought Grey and Blaise here," Cade began. "But I'm going to need Greyson from here on out. Just easier to brief him at the same time. And, I figured you could use the extra support from Blaise."

Well, shit, Ellie thought miserably. *This is not going to be good news.* She held tightly onto Hunter's hand. "Okay."

Cade crouched next to Ellie. "Listen, I can tell you this on your own first if you prefer. I should have been more sensitive."

"No, it's fine. Hunter is my fiancée and she should know everything. Greyson is your partner and Blaise is my best friend. You can say whatever you need to say in front of them. I'm ready." *I hope.*

"What's this all about?" Hunter asked.

"I found the evidence we need for authorities to make an arrest for the attempt on Ellie's life," Cade announced solemnly.

Epilogue

"Miss Montgomery."

Ellie leaned closer to the mic and cleared her throat. "I'm sorry, but for the record, my name is now Elena Vale. Dr. Hunter Vale and I got married over the weekend."

The defendant side of the court room erupted in curses and shrieks.

"Order!" Judge Peterson banged her gavel with authority and scowled at the defense attorney. "Mr. Stevens, I suggest you control your client."

"Yes, I'm sorry, your honor."

Judge Peterson gave him a glare and then – poof – a pleasant smile graced her face as she turned to Ellie. "Congratulations on your nuptials. Now, can we get back to the trial?"

"Thank you," Ellie cleared her throat again, sat up a little straighter, and waited.

"My apologies." District Attorney Nunez smiled amicably at Ellie. "Mrs. Vale, could you tell the court how you know the defendant?"

Instead of looking over in that direction, Ellie looked at Hunter, who sat in the first row of the court room. She gave Ellie a little wink and an encouraging nod, provoking a small smile in return. She took a steadying breath, then brought her attention back to the D.A. "She's my mother."

"And, how would you describe your relationship?"

"Well, she tried to kill me, so I'm thinking it's not great."

"You weren't supposed to be in that monstrosity!" Grace Montgomery screeched and pointed angrily at Hunter. "It was supposed to be *her!*"

"Oh, I'm sorry. She tried to kill the woman I love," Ellie amended dryly. "But, got her own daughter instead. I'd say we still have a few issues."

ELLIE SCRATCHED ABSENTLY at her newly freed-from-a-cast arm as she and Hunter sat side by side in the court room. It was the fourth day of the trial and for most of the day today, the jury had been in deliberation. If she could stand for more than a couple of minutes at a time and walk without a cane for more than two steps, Ellie would be pacing. She had to make do with bouncing her leg. It was slow and sporadic, but it helped.

Hunter placed her hand on Ellie's, hampering her fidgeting. "*It's almost over, baby*," she whispered close to Ellie's ear.

"Only to begin again with Father," Ellie replied. She leaned against Hunter's shoulder, wondering how long the judge would make them wait before she made her appearance. "Do you think he'll plead guilty to avoid all of this if she's convicted?"

Hunter lovingly kissed the top of her wife's head. "He's a 'man' who didn't hesitate to let his wife take the fall. I think he'd do just about anything not to face a judge. Or you. He hasn't even had the decency to show up here." *Stand by your man, but don't expect him to stand by you*, Hunter thought with repulsion.

"I hope you're right. I don't know if I can do this again." She sighed. "I know Jessie doesn't need any more of this shit." There had been a mutual agreement that Jessie would not be at the trial. Ellie refused to allow Jessie to testify regardless if it helped the case or not. The teenager was well on her way to a happy, stable, stressed-out college life. Ellie would be damned if she'd let John and Grace Montgomery ruin that.

Hunter put her arm around Ellie, holding her close. The world had changed so fast for her wife, Hunter was impressed that Ellie was able to keep her sanity through it all. A few moments of a bad attitude were certainly excusable.

The night Ellie had told her that she was having Cade investigate her parents, Hunter was beyond shocked. Though she never questioned Ellie's suspicions, to think parents could be so cruel and uncaring to their own flesh and blood — especially a human being as sweet and loving as Ellie — was unfathomable. It killed her to see the anguish her then-fiancée tried so valiantly to hide, from her daughter particularly. And the desire to run to her own parents and thank them profusely for being who they were was powerful.

When she did break the news to Cece and Alton, they were livid. Hell, Cece was ready to confront them herself, professing "your father needs fertilizer for his garden". Blaise offered to help in her fiery, colorful way. As devastated as Ellie was to learn she was right, even she had to laugh at the vision of Cece and Blaise cracking their knuckles and going over some of the ideas Cece came up with when she had wanted to make fertilizer out of Susan. Which she still did.

Jessie, on the other hand, had been completely destroyed. Who wouldn't be after finding out that their grandparents had hired someone to kill their mom? It was almost too much for the teen to handle. Ellie spent the night holding her close, telling her everything would be okay while Hunter took it upon herself to ask Dr. Woodrow for advice. The three of them had their first session with the shrink that following day and any other day Jessie needed it.

Hunter would do whatever it took to get Ellie and Jessie through this.

"All rise!"

Hunter stood and helped Ellie up. Physical therapy had begun barely two months ago and Hunter couldn't be prouder of Ellie's progression. She still had to use a wheelchair most of the time, but here she was, defying the doctors. Standing and walking a few steps was just the beginning. Running again was not too far off.

Judge Peterson glanced at Ellie, who was holding on tightly to Hunter, and nodded. "Be seated. Will the foreperson please stand? Have you reached a verdict?"

"Yes, your honor."

"Will the defendant please stand?" Judge Peterson watched as the defiant older woman sat for as long as she possibly could before her lawyer "helped" her up. "You may read the verdict."

The middle-aged, nondescript woman stood tall. "On the count of attempted murder, we the jury find the defendant guilty. On the count of solicitation to commit murder, we find the defendant guilty."

Ellie's eyes closed and she felt Hunter's comforting arms squeeze her tighter. She didn't know if what she felt was relief or heartbreak. Perhaps it was both. Or perhaps she was beyond feeling much of anything for the woman who raised her.

"So say you all?"

"Yes, your honor," they all responded as a group.

GRACE MONTGOMERY WAS sentenced to nine years in prison and fined $10,000 for the attempt on Ellie's life. Hunter would have preferred a harsher sentence, but at least the woman was being punished. The look of disgust and hatred that Grace shot the two women as she was escorted out of the courtroom would have stung if either one of them cared enough to let it. In response, Hunter kissed Ellie deliberately on the lips.

"You okay?"

Ellie shrugged. "My mother was just convicted of trying to kill me. I'm as okay as I can be." She leaned over and kissed Hunter again. "Let's get out of here."

"Sounds good to me." Hunter stood, stretching her long limbs. "Let me get your chair."

"I can walk to it, honey."

Hunter loved Ellie's gumption. She just hoped she didn't overdo it. "'Kay. But hold on to me, yeah?"

Ellie scoffed teasingly. "Such a hardship." She grabbed Hunter's hand and gingerly got to her feet. Sitting for long periods of time often caused her legs to cramp when she stood, but Ellie gritted her teeth and pushed through.

"Good?"

Ellie looked up into Hunter's beautiful face. "Perfect."

"Ellie?"

Her head turned at the male voice and was greeted with a sight she never thought she'd see again.

"Trevor?" A moment of uncomfortable silence followed until Ellie shook her head. "Honey, this is Trevor, Jessie's, um . . ." Nothing. He was nothing to *her* daughter. "Trevor, this is my wife, Hunter."

Trevor held out his hand. "Nice to meet you."

"Mmm." Maybe it was immature, but she didn't want to shake the man's hand and it wasn't nice to meet the person who abandoned his daughter.

"What are you doing here?" Ellie asked.

Trevor took his hand back, understanding the snub perfectly. There had been no expectations of a warm reception. "I, uh, came to make things right."

Ellie frowned. Her legs were beginning to shake, but she wasn't about to let any kind of weakness show. "I don't understand." She watched as Trevor reached into the inside pocket of his suit. A cursory glance showed her that the years had been kind to him. He still boasted thick, blonde hair and his face was still boyish, yet held faint lines of years gone by. He was a bit stockier than his lanky, high-school self, but it seemed to work for him.

He handed Ellie a folded document. "I needed to give you this."

Ellie let go of Hunter long enough to take the paper. She unfolded it and frowned again. They were signed legal documents terminating Trevor's parental rights. "But, you signed these years ago."

"I did," Trevor confirmed, then shifted uncomfortably. "It was never filed. I didn't know that until your parents found me."

"Found you?"

"Yeah, um . . ." he adjusted his tie as though it was too tight. "They sought me out, imploring me to help them. They said they were afraid for Jessie. That you were unfit to be a mother and they needed me to get Jessie away from you."

Ellie visibly recoiled. The pain of losing Jessie would have been a hell of a lot more painful than what the crash did to her and her parents knew that.

"I just couldn't wrap my head around you being a bad parent," Trevor continued when Ellie said nothing. "It just didn't jibe with the girl I knew. When I tried to get out of it by reminding them I had no legal standing to get involved, they told me the papers had never been filed."

"Obviously, you didn't help," Hunter prompted. Her body shook from anger and she knew then that nine years in prison was absolutely not enough.

He looked up at Hunter who stood an intimidating inch or two taller than he. "I asked them for more information. If Jessie was in real danger, I would have stepped in." He ignored the soft snort from Ellie. "But, I found out they were just upset that Ellie was, well, with you. That's the reason they neglected to file the papers. They said they were afraid you might 'regress' — their words — and needed leverage if that ever happened." He looked at Ellie. "I never imagined you were . . . but that doesn't make you a bad mother. I guess when I refused to help them, they tried a different approach."

Hunter took a menacing step towards him. "Did you know they were going to do this?"

"No!" Trevor held up his hands in defense. "I swear to you, if I had any idea they were going to do something like this, I would have found a way to tell you, Ellie. You're the mother of my . . . you're Jessie's mother. I would never condone this."

Ellie placed a calming hand on Hunter's arm. "I believe you. But, how did they know about Hunter?"

Trevor relaxed slightly and shrugged. "They said they saw a photo of the two of you on some social media site of Jessie's that they were monitoring. Anyway, when I heard what happened, I thought I owed it to you to hand-deliver these and let you know that you have nothing to worry about from me."

Ellie nodded. "Thank you."

Trevor smiled. "I'm happy for you both. I'm getting married soon myself and moving to Oregon."

"Oregon?"

He shrugged again with a grin. "That's where her job is taking her, so I'm following." He hesitated. "Do you think it would be okay for me to meet Jessie before I go?"

Ellie shook her head. "No. I'm sorry, but I don't think that's a good idea. With everything she's been going through, it would be confusing for her to see you only to lose you again."

He was disappointed, but still agreed. "I understand. Maybe one day you can tell her that I've thought about her every day. And, that I made the right decision. Back then and now. I would have been a terrible father, Ellie. You're all she ever needed." He turned to leave.

"Trevor?" When he turned back, Ellie smiled. "She's going to Harvard."

His grin was huge and proud. "She definitely took after you." He paused, taking in the information, and then nodded with satisfaction. "Have a good life, Ellie."

"You, too, Trevor. Congratulations on your upcoming wedding."

The two women watched him walk out of the courtroom and out of their lives. Hunter didn't have to like the man, but he could respect what it took for him to come here and tell Ellie the truth.

She shuddered to think how differently this could have all turned out. Ellie could survive a car crash. She never would have survived losing her daughter.

Hunter — ready to see Ellie laughing and living life fully again — made an executive decision. "We're going on vacation," she announced.

Ellie smiled up at her wife. *Wife.* God, she loved that. "After this past weekend, I think that's called a honeymoon, love."

Hunter grinned her lopsided grin and took Ellie in her arms. She sent silent thanks that everyone had left the courtroom during their chat with Trevor and they were now alone. "Even better. You know what couples do on their honeymoon?" She kissed Ellie, giving her a small preview.

Ellie sighed happily against Hunter's lips. It had been a horrible few months, but she felt in her bones that this was the turning point. It had to be. How much more could any of them endure? "I think I'm done standing, honey."

Once she made sure Ellie was secure, she rushed to get the wheelchair from the back of the room. She could kick herself for letting Ellie stand there for longer than she should have at this point in her recovery. But, she knew better than to voice her self-blame. Ellie would just tell her that she was an adult who knew how much she could take. So, she stayed on the much happier topic of their honeymoon. "Where do you want to go, baby?"

Ellie accepted Hunter's help getting settled into her chair. She had long since decided that it took way too much energy feeling sorry for herself. She also knew that it made Hunter feel better when she was able to be helpful. "We can go anywhere we want. Eve offered us the use of her private jet."

Hunter's eyes widened. "No shit?"

"No shit," Ellie chuckled. "All we have to do is give them destinations."

"Destinations with an 's'?" Ellie nodded and Hunter smiled, kneeling at Ellie's side. "How about we make Cambridge our first stop. We can show Jessie around Harvard."

Ellie's eyebrows rose. "You want to take our daughter on our honeymoon?"

Hunter shrugged. "School is out and she's had a really tough time. I just think it would be good for her and us. Is that okay?"

Ellie caressed Hunter's cheek. "This is why I love you so much." She brought Hunter to her and kissed her sweetly. "Let's go home, honey."

ELLIE LIFTED HER head to the sun, letting the warmth wash over her. She smiled with a happiness born of feeling as though the weight of the world was finally off her shoulders.

As it turned out, her father did plead guilty to accessory after the fact and received three years in prison. She would never admit to how satisfying it was to know her parents were the ones being punished now after everything they put her through over the years.

The person who was paid to hit Ellie was also convicted of first-degree attempted murder. He is currently serving a life sentence with a possibility of parole in ten years.

Then there was Susan. Cade's Department of Justice friend had come through. With a warrant, Susan's computers and financials – as well as those of her husband's shell companies – were searched with a fine tooth comb. Since Jules already knew where to look, it was easy to lead the authorities to the data they were really looking for.

As a result, Susan Hinde now faced multiple counts of child pornography and statutory rape. Sadly, Hunter was not the first, nor the last, underage girl unable to avoid Susan's talons. Though the statute of limitations was far exceeded for Hunter, which Ellie hated, Susan would be punished for others. That would have to suffice.

Ellie knew that Hunter felt responsible for the young girls that now had to live with this burden. If she had just told someone, Susan would never have hurt anyone else. It took a lot of listening, understanding, therapy sessions, and love to convince Hunter that the only one to blame was the immoral bitch who preyed on innocent, confused girls. The punishment would never be enough, but maybe Hunter would sleep a little easier knowing Susan would be going to prison for a long time. As a bonus, her reputation was ruined, she was made to register as a sex offender, and she was facing a very messy divorce from an irate, embarrassed husband.

"Mom? You ready?" Jessie bounced on the balls of her feet as though she were ready to run a marathon and be happy about it.

Ellie chuckled at her jubilant daughter. "I'm ready. Go on ahead. I'll catch up." She felt Hunter's presence behind her and leaned back into her when strong arms enfolded her.

"You good, baby?"

That voice, the soft breath in her ear, the feeling of that body close to her, never ceased to create havoc in Ellie's body.

"Mmm, very."

"Sure you're up for this?"

Ellie raised a brow and looked back at her wife. "Do you not remember last night?"

Hunter groaned. "Baby, I'll remember last night for the rest of my life. But, *I* did most of the work. This is different."

"You're worrying again."

"I'll worry about you and Jessie until I die, baby. That's not going to change."

Ellie turned in Hunter's arms. "I've been feeling much stronger, honey. I'm standing and walking for much longer periods of time. I can do this. I promised you I would start out easy and I will, okay? You and Jessie are right here with me." She pulled Hunter's head down to kiss her. "We're in Hawaii at these beautiful falls. The world is right again. Let's enjoy it."

"I'm enjoying ever second, wife. Every city, every country, every step with you and Jessie has been a blessing." Hunter sighed lightly. "You'll be careful?"

Ellie raised three fingers on her left hand. "Scout's Honor."

Hunter laughed. "No more time with Mo for you. It's the right hand and you were never a scout."

Ellie shrugged with a smile. "How about this?" She kissed Hunter deeply. "Enough of a promise?" she asked when they finally came up for air.

"Oh, yeah."

"Come on, guys! We're losing daylight!" Jessie called out.

"The boss has spoken," Hunter snickered.

"Oh, God, don't say that to her. Let me keep some semblance of authority before she goes off to college. Ready?"

"Ready."

Ellie took a deep breath and with Hunter and Jessie by her side, she began to jog slowly.

Acknowledgments

This is my eighth book I've published and there are so many other stories I still need to tell. The thing is, as a writer, each book, each character takes a piece of me with them. Once I finish writing for a couple, I feel a bit of a loss. I know they'll be there in other books, but it takes me a minute to switch gears and learn about another character that resides in my head. 😊 I think I would go a little crazy if I didn't get all of this stuff out of my head. Heck, maybe writers ARE a little crazy, regardless. I'm okay with that. But if I can bring my characters to 'life' and have them entertain you for a bit, that means the world to me.

This book dealt with things I have no clue about (surgery, doctor stuff, injuries, baking, legal stuff, etc.). I did my best to research, but I hope you'll forgive me if I got a few things wrong or stretched the imagination just a tad. The wonderful thing about books is their ability to make you suspend your disbelief. However, I tried to make it as believable as I could.

I also wrote about things I did know about. It's what made this book one of the most personal books since Something About Eve that I've written. After I released Coming Home and started reading the reviews about how the readers wanted Ellie and Cade together, I *almost* changed my mind. But, alas, that's not who Ellie is. I think once people have read her story, Ellie's character in Coming Home will make more sense.

Something did change as I began writing this story. My first inclination was to have more sex in the book. I apologize to anyone who thinks I should have. 😊 Thing is, as I began to write Ellie's story and her personality came to me, she turned out to be a much more private person. She didn't mind if you knew she was being intimate. She just didn't want to be on display all the time. If you're looking for a couple who don't mind being "watched", I suggest you read *Fifty Shades of Pink*. Whew! 😊

Okay, now on to the real acknowledgments.

Daisy — Even though you don't read my books, you still support me in all that I do. You even have conversations with me about the content! It may be wrong, but it sure is entertaining to "discuss" my characters and what's happening to them with you. As always, thank you to my favorite "professional spectator".

Lisa — You're an awesome beta reader! You're edits and comments helped me so much. The gallery scene happened because of you and I'm beyond grateful. Thank you for taking the time to read and discuss this book with me. I hope you're ready to continue being a beta reader for me. Even if you're not, I'm still coming to you for opinions. 😉

Karen — You're contracted to be my beta reader until the end of eternity. Deal with it. Your enthusiasm for my characters (and, in particular, this book) was contagious. If I ever felt a little daunted by the amount of story I had to tell, I just had to come to you and talk about Ellie or Hunter. It's readers (and friends) like you, Lisa, and Wanda who help me feel like I'm not *too* crazy for seeing these characters as real. Thank you! 😊

Wanda — My beastie since I was a mere pipsqueak. I love how angry you get with my characters (and me). It means I'm doing something right and bringing out those emotions! Though, if I went with half of your ideas, I'd be writing an MMA book or killing people in horrible ways. I love it! Even if I'm not hitting or killing people as much as you would like, you still support me! Thank you! 😉

All the Sunday Ladies — Thank you. Your support and love has not waned a bit in the last two years. I'm grateful for all of you who continue to be in my life and call me friend. #TRFL

Jim McLaurin – As always, your insight and humor makes the editing process fun! Thank you!

Drue Hoffman and Debra Presley from Buoni Amici Press – Thank you for the book interior design, and all you do for me for promotion!

To my readers — I get quite a few requests to write more about certain characters. I have to say, sometimes it works! I hadn't really thought about writing another book for the Eve Sumptor novels. Now, there's a story brewing! So, thank you. I also know that some of you are waiting for a conclusion to my online stories, and I appreciate your patience! I promise I will get to it very soon!

Writing is a very personal thing because you put so much of yourself into it. You then put it out there for everyone to judge. Now, you know you're not going to please everyone and harsh reviews can sting. But, honestly, if I can inspire *one* person with my writing, it truly is worth it. "Just one more chapter!" Peace, love, and light!

About the Author

I reside in the Houston area where I live in a bit of a zoo. 😊 With five dogs, two cats, and various other creatures, everyday is certainly an adventure. If I'm not writing, I'm training for triathlons. I'm terrible at them, but I do them to challenge myself and to raise money for charity. It's a good way to keep myself feeling young. That's what I'm choosing to believe anyway. 😉

As for what's next for the writer in me? There's so much I want to get to that it's hard to decide which direction to go. Another Eve Sumptor book may be in the works for all you Eve fans. And the LA Lovers series will most likely continue with Cade's story. Of course, each LA Lovers book will be a stand-alone, HEA. But, as always, look for Ellie & Hunter, Blaise & Greyson, Rebecca & Cass, Eve, Lainey, and more to show up here and there. I truly hope you enjoyed getting to know Ellie and Hunter as much as I love writing for them.

Where you can find cameo characters

Blaise Steele

- Coming Home
- Flawed Perfection
- Destined to Love

Greyson Steele

- Coming Home
- Flawed Perfection

Eve Sumptor-Riley

- Something About Eve
- Flawed Perfection
- Coming Home

Adam Riley

- Something About Eve
- Flawed Perfection
- Coming Home

Lainey Stanton

- Something About Eve
- Flawed Perfection

Rebecca

- Fifty Shades of Pink

Cass

- Fifty Shades of Pink

Cade Drake

- Coming Home

Dr. Woodrow

- Fifty Shades of Pink
- The Eve Sumptor Therapy Sessions (online only)

Kiara Adler

- The JasAnni Fanfic (Online only)

Soundtrack for Coming Home

I was stoked to have two awesome albums that came out during writing this book that helped me. The first was Wings of the Wild by Delta Goodrem. The second came from the most incredible, inspiring movie: Wonder Woman. My characters went through quite a bit. It was nice to be able to listen to something like "Wonder Woman's Wrath" to help get them through it. Since I listened to practically every song on both of those albums, I won't list each individually. However, I do encourage you all to take a listen!

Connect with Jourdyn Kelly online

My Website (http://www.jourdynkelly.com/)
Twitter: (https://twitter.com/JourdynK)
Goodreads
(http://www.goodreads.com/author/show/2980644.Jourdyn_Kelly)
Facebook (https://www.facebook.com/AuthorJourdynKelly)
Instagram (https://www.instagram.com/jourdynk/)
Amazon Author's Page (http://www.amazon.com/-
/e/B005O24HK8)